THE WAY TO BABYLON

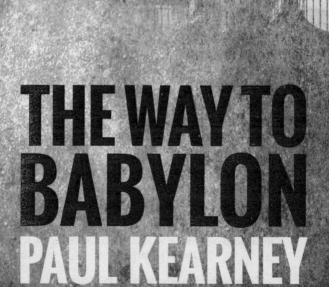

THE WAY TO BABYLON

PAUL KEARNEY

SOLARIS

This edition published 2014 by Solaris
an imprint of Rebellion Publishing Ltd,
Riverside House, Osney Mead,
Oxford, OX2 0ES, UK

First published in the United Kingdom
in 1992 by Gollancz

www.solarisbooks.com

ISBN: 978 1 78108 189 1

Copyright © 1992, 2014 Paul Kearney

10 9 8 7 6 5 4 3 2 1

A CIP catalogue record for this book is available from the
British Library.

Designed & typeset by Rebellion Publishing

Printed in the US

For my father

Acknowledgements to:
John Wilkinson for a lot of hard work
and encouragement, Martin and Suzie
for many excellent dinners and my family
for their unfailing support.

CHAPTER ONE

HE FOUND IT hard to believe, looking back; hard to believe in that older, sunnier time when his mind and his body were whole. Before the world came crashing down on him. In a single screaming instant, he had seen all he loved taken away from him. And now he was alone.

Yes, someone up there really has a bastard sense of humour. Well, I hope you're amused at my antics—at the smashed bones and the red pain and the months of putting the bits together. And the anxious friends. Christ; that's the most hilarious part—the agonies they had, debating when to tell me she was dead. Crushed. Because of a rope I had stretched one too many times. It was always too expensive to replace. Now that must be funny.

So die laughing.

The sun was warm on his face. He opened his eyes and saw the familiar stretch of river and woods, separated from him by a wide lawn. The figures in dressing gowns seemed totally out of place. And the white-clad nurses. It was a world away from the heather and the eagles. And the mountains.

You don't get much more civilised than Berkshire.

His fingers rubbed the armrest of his wheelchair absently. They were so bloody old here. Old men and old women who were on their way to a deck chair in Bournemouth but who needed an MOT first. So they wouldn't keel over and spill their ice cream. A gentle retirement.

That's what I need. A quiet slide into oblivion with slippers and a golden labrador, and perhaps a walk on Sundays. He almost laughed, but the twitch in his jaw sent lights splashing through his skull. He cursed fervently and silently instead, touching with a ginger hand the metal rods implanted in his face like some hideously inept form of acupuncture. Man in the Iron Mask, that's me.

The pain sank, and there was only the sun on his face.

I'm lucky, of course. Should be dead, by rights, after falling two hundred feet. She was. Very dead, by all accounts. Real-life ugly dead. It shouldn't happen to people in that way. They ought to have time for a dying wish and the rest. A last kiss—

Oh, hell; here we go again. You stupid bastard.

He gouged his eyes until they were dry, until his head ached again.

Well, I'd rather have the bloody headache anyway. Life's a bitch.

And a thousand years away a laughing, silver voice rejoined: 'And then you marry one!'   .

His right hand worked at the control knob, and with a jerk and a whine he was off down the patio, zigzagging to avoid chairbound patients.

Hold on to your bedpans, you retired bankers!

Then a white body right in front of him; a tray of bottles and pills that erupted into the air; a collision and a woman's startled shout.

Oh, shit. He sped away, deaf as well as dumb, with pills caught in the folds of his blanket and syrupy medicine down his neck.

'Mr Riven, come back here! What do you think you are doing?'

I must get this thing souped up. It's still not as good as a pair of pins.

The engine sank to a halt and he waited patiently as a burly nurse stalked towards him.

Jesus. With legs like those, she could be an oil rig.

'Mr Riven, I have told you before about speeding with your chair. Don't you ever listen? There are other patients in this centre, Mr Riven, and most of them are old and frail. Don't you care about the accident you could have been responsible for if you had hit one of them instead of me?'

Talk to me about accidents then, you fat cow. Talk to me about responsibility.

'I'll push you out on to the lawn. There you can't get up to any mischief. Be good and sit in the sun while it lasts. You ought to be grateful for the chance to get out of doors, Mr Riven. I understand you are an outdoor sort of person...'

Oh, yeah. Running, jumping, climbing. The great outdoors just kills me.

'There we are. You can sit here and enjoy the sun.

Your lunch will be in an hour. I'll come out and get you and you'll have a nice big appetite with all this fresh air.'

And off she goes, with seabirds trailing in her wake and a smell of land in the air. Ahar.

Christ. Even retirement couldn't be as boring as this.

He twiddled the armrest knob again, but the engine could not cope with the bumpy grass. It lurched a few feet and stopped with an ominous crunching sound.

Ouch. Must have forgotten the clutch again. Wonder if you can get four-wheel drive in these things. Or an estate. I could put the golden labrador in the back.

...I can't even bloody well whistle.

He sat, scowling theatrically, until his head hurt again, then sighed and stared at his knees. Twisted, thin, even under the blanket. More metal than bone, now. We can rebuild him, make him better than he was before... Pull the other one; it's got pins in.

Well, another hour of this marvellous southern air and then I'll be wheeled in by Nurse Bisbee of the Hairy Forearms—she-who-must-be-obeyed—to a gourmet meal of minced bangers and smash. Or if the cook is feeling adventurous, maybe a little steak and kidney with a delicate whiff of ketchup. And afterwards we'll retire to the drawing room, sniff some liqueurs, pop our painkillers and wait for supper, after which we'll toddle merrily off to bed. Ah, for the life of a country squire.

Wait a moment: it's old mad Molesy, come to say hello. Certifiably insane and he's the only one who'll talk to me. Hiya, Molesy. What planet are we on today, then?

The old man had a face like a rumpled rug, red as an apple, but with two brilliant blue eyes; blue as a lochan under a clear sky. His jaws munched moistly for a moment, then he looked slantwise and whispered: 'You haven't gone, then. You're still here?'

No, you old twit. I'm a mirage.

'I only asked, see, because I thought you'd be off any day now, what with you having been there and all.' He lowered his voice even further, looking about furtively. 'You and me's the only ones who know.' His voice was whisky-roughened, with the lilt of the Highland Scot, and some accent behind it that could not be placed. 'We've been there, and that's where it is.'

Some day, Molesy, I'm going to bop you one on your big red nose. You and your Celtic bloody twilight. You're a whisky-sodden jock who's lived too long on his own and got hill mist in his hair.

'Don't worry. I know you can't tell anyone. I know you can't talk. That's why the rest never talk to you. They think your head's gone along with your voice—like they think mine is gone.' He chuckled, for a moment seeming startlingly shrewd and somehow younger.

'Ach, well. We'll keep our secret for a wee while yet, eh, Mr Riven? There's time, and there's time enough...' He trailed off. 'Ach, my old head wanders like drift these days. It was better on Skye, back in Minginish, with the wind and the salt smell. Better when I was at home, in my own place.'

Aye. Maybe you do have a point at that. But I'll never be going there again.

'I'm off. I must be going. Bloody nurses...' And

away he went, weaving a precarious trail across the lawn to the ward buildings.

There's time, and there's time enough.

Using a mixture of motor power and his good hand, he managed to manoeuvre the chair back on to the patio, though his head felt as though it were about to explode by the time he got there. That's it, you bastards; don't offer me any help. It might aggravate your ulcers—

Bloody hell, my skull hurts. I bet it's still cracked.

Patients were making their way towards the buildings in time for lunch. The autumn sun was warm and down where the river glittered there were willows. Their limbs dipped in the flow and the thin leaves floated in fleets on the water. He liked to sit where the bank shelved into gravel and the light spangled on the bottom. It was a southern place, very sleepy and slow. He looked back, and half wished he could go and sit there now. But the old man had put the northern mood into him again. The mood of stone and bracken and peat. That was the worst mood to be in, for in an instant he would be belaying on the top of Sgurr Dearg again, staring in horror at the severed rope.

A stereo was playing in the recreation room. He listened to it for a moment, face twitching, then shoved the chair into life and whirred inside, whistling in his mind, watching other mountains.

'MOUNTAINS. THEY WERE the world's backbone. In the north they were the black, snow-eaten teeth of the Greshorns, high enough to lose themselves in perpetual cloud and to squat, vast and sullen, like a tribe of savage giants in conclave with the north wind. They loomed over the green lands below, a drop as long as a river separating them from where men worked the softer slopes and meadows.

'To the west yet more peaks reared up to snatch at the skies—less brutal, these, more broken, with wide slopes of scree and heather-tangled rock. They curved down the land in great gentle swathes of dull stone, rolling for hundreds of miles to the south, to where the sea swept into the coast and battered it into shingle.

'To the east another great barrier of high ground was pushed up in escarpments and cliffs, shattered and frowning under ice and snow at their highest points, leaning off into wastelands of stone and sand farther east, where the sunlight became harsher and the character of the land changed and shifted, becoming scrub, savannah and, eventually, arid desert.

'Mountains. They bounded three parts of the world and left the last part to the grey, murderous sea. Within their gnarled horseshoe, the world was a green and pleasant place, wrinkled with silver rivers and scattered with forests that no man had ever cleared. The world was wide and fair, hung over with a haze of sunlight and shimmering with warmth. It was uncluttered, empty; wild as a wilderness and serene as a summer afternoon.'

And it did not exist, save in the mind of a cripple who whistled in silence.

THE MEALS OF clearly-defined meat and vegetables that sat on other plates had on his mutated into a single pile of neutral-coloured mush, which he siphoned carefully into his broken mouth. Around him, the dining room was full of talk. It was set aside for the more mobile patients. The rest ate in their beds, in their respective wards or rooms.

'Would you like some more, Mr Riven?'

He rolled his eyes at the young nurse with an are-you-kidding? look. She laughed. 'I get the hint. At least you can't go on at us like Mr Simpson does.' She turned away.

God, I could murder a pint.

It was months since he had had a drink. The drugs that were continually in his system did not permit it. The idea of getting drunk both attracted and repelled him; though it was, he had to admit wryly, a useless exercise now for him to get legless. Sometimes he wanted to drink to make himself unconscious; a darkness without dreams, without the sight of that frayed rope end swaying in front of him. And sometimes he wondered if it would bring it all back, make it even more vivid.

He sucked the remainder of the liquid meal into his mouth without tasting it. Across from him, a middle-aged man was eating his own meal precisely and deliberately. He looked as though an earthquake would not have hurried him. Riven felt trapped—by the drugs, the chair, the liquid food, the age of the people around him. He looked about and finally saw Doody, the orderly, at the other end of the room. He waved his arm.

Doody was a black from London, ex-Army like Riven himself, and ex-RAMC. He had a streak of recklessness in him several miles wide.

'Wotcha, sir. What's up?' Riven raised his eyebrows helplessly, and then put one finger to his head with the thumb as the trigger.

'Fucking hell—like that, is it, then? We can't have that. Hold on a mo' and I'll have you out of this.' He went up to the charge nurse, and came back a few moments later. 'Come on. Let's leave these old farts to stuff their faces, and get a bit of air.'

He wheeled Riven outside again, into an afternoon of blue and gold with the river and the traffic in the background. Suddenly the air seemed easier to breathe. Sitting down the whole time made Riven feel as though his lungs were being cramped. Once upon a time he had run a lot, run for miles, until his lungs had seemed bottomless. But all that stamina he had left behind him at the foot of the mountain.

'Here, have a go on this, sir.' Doody handed him a notebook and pencil. 'Left it behind this morning, didn't you? Mind you, I don't blame you for not wanting to use it sometimes.'

Sometimes it's easier not to, Riven wrote quickly.

Sometimes—he paused. *Sometimes I really don't give a shit*. Doody looked at him with unaccustomed gravity.

'You don't, do you? A lot of people say it, but you're the only bloke who really knows what it means, I reckon.'

The pencil was silent. Doody leant forward. 'Any day now, sir, and those fucking rods will be out of your face. You'll be able to eat and talk and puke in my lap if you want to.' He straightened a second and made a show of looking over his shoulder. 'And what is much more important, I'll be able to pour some beer down your neck.' He smiled, his face becoming even more ugly for a second, then he and Riven exchanged a rapping handshake.

You fucking marvel. You keep me sane.

And sanity is a wry thing; a shivering gangway between light and dark.

He remembered the rocks flashing past him, the momentary feeling that he was being granted a sight of something not often seen by those who could speak of it afterwards.

Death.

I'm here, Death had said with a grin. I always have been, waiting in the wings of every story. The uninvited guest.

And that had not mattered.

Riven smiled slightly, unconsciously. I was happy to meet him and shake his hand. He was taking me where I wanted to go.

The grief bubbled up again, relentless as ever. It was irritating to be continually caught unawares like this. Undignified. It never happened in the best stories—in his own stories. Grief becomes boring to hear about, after a while.

He shook his head as far as he was able, freeing it from the hill mist and the smell of the heather. There was a face in his head: a dark girl with heavy brows and a determined set to her jaw. She was very young. Who was she? One of his characters, perhaps. A maiden from the land of dreams and stories.

It's a bugger having a tireless imagination sometimes.

He whirred the chair round. Doody was talking to one of the other nurses. Her face was suspiciously similar to that of the girl in Riven's head.

So much for a tireless imagination. Doody looked over and waved.

'You've an appointment with the head bone-carver, sir, it seems. I'll take you in a minute.'

Riven gave his version of a nod. The nurses's smile went unreplied.

An appointment to keep. Ach well. And no doubt promises to meet, too. Bring on the bone-carver.

He did not see Molesy watching him from the shadow of the veranda, his face briefly that of a young man with calculating eyes.

'WELL, MICHAEL, YOU appear to be making progress... one last jab... that's it.' All he could see was the bright light above him. He could feel the deft hands working at his face, the slight grate of metal on bone. Like being at the dentist. Strange, to feel the jaw slackening. To feel the possibility of movement there after so long.

'Lovely. There's going to be hardly any scarring. If your limbs heal as well, you'll be laughing—' The surgeon checked, grimaced. 'I'm going to let you move it in a moment. Just take it very gently to begin with. Nothing sudden. There...'

It works. Holy shit, it works.

'I can talk,' he said thickly; the first time he had heard his voice in months. He had to fight back the tears. She had been the last person to hear it.

'Have you any pain, any discomfort? Apart from general stiffness, of course.'

He shook his head. No more than usual.

The doctor bent over him. A grey-haired aquiline profile with large black-rimmed glasses.

'Hey, doc, you're not so ugly after all.' He grinned, ignoring the pain that shot through his jaw.

'Neither are you, now. You look a lot less like a TV aerial than you did. Try and sit up.'

He did so, his lower jaw immediately pulling at him. Odd to feel its unsupported weight, like a pendulum attached to his lower skull. He felt himself dribbling and wiped his mouth.

'Christ, it's like learning all over again.'

'It'll be like that for a day or two, until you get used to being responsible for it.'

'What about the rest?'

The doctor paused. 'Longer, I'm afraid. You won't be able to begin walking for some time yet, but the arm should be gaining in strength all the time...'

Time. Well, I've plenty of that.

The words he made were large, clumsy, with no sharp corners. It was as if they had been wrapped in dough. He still carried his notebook with him to cope with those occasions when he was too tired to make the effort to speak, or when those who tried to understand him were particularly obtuse. Doody, being Doody, understood every word he said, and frequently told him off for mumbling on purpose.

'Now you've got that space-age hat rack off your face, you should try and have a go at the old cow Bisbee, sir. She thought your dogs weren't on one leash, if you know what I mean. She's a one to fucking talk. All she's got between her ears is aspirin and elastoplast.'

And Riven laughed for the first time in a long time, though his face ached when he did so.

The white bulk of Nurse Bisbee entered the room like a ship in full sail. Doody rolled his eyes. 'Oh, shit, wait for it. I'm probably supposed to be wiping arses or licking floors or something.'

'Doody, shouldn't you be somewhere else at this time of day?' asked Nurse Bisbee, frowning. 'Like the laundry room?'

'Why yes, massah, I is on my way,' Doody retorted, exiting with a nod and a wink to Riven. Nurse Bisbee continued frowning in his direction after he had gone, and then she became brisk. She plumped up the cushions at Riven's back, manhandling him like a child. 'Now, Mr Riven, I hope you're feeling strong today, because you have a visitor, and a very important-looking man he is. I think he must be a lawyer or something. I'll just make you comfortable and then I'll send him in. Have you got your notebook handy? Good. I'll go and tell him to come in.'

A visitor, come to talk to the newly vocal Michael Riven. Shit. A short, thickset man in a sober suit that hung on him uncomfortably, as though it wished it were somewhere else. His face was square and ruddy, the black hair almost militarily short. He might have been a blacksmith, or a sergeant major, were it not for the softness of the eyes. There was a smile on the face, aimed at Riven. His hand jutted out.

'Hello, Mike.'

Riven returned his grip momentarily, a smile poking its way on to his lips. 'Hugh,' he said clearly. The man was his editor, midwife to the stories he had written back when the world was young.

The man called Hugh sat down beside Riven's wheelchair. His chair scraped as he pulled it forward. He seemed reluctant to meet Riven's eyes.

Christ. Is it that forbidding?

Finally he did. He shrugged. 'Oh, hell. There's not much to say, I suppose.'

'No,' said Riven, the word clear as glass in his mouth.

Hugh flapped a hand. 'I'm supposed to be here to give you a bucketful of sympathy and then get down to the nitty-gritty in a decent space of time and ask you about your writing.' He grinned, looking boyish for a brief moment. 'My tongue's as dry as day-old bread. This sort of thing is much easier under the civilising influence of alcohol. But that's taboo, I hear.'

Riven nodded. 'I'd sell my bloody soul for a pint.'

The ice broken, Hugh relaxed visibly. He glanced about and then sneaked one of his foul-smelling cigarettes from his pocket and lit it with relish.

'Drugs. I know. I spoke to your doctor. You must be high as a kite, the amount they're pumping into you...' He trailed off, and contemplated his glowing cigarette. 'I'm sorry, Mike. Sorry for you—for her. For the whole bastard thing. But what do you say that hasn't been said already? You know how I felt about her, Mike. I adored her. She was a bewitching woman. Such a waste.'

Riven nodded again. Grief is not only embarrassing. It is banal. It is wholesale.

'I know,' he said savagely, the words slipping in his clumsy mouth. He sounded as though his batteries were running down. 'Forget it, Hugh.' Leave it.

His editor pointed, smoke dribbling from his fingers. 'Good job you're left-handed.'

Riven frowned. What? Then realised. My one good limb. My writing hand. Now there's irony.

'I'm not writing. I won't for a long time—a long time, Hugh.'

The square-set man nodded, embarrassed. 'I didn't expect otherwise, to be honest. You'll need time. It would be obscene of me to start spouting about deadlines and advances...' But he looked as though he would have liked to, just the same. 'You're making progress, that's the important thing. Last week you couldn't even speak. The doctors think you'll make a complete recovery... We won't hurry you.'

You're damn right.

'There is one thing, though, Mike: the third book. Everyone is clamouring for it—the last of the trilogy. We have fans writing to us about it.'

Riven chuckled, startling himself. Fans! I have fans. Jesus Christ!

Hugh smiled in response. 'I know. Sales have almost doubled since the accident. Human nature is a weird and unpleasant thing at times. A real-life tragedy, and suddenly everyone wants to read the fiction. I've never been able to explain that sort of thing.'

Riven's laughter curdled in his throat until he felt like spitting.

'Maybe I should write it into the next book,' he snarled. His eyes glittered.

A rock face on Skye, and he sitting on a ledge and the rope gone slack, swaying. He could still hear the scream.

Why did it seem so terrible that she had screamed his name?

'I'm sorry,' Hugh said again, shifting on his chair. He looked at his watch. 'I'll go. You can do without this. Give me a ring when you've... sorted yourself out a little.' He stood up and seemed about to offer his hand again, but thought better of it. 'I'll go,' he repeated. 'Hang in there, Mike.' Then he turned and left. Riven toyed with the control knob of his chair.

Why are these such fearsome things? Sit in one for a while, and you're a metal centaur and people's eyes shrink away. Dan Dare, eat your heart out. Here comes Michael Riven in his fantastical rocket sled.

He directed the chair over to the window and gazed out. Autumn. Autumn on Skye. The bracken will be turning brown.

You might get the first snow on the Cuillin hills. Mind you, November can be quite mild up there...

'Your visitor doesn't look too chuffed with life,' said Doody cheerfully. He pushed in a laundry trolley and rolled it to a halt beside Riven's chair.

'Red tape,' said Riven absently. 'There's a lot of it about.'

'I'd have thought you were well clear of that now, sir. Being in hospital does have its advantages.'

Aye. It does. 'What's the date, Dood?'

'Twelfth of November. Bloody hell, these sheets are a mess. It's Mr bloody Simpson being careless again. You'd think a merchant banker could control his bum. He's in, but the light's not on, if you get my drift.'

I've been here four months. Christ.

'Doody, how many visitors have I had since I came in?'

Doody stopped to consider. 'Oh, loads. At least, they've been here loads of times. Not that you've ever seen any. They only got to see you when you were unconscious.' His brow furrowed. 'And you've never said why you wouldn't see them.'

Memories. Sympathy. Ye gods.

He stared out of the window again, watching the

river with its willows. Once he had seen the blue flash of a kingfisher there. A kingfisher summer... .

How did he get in here to see me? ...The white whale, of course. What was it? Like a lawyer. Ah, the trappings of respectability. Poor old Hugh.

'You know, sir, this may sound fucking stupid, but you're getting bloody quiet these days. You used to say more with that notebook than you do now you've got your voice back.' Doody was looking at him keenly, one hand clutching a forgotten bunch of linen pillowcases. Riven met his eyes.

'Well, Dood, you know what it is, don't you?' he asked sadly.

Doody shook his head.

'It's alcohol withdrawal symptoms, you soft git.'

'Ah!' Doody nodded sagely, then went out, pushing his trolley in front of him. 'Now you're coming off the drugs, I'll have to see if I can organise the proper medicine, Mr Riven, sir...'

CHAPTER TWO

THE BEECHFIELD CENTRE was a nursing home for those who preferred to be nursed in private. While not being what could be termed as 'exclusive,' it nevertheless tried to cultivate a certain calibre of clientele. One of its prime aims in life seemed to be to prepare members of the older, more privileged generation for the rigours of retirement. Thus, arthritis, rheumatism and wandering wits were high on the list of maladies encountered within its white walls. Riven was an anomaly in the system, but he had been welcomed at the centre nonetheless. He had something of a name in 'literature'; he had written two fantasy novels that had done quite well, earning him a modest income which sufficed—just—to keep him, with only a few odd jobs to supplement it. His parents had always wanted him to get a 'proper' job, and though they had not been ecstatic, to say the least, about the army, at least it was that. But Riven had left the army as a lieutenant, deciding he had seen enough. It was not to be missed, but it was not for life, either. Still, he would always be proud of having been a soldier; it had fulfilled one childhood ambition, and had given him time to think.

The trustees of the Beechfield Centre were glad to have him, eccentric though some of his behaviour appeared. The fact that he refused to see visitors, for instance, or that he would not communicate in any way with certain of the staff. But there was the double tragedy of his dead wife and his terrible injuries to think about. They made allowances for him, as long as his insurance paid for him to be there.

The consultant, Doctor Lynam, dropped in often, in his smiling, pleasant way. He was the sort who smokes a pipe with consummate incompetence, but who sticks to it manfully, knowing that it will be conquered by the time he has retired to his house in the Cotswolds. He gave the patients the same kind of absentminded affection he gave to his dog, which did not make him a bad doctor, but which made those under his care think uneasily that by troubling him with their ailments, they were interrupting the gracious, even flow of his life.

There were two nurses: Nurse Bisbee and Nurse Cohen. Bisbee was a relic from a Victorian schoolroom, benevolent as a South American dictator. Her face resembled a large pink crag, with the hair pulled back from it so tightly that Riven half believed when it was loosed her face would bunch up like a bloodhound's.

Nurse Cohen, on the other hand, was young and slight, with mischievous eyes and dark hair which it sometimes hurt Riven to look at.

There were several auxiliaries also, as well as a small kitchen staff. Doody combined the jobs of porter and nursing assistant, and sometimes helped out in the kitchen as well. No one seemed to know exactly what his job was.

When he was a nineteen-year-old corporal in the Buffs, he had chosen premature voluntary retirement rather than face a court martial for striking an officer. It was in Ireland, and his brick had come across a suspect van. Intelligence said it contained a device, so they set up an observation post on the hill above to monitor the area. When the platoon commander came on the scene, he demanded that Doody's brick go down and check the vehicle at close quarters. When Doody refused, he was called a coward, and a few other names; he flattened the officer. A few moments later the bomb in the van exploded. It was then that Doody applied for the Royal Army Medical Corps. He was good at his job, but the officer had many connections. So it was, at the age of twenty, Corporal David Doody found himself unemployed, having learned in the army the twin skills of killing and healing. And that, he used to say, was about as logical as the army ever got.

'So here I am,' he would add, 'wiping old geezer's backsides and trying to keep on the right side of Stalin in a white uniform.'

'IT'S SUCH LOVELY weather we're having,' said Nurse Cohen. 'A real Indian summer.'

Riven nodded. She was pushing him across the lawn behind the Centre. He was wrapped up against cold, with a blanket across his knees, but the sun was bright and warm and there were starlings darting around the willows. Like spring.

'I'll leave you here and be back in ten minutes to make sure you're not getting cold. All right, Mr Riven?' He nodded again and managed to smile for her.

Wonder how long her hair would be when let down... shit.

He sat and listened to the river and the squabbling starlings. The sky was clear, winter-clear, and though it was only mid afternoon, the sun was beginning to set. He could see it in the faintly tawny light and the long shadows.

A heavy hand placed itself on his shoulder and he turned sharply. Molesy.

'Ah. Mr Riven.' He looked about craftily. 'I hear you're talking again.'

'That's right.' You give me this shit about Skye again, Molesy, and I'll plug you one, cripple or no.

The old man was less than perfectly clean, and there was a smell off him—sweat and earth—which surprised Riven. The Beechfield staff were usually very efficient about hygiene. Molesy seemed to have escaped their attentions. If it came to that, he had never yet seen the old man in the company of a nurse or an auxiliary. Riven felt a twinge of uneasiness. Almost as if they did not know he was here.

Molesy glanced about once more, watchful as always. Was he worried about being seen? Riven shifted in his chair.

'How long have you been here, Molesy?' he asked.

The old Scot ignored him. 'We share a secret, we two,' he said—and again there was that accent which Riven could not place jangling behind the brogue. 'But don't worry, the secret is safe with me.'

'What secret?' Riven demanded irritably.

'Ah, now, don't be mocking me, Mr Riven. You're from Eileen A Cheo. You know what lies in the mountains above the sea, where the waterfall comes down to the Cape of the Wolf's Heart.'

He's gone. He is as loopy as a kangaroo.

But the old man's face had become shrewd, and the stare of the eyes had focused. For a second the jowls of his face seemed to tighten. Riven had the momentary impression that Molesy was not old. But then it was gone.

'When you have your legs, and the broken pieces of you have put themselves together, remember to go home. We must all go home in the end,' Molesy said earnestly. 'That is where you are needed—where the mountains meet the sea.' His blue eyes twinkled. 'There are things to be done up there.'

Riven saw Nurse Cohen walking towards him across the lawn. Molesy followed his gaze and flinched. He swore under his breath.

'Time I was off,' he said in a muttered sing-song. 'Time to walk the Northern Road again. Remember the smell of the sea, Mr Riven, and the curlews calling through the peaks of the Black Cuillins. Don't be forgetting it in this southern place, where the air is full of smoke and the water is stale. Remember where you must go.'

And he lurched away swiftly across the grass, bumping into another patient as he went. He disappeared into the trees, and there was only the faint, earthy smell left in the air to mark his passing.

'All right, Mr Riven?' Nurse Cohen said cheerfully, taking the handles at the back of his chair.

'Who the hell is he?' Riven asked her.

'Who?'

'The old man—the old Scot. Has he been admitted here?'

'We've no Scots at Beechfield, Mr Riven. Just one Irishman, who is ready for his dinner. It's getting chilly, don't you think?'

And Riven shivered slightly in answer, though not with cold.

HE SPENT A lot of time in the recreation room these evenings, as it got dark so early. There the patients watched television, played cards or argued half-heartedly amongst themselves. Riven read. He was attempting to keep abreast of the current fantasy scene, as his editor called it. He wondered sometimes if he would write again, but there was something there, something black and futile, which stopped him every time his pen touched paper and made every word he wrote into nonsense; useless nonsense. So he waited out the long evenings into the winter that was coming. Apart from Hugh, he had spoken to no one from his former life since he had left hospital. Former was what he called the life before. He could not quite believe that there had been a life before. The laughing platoon commander, the lover, the husband, the writer. All that had been someone else.

He looked out of the window to where the river ran off in the darkness. Where Molesy had disappeared.

It's going to be one of those nights. Well, it's not the first and it won't be the last. How long ago was it, when I first went to Skye? A never-to-be-forgotten visit while I was still in the army. One winter, long ago.

STARING OUT ON the loch, he watched the greylags wheel round and honk their way into the water. The last light was going down behind the mountains, leaving herring-bones of pink cloud trailing across the sky, throwing sunset into the water, making the ripples incandescent.

His feet were wet, and the fire was sinking along with the sun. His mess tins sat at his side, undersides blackened, insides smeary with curry. He'd wash them in the stream later.

No tent, and it looked like rain. He did not trust the bivvy-bag entirely. Screwing up his face at the darkening sky, he rubbed pine resin from his fingers. He missed the sound of the sea, for he had slept on the shore for the past few nights. Now all he could hear was the rising wind in the peaks—and the settling of the geese on the loch.

Beats the hell out of traffic. He grinned at the fire and his faintly steaming boots. Stretching, he felt a bright prickle of rain on his upturned face. Not the first night he would be soaked through whilst sleeping. A few days ago he had woken up, bivvy stiff with frost. The nights were long these days, getting longer. Snow had held off, though. Only the mountains were dusted with it. The mountains he would begin scaling tomorrow.

*   *   *

'YOU KNOW, SIR, I sometimes think that if it wasn't for me, you might dig a hole and hide in it. What do you think you're doing, sitting there staring at nothing?'

Startled, Riven turned away from the window to see Doody watching him with disapproval. He whirred the chair round almost sheepishly.

'Anyway, I come here on a mission.' Doody moved to the back of the chair and took the handles. 'We're off to see the wizard, me old son—but if anyone asks I'm taking you to the bog.' He wheeled Riven out of the recreation room and away from the clamour of the television. Then, looking about him as if he were on patrol, he took Riven down a side corridor, whistling tunelessly.

'Can I ask what's happening, or is it a state secret?' Riven demanded peevishly.

Doody laughed. 'Tonight, sir, since you're off the drugs, you and me is going to get paralytic.'

Eventually they stopped outside the door of a storeroom. Doody produced a bunch of keys with a flourish and, opening the door, bowed deeply. Riven motored the chair inside.

'Fucking Aladdin's cave or what?' Doody asked, closing the door behind him and switching on the light. Riven began to laugh. Piled on a table in the middle of the cluttered little room were several six-packs of beer, and a large bottle of Irish whiskey. Two pint and two short glasses shone there also.

'Don't say I don't think of everything. I made sure the beer got chilled, too.' Doody smirked.

A can spat as Riven pulled the ring. 'Music,' he said, and began pouring. Doody joined him. 'Anne Cohen is covering for us,' he said, 'so we don't have to worry about tin-knickers.'

'How the hell did you get it into the building?'

Doody took a long gulp, swallowed, and closed his eyes for a second before replying. 'Piece of piss. I wheel laundry baskets. Laundry baskets are big. You put things in them. I could probably get a dance troupe in here if I really tried.'

Riven half-emptied the glass at one gulp, and then put his head back to stare at the ceiling with its single light bulb.

'You know, Doody, tonight I am going to get totally—'

'Utterly,' Doody put in.

'Completely.'

'One hundred per cent.'

'Shitfaced.'

'Here's to oblivion, sir.' And their glasses clinked together.

THEY MOVED QUIETLY down the street. His eyes glinted in his camouflaged face and he waved his hand downwards. The brick went firm; four soldiers merged with doorways, their rifles pointing out in covering arcs. In the dark they looked like full bin liners huddled in porches.

They moved on. The radio hissed slightly. Around them the dead windows and closed doors frowned on them. Some were boarded up, some had broken glass glittering in them. A dog barked, and there was the faint, far-off rumble of nocturnal traffic.

'Hello, mike one zero, this is zero; radio check, over.'

He thumbed the pressel switch and felt the pressure of the mike at his throat.

'Mike one zero alpha, okay, over.'

'Zero, roger, out.'

They came to a junction lit by a single amber street lamp. Broken glass was strewn across the road, and a burnt-out car that the day before had been a barricade squatted black and tangled on the tarmac. One by one they scuttled across the dangerously lit space, breathing heavily as they took up positions in the darkness on the other side.

Then they set off again down a darker, narrower street that had more than its fair share of derelict houses and graffiti. One of the soldiers kicked a stone, and it rattled across the road, making them all start. The other three cursed him softly.

Then the night vanished. There was a brilliant flash, and a concussion that blew them off their feet and sucked air out of their lungs. A moment later came the noise, and the rain of rubble and dust. The point man of the brick was engulfed and disappeared.

Riven was blown across the road and somehow his rifle went off in his hand, although he had thought the safety catch on. He lay in a tangle of bricks and the remnants of a small front garden, thinking: I've had an ND.

Flashes and cracks started from a house up the street, and thumps as rounds began to go down around them. He pressed the mike button.

'Mike one alpha, contact—'

Then he crawled to cover as the tarmac in front of his nose erupted in bullet strikes.

'Belsham! Johnson! George!' he screamed, vaguely realising that Johnson had been point and was now perhaps beyond hearing him.

Answering cracks came from an SLR close by, and a voice shouting: 'Belsham here, sir; George is hit. I don't know where Pete is!'

'Mike one zero, contact'—he looked about him—'corner of Creggan and Wishingwell Street. Two casualties. Under fire from at least one enemy. Request QRF. Over.'

'Zero, roger. QRF on its way. Out.'

He peered cautiously around his little garden wall. The flashes had stopped. The gunman was making his getaway. 'Belsham! Where the fuck are you?'

'Here, sir; behind the shed.'

He ran over. Belsham was kneeling beside a prostrate George, ripping up field dressings furiously. Riven felt sick.

'Where's he hit?'

'Chest, sir. I can handle it.'

'Right. I'll go and look for Pete.' He doubled off again to where the explosion had happened. A mass of rubble blocked the road. He stumbled across an SLR with a bent barrel, then found what was left of his point man. He vomited whilst the whine of the Quick Reaction Force's Land Rovers filled up the street behind him.

THE LIGHT BULB grew brighter, the pile of empty cans higher; the talk louder.

'What was the first battalion like, then?' Riven asked.

'Laid back. What about the third?'

Riven belched. 'Stuck up. They didn't like Irish subalterns.'

'Funny us being in the same regiment, sir.'

'I was in Ireland when you were in Belize.'

'Why'd you leave?'

'Got married.'

'Oh, shit. Sorry, sir.'

Riven waved his hand. 'Doesn't matter. Doesn't matter.' He grinned crookedly. 'Life's a bitch.' He sat staring at his empty glass. 'Doesn't matter,' he slurred again.

Doody refilled them both, spilt some, and sniffed. 'What was your wife like?'

Riven continued looking beyond the pint glass in front of him, head swaying slightly. 'My wife. Bloody hell.' He blinked. 'She was tall. Tall and dark. Quite a lass. Her eyebrows met in the middle. I used to call her a witch.' He smiled, remembering. 'She put a spell on me, anyway. Jennifer MacKinnon, from the Isle of Skye—the Isle of Mists, in the Gaelic... Ach—' He downed his drink in a succession of throat-scraping gulps. The empty glass glittered in the artificial light, and he smacked his lips loudly. 'Fucking beer didn't last long, did it?'

Doody broached the whiskey with great ceremony, and they toasted each other in loud voices before throwing it back. Riven felt the raw liquid burn its long-lost way home down his throat, and the room wavered a little.

'Bloody hell,' he said again as Doody refilled the glasses. 'Good stuff, this.'

'Only the best,' Doody affirmed. He sloshed whiskey on the table and scowled at the bottle.

'Fucking bad craftsmanship, that.' Again, they threw back the spirit as though it were water. Riven was beginning to have trouble focusing. There was a window behind Doody's head, blue with the night, but he could have sworn there had been a darker silhouette framed there for a second—a strange shape with sharp ears...

Ah, I've no head for this stuff any more.

Doody began singing quietly, an army song not noted for the delicacy of its language, and Riven joined in with a will. They bellowed out the chorus together. A sweep of Riven's good arm sent his glass to the floor, where it shattered. They peered at it owlishly. Then there was a knock at the door, and the pair gazed at each other.

'I'm only a cripple!' Riven protested. 'He made me do it!'

The door opened and Nurse Cohen entered. 'Are you two still in here? Couldn't you keep it a little quieter?'

Doody looked blank for a second, then recognition dawned.

'It's our guardian angel,' he hiccuped. 'Our lookout. Is the coast clear, Anne?'

'You two are utterly smashed,' Nurse Cohen whispered.

'I am,' Riven volunteered absently.

'Doody, for God's sake, did you have to get him *completely* plastered? Old Bisbee will be doing the rounds in under an hour. I can handle the auxiliaries, but not her. We've got to get him back to his room.'

Doody saluted with a beatific smile on his ugly face, and then, infinitely slowly, he fell over. Nurse

Cohen swore, went over to Riven and prised the other glass from his hand.

'Come on, I'll get you out of trouble, at least.' With a final despairing glance at the mumbling Doody, she wheeled Riven out.

'Nurse,' said Riven plaintively. 'Nurse—'

'What is it?' she hissed, looking warily over her shoulder.

'I have to have a pee, nurse...'

'Oh, Christ! You're kidding!'

Riven shook his head dumbly. She pushed him to the toilets used by the walking wounded of the Centre, then stood in front of him.

'I'll have to support you. Come on.' She lifted Riven easily, for he was painfully thin, and half carried him to the urinals. Then she held him as he relieved himself.

'This is the first time I've been upright in months,' he said. But he was suddenly and painfully aware of the woman holding him. The feel of her, the smell of her hair. He clenched his teeth, and nodded when she asked him if he was finished. She took him back to the chair and laid him in it like a baby.

'There. Now perhaps I can get you to bed.' And she smiled at him, pushing a lock of hair up under her nurse's cap.

He looked away and whispered, 'I'm sorry.'

She actually laughed, and began trundling him along the corridors. 'Boys will be boys, I suppose. But your head will hate you in the morning, Mr Riven.' She put him to bed and tucked him in. 'I think you'll survive, but I wouldn't try that again in a hurry. Go to sleep now. I've got to do something about that idiot Doody.'

She left, turning out the light as she went. Riven lay open-eyed in the darkness.

Didn't quite make the oblivion stage.

He closed his eyes.

THE SLEET LASHED his face, screaming out of the darkness. The ice axe slipped fractionally. He dug in deeper, hauling himself upwards and feeling for handholds. Jagged rock iced and bled his hands. He shut his eyes to the gale that hammered him, and felt his way forward.

Why? Why do it?

His boot moved up, searching for a crack in the frozen rock. Snow piled itself in every crevice of his clothing, clung there in folds and lines, clogged his ears.

I will do it. Because—

Slipping. A lightning rebalance that tore a groan past his lips, bared his teeth in a moment of helpless anger. Then he was secure again; buffeted by the storm, but holding.

Because I am one stubborn son of a bitch.

THE FACE HE was staring at was pale and thin. The cheekbones stood out below the eyes, making them into dark hollows, though the eyes themselves were steady and grey. Fair hair fell over the scarred forehead, and a beard of the same colour sprouted on the lower face. A hand rubbed it thoughtfully.

Jesus. So this is the new me. What happened to the broad-shouldered soldier? He turned the chair away from the sink with its mirror, and made for the passage beyond it that led outside.

I was never overly tall, but I was thickset, at least. I look like a rotten stick.

The weather was cold and fine, with a mist that wreathed up from the river in the mornings and vanished by noon. He looked across the lawn to where the willows stooped, and the water glittered.

I'm going to paddle in that some day, if it kills me.

'How's your head then, Mr Riven?' asked Nurse Cohen, coming up behind him.

'It's been better, but on the other hand it's been much worse... How is Doody?'

'Taking the day off. He has a stomach bug.'

'Ah! Hope it's not catching.'

'I doubt it, somehow.'

'You didn't get in trouble, did you?'

She shook her head. 'In the end, I simply locked the storeroom and left Doody in there to sleep it off. Luckily, he didn't throw up. I let him out this morning and he made a mad dash for the toilet. Seems he had been crossing his legs and praying for hours.' She laughed. 'Well, I have to go and prepare Mr Simpson to meet the day.' She laid a light hand on his shoulder for a second, and then left.

Riven sat quite still, feeling the cold air on his face and watching the starlings squabbling in the bird bath in the middle of the lawn. Then he shoved the chair into motion and rattled across the patio. He hit the grass with a bump and a protesting whine from his steed, then continued more slowly, the motor bickering loudly. The chair lurched and shook as it hit sudden dips and hollows. The lawn was not as flat as it appeared. He wobbled dangerously and ground to an ignominious halt on the last steep slope before the river. The chair teetered at a crazy angle. He swore and leaned away from the slope, but too late. He fell over and hit the ground with a sodden thump and a flash of pain in his legs.

'Shit!'

There was dew-wet grass at his cheek, and the smell of soil under his nose. He rolled free of the chair and managed to sit himself upright, earth on his face and under his nails. His blanket was twisted around his legs, a tangle of tartan on the grass.

You asshole, Riven. You really make a habit out of this sort of thing, don't you?

He looked round. He was invisible from the Centre, hidden by the slope. The river was fifty yards away, beyond the dipping trees. His legs and arm were screaming at him.

He tried to right the chair, but it was too heavy and in too awkward a position. And he was too weak. The weakness enraged him. He punched the grass with his only useful limb.

You bastard! You utterly useless bastard!

Right on cue, the rain began. It started as a breeze in the willows that stirred his hair, then a fine mist of moisture that drifted down and finally a wind-driven shower that drove into his eyes and soaked his shirt. He started to laugh.

Fucking typical!

He began to crawl, pulling himself through the muddying ground with one arm.

Couldn't be more than a hundred yards. Christ, at Sandhurst I've crawled ten times that in full kit with a Jimpy rattling live overhead. Come on, Riven, you wimp, are you a man or a mouse?

He stopped, gasping, when he got to the top of the slope. Runnels of water were flowing down it. He was chilled to the bone, and to the bolts. He looked up to see a sullen, glowering sky above his head, and then peered through the rain towards the Centre.

He waved at the figures in the windows.

Come on, you senile old bastards. One of you has got to see me.

He bent his head into the mud.

I don't believe this. I can't die of exposure in bloody Berkshire. I'd die of shame first.

He began crawling again. He made the bird bath his goal and refused to look at the buildings. He felt himself going numb. The rain was turning to sleet.

Winter has picked a hell of an auspicious moment to arrive.

Then there were white-shoed feet in the soaking ground beside him, and strong hands took hold of him.

'What happened to you, Mr Riven?' He was being lifted up, and found himself looking at Nurse Cohen's face.

He smiled wanly. 'You took your bloody time.'

Her cap was gone and the rain had streaked hair across her face. He closed his eyes.

A FACE BENT over him, dark hair spilling around it. Beyond it was the brightness of sunshine reflecting on snow. His eyes watered, and he blinked, bringing the face into focus.

Grey, grave eyes and a mouth with a smile. Shoulder-length raven hair that was shining in the light.

'How do you feel?' The voice was low, with a Highland Scot accent.

He was lying in a bed draped with brightly coloured blankets. Behind the girl's head was a window of pure blue sky. He could hear wind in the rafters.

'I'm... fine, I think. Where am I?'

'You're near Glenbrittle,' she answered musically. 'We found you last night lying on the western scree of Sgurr Dearg, battered to bits. You had your torch burning beside you. That's how we found you.'

He touched the bandage on his head, and blew air through pursed lips. 'I remember now. I lost a crampon and went flying down the mountain.' He winced. 'Christ, how did I survive it?'

'You're badly bruised and you gashed your head, but apart from that, you are as healthy as I am. A wee bit peaky maybe, but right as rain.'

He raised his eyebrows and sat up laboriously. The girl helped him. He grimaced as his bruises shouted.

'Lucky, I guess.'

'More like miraculous,' she retorted, and helped him out of bed. To his embarrassment he found he was dressed in an old-fashioned nightshirt.

'It's all we could get on you,' she said, smiling mischievously.

Reddening, he stood up. The girl's arm encircled his waist, steadying him. She was as tall as he was. Dizzy, he swayed, and she leaned herself against him. He caught a fragrance of windblown hair. He felt like kissing her, but settled for asking her name.

'Jennifer MacKinnon. My father is Calum MacKinnon, and it is our home you are in.'

'I'm Michael Riven. Thanks.'

She shrugged. 'We'd hardly leave you lying up there. Come and have a look at what sort of trip you had down Dearg.' She led him over to the window.

Outside, blindingly white snow covered everything, and rearing up massively in front of him was the mountain, stern and blunt, dark granite faces scattered on it where the wind would allow no purchase to the snow. He looked at the pocked scree face. He had fallen down that, head over heels.

'I survived that?'

'Aye,' she said quietly. 'You did. There's many a one wouldn't, I'm thinking. What made you climb during that storm anyway? Had you a hound at your heels?'

His face clouded. 'Maybe. One that followed me all the way from the south.'

And follows me still.

'IT'S DISGRACEFUL, THAT'S what it is. You've been told so many times, Mr Riven, never to drive your chair on to the lawn. Now it will take an electrician to get it working again. Until then, you can stay in your bed— hopefully that will keep you out of further mischief. Don't you ever think of the staff of this Centre, Mr Riven? Your attitude is incomprehensible. It had better improve, or I shall be having words with the consultant about the advisability of keeping you here.' Nurse Bisbee paused. 'Haven't you anything to say for yourself?'

Riven continued staring out of the window at the blue night and the rain that tapped on the glass.

'Well, I'm not wasting any more time with you. There are patients who need me more, Mr Riven.'

And off she goes, steam coming out of her ears. Righteous indignation oozes out of every pore.

He lay and looked at the ceiling, unable to push out of his mind the way Nurse Cohen had manhandled him inside. Her hands on him.

Christ, that's all I need. A bout of horniness.

The window rattled under the battery of the wind. He shut his eyes and heard again the gales in the Cuillin hills, the curlews, and the sea.

I haven't left this place in four months. Didn't even go to the funeral. I was unconscious in a hospital getting wired together.

THE CHAIR WAS not in operation for nearly a week, during which time Riven lay in his bed and fought a running battle against the memories. Doody called in frequently, and teased him about morning afters and wheelchair acrobatics. Riven did not see Nurse Cohen much. Nurse Bisbee took care of most of his needs with a tight-lipped silence, or neutral remarks about the weather which she usually saved for the elderly in the Centre. Or she talked about Christmas, which was drawing near; and which made Riven hate her. His memories of last Christmas were too close.

He was taken to see Doctor Lynam, to have the progress of his legs monitored. They were pronounced 'fairly sound,' and the good man recommended, with a tap of his pipe, that Riven try them out after a few days and see how they went; as though they were a new car.

So Doody and Nurse Cohen took it upon themselves to haul Riven out of bed, procure for him a walking frame, and help him down the corridor in a string of lurches and bumps and near-falls and pain and gritted teeth. By the time they had gone twenty yards—at Riven's insistence—his head was in a red mist and the sweat was trickling down his back. He had to be put in the chair to return to his room.

'Don't worry, sir,' said Doody. 'What's-its-name wasn't built in a day, was it? We can have another go tomorrow, if you're up to it.' Riven nodded faintly. Nurse Cohen tucked him in.

'We can always have a rest tomorrow if you like, and try the next day. It's up to you.'

He managed a smile for her.

I'm as weak as a half-drowned kitten. My legs are in bits. How in the name of God will I ever be as I was again?

He could not help but think about the army, when he had run and jumped and crawled and marched. And marched. Why did everything he wanted to do seem to need mobility? All that walking in the Highlands, all that climbing. If his legs were taken away from him, he had once supposed he could fall back on writing. But that was... gone, now. That was no longer a way out.

Alone. As I was in the beginning. And I've gained so much and thrown so much away that I'm left with what I had at the start.

The shadow of another world.

A refuge, maybe, or a handicap.

Time was when his world, the world of his novels, sat at his elbow always waiting for him, and he could turn and look into someone else's eyes in a room that was empty, and see them laugh back at him. He had made a world of simple, open people who saw right and wrong as black and white with no grey in between. But then, in stories, things are always simpler. His books were of a world ringed by mountains and the sea; a wide place with room for some mystery in it— maybe even some magic. There was something of Skye in it. Stone and heather, and clean air. Just as Molesy had said. And magnificent, make-believe characters— people who ruled what he did just as surely as if they drove cars, played squash and got drunk in the real world. He had almost killed himself trying to prove he could be one of them. They had made him become a soldier and they had pursued him up mountains, until he had fallen and found the girl who was to become his wife at the foot of one. He had failed, but he had told their stories still—tales full of fighting and honour, and desperate deeds done with bright swords. Oh, yes. But he had betrayed them somehow, by giving his love to someone in his own world, and he was not sure if they would have him any more now, that he was bruised and bleeding from a loss so great as to leave his life empty of anything else but those stories, and the people in them. In the beginning they were all he had thought he had ever wanted, but now he did not know. Now that he wanted the world to be simpler, cleaner, he felt he had muddied whatever his imagination had given him.

He could write no longer. There were no more stories left in him.

* * *

RIVEN HAD NEVER been the most patient individual in the world, and the progress his legs made, though applauded by his coaches Doody and Nurse Cohen, was to him like pecking at a mountain with a needle. He chafed as he had not done before, and realised dimly that his time in Beechfield was nearly over. The thought chilled him. He did not know what would happen next.

Leave it to the next year. This one is nearly over.

'We'll have you running a fucking marathon before Christmas, sir; then you'll be able to outdistance the nurses who'll be after you.' Doody was watching over him as he thumped down the passage with the frame. 'Still, I reckon Anne will keep them off you well enough,' he added, smiling wickedly.

Riven looked round sharply. 'Don't give me that shit, Doody. I'm bones and bolts, and I've got to get used to it.'

Doody shook his head. 'Your eyes must have been damaged in the fall then, too, you twit.'

Riven kept the frame crashing along, with his feet following as though they were drunk. 'I... couldn't, Dood.'

Doody's eyebrows shot up his black forehead. 'Looks like it'll be you and me getting hammered again, then, sir. You're hardly in a fit state to dance the night away.'

Will I ever be?

And he smashed the frame down, and sent his feet following after.

* * *

AN IMMENSE EXPANSE of whiteness piled in mountains, falling away on one side to a blue sea. It shone in the winter sun, blazing soundlessly in a still cold. He breathed in the shrill air, bruises aching. The snow crunched slightly under his feet in the silence.

'Bla-Bheinn, Sgurr Alisdair, Sgurr nan Gillean...' the girl beside him said in her lilting voice, pointing with one gloved hand at the monolithic, jagged ice hills all around them. The names were like a pagan litany.

He looked at her. Her face was healthy with raw air, eyes sparkling, lips slightly parted.

She caught his gaze suddenly, and reddened at once. 'It's rude to stare, you know.' And she smiled.

'Maybe,' he said simply, 'but I like the scenery.' They both laughed, with only the mountains to hear them. He wanted to touch her face, but took his eyes away with the thoughts moiling within him.

'Dangerous, busy Belfast is a long way away,' he said, breath steaming.

'Aye,' she said. 'I hate cities, even Edinburgh. And especially London. Mountains and the sea are in my blood. I'm a Skye lass through and through.'

'A Skye lass,' he repeated, testing the words. A nice sound. She turned with a crunch of the snow, and pointed eastwards. 'See Bla-Bheinn? It leans over Glen Sligachan, that runs right through the Cuillins. There where the glen ends at the sea is Camasunary. It's an old shieling, and my father has a bothy there. It's the loveliest spot on earth. No road to it, only a path that leads over the ridge to Torrin. I spend summers there.'

'I've seen it. I camped there on my way round the coast to Glenbrittle.' He smiled wryly. 'When I was there, the rain was driven horizontal by the wind, and if you faced seaward it was impossible to breathe.'

She grinned. 'Aye. Well, you take the rough with the smooth up here.'

The impulse was too strong, and he raised his hand to touch her cheek, caress her hair.

'I wish I lived here, and didn't have to go back south.'

She stared at him with that smile he had already come to know. Secretive, conspiratorial; one corner of her mouth quirking upwards. She touched the plaster on his head lightly.

'Stay a while, then,' she said.

BEECHFIELD CRAWLED ITS way through the darkest heart of the winter towards Christmas, and what passed as a festive spirit resurrected itself on the wards. Riven held himself apart from the preparations, eyeing the spectacle of elderly people making paper chains with profound dislike. He took to spending long hours by the windows that looked out on to the lawn and the river with an unread book on his lap, trying to avoid the well-meant attentions of the staff—even Doody. To keep thoughts of Sgurr Dearg out of his mind, he was thinking of higher mountains.

'To the east of the western peaks, north of the sea, the land rose and fell in Dales and moors. In the Dales, herdsmen grazed their sheep and cattle, and there were small fields of barley for bread and beer. The people were scattered, coming together only to buy and sell, and for defence in the wintertime against the wolves and the other beasts that came hungering out of the mountains. There were old fortresses there in the heart of the Dales, at the crossing of the rivers or where the soil was very rich. They had been built by the first men to come out of the north, ringed with turf ramparts and stone walls. These were the Rorim of the Dales peoples, where the fighting men lived with the Dale lords and issued forth in their defence. They fought the wolves and the Giants from the ice, and the other creatures which few men saw except as brief glimpses outside their windows in the night...'

Riven blinked. He had been recalling one of his own books almost word for word in his head. It sounded as portentous as a bible in his mind, and he looked out at the night beyond the window as though he were peering from a fortress. Was Molesy out there now? He was not a patient here, that was certain.

Something moved down by the willows at the river—a shape that loped from one shadow to another. Riven jumped in his chair. A dog, a stray hanging around for scraps.

And it was there again—no, this was another one. He was sure there were two of them out there, crouched in the deeper darkness underneath the bare limbs of the trees. The hair rose on the back of his neck. Dogs, merely. But he felt their eyes on him. They were sitting patiently on their haunches in the night, gazes fixed on the bright windows of the ward buildings.

Dogs—yes. But they stirred some old, forgotten fear in him. Getting the bloody jitters sitting here by myself, that's what I'm doing.

Dogs—but they had looked like wolves.

'Christmas may be coming, Mr Riven, but you are one goose that is not getting very fat,' said Nurse

Cohen from behind him. She came forward and looked at his bony frame disapprovingly. 'We'll have to try and build you up, especially now you are doing all this walking.'

'Walking!' Riven exclaimed. 'I've never heard it called that before. I've never walked like that before.'

'It's a start, Mr Riven, and you're doing very well. I can see you are determined to enjoy Christmas upright.'

Riven bent his head. 'Do you go out of the Centre much, after dark?' he asked her, feeling foolish.

She seemed puzzled. 'There's not much cause to be going out on a cold night like this. I generally make a run for the car as soon as my shift is over and beetle off home. Why?'

He scowled. 'No reason.' But he wanted to be out there, in the night, by the cold brightness of the river. It was almost as if he were being called. And at the same time he knew that nothing would persuade him to go out alone in the dark.

What's there? My imagination? Nothing. Bugger all. Don't be a fool.

Nurse Cohen set a hand on the back of his neck, light as thistledown. Her fingers were cool on his nape. He could smell the clean linen smell of her uniform, and froze. His jaw muscles bunched wildly. Her face was suddenly that of the young, dark girl he had envisaged days before. He twisted away from her hand, and she gave a small sigh and patted him on the shoulder.

'Don't sit there too long on your own. Why don't you come in and join the others? They're getting quite lively with Christmas coming. Like a bunch of kids, really.'

He shook his head slightly, and after a moment she glided away, back to the light and warmth of the recreation room.

THAT NIGHT, HE had a dream.

It was bitterly cold, and the snow lay thick on the ground. The rivers had become hard and grey as sword blades in the shadow of the hills. And the Giants were abroad, coming down out of the high mountains for the first time in generations.

They were three days out of the Rorim when the blizzard struck, and the world became a whirling void of snowflakes two steps wide. They cast about for shelter in the lee of a hill and eventually came upon a bank of broken stone that kept the worst of the wind off them. They sat there with the whiteness piling around their calves and the slow, numbing chill eating through their winter furs. There were three of them. One was slight and dark, the other burly and red-bearded, and the third a scarred man whose legs were of different lengths.

It was the dark man who started, his head snapping up and his eyes narrowing to stare out at the flapping curtain of the snow.

'What is it?' the red-bearded man asked at once. 'What do you see?'

The dark man grimaced. 'I'm not so certain. Nothing, maybe—a shape on the wind.' But now they all strained silently to pierce the blizzard with their tired eyes.

'What was it like?' Riven asked, rubbing his aching legs.

'It was big,' the dark man said shortly, and Riven cursed.

The sound of crunching snow came to each of them at the same moment, and they froze.

'Listen,' Riven said urgently.

'Shut up!' the dark man hissed.

They made no sound for many heartbeats. The wind had dropped slightly, and the snow was falling in a near-hush. They heard the sound again—a bulk moving through the deep-lying drifts. Perhaps a rasp of breathing.

'Where is it?' the red-bearded man demanded.

There was a click of rock behind them, and they turned as one, scrabbling through the snow that covered them.

Something rose up like a grey wall out of the snow, ten feet tall and pale with ice. Two eyes burned like blue balls of fire in a misshapen face, and the shadowy blur of a great arm swept through the air and smashed the bearded man ten yards through the air. Riven yelled with fright.

'Run!' the dark man shouted, tugging at his sword, but Riven could not move. The snow had frozen into ice around his knees, locking him into immobility. He saw the dark man smashed aside like a broken stick, and the blue fires of the Giant's eyes were upon him. They knew him.

'Never marry a woman whose eyebrows meet in the middle,' the Giant said with Jenny's voice, and then it laughed, the sound clear as a bell in the falling snow.

Riven shrieked.

*　　*　　*

THE NIGHT WAS silent. Had he screamed? All he could hear was the pumping of his own blood in his ears, fuelled by a racing heart. His legs had become tangled in his blankets. The moon poured a bright eldritch light in through his window. He sat up, rubbing his scarred temples. The door to his room was closed. If he had screamed, it was possible no one had heard him. But no; the nurse would have.

Only a dream, for Christ's sake.

But the Giant was straight out of his books, one of his pet monsters. And the other two men... He knew them from somewhere.

'Fucking potty,' he murmured.

The dream had left him with a bad taste in his mouth, as though something somewhere were not quite right. There was a jangling feeling of unease in him that was allied to but separate from the miasma of grief he was continually fighting. Absently, he wondered if the weather was fine up at the bothy. On a night like this, the sea would be shining like a lamp and the waves would be a gentle sussuration of water on shingle.

Ach, shit.

He swung his legs off the bed and groped for his dressing gown and crutches. Sleep was a long way off now. The cold floor chilled his toes, like the clutch of winter's ice. He shook his head. Dreaming of giants. What next?

His crutches clumped on the linoleum as he laboured over to the window and manoeuvred himself into a chair. Outside, the gardens were a maze of silver and grey, the trees standing in ponds of shadow and the river glittering coldly in the light of the moon. He stared at the deep shadows a little anxiously, but there were no dogs there tonight. Or bloody wolves either, come to that. He smiled. Imagination is one thing, but paranoia quite another.

Savagely he pushed the encroaching memories away and strove to think of other things. His books. There had been two characters like those of his dream in the second, he remembered, but their names escaped him, which was irritating. And the giants from the mountains—Rime Giants, creatures of the glaciers who marauded the lowlands in the depths of the bleakest winters...

Moonlight on the lawn turned it into a flawless snowfield, and he winced. Winter. He felt he would never be free of it. So many doors in his mind had been frozen up and were closed to him. His imagination creaked with ice. My livelihood, he thought glumly, and he remembered Hugh's words. So the fans were hungering for the last of the trilogy. Well, maybe if he could churn it out somehow, it would be enough.

But Jenny was in there, in that world of mountains and giants and desperate swordsmen.

He flinched away from the thought. Time heals, he reminded himself bitterly. But when will I have the guts to finally go home? He recalled Molesy's ramblings. *Remember where you have to go.* Easy for you to say, you loopy old bastard.

He thumped the arm of the chair. Come on, Riven. What happened to the soldier in there? Where did he go?

There had been a Greenjacket officer who had been to Oxford with him, an impossibly good-natured gentleman who had once led his platoon in an attack whilst chanting the Anglo-Saxon *Battle of Maldon*. And that had completed a circle somehow—the myth had met the reality and had in a strange way become the same.

It's why I began writing. To make my own myth. But the real world has a way of mocking things like that.

The door opened and he jumped like a hare, half expecting to see a hulking monster stoop into the room with its eyes blazing. But it was only Nurse Cohen, her white uniform making a wraith of her in the moonlight.

'Mr Riven, what are you doing up?'

He shrugged. 'Couldn't sleep.'

She laid a hand on his bare arm. Her fingers were warm against his skin. 'You're freezing! Come on, let me get you back into bed.'

He shook his head. 'It's all right. I'm fine.'

She studied him for a long moment, standing in the shadow at the side of the window. 'Bad dreams?'

'Maybe. How do you know?'

He thought she smiled slightly. 'I look in on you now and again while you're asleep. It's my job. You cry in your sleep, Mr Riven.'

Riven swore briefly and turned his face to the bright window again. 'It's not a fucking spectator sport, you know.'

'I'm sorry.'

'Everyone's sorry. I don't want anybody's sorrow. I just want some peace.' He closed his eyes. 'Sorry.'

'Everyone's apologising,' she said quietly.

'I am sorry, really. I'm a cantankerous bastard at times.' He paused. 'And foul-mouthed, too.' Jenny had always hated him swearing.

'It doesn't matter,' she said, and sat on the windowsill so that the moonlight limned her in silver and made her face indecipherable. Riven caught himself wondering how old she was.

'Will you ever write again?' she asked unexpectedly.

He did not reply, and she added: 'I've read your books. They're beautiful. All mountains and horses, and strong silent types.'

He laughed despite himself.

'Will you finish the story? Will you write the third?'

He could not speak. The story finished me. My part in it is over. And Jenny's. There will be other characters in it now. And he felt the damned tears crowding his eyes.

'Shit,' he muttered.

'It's all right,' she said. 'Listen, I didn't mean to—oh, hell.' She leaned over and suddenly hugged him close, so that his tears wet her neck. He clenched his teeth. Get a grip, man. He could feel the soft push of her breasts through the uniform.

She withdrew, leaving him strangely desolate.

'I'd better go,' she said. 'I'll be missed on the wards. Will you be okay?'

He nodded dumbly.

She stared at him as if unsure, and then leaned forward again to kiss his scarred forehead.

'Is this regular nursing procedure?' he asked lightly.

'There's nursing and there's nursing, Mr Riven.' She stood up. 'Remember, if you need me, just press your buzzer.'

'Handier than whistling,' he said with a thin smile.

'Don't let yourself get too cold. I'll check on you a little later, and I want you asleep in bed. Good night.'

His eyes followed her to the door. 'Good night, lass,' he whispered.

'I MUST MOVE on soon, Jenny.'

The fire crackled, turfs shifting slightly in a momentary flare, throwing larger shadows behind them.

'I've been away ten days.'

The wind howled anew around the windows; they rattled as it rushed down from the mountains. Down from the heights of Sgurr Dearg, whose slopes had brought him here, bruised and bleeding. It was fitful, roaring and silent by turns.

'Will anyone have missed you?' she said quietly, eyes fixed on the fire. Her hair glinted in the flickering red light.

He chuckled bitterly. 'I doubt it, but I have things to do, I can't stay here for ever.' He turned his head to regard her lovely, dark profile. 'Much though I'd like to.'

Without looking at him, she moved her hand on to his and let it rest there.

'Do you really want to go back, Michael?'

'I have to. My leave will be over in two weeks.'

'You could stay here. You're good around the place, and I know Dad likes you.'

He did not answer. A penumbra of dreams rose out of the fire and swayed tantalisingly in front of him. How often had he dreamed of something like this?

'For another two weeks,' he said.

Jenny smiled, and cocked her head to listen to the wind. 'Well, I suppose there's time enough...'

*   *   *

RIVEN SLEPT, BEREFT of dreams. Outside, the moon flickered through feathers of cloud, burning bright their edges. In the shadow of the trees, a figure waited patiently. A pair of wolves sat by its side. They were winter wolves, fully grown, and grey as ghosts in the moonlight.

CHAPTER THREE

RIVEN HAD NOT seen a white Christmas for as long as he could remember. December was cold and dull, with flurries of rain that whipped the willow limbs about and rippled the surface of the normally tranquil river. On the wards, tinsel and a few bravely decorated trees appeared.

'They'll have me dressing up as Santa Claus next,' Doody said, grinning.

When the daily purgatory of his morning walk was over, and Riven was tired enough to lie still in bed for a while, he sometimes drew a little—mostly horses and landscapes—and sometimes he thought. It was good to retreat to that other world, which stretched wide and green in the middle of the mountains; the place where all was ordered as he loved best. It was good to forget his shattered body for a while and walk the wide Dales with legs that did his bidding, or on the back of a willing horse with only the characters of his imagination for company.

They were many and varied. Like a pilgrim, he shared the road with others who came and went in his mind, travelled with him for a while, and then took another way and disappeared again. There were farmers and shepherds, peddlers and rogues, beautiful ladies and hard-eyed soldiers. They sprang into his mind fully grown, clad in leather and linen, smelling of earth and sweat, or redolent with perfume and spice. Their colour put the dull days of December to shame.

He rode up and down fertile Dales dominated by turf and stone fortresses, where companies of sashed warriors patrolled the ramparts. He stayed in inns where the beer was pungent as wine and the fiery barley spirit scorched his throat. He laughed at travellers' tall tales of far-off lands beyond the mountains, but told none himself. For he had none left to tell. Instead he listened and watched, and marvelled. He spent days with an innkeeper called Gwion, who fussed over his guests as though they were children and whose bald pate glinted like a mirror in the candlelit evenings. He drank himself roaring drunk with the red-bearded man of his dream and found him to be a fountain of homespun philosophy with an unquenchable good humour. His name was Ratagan. There were others also. A young man with blue eyes and a sardonic turn of the mouth regarded him unsmilingly and rubbed the ears of two tame wolves who were always at his side. He was Murtach; Murtach the shapeshifter. And the fine lady who was a demon on horseback and who dressed in black—well... and there the daydreams broke down, and he stared at the gentle rain that trickled down the window.

He marvelled because they were characters from his books, but in his daydreams they took on lives of their own and had their own stories to tell. They became his companions, their faces eventually as familiar to him as those of Doody, or Nurse Cohen. They held the black memories at bay, and only when they had left him for the day did the despair come crowding round him again, knifing in at all the familiar weak spots.

'You're at it again, sir,' Doody said to him.

'What?'

'Wandering.'

Riven rubbed his eyes. 'Gives me something to do.'

'I'll give you something to do.'

'Not making fucking decorations along with the other lot. I'd had enough of that by the time I was twelve.'

Doody shook his head. 'Getting worse, you are.'

Riven scowled. 'Santa Claus can't bring me what I want for Christmas.'

There was a pause.

'I know, sir—but this won't bring her back either. Come on. Give the world a break.'

After a moment, Riven laughed. 'Why not? It's given me a bodyful of them.' He thumped Doody on the arm. 'Sorry, mate. Next time you find me like this you have to kick me down the corridor.'

'That's more like it. But remember, I got done for striking an officer once before.'

Christmas was for the more elderly and less mobile inmates of Beechfield. The Centre did quite a creditable job of making it traditional, and there was a service in the morning for those so inclined. Riven was not. However, he managed to paint two cards, for Doody and Nurse Cohen. Strangely, he could still paint well enough. It was writing, the less instinctive skill, which eluded him.

His walking had progressed, if not by leaps and bounds then by several dozen steps. He had dispensed with the frame by now, and muddled along with a single crutch. He was twenty-eight years old, but with beard, stoop and crutch he looked forty. Every day the face that met itself in the mirror grew grimmer, and the new lines at the corners of the mouth deeper.

The pins in his limbs would baffle airport metal detectors for the rest of his life, and the scars he bore would never fade completely, but his body was fighting for health and wholeness whether he wished for it or not. The headaches he had been subject to decreased in virulence and frequency, and the pains in his legs gave way to a feeling of weakness.

For Christmas, Doody and Nurse Cohen together got him a hip flask full of malt. 'Keep you warm in the winter nights, sir,' Doody said with a wink. Riven's watercolours seemed inadequate in exchange, though the pair expressed delight over them.

Christmas Day, and Christmas lunch, and that boring Christmas afternoon with the Queen on television and patients happily dozing. Then a dark evening strolling into night, and it was over. One taboo time was behind him, and now crouched in waiting for next year. That night he lay quiet as a corpse in bed, and viciously beat back the siege of his memory; pushed it away until he had walled it off in a dark corner. In the morning the struggle showed in the tiredness, and the sombre set of his face.

The holiday deadness that would last until the eve of the New Year then set in. Doody and Nurse Cohen took their well-earned holiday. Riven watched them drive away together: Doody was getting a lift to the station. That left him to the tender mercies of Nurse Bisbee. He was glad, in a way. They were the ones who were drawing him back into the mainstream; something he did not yet want.

He had received Christmas cards from old friends, most of whom he had known at Oxford; and also from one or two of his colleagues in the army. He mulled over them for hours, not yet ready to believe that these people had any claim on him. The world outside was a lawn and a willow-fringed river; no more. If he began thinking about things beyond that, the wall began to crumble, revealing the darkness behind it.

He actually discovered a patient reading one of his books, on a wet morning as he hobbled through the recreation room on an expedition to the toilet. He felt a moment of pride and pleasure, then a weird panic, as if his den was being infiltrated, or his disguise being whittled away. That world, which had once driven and uplifted him, being brought here by others. Even here. First Nurse Cohen, and then this. How could he forget, or begin to heal, since Jenny was in that world also, in every word he had ever written, as surely as if her picture smiled behind every sentence? He stole the book when the old man left it behind for a meal, and took it back to his room.

Flame of Old. The first one. The one I began as a boy, and left again; until I met her. The glad one. The story which believed in happy endings.

He opened it.

THE LAND WAS hard, but good. In the Dales, there was fine soil, rich enough for barley in the more sheltered parts. Down there also there was kale, and the shimmering mouse-fair hayfields. But the hills clawed out of the valley like blind, blunt breakers of granite that foamed into serried patches of boulders, encrusted with moss, straddled with heather and humps of yellow grass. Thorn trees gnarled there, bent by the icy northern blast that men chose to call wind. They looked like leering cripples, hardy as the rock on which they perched.

And there the Rorim was. Ralarth Rorim, fortress of the southern Dales. It encircled a low hill that some said was made by man and others said had always been there. The ramparts overlooked a wide valley spangled with the bright circles of a deep stream, and in the valley were the crofts and huts of the Dales peoples. Fields were marked out in straight lines, and animals grazed in dotted herds. Ribbons of blue smoke rose up into the clear air from houses and inns, smithies and byres. The bustle of a market could be heard when the wind permitted. It nestled like a patchwork in the slopes below the Rorim itself, and there folk bought and sold, bargained and argued, their voices a mere murmur on the breeze.

Beyond the Dale of Ralarth the hills rolled in a sombre sea to a blur of mountains on the horizon.

They were flecked with stone, drowned in heather and coarse upland grass; a tableau for kites and buzzards to wheel over, for wolves to roam, for deer to tread warily. To the south, a stain of forest darkened the slopes of the hills like a silent sea in the valleys and crested the stone-ridden heights with pine and fir, spruce and beech, occasional oak and a riot of ferns and brambles. Scarall Wood was its name; a home for wild things. And to the south of the wood, the land dipped sharply in grey cliffs, tumbling down past waterfalls to the rocky brim of the sea itself, that beat unceasingly against the ramparts of the earth in its ancient battle.

The troop of horsemen came riding out of the north, with the wind at their backs and the sun of a waning day to their left. There were ten of them mounted on tall, dark horses whose necks were pale with foam. They were dressed in metal-studded leather, belted with blue sashes. Swords rattled at their thighs and empty provision bags bounced from their saddles.

They halted within sight of Ralarth Rorim and stood in their stirrups to watch the great dip of the Dale cup the gathering twilight in its folds. A few fires twinkled like gems in a mine, and they could catch the distant lowing of cattle being driven in for the evening.

'Home,' the big red-beard, Ratagan, said with satisfaction. 'I told you we could make it before nightfall if we pushed on.'

The dark, slight man with the sharp face who had reined in beside him nodded. 'Though the horses have paid for it. But it will be good to be under a roof this night.'

'And within walls,' Ratagan added. He scanned the surrounding hills. 'I had no mind to be staving off the hunting packs yet again. I've had enough of the wolf-folk to last me a long while.'

'Then will you be steering clear of Murtach when we get back?' the dark man asked with a grin that was like the flash of a knife in the twilight.

Ratagan laughed, his voice a boom of sound in his beard. 'Those curs of his! They're afraid of their own shadow. I think their dam must have been a strayed lamb. But they look the part, I'll admit.'

'Murtach says appearances can be everything,' the dark man said.

'Aye, and he would know—shapeshifter that he is. Ah, the beers he will ply me with tonight for the stories I have gathered!'

'You are the one to tell them.' The dark man smiled. 'But come, we must be on. The wind grows cold, and we have a mile or two yet to do before dark.'

They spurred their weary mounts, and the little column set off once more on the descending slopes to where the lights of the Dale were burning in the deepening darkness.

AYE. BUT FOR some, the darkness comes too quickly for us to go any farther.

He closed the book and then his eyes, still seeing the evening hills of another world. Then he got up slowly, retrieved his stick and, making the laborious way to the recreation room, left his work where it was.

As Christmas was for the less lively of Beechfield's inmates, so New Year was primarily for those who, as Doody put it, had less than five pinkies in the grave. Many patients went home for the holiday season, but a fair percentage remained, as did the staff who looked after them.

'Well, sir,' Doody said when he returned on New Year's Eve, 'I intend to party it anyway, whatever that old cow Bisbee says. Orange juice, my fucking foot! Anne and me are trying to get some booze in for the old boys who are up to it. You'd be surprised how many of them perk up at the mention of the hard stuff.'

New Year. It was always a big thing in Scotland. Should auld acquaintance and all that.

Nurse Cohen took him round the garden in his chair that afternoon. He listened to her as she talked about the New Year and the party, and Bisbee's tyrannies, not so much aware of what she said as the way she said it.

It was cold, but it had stopped raining, and a fitful sun was drifting through a wrack of clouds. The river was full and noisy, throwing away sunlight as it broke over stones, and the willows were almost bare.

'There will be snowdrops here soon,' said Nurse Cohen. She imprisoned some hair that the wind had freed. 'Then the daffodils come up in the spring, and this whole bank is covered with them. It's quite a sight; sort of cheering.' The chair halted. 'Will you really not be here to see it, Mr Riven?'

He shrugged. 'Maybe. I'm pretty much put together again now. I've no excuse for staying any longer.' *And I have things to do.* He forced a smile. 'I'll tell you next year.'

'Next year. Well, I've no resolutions made, so I won't be breaking any as I usually do. Doody promises to behave himself a little more, though I've never seen bacon with wings. I reckon old Bisbee could make a resolution to take that poker from up her backside.'

Riven laughed.

'Mr Riven?'

'Yup?'

'You can call me Anne, you know, if you want to. Most of the other patients do.'

'Okay. Anne it is.'

'Good.' She looked at the sky. 'Rain. I'd best get you inside. Patients aren't supposed to get wet.' She wheeled him back towards the Centre.

The meal was not as big an occasion as at Christmas, but it was certainly livelier. The staff ate with the patients, and there was a good deal of merrymaking at Riven's end of the table, where Doody and Nurse Cohen—Anne—had stationed themselves. In front of them sat several innocuous-looking bottles which housed rather fiery liquid. Hence the noise level, at which Nurse Bisbee shot more than one suspicious look.

Some electronic wizard had rigged up a system whereby Big Ben chimed on speakers set in the wall. As the meal ended, and the magical moment approached, it grew quieter. Riven wheeled himself away from the table and took up position near a window that looked out on to the garden, which was now lost in the dark.

A fine night for Hogmanay.

The stars were so bright that he could make out Sirius, even from inside. He wanted to be out, alone under the sky as he had so often been in his life. The lights in the room dimmed and the speakers began to crackle. A voice began telling of the crowds in Trafalgar Square and the antics in the fountains. Doody was dancing a jig with an old woman who was whooping with laughter. She looked as though she had not danced in decades. Nurse Cohen joined them, along with an octogenarian who on other days would be grumbling in his bed.

The chimes began to ring out, and the dancing stopped. Glass in hand, Riven stood up.

Nine, ten, eleven...

On the last stroke he drained his glass, and raised it to the ceiling.

For you, my bonny lass. A New Year.

As he limped out of the room he saw Nurse Cohen being kissed by Doody. The patients were giving each other elderly pecks.

Shaking arms entwined, and 'Auld Lang Syne' began. It followed him as he made his way outside into the still air and the cold stars, out to the lawn and the quietly churning river.

The grass was wet and slippery, and his progress was slow. He stopped to place the constellations. Orion with his shining belt. The Plough, and the North Star. Venus down near the horizon, and bright Jupiter. They had guided him in times before this. They guided him now, as though the time could be taken back and he was on Skye again with a heart that was whole and in the keeping of someone who loved him.

The river flashed back starlight and brimmed under the bare limbs of the willows. He sat down and fumbled with his shoes, hands quivering with tiredness. Then his socks; and the chill dew was wet on his bare feet.

The water was so cold at first that it burned, but then it merely tingled, glittering around his calves. He stood there and let it pour around him, and stared at the high arch of the sky. It seemed to wheel in a velvet immensity. He was its hub, the pivot on which it turned. He knew his time at Beechfield was over. It was time to go. Time to return to the mountains.

CHAPTER FOUR

RIVEN WAS NOT going back to Camasunary to write a book. He was trying to lay a ghost to rest, to heal himself. He thought that perhaps the writing would be a part of that, but he could not be sure. Whatever was to happen, he was here, now, on a train, his belongings crumpled in a rucksack at his crooked feet, Beechfield half a dozen counties to his back, and a new year opening out like a dark flower in front of him.

A night train journey. He never bothered to get a sleeper; it was a sort of tradition that he pass as uncomfortable a time as possible getting to Skye. It seemed to make the first sight of the Cuillins across the Sound of Sleat all the more worthwhile. Mind you—he peered at the blue gloom beyond the window—if it keeps like this I'll see nothing but the usual drizzle.

Carlisle went past, and with it England. The motion of the train lulled him into a doze. He woke hours later from his cramped sleep to feel the pains in his legs and see dawn break out over high land. It was already spotted with snow. He wondered if there would be any on the islands; and for the first time considered the difficulties of getting to the bothy. There was no alternative to hoofing it over the ridge. He could hardly get someone to carry him.

He got off the train on a grey, damp morning at Mallaig, and walked the short distance to the harbour. Around him were fishing boats, and a tangle of lobster pots and fish boxes. Gulls screamed overhead, the first time he had heard them in what seemed like years. He looked up to see the housing estate perched incongruously on the side of the mountain above the harbour. The slopes were brown with dead bracken, but he could see Skye across the sound. He was back again, back in the land of sea and stone.

He was in time for the noon ferry, and boarded the small vessel with a feeling akin to fear. To be this close again. Was it the best thing? But there was a determination in him.

He stayed on deck during the short voyage, and let the wind mock his beard. Armadale, low-lying and wooded, was approaching. From there it was a long bus journey, and then the hike over the ridge.

Speed, bonny boat... I think.

The ferry pitched and tossed below him, and the gulls followed in its wake. What was he coming back to? The thought of Camasunary, dead as she was dead, with her things inside, left as they had been left that summer morning, made him squirm. Made the black mood hover close to his head and nestle on his shoulder.

Maybe Molesy's advice was not so hot.

From the pier at Armadale he was subject to the vagaries of the island bus system. He managed to get to Broadford without much trouble. From there he could catch the post bus which went through Torrin; first, however, he ensconced himself in a hotel and fortified himself with a few drams of McLeod's whisky. A head for the hard stuff was a vital social skill, and it was something he had picked up in his time in Scotland.

The little red bus that took post around the island arrived late, as usual. The driver did not recognise him, for which Riven was profoundly thankful. He sat in silence as the vehicle wound its way around the knees of mountains, south beyond to Torrin. For Riven, it was like going back in time. The months in the Centre seemed like a grey and hazy dream from which he had finally woken.

And at last the ridge, leaning tawny with the bracken above him, its head powdered with snow. He breathed deeply and fingered his stick, looked about him. From a dripping stand of hazel nearby, he cut himself a staff better suited to the rough ground, and began the long haul upwards. The whisky glow left him after a few moments of wind-driven drizzle. He bent forward, took small steps and tried to regulate his wild breathing.

Noisy rills crossed what path there was, soaking his feet. He felt the beginnings of sweat on his back and under his armpits, though his face remained wind-cold. Stopping for a moment, he straightened up and stared at the climb ahead, trying to ignore the pains in his legs.

I must be mad.

But he lurched forward again, leaning on the hazel staff. There were a few Highland cattle on the hillside. They eyed him with placid curiosity, chewing cud under a shaggy fringe. He splashed past them and stole a glance at the sullen sky.

Looks as though it's about to dump something really unpleasant. He was familiar with this path, this ridge. He knew most of the twists and turns, the false summits, the areas of bog and black peat water, but the body which ached up it now was unfamiliar. New weaknesses mapped his ascent, so that he was taking this path for the first time, ignorant of the effort required to follow it.

He crossed the snowline, and the rain turned into sleet that gathered on the rocks and the clumps of heather and then degenerated into slush, only to be replaced by a fresh flurry. A soft day, Calùm would have said, with his imperturbable pipe in his mouth and his eyes gazing out from a face which had seen much worse. But Calum had died a year before his daughter, with his dog whining at his feet on a clear night of moon and silver surf, bowed under a load of drift which his heart had refused to bear.

Riven reached the summit of the ridge, and sat down on a stone with the sight of Sligachan glen blooming out before him in the gathering darkness and the whipping sleet. A mountain loomed opposite, and to his left the sea hissed in long spumes that crashed on the beach below. Aye. A soft day; but not a soft night to follow it. He rubbed his legs, utterly alone and near to tears. Only some stubborn, partly military thing prevented him from sobbing, as it had prevented him from weeping when his corporal had been blown to bits in front of him in Ireland, or when he had known Jenny was dead.

And, again, he could see her, hair tossed by the wind, wrapped up against the winter, laughing and telling him to hurry on. To hurry on down this hill I've climbed. So he started off again, swearing at his legs, the mud, the water and the winter, and most of all at himself.

The way down was harder, hurting his calves and jarring his bones. He had to grasp heather and boulders to control the rate of his descent, jam the staff in the sodden ground before him. The way was so steep that the path had to double back on itself every so often, creating a pale zigzag down the side of the ridge. Streams took the more direct route down, bisecting his way frequently. His wet feet ceased to feel uncomfortable, but the pain bothered him. He had visions of bolts coming loose, screws floating away inside muscles, metal scraping bone.

The sleet turned to rain again as he descended. Chill, stinging rain propelled by a wind off the sea. The breakers were roaring into the bay and smashing in a white fury on the headland beyond. His eyes followed the beach as he stumbled down, and he thought he saw the dark dot of the bothy on the far end of the bay.

Then he slipped on a green boulder and fell heavily, rolling a little down the slope and landing with his face an inch away from black peat water. He lay there a moment as the water calmed and the beginning of his reflection was created; then struggled on to his hands and knees, sinking in the ooze to his wrists. Soaked to the bone and black with mud, he levered himself to his feet and staggered on, mouthing curses, head bent against the wind.

'LOOK HOW BLUE the sea is today,' he said, stopping on the top of the ridge and easing his thumbs between the pack straps and his shoulders.

She looked at him, hair whipped by the wind to a dark, flickering mane. 'It's all blue and green here in the summer, and calm as milk down in the glen. Lots of midges, though.' She took off her pack and dropped it to the ground. 'Let's stop a wee minute and have a breather.'

He joined her.

The wind swept across the hills in erratic waves of air, flattening grass and making its underside glisten in the sunlight. The clouds were white and billowing, tumbled across the hard, pale blue sky. The day was clean and fresh; they could see with crystal clarity the stony peaks of the Cuillins parade in the long ridges to the edge of sight.

They lay in the crackling bracken, Jenny's hair spread out like a fan. She pushed it back from her face and leaned on one elbow beside him. Overhead a curlew arced, calling shrilly, and the shadow clouds covered them more frequently. Perhaps a mizzle of rain was forming out over the sea, and readying itself for the assault on the mountainous coast.

Jenny stirred. 'People are like the seasons, you know,' she said absently. Riven frowned at her. She lay now on her stomach with her chin cradled in her hands. Her eyes flashed with laughter at the puzzlement on his face. 'It's true,' she said, 'they are.

Some are winter, some summer, others spring and autumn.' He laughed at her, and she tugged his hair.

'What does that make me?' he asked.

'An idiot,' she cried.

He grabbed her and held her captive, but she struggled. 'Idiot!' she yelled again, triumphantly, and twisted in his grasp, but could not break free. Finally she lay quiet in his arms. The wind blew her hair out behind her, sweeping across the hillside and tossing the gulls overhead about like leaves. They grinned at each other, their faces inches apart.

'You,' Riven said breathlessly, 'are spring, with the wind and the showers, and the shifting clouds...' He kissed her lightly on the lips. 'And autumn,' he murmured, 'with the richness of harvest.'

Their lips met again as the wind hissed around them, and the clouds massed steadily, obscuring the sun.

IT WAS DARK, and he was stumbling through knee-deep mud that marked the end of the descent. The mountains were vast dark shapes against a slightly lighter sky. The wind had battered away most of the cloud, and the rain had lessened. Soon it would be moonrise. He splashed on through the rushes that carpeted this part of the valley floor, the pain in his legs becoming a bright light in his head.

Hard part over, me old son. Now just a plod across the bay. The rain finally ceased, but a fine spray whipped off the water to sting his face and salt his lips. The beach was awash with foam and moonlight, the breakers shining in long lines out to sea.

He was past the mud and crunching on shingle,

his feet sliding on the larger pebbles and the staff slipping off smooth stones. It kicked up the odd shell to reveal sudden mother-of-pearl palenesses.

He stopped, breathing hard. The bothy could be seen clearly. It was dark, with the bulk of the mountains behind it and the bright marriage of sea and sky beside it.

No lights. No fire.

A stab of grief went through him and then drained away, leaving him as cold as the shingle.

Fuck it.

He jabbed his staff at the ground and hauled himself forward, the sea spray making him squint. There was a storm of wind rushing down the glen. He could imagine it beating at the windows and howling down the chimney. Making the door bang.

This door. This threshold.

He fumbled with the keys, chill in an outer pocket, as the wind battered him relentlessly.

Numb, useless.

And the door opened.

He stood swaying with the storm a black and silver roar behind him and his legs a painful abyss away. The door banged against the wall and the wind rushed in past him, sending up a flock of ashes from the dead fireplace, ruffling the pale pages of a book left half-read. Flapping the sleeve of a jumper flung on a chair. Flung, where she had left it.

'I don't need it—it's too nice a day, and it would make me boil. Come on, Michael, you old woman, let's get out while the sun lasts. It's beginning to darken earlier these days.' And the sound of the gulls outside, screaming.

He closed the door behind him, thrusting it shut against the wind's insistence; and the room became dead again, dark save where the moonlight came in the windows.

He dropped his rucksack and staff with a clatter and sank to his knees on the flagged floor, his clothes dripping and his hair lank across his forehead. Their picture peered at him from the shadowed mantelpiece, and the two brass candlesticks glinted coldly in chorus. There, on his desk, his typewriter and a thick file of paper weighed down by a rounded rock from the beach. A coffee mug sitting there.

'—But I haven't finished this—'

'Oh, leave it. Your head needs some mountain air in it.'

Here, by the door, wellington boots. His hiking boots, also, along with a smaller pair. He touched a lace idly, then turned away and lurched to his feet.

Tired. God, I'm tired.

He navigated across the room and stared into the black hearth, thinking of past fires. Of carrying in peat through lashing rain, feeling the warmth of the first flames lap his face. Sudden anger flushed him.

'I don't need this. By Christ, I don't need it!' He thumped the mantelpiece so that it quivered, then flinched away from the photograph there. The door to the bedroom was open. Mouthing curses, he plunged towards it.

Into the bedroom, to see the bed unmade, pillows awry. One with the dent of a head in it still. And her nightshirt lying across it.

A warm tangle of hair and flesh, smelling of lavender and curled up in his arms, frowning slightly in sleep; the cold toes seeking his legs to warm themselves, the face nuzzling his shoulder.

Something between a snarl and a sob escaped his chest. He felt the old black wings beating perilously close to his head, but knelt on the bed and took up the nightshirt in his fists. It smelt musty, damp, but he buried his face in it, and sank down on the cold mattress. Then, still dripping, he curled up there and hid his head; blind and deaf to the storm, the battery of the sea, the howling mountains.

CALUM TAMPED DOWN his pipe with a finger grown fireproof through the years, and let slip a skein of blue smoke from between his teeth.

'So you've a mind to marry her,' he said quietly, his grey eyes on the breaking waves that the southerly breeze was pushing on to the beach.

'Aye,' Riven answered him.

Calum wore an old tweed coat with more than its fair share of patches, and his cap, as always, perched on his head. There was a lean cast to his face; the grey eyes looked out from a network of wrinkles and laughter lines, and the mouth had a good-humoured quirk to the corner of it that was seldom absent. It was there now, as he considered giving his daughter away to this Irish soldier who had literally fallen into their lives one winter evening, and had been appearing regularly ever since.

'Will you leave the army?' he asked.

'Yes, as soon as I can.'

'In some parts they'd say it was old-fashioned,

these days, to be asking a father for his daughter's hand,' Calum said, and the grey eyes twinkled.

'Maybe, but you're all the family Jenny has, and it's important.'

Calum nodded approvingly. His eyes shifted to take in the flight of a curlew across the bay, the long curved bill clear in the light of the evening, silhouetted against a darkening sky.

'Her mother was a marvellous woman,' he said at last, and the eyes lost their focus, seeking somewhere else. 'Jenny is made from the same mould. Her like doesn't come round too often.'

'I know,' Riven said softly.

Calum puffed smoke again. 'Aye, you do. I know that, Mike.' And then a smile etched its way across his face. 'What about a dowry?'

'What?'

'Since you're being so old-fashioned about it, we may as well go the whole way.'

'No, Calum. There's no need—'

'You love Camasunary, the bothy; the pair of you.'

'Well, yes.'

'It's rough, and it would need some work, but it would keep you out of the clutches of the bank and such.'

Riven smiled. For the first time, Calum looked him in the eye, and the quirk at the corner of his mouth twitched into a grin. 'How about a wee dram to wet the head of the evening?'

'Why not?'

And they walked back up the glen, to where the light shone out of the open door, and Jenny had the supper waiting for them.

* * *

CHILLED AND ACHING, he woke at dawn, eyes fully open in an instant. The cramp in his limbs filled his head with fire. He sat up and saw the wreck of the bed, mudstained and wet, sheets awry.

'Oh, Christ.'

He rubbed his face groggily, and when his hand dropped away his eyes were empty.

So I'm here, after all.

He stood up, swaying. Around him the familiar jetsam of two lives stared at him from the dressing table, the wardrobe, the shelves and the walls. His breath steamed. The bothy was as cold as stone.

He stopped to touch a photograph of them both, face expressionless, then moved into the main room. His rucksack squatted forlornly in a puddle by the door, the staff lying beside it. He picked up the hazel and fingered its smoothness. It was comforting, somehow. To possess something which had nothing to do with this past.

He looked about. A haven, this place had been. But not again.

He felt like putting it to the torch. She'd like that. He settled for cleaning out the hearth. Gazing at the remnants of the last fire there, he was reluctant to sweep them away. They were a relic. But a reminder, also. He got rid of them, and in a little while had a defiant blaze going. His clothes curled with steam, but he hardly noticed. So much, in here, to remember. He shook his head as though a fly buzzed at it.

He prepared coffee, heating water in the kettle and skirting the thought of the whisky-filled hip flask.

Time enough for that, later. Outside, the morning was dull, windy still. A sun was fleeting through the clouds with a mizzle at its throat. He could hear the sea.

The kettle whistled loudly, and he drank black coffee. All the perishables had perished long ago. Idly he scanned what he had been writing, flipped through a few pages which had pencilled criticism, suggestion and ribaldry scrawled in them from Jenny. She had often done that.

He turned away hurriedly. Too close, too near. Not yet.

He rescued his rucksack and spread out his belongings to dry before the fire. The flames mesmerised him, as they always did. He gulped the scalding coffee down, mustering courage.

And so, to work.

He began in the bedroom, collecting her things; their things. He made a pile of them: photographs, a teddy bear, clothes, shoes, a brush with raven hairs clinging to it. Like drift after a storm it mounted, as he methodically checked the drawers, cupboards, under their bed. Then he did the same for the other rooms. Their picture came down also, leaving a gap on the mantelpiece. He refused to look at it as he put it with the rest.

And when he had gathered up the memories, he placed them in the wardrobe and locked the door, turning the key with a creak, and putting it on the mantelpiece. The fire cracked at him, spitting sparks on to the stone floor. He changed his still-damp clothes before it, hanging them with his other things. For a moment, he examined his naked legs. They were pale, thin and scarred. He thought bitterly of past running and climbing, then dressed, lacing up his hiking boots grimly.

Feeling better for the dry clothes and the fire, he unpacked the provisions from his rucksack. The sugar was wet, so he set it on the hearthstone. He propped the hazel by the fireplace, drew up a settle, and sat down.

And now... what?

A glance towards the typewriter. He cursed. Those sheets were still there. Well, maybe he'd burn them sometime. Maybe.

He looked around the room. Nothing to show, now, that she had ever existed. Except the grave in Portree, and perhaps the remnant of a splash of blood up on Sgurr Dearg: the Red Mountain. But that would be long gone, washed away by rain off the sea.

No—nothing.

It wasn't fair. It just was not fair.

He went out, taking the hazel, found a day of iron sea and sky waiting for him, and the waves hissing at the shingle.

He began collecting drift, partly through habit, partly to wall off his mind. There was a good selection in the wake of the storm the night before. The inevitable fish boxes were prominent, along with remnants of rope, a plastic bottle, some rounded fragments of wood and a dead seal. A grey seal, it was, and half its head had been sheared cleanly away, so the still-moist brown eye stared at him on one side, and a grinning skull on the other. Propeller, probably. He kicked it, and the body quivered from top to bottom.

He piled the drift before the house, as was his wont. There were no windows on that side, the seaward side. The wind tugged gently at his beard, and he rubbed his chin.

HE CLEANED THE bothy out thoroughly, washing the stone floor and airing the bedclothes in moments of rainless weather. He had more than enough peat to see him through the winter, the bothy having been deserted until mid-January. The nearby burn supplied water, if he trudged far enough upstream so that it left the salt behind. Food was his only problem, as it had always been a problem at Camasunary. There had been a good store set by in the freezer which chugged quietly along on the generator, but the months of neglect had left it all to spoil. Riven had an unpleasant time cleaning it out and scraping the sea rust from the generator engine until it would burble happily to itself.

Stags bellowed across the glen at night and in the early morning. The call was old, primeval. Staring into the flames of his fire, he listened to them and could have been a caveman at the world's dawning, waiting out winter and turning his back to the darkness outside.

The coast around the bothy was steep and rocky; the way round to Loch Coruisk and Glenbrittle was hair-raising in winter, especially at the Bad Step which was a rock climb at the best of times. Riven began to reacquaint himself with the place by scaling the cliffs and boulders that overhung the foaming sea to the west, looking up at the heart of the Cuillins as they frowned darkly over the coast. He followed deer tracks for the most part, often on all fours, scrambling for heather-choked ledges. He watched an eagle sail out from the heights of the cliffs above, wings feathered like fingers.

Then he stopped, utterly spent, and clung to a wet boulder until the fire in his limbs subsided and he was able to continue. He was trying to make himself fit brutally, with no time for his weakness. And there was the added bonus that his exhaustion threw oblivion round him as soon as his head hit the pillow that night. So he decided to persevere, push himself with savage satisfaction, pick the difficult routes around the coast and the lower slopes of the mountains.

The following day he saw an otter, off the coast leading to Coruisk. It bobbed dark-headed on the water and at first he mistook it for a seal; but then he saw the prehensile hands holding a fishing float and stopped to stare. The float was yanked underwater and then released so that it shot up into the air. Again and again the otter repeated the game, mere yards away from a rocky smash of coast. Entranced, Riven only left when hunger drove him home. The otter continued playing, totally absorbed.

To help the food situation, he resurrected the .22 rifle from the closet and went out to kill some of his neighbours. It was only a matter of time before his progress down the glen raised some grouse. He shot two brace, and a hare, before turning back as the weather drove in. Once at the bothy, he set about the task of plucking, skinning and gutting them almost with relish. It was a skill he had not been called upon to use in a long time. He remembered dripping bivouacs on Dartmoor, and trying to boil a skinny rabbit over an inadequate fire. Survival training, it was called. Everyone hated it, but, as usual with most military experiences, was glad he had done it later, over a beer in the mess.

He stopped his gory work at the sink momentarily, feeling a small pang of loneliness. Not just because of Jenny, but missing the mad horseplay of his youth. Then he chuckled aloud. Youth! I'm not exactly pensionable yet, no matter how old I feel. He packed most of his prey in the freezer, and then set to work making a broth out of the odds and ends. He whistled noiselessly as he worked, but raised his head as he noticed the wind drop. It was no longer rattling down the glen. Now there was only the quiet sighing of the sea: his favourite lullaby. That, and the chugging of the little diesel generator. He listened to the almost-silence for a few moments, and then the hairs on the back of his neck and on the crown of his head rose, for no reason. He turned around quickly, hands red, but there was only the bothy and the hissing of the fire. The generator continued its subdued monologue; the sea sighed on.

But something had made him turn.

He walked away from the sink and took the staff from the corner, still listening. Nothing but the normal night noises. A late curlew shrilled its way across the glen, and was gone.

Then the sound of the generator died.

His breath caught in his throat as the light of the kitchen went down into darkness. The only radiance was the saffron glow of the fire. There was no sound save the waves on the shore and the drubbing of his heart.

He went out into a calm night of clear sky and new moon. Shingle crunched under his feet. He could see the black shape of the dead seal off along the shore. Not a breeze stirred.

But the night was empty, tranquil. His grip on the hazel relaxed. Bloody generator. He turned, thinking he had caught a movement over by the burn, and stood a moment, irresolute. Then he swore. Hill mist in your hair, boyo.

He set the generator going again, though he could find no reason for its failure, and when he went back into the bothy, the kitchen light was bright and defiant. There was a peculiar half-smell in the house. He wrinkled up his nose; but as soon as he caught it, it seemed, his sense became used to it and it faded. Musky, like an animal. Must have been the game he had killed.

He returned to his work at the sink.

CHAPTER FIVE

WRITING: MAKING PATTERNS on paper, like squeezing blood out of aching fingertips and watching it mark the whiteness.

They were becoming clearer around him again, his characters. They refused to allow themselves to be printed on paper, but their shadows fell over his shoulder as he sat at his barren desk and tapped the keys of the typewriter aimlessly.

He plotted the rise and fall of lords and ladies, struggles for power in the wide, green land of his stories, battles and sieges, and forlorn love liaisons which he could never quite bring himself to visualise fully.

No, it's no good. It's gone.

His world was flat and lifeless, the characters like puppets across a badly painted backdrop. The picture he was creating darkened, grew colder. His imagination drifted into an icy gloom without stars.

Battles became ugly, desperate affairs and corpses piled in the snow. Wolves worried at the bodies, and the stench of burning hurt the air. His fingers clicked the keys into a glittering immobility. He ploughed to a halt.

I have become a season, he thought. I am winter, waiting out the long night before spring.

Sullen days broke and set as he sat there, staring out of the window at the glen beyond and the vast intruding bulk of the mountains. He watched the gulls squabble over the corpse of the seal, and wished he had buried it or burned it or something. Then he bent his head and the keys clicked slowly again. Like the seal's body, his story quivered with life; but only through the blows he dealt it. He was heavy-handed as a crab, and the words he made lay on the page as though rigid with ice.

He went out, looking for release in the watery sun and the fresh wind. Taking the staff, he limped down to where the burn became brackish and sat at the edge of the rust-coloured water, swigging his hip flask defiantly.

He stared absently at a huddle of boulders across the burn, tracing with his eyes the patterns of the lichen, the pale shades of drier rock, the dark recesses where moss clung. The whisky warmed him, made his head swim. His empty stomach began to glow and he rubbed his knees thoughtfully. The gulls had left their noisy argument and had gone swooping around the sea cliffs in figures of eight.

He stared again at the rocks. The patterns had changed; they shifted even as he watched. He squinted, making shapes and silhouettes. Now a horse, then a tower, a crown, a face... A thin, dark, pointed brown face with black eyes as bright as beads, and a sharp beard split by a grin.

'Jesus Christ!'

He jumped up, the flask falling aside with a hollow thud. His swaying eyes shrilled out on to the rock— but there was only lichen there, and goosepimpled granite. He knuckled his eye sockets.

Shouldn't drink in the afternoon.

That evening he sat before a high fire and cleaned the rifle. He took more time than usual about the task, both because the weapon had not been cleaned for a time, and because it was comforting to feel its wooden smoothness in his hands, to sight on imaginary targets along the beach in the dusk. He had always liked guns, liked dismantling and cleaning them; except when cleaning them became a drudge, as it often had in the army. It was an arcane skill, concrete and satisfying.

He worked the bolt back and forth until he was sure it was free of rust and carbon, and then loaded the rifle methodically. He still could not readily admit to himself that what he had seen that afternoon had been only imagination...

Night came. He dozed, lulled by the fire and the sea. The rifle lay by his side on the floor, the oil on it glistening in the firelight. He had not switched on the electric lighting, and the flames threw his lean, bearded face into sharp relief, accentuating the scars on the forehead, the lines that marked the eyes and mouth even in sleep.

The warmth soothed the long ache of his legs and the sound of the waves soothed his habitual frown.

He breathed deeply. A turf in the fire collapsed with a tinselly rustle and the rafters creaked in a wind off the sea.

His eyes slitted at a small sound.

There was someone else sitting at his hearth, gazing into the fire.

His breathing stopped. The chair cracked under him. Pent-up air became a quiet thunder in his temples. He dared open his eyes a little farther, forcing himself to take an unhurried breath into his lungs. His heartbeat rose to drown the quiet sea wind, and leap like a fish in his throat.

One hand reached out to bask in the heat, the fingers wriggling with pleasure. There was what sounded like a sigh, and the shape on the hearth— half shadow and half firelight—moved closer to the warmth. Riven saw a dark-eyed face framed by raven hair; and then the tears gathered in his eyes and spilled over, sparkling in the firelight, and he knew he must be dreaming.

The face looked up at him suddenly, and he saw its beggar-thinness, the dirt on the cheekbones, the tangle of the hair; and at the same time, he smelled the musky body smell which faded almost as soon as it was identified. But the eyes—the eyes. They looked at him from across an abyss of loss and nightmare, stared out at him from a hundred photographs and a thousand memories. They met his own from under brows that met above them, and he almost gagged in disbelief.

For a second or a century, they looked at each other, as once upon a time they had been wont to do here, on clear nights when the fire was high and the wind had soughed down the glen beyond. She had sat by the hearthstone so that her face had lifted up to his with a laugh in the eyes. And then the hearthstone had gone cold, and her place was empty.

There was nothing in the eyes... Almost nothing. He could see no recognition there. It was as though she were a husk, a beautiful filigree empty of life.

But it was her. Here, in his dream.

'Jenny—' he croaked—and she bolted, ran across the room with a spatter of bare feet, clashed the latch, and was off into the night.

He was after her, lurching and cursing. The night met him like a black wall and threw rain at him as he went through the door. 'Come back! Come back, damn it!'

But the beach was empty, the waves tumbled undisturbed on the shingle, and the wind caressed his beard.

Come back.

Away over the bay the dead seal lolled. He thought he saw another splashing into the shallows, but he could not be sure. The sky was huge and starlit, the air cold as sea water and his limbs as weak as a pup's. He leaned on the doorframe and closed his eyes.

THE STARS WHEELED, the Plough revolving about the Pole; and midnight crept round.

He sat in the chair with a dying fire at his side and the rifle propped by the hearth. He wanted to go home, but knew there was no longer anywhere named home for him. He was a misfit wherever he went.

But his mind was sound. He had seen her; he had heard her fingers panic at the latch. The door had been open when he had followed her through it, but he had not opened it. She was real. He had not been dreaming.

A gipsy, perhaps? A wanderer, a vagabond? A child abandoned?

In these mountains?

He tried to remember her again; her face, what she wore. A vague impression of a dark slip. Bare feet—at this time of year! But the eyes, looking at him. Jenny, staring out at him. Eyes to catch his soul.

Impossible.

Perhaps someone from the hotel at the other end of the glen—lost, maybe. He shook his head tiredly. Where had she run to? And he slept, at last, with his chin sunk on his chest, one hand trailing floorwards.

CRIPPLING STIFFNESS TOOK him the next morning and he hissed and grimaced to stand up, cursing the cold of the bothy and the pallor of the fireplace. He was sick of sickness, sick of being alone, and yet the thought of people made him sick.

Another grey day.

Drizzle, and a massed bank of storm cloud. The mountains were about to don their veil again.

Sick of rain, too.

He wondered if it would snow. It felt cold enough for snow, though it rarely lay around the sea-level bothy. Perhaps the mountains would receive an icing. Perhaps then the cloud would lift, and he would see some sky.

A tap at the window spun him round, and staring in at him was the bearded face, smiling. The mouth made words, but he could not hear them. He bent and seized the rifle and threw back the door.

A momentary glimpse of surprise on the face; awkwardness so swift in passing it was scarcely noticeable.

'I'm sorry. Did I startle you?'

He followed the other's eyes down to the rifle barrel, and lowered it, embarrassed; and suddenly ashamed. Hospitality was a tradition in this island.

'Sorry, you made me jump.' There was a small silence as invisible speculations filled the air between them, but it dissolved in a loud rattle of thunder that split the air above them and wrecked on through the glen. Riven flinched.

'It's going to be a rough day. I've watched the storm come in this morning,' the stranger said. 'I think it'll be a big one.' His voice was level, low, but the accent was unfamiliar, though Riven was momentarily sure he had heard it before. 'Could I come in for a moment?'

And Riven retreated. 'Yes, sure,' just as the first rain pocked the ground outside.

'My thanks.' The latch clicked shut behind him. He wore a rucksack, hiking clothes. 'I've been walking and climbing for the past few weeks. This is my second visit here.' The rucksack descended to the floor. 'But it was deserted last time, so I slept in the shed at the back with the machine in it. I thought it might be a summer place for someone. I never expected to find anyone here. You live here?'

'I live here,' Riven replied. 'I've... been away.'

'Ah. That explains it.' The rain drumming down outside now. 'Yes.' A peer out of the window. 'The storm caught up with me, all right.' A peer at his feet. 'New boots. They've crippled my feet. I've got blisters like sea pebbles.' He looked up. 'Oh, I am sorry—' A hand, proffered. 'I'm Bickling Warbutt.' A dry, firm handshake, the grip stronger than the slender fingers suggested.

'Bickling?'

A laugh, clear as a sleigh bell. 'Yes, my parents had an old ancestor they named me after. Most of the time I'm called Bicker.'

'I'm Riven, Michael Riven.' Had he heard the name before?

There was something familiar here, like an unremembered dream.

'Pleased to meet you—and grateful you've let me in. Would you be minding it much if I stayed in here until the rain eases off?' The grin again.

Get a grip, Riven.

'No, of course not.' He roused himself. The host role. 'Take your boots off, if you like.' More thunder, louder this time. 'I'll just get the fire going.' As the stranger, Bicker, fell to his boots, Riven occupied himself at the hearth, but stole glances at his visitor as he did so.

He had about him a neatness which was more an air than a physical fact. Perhaps that beard and those eyes would always look dapper irrespective of any muck. His hands were the right size, his feet small, his entire frame sturdy as an otter's, with no limb at a loss as to where to put itself. He was well-dressed for winter, but seemed to have escaped its effects. He did not look as if he could ever have suffered from blisters, tiredness, or anything else. He exuded health like a steel spring, and his ready grin was unconquerable. Riven disliked him for no rational reason, and felt ashamed in doing so, for it was like a sick man distrusting health. But there was something more here that worried him, intangible as peat smoke. If he could only remember!

The flames leapt up in the hearth, warming him and lending a kindlier glow to the room.

Too much was happening. Too many things. He did not want company—not now.

'Ah, that's better.' Bicker was wriggling his bare toes. Thunder rumbled again, and the rain became a steady rattle at the windows. Riven stared at the glowing peat in the fireplace, lost for a moment.

'I must say, it's nice of you to invite a perfect stranger over your home's threshold.' The dark man stood up, his boots dangling by the laces from one hand. 'Is there anywhere I should leave these?'

'By the door is fine.' He poked the fire without looking at his guest, watching the sparks sailing up into the blackness of the chimney.

'I hope you don't mind me asking, but you're from across the sea, aren't you?'

Riven blinked. 'Northern Irish.'

'Ah, I see. Came over here to forget about the Troubles, I suppose. Don't blame you. Tragic place.'

Riven poked the fire savagely. 'You'll be hungry, I expect. I'll fix something.' He stood, then frowned and remained with his back to the fire and his hands splayed to the heat. Bicker was rummaging in his rucksack.

'Were you on the slopes leading down to the burn yesterday?'

The other man looked up. 'Why yes, I was. Did you see me?'

'I think you saw me. You grinned at me.'

That grin.

'I may have been smiling, my friend, but I don't remember smiling at you. Mind you, I never look about me much when I'm climbing—tend to be a bit absorbed, don't you know?' And Riven, seeing the dark man's darting gaze, knew he was lying.

'Nice little weapon you've got there,' Bicker went on, nodding to the rifle as he restrapped the rucksack. 'For hunting, you use it?'

Riven nodded, and sucked his teeth. 'You didn't see a dark girl wandering about the glen, did you?'

Bicker seemed almost startled, then he appeared to consider the matter. 'No, can't say I did. Does she live here?'

'No. I don't know... where she lives.' He was uneasy. He felt as though the storm was in the room, breathing on his neck. He wiped his hands on the seat of his trousers.

Must have got used to being alone.

He went into the scullery and set about reheating some of the broth to which the local wildlife had contributed. He heard his guest moving about in the main room, and fought a desire to peek round the doorway at him.

Thunder growled overhead, and a barely noticeable flicker of lightning winked at the window.

'Is it always like this at this time of year?'

'Not always. It's usually pretty stormy, though.'

'You take the rough with the smooth up here, I suppose,' Bicker responded.

Riven stopped what he was doing for a second, forehead gnarled, then began stirring the broth again.

The storm became more violent as the evening drew in. There was less rain, but the wind grew and whistled like a train around the sea cliffs and the headlands. Riven occupied himself with some aimless typing—anything so he would not have to make conversation with his guest. Nursery rhymes, poems, anything. One rang in his head with infuriating insistence, and he could not get it out:

> *How many miles to Babylon?*
> *Three-score miles and ten.*
> *Can I get there by candlelight?*
> *Yes; and back again.*
> *If your heels are nimble and light,*
> *You may get there by candlelight.*

'I like that one,' a voice said. 'It's old, isn't it?'

It was Bicker, or Warbutt, or whatever ridiculous name it was he called himself by, leaning, as Jenny had used to do, over his shoulder and reading what was being typed. He flared up in anger. 'Do you mind?'

'Oh, I am sorry.' Bicker retreated with the right amount of contrition. 'I know it's an irritating thing to be doing—I dislike it myself.'

Riven felt like flinging the typewriter at his head, but turned back to his work with a silent curse and a, 'Doesn't matter.' He was not sure if he was angrier at himself or Bicker.

I can be polite, can't I, for Christ's sake? The keys ground to a halt.

Oh, fuck this.

He was in a savage, tearful mood. That's what people do for you.

He got up. Bicker was reading a book with great concentration. Riven could have sworn that his lips were forming the words as he read. He shook his head, then retrieved a bottle of malt and two glasses from the scullery. He clinked one down in front of Bicker, and settled himself opposite him at the fire.

Might as well redeem his notions of Highland hospitality.

'Here,' he said, and poured the shining stuff into Bicker's glass and then his own. 'I'm not a great host, but I do have good malt on me. It'll keep the cold out, if nothing else.'

Bicker smiled; the first real smile Riven had seen on him. 'My thanks. Shall we have a toast?'

'Slainte.'

'What?'

'Slainte. It's Gaelic for bottoms up. Listen: *slonsha*. I probably say it in the Irish way. The Scots Gaelic is broader.'

Bicker raised his glass. 'Well—slainte, then, and your good fortune.'

'May you be in heaven an hour before the devil knows you're dead,' said Riven, and polished off his glass. He poured another, refilling Bicker's as well. 'This'll keep the wolf from the door.'

Bicker glanced out of the window, then laughed his careful laugh and sipped his whisky.

'Have you lived here long?'

'A fair while,' Riven replied, watching the fire. 'I've... been away.'

'Ah, yes. You said.'

'Did I?' He sipped the powerful liquid, feeling warm and logical. 'I was in the army a while.' He always said that. It gave people a good excuse to categorise him.

'So you have been a soldier, then?'

'Only four years. Left, and came up here.' Careful, Riven; that's enough. Leave the rest.

'What is it you type on your machine, apart from nursery rhymes?'

'The odd book. What is it you're reading?'

'An odd book.' Bicker did not volunteer to show him the cover. 'Do you mean you're a teller of stories, a writer?'

'Yes. I mean I was.' Shit. I don't even know myself.

'Run out of stories?'

No. The story ran away from me. I never caught up with it. 'You could say that.' He listened to the wind, and a great surge of self-pity welled up in him. He stared hard down into his glass and blinked furiously, swearing at himself.

'It must get lonely up here.' Riven could not answer. 'I'd have thought you would have had a dog or something to keep you company.' Bicker's voice was light, conversational, but Riven knew he was watching him. The whisky mourning fled, and he felt uneasy. Who was this guy?

'What is it you do, Bicker?'

A swift flash of surprise. 'Oh, I'm not doing anything of much importance. Just wandering the land in between things.'

Riven stifled his annoyance. 'What sort of jobs do you do?' *You're no bricklayer, that's for certain.*

Bicker shrugged. 'Anything that pays, really.' He set down his glass, and stretched. 'I know I shouldn't be the one to say this, but it's getting late and I'd like to make an early start tomorrow morning. I think I'll turn in, if you don't mind.'

Riven got up, realising he had to leave the main room and the fire to his guest. 'Hope the floor's not too hard.'

'Oh, I've slept on worse. Good night, and thanks for the drink.'

Riven waved his hand vaguely and wandered into the dark bedroom clutching the whisky bottle. ''Night.' He closed the door, shutting out the firelight, and sat down on the bed with a yawn. *He's right. It is late. Must be the drink.*

He set the bottle down by the bed, undressed and got in. *The familiar pang at lying alone there.* He listened to the roar of the wind and the waves, and then slept without a dream.

BIRDSONG JUST OUTSIDE the window, and sunlight streaming in along with it. He smiled, listening to it and the sea.

Good morning, Riven. Well, thank you. He could smell bacon frying, and stretched in bed. *She's—*

Dead, Riven. That is your house guest, making himself at home.

He lay still, listening to gulls and enjoying the sun from the window. He contemplated staying in bed until Bicker had gone, but the civilised side of him would not. Besides, the smell of the bacon was calling.

Bicker was in the scullery when Riven shambled in, scratching his head and yawning.

'How do you like your eggs?' he asked him.

'Eh? Oh, fried.' He stopped. 'I haven't got any eggs. Or bacon, come to that.'

'I had some stowed away. Thought I'd make use of myself in return for the night's lodging. You don't mind?'

Riven filled the kettle. 'No, that's... fine. Sure. Go ahead. I'll have two eggs, thanks.' Oh, wake up, you slob.

He stretched, then went outside to be met with a sweet breeze tasting of salt and a spangle of sunlight off the sea.

Now that's more like it. More like spring, perhaps. Jenny's season.

'Breakfast is ready,' Bicker called.

He remained staring at the sea for a moment, the familiar words biting into him. Good morning, my lass. I hope you can feel the sun, wherever you are.

'It'll get cold.'

He went inside quietly to a fried breakfast.

'What a day, eh?' Bicker grinned, bright as a squirrel. His enthusiasm was almost infectious. That, and the sun flooding the room. Riven smiled, feeling a tinge of the old restlessness.

'It is, isn't it?' He began to think that Bicker was not such a bad bloke after all. Especially after he had tasted the food.

'I'm going to walk the coast path to Glenbrittle today,' Bicker was saying. 'It's about fourteen miles, but it should be possible. I've already done the bit round the memorial hut. It's the Bad Step I'm a mite worried about.'

Riven gulped his tea, filling up with bonhomie. 'Oh, that's no problem in good weather like this. You just have to be careful. I did it in a gale once, when the rock was wet and I was carrying a sixty-pound bergen.'

'Really?'

Riven stopped. I bet this guy has climbed the Eiger, and is secretly laughing his socks off at me.

'I thought I might stay in the hostel at Glenbrittle, and then pit my skills against the Red Mountain—Sgurr Dearg, it is called.'

Riven put down his mug. 'You must be careful on that mountain. You know what else they call it?'

Bicker shook his head.

'The Inaccessible Pinnacle.'

'I see—yes,' Bicker said thoughtfully. 'I had heard that there was someone killed on it last year.' Riven began to butter his toast. 'Why don't you come with me?'

Riven looked up, startled. 'Eh?'

'Come round the coast with me. You can be my guide. It's a fine sort of day, and you don't seem to be too busy here at the moment, if you don't mind me saying so. I was going to walk on to the Sligachan Hotel and stay there a few nights. Come with me. I owe you a return for the hospitality you've shown.'

'The Glenbrittle hostel is closed this time of year,' Riven said, but he knew he was fighting a rearguard action.

'Well, I have a... tent.' Bicker seemed to choose the word carefully. Riven was silent. The gulls were loud outside. Probably fighting over the seal.

'Yes, why not?' he said at last. 'It'll do me good. But I'm not climbing on Sgurr Dearg.' Bicker shot him a strange look, but before he could say anything Riven stood. 'If you clean up, I'll chuck a few things in a rucksack. I won't take long.'

He entered the bedroom before Bicker could reply.

CHAPTER SIX

IT WAS WHAT Jenny would have called a glorious day. From the slopes of the headland they could see Soay in the sunlit sea. Farther off were the dark cliffs of Rhum; Muck and Eigg were somewhere behind it. Riven sat down, breathed in the clean, bright air, and smiled. He had been right: this was what he needed. A blowing away of cobwebs. A new perspective.

I love this place.

Bicker was studying the map. 'This is Ulfhart Point,' he said. 'The cape of the wolf's heart. The hardest part is over us now. It'll be well after dark by the time we get to Glenbrittle, though.'

Riven was hardly listening. He wanted to drink in the view, store it away in his mind like a jewel.

It's worth it, Jenny. As long as I can remember things like this, it's all worth it. He turned to his companion.

'If we go on this way for a little while, we come to a small strip of oaks on the side of the mountain.

Through them, then we start climbing up on to the plateau. There's a place there where the way is less steep, and a waterfall flows down to the sea; when we see that, we make our way to the plateau. Then it's flat and boggy nearly all the way round to Loch Brittle, but easy enough going, even in the dark.'

Bicker put away the map. 'I can see I won't be needing this,' he said with his ready grin.

Riven turned back to the view before him. He rubbed his legs absently. They were sore and stiff, but he thought they would carry him to Glenbrittle well enough. It was the climb to the plateau that would really test them. He stood up, knowing that the best things are better not savoured too long, and turned away from the view to the path ahead. It was early afternoon. They had made slow time around the coast, mainly because of his own weakness. He had a grudging respect for Bicker's fitness; the dark man could probably have been in Glenbrittle now if he had been on his own. He had a curious habit, Riven noticed, of taking out the map and staring at it with eyes that were unfocused, elsewhere; as though he were not really paying it any attention.

They laboured on round the steep coast, disentangling their way through the strip of stunted oaks. It was a hot and awkward business, made worse by the packs they carried. Riven was a great believer in packing everything which might possibly be needed when he went walking. He even had a length of gaudy nylon rope in his rucksack, though he knew he would never again let himself get into a situation where he might need it. A strange thing is habit.

'There's the waterfall,' said Bicker breathlessly, as they cleared the last of the trees. They were close to where Riven had seen the otter. He stared out to sea, but there was nothing in the waves today, not even a fishing float.

They stopped for a moment so Riven could get his breath back.

'They call the land beyond Glenbrittle *Minginish*,' Bicker was saying, 'and Skye itself is called Eilean something-or-other. Island of the Mists.'

'More like island of the drizzle,' Riven retorted, short-tempered because of his physical inadequacy.

'Strange names. They don't all sound Gaelic, either.'

'They're not. The Vikings colonised these islands off and on. A lot of the names come from the Norse.'

'Vikings!' Bicker seemed amused. 'You mean blond giants with horned helmets and axes from the far north?'

'They weren't like that,' Riven replied testily.

'I thought they came from beyond the sea, not Scotland.'

'This coast was mostly harried by Norwegians. Orkney and Shetland belonged to them, too, and the land up along the Pentland Firth.'

Bicker whistled. 'They got around.'

'They discovered Newfoundland.'

'I thought a... Spaniard did that.'

'Columbus was in the Caribbean, four hundred years later.'

'Where did you learn all this?'

Riven shrugged. 'College. But I thought everybody knew about Columbus looking for the back door to Cathay.'

It was Bicker's turn to shrug. 'Shall we attempt the slope, then?' he asked, losing interest. Riven nodded sharply. For someone so assured and obviously intelligent, Bicker had some strange ideas about history. Or perhaps his own field of knowledge was very narrow.

The slope reduced them to their hands and knees, and Riven was in silent agony as he toiled upwards. There was nothing but rocks and the swell of the sea to be seen below, and the yellow grass under his nose.

'It's a hard haul, this,' Bicker panted, a little way ahead. 'But it's the last hard part.' Riven grunted assent, wanting only a respite. He had not even the breath to swear.

And then they were at the top, sweating and breathing deeply. It had become suddenly warmer. Riven took off his pack and lay on the grass. The sky had cleared and was more free of cloud. It could almost be summer. Bicker stood with his back to him, eyeing the way ahead. Then he bent to fumble with his rucksack.

Riven sat up. And swore.

There was no Loch Brittle; no Cuillin mountains. The Skye he had expected to see was simply not there. Instead he was looking out on a wide expanse of rolling hills, green with new bracken and golden with buttercups, stretching like a vast sunlit sea of light and cloud-shadow into purple heights beyond, barred here and there with the glitter of a river, dotted with clumps and copses of dark trees, silent under the immensity of the sky except for the sigh of the wind that brushed the grass in waves. Far to the west—or what had been west until a few moments ago—there were the blue shapes of high mountains. They were a long way off, but Riven knew, without knowing how, that they were higher than any in Scotland. The sun lit up distant snowfields on their slopes.

The air was balmy, pushing at his hair like a caress. And the smell—here was a place which had never known engines or factories. There was a smell of grass and new bracken on the breeze, a hint of pine resin from the woods on the higher slopes, a smell of soil, of growing things. It filled his lungs like a draught of spring water, and for a moment tears stung his eyes. Then the panic rose like a cloud in his throat.

'Jesus Christ!'

He whipped round to stare at Bicker, to see if the dark man were sharing the hallucination. His companion was studying the spectacle before them with something like rapture.

'Bicker, what's happening? What's going on, for God's sake?'

The dark man laughed. 'Calm down, Michael Riven. There is no need to be alarmed.'

And Riven felt a thrill of terror lance up his backbone.

'Who are you?' he demanded. His voice shook. 'What is this? What have you done?' He stared at the wide land below, then looked behind him and saw the familiar headland where he had seen the otter, the waterfall sparkling down to the sea.

'I have not done a thing,' Bicker answered.

'Who are you?' Riven shouted, and as Bicker smiled at him he suddenly knew. He recognised him. And realised where he was.

*...The world was a green and pleasant place,
wrinkled with silver rivers and scattered with forests
which no man had ever cleared...*

No. I must be out of my mind.

'I am Bickling Warbutt, heir to the Lordship of
Ralarth Rorim, a fortress of the Dales peoples.'

*The land was hard, but good. In the Dales, there
was fine soil, rich enough for barley in the more
sheltered parts...*

No. It cannot be.

'It can't happen,' he whispered.

'This is your country,' Bicker said gently. 'Here,
real, in front of us.' He spread his arms. 'These are
the labours of your imagining.'

He found it impossible to think. His brain had
seized up, had gnarled on to neutral. Part of it was
already considering the implications of what Bicker
had said, and part of it was screaming quietly to itself.
Riven met the eyes of the man who had encountered
the Rime-Giant with him in a dream. The man who
was a prince in his own books—standing here now
in hiking boots and a red anorak with a rucksack at
his feet. Bickling Warbutt, heir to Ralarth Rorim.

It doesn't exist. It never has.

He squeezed shut his eyes, refusing to think.
Already a madcap race was going on inside his
head as his imagination raced to understand this, to
extrapolate reason from it. The rational part of him
was still quietly gibbering to itself.

'This-cannot-happen,' he said in a low, steady
voice. He stood up carefully, his legs like clay
underneath him, and eyed the dark man warily.
'How did it happen? How did I get here? Where has

my world gone—where is the real world? *What's going on?'*

'Many questions. I can't give you all the answers you seek, I fear. Some I will try for, others you will have to wait for.'

'Tell me!' Riven yelled, an edge of hysteria in his voice. His legs quivered and he half-sat, half-fell down again.

Bananas. That's it. I've flipped. Gone apeshit. Or I'm on one hell of a trip.

'You are not mad,' Bicker told him. 'You must try to accept what you see here—what you find yourself in. I myself know something of how you feel, as have all of us who have been through one of the doors.'

'Doors?' Riven croaked.

'We have come through a door from your world to mine—from the Isle of Mists that you name Skye to this place. To Minginish.'

'Minginish,' Riven repeated. 'That's on Skye.'

'The land beyond the Cuillin mountains. I know. It is our name for our world.'

'"Our"?' Riven echoed. He blew air out through his lips. 'I never called anything in my books Minginish.'

'Not everything is as you imagined it to be,' Bicker said. 'I have read your books, Michael Riven. There is much else besides what is in them in this land.' His face darkened. 'And more arising every day.'

Oh, boy.

Riven gestured back the way they had come, to the familiar headland below and the waterfall. 'That's Skye there, down on the shore. That place exists in my world.'

'It does,' Bicker said. 'But you cannot go back that way. If you tried, you would merely find yourself on the shore of the southern ocean—our ocean, not yours. The doors open only one way.'

Riven held his head in his hands. 'There's got to be some sort of explanation for this. Quantum physics or something.' After a moment, he looked up. 'You're saying that this corresponds to what I wrote in my books?'

Bicker nodded. 'For the most part.'

'So you have Rime Giants and wolves and suchlike?'

'Yes. More than enough of them.'

'And... characters,' Riven said in a wondering voice.

'Ratagan, Murtach, Gwion... they are here, as I am,' Bicker said softly. Riven felt the hairs rise at the back of his neck.

Jenny.

'Is there a dark lady here—or a girl? Shit.' He remembered. The girl at the bothy who had not been a dream.

'There is not,' Bicker said hastily. Too hastily.

'There may be.' Riven groaned. Mother of God, what have I done? 'No,' he said. 'This I can't take. It is obscene. I don't know what the fuck you want with me, but you're not getting it. I'm going home, and you're not stopping me.'

'You can't go back that way,' Bicker told him harshly.

'Go find yourself a bloody quest or something, but leave me alone.' He threw on his rucksack and started off down the slope to where the waterfall fell into the sea.

'You can't go back!' Bicker shouted at his retreating shape. Just watch me, he snarled silently.

Behind him, the dark man sighed and began unpacking gear from his own sack.

BY THE TIME Riven had toiled down and up the headland again, it was nearly dark and his legs were screaming outrage at him. He was shivering, for with the setting of the sun it had grown cold, and the stars—strange stars—spattered the sky. At the top of the slope he found Bicker waiting for him beside a bright fire, wrapped in a cloak. He threw down his pack and croaked, 'Son of a bitch.' Then he collapsed by the embers. He did not care if this was Skye, Earth or Oz. He was exhausted, and sure he had sprung something loose in the climb. When Bicker, dressed now in dark supple leather and belted with a sword baldric, threw a cloak around him, he did not protest.

The fire crackled, fluttering in a breeze off the sea. Bicker's eyes were watchful and flame-filled as he reclined beside it.

'Are you hungry?'

Riven nodded. Bicker nudged a small black pot out of the fire. He wrapped his fingers in the hem of his cloak and passed it over. Riven took it in the same manner. It was broth. He bent over it and the appetising smell curled up round his nostrils. He blinked rapidly, and then there was a great, dry sob in him that felt as though it would break his breast. He fought, but it mastered him and racked out into the fire lit darkness. Another followed it, and he clutched at the pot until his hands were burned through the cloak.

'Ah, Christ,' he said thickly. Stop it. Stop it, man. But the golden tears sliced like knives down his cheekbones. The air seemed close and full of unseen faces, crowding round him. He sobbed again, his teeth grating and the lovely wholesome smell of the broth filling his head. Something that had been broken in him stirred again, and he thought the pain of it would kill him.

He blew on the broth, and drank it in scalding sips at last. When it was finished he lay back on his rucksack and stared at the night sky.

'Bicker,' he whispered, 'what's happening to me?'

The dark man's face was twisted with a pity that would once have set Riven snarling. 'If I knew that, then many of my own life's questions would be answered also. Let it lie for a while. You need rest, and the daylight is a better time for the answering of questions.'

Is it? Riven wondered, and he stared out at the blue darkness beyond the fire, suddenly afraid of what the morning would bring him.

'How did you get to Skye?' he asked.

'Through another door, one up in the northern mountains—' Bicker hesitated.

'The Greshorns.'

'Yes. The very same. There is a mountain there called the Staer. On a ledge near its summit it is possible to pass from Minginish to your world—to the Isle of Mists.'

'What started this? How did you find these doors? What do you want of me?'

Bicker shook his head and threw more of the dried heather curls on the fire. They flamed up brightly and their scent filled the night air.

'The story is a long one. I will not tell it this night—' Here he flashed a glance at Riven that said he would argue the matter no further. 'Tomorrow I will try to explain a few things...' He sighed, looking tired himself. 'It is not an easy thing to tell, but you have the right to know. Indeed, you will have to know. For now, go to sleep. I will watch over us for a while, though the fire should keep the beasts at bay.'

'Beasts?' Riven queried.

'Go to sleep,' the dark man repeated.

THE DAWN WAS bright and cold, the sun burning its way through streamers of pink and scarlet cloud on the western horizon and lighting up the dew on the grass and the stones. Birdsong flickered up and down the hills, but there was no other sound.

Riven lay watching the sky for minutes after waking. Bicker was already up, doing something to what was left of the fire. Riven felt the damp of the early morning through his sleeping bag and the beginning of protest from his wrecked limbs. Walking would be hell today.

It was not winter. This was not the same place he had set out from the morning before. This thing was truly happening to him. It was as real as the brilliant dew on the ground, or the rising breeze that pushed the clouds aside and left the sky a deepening blue—more blue than he had ever seen before. No pollutants here. No cars. No smoke worth mentioning. The air was as clear as sunlit diamond.

This is not Skye. It is not even Earth.

He closed his eyes briefly, feeling slightly sick. Bicker had promised to do some explaining today. He had better.

He sat up, wincing. His companion was heating a mess tin full of mush over a primus. Evidently the fire had been beyond resurrection.

'Good morning,' the dark man said. 'I trust you slept well.'

Riven nodded, and crawled out of his sleeping bag. 'Shouldn't you be cooking rabbit on a spit or something?'

Bicker tested the steaming mess, and seemed satisfied. 'For the moment, this is more convenient. We have a fair few miles to make today.'

Riven stifled a groan. *Just what I need.* He noticed that the rucksack had been replaced by a leather holdall, and there was a scabbarded short sword lying across it. He shook his head.

I don't believe it. Swords and bloody sorcery.

'Should I call you Prince Bicker?' he asked, struggling into his boots.

The dark man smiled. 'Here in Minginish we are not so formal. Bicker will do. The word "Prince" is only used in your book. It does not correspond to my rank in my own country.'

'My apologies,' Riven rasped. 'I'll try to get it right next time.' He fumbled in his rucksack for provisions. He needed coffee before he could even think about functioning. Bicker watched him with keen interest, spooning gobbets of his unspeakable breakfast into his mouth.

'What the hell is that?' Riven asked him when he had his coffee bubbling nicely.

'Bacon and beans in a bag,' Bicker answered. 'It is another of the things from your world which I will assuredly not miss.'

Riven sipped his coffee. 'How well do you know my world?'

'I have spent a long enough time there. At first it was terrifying, for I was not sure if I would find my way home. It was I who found the first door, by accident. And it was a long, weary time before I found the one that would take us back—the one we have just passed through ourselves.'

Riven frowned. 'What the hell is going on? What is the point of this? How did it happen?' He knew there was something like hysteria edging into his voice, but he was too bewildered to care. These things do not happen in real life. Another world. *His* world, for Christ's sake.

Bicker finished the last of his food, and stood up. 'We had best be moving on. We can talk as we travel.'

They packed their gear. Bicker stowed the primus away and slid his sword into the baldric, which made Riven stare. He would have laughed, had he not been afraid of how it would sound. In a few minutes, the blackened fire circle was all that remained of their camp, and Bicker covered even that with stones and plucked grass. Then they set off northwards.

*   *   *

DESPITE HIMSELF, RIVEN found that he was responding to the beauty of the land they were traversing. As the morning wore on, it became warmer, and he sweated under the rucksack with his legs complaining ceaselessly, but even so there was peace of a sort to be had here. He could enjoy the simple emptiness of the land, unscarred by man, untenanted. There were no roads, no telegraph wires, no jet trails in the sky; no litter. And almost no sound. Except for the wind and a few birds, the country was silent, quieter even than the bothy had been, for there the sea had been a constant companion. He could have enjoyed this were it not madness to be even seeing it, walking on it. He tackled Bicker again.

'You promised to tell me how this came about—why you came to Skye. Why you have brought me here.'

The dark man sighed. 'Indeed, I did.' He walked on for a few seconds, his face closed. 'It is a long and tangled tale I have to be telling you, so you must bear with me. Storytelling is not my strength. Ratagan is the man for that.' He glanced at Riven quickly. 'But you would know that already.'

Ratagan, the bluff red-bearded giant. The drinker— the storyteller. Riven knew him already. Oh, yes.

'Well, I will begin at the start.

'It was last year, in the height of summer. I was wandering in the north of the land, beyond Talisker—' He waved away Riven's attempt to interrupt. 'It was a fine day, a day of haze and buttercups, and the barley ripening. It came upon me that I thought I would climb the Red Mountain and look out on the land, for I was a scout then, in the pay of a lord named Quirinus, though I had little to do. It had been a quiet spring, a summer of plenty. The weather was so fair that the passage of the mountains was but little trouble, though in the winter that is another tale. I was a long way up on the western face, and the sun was hot. I found a ledge that was out of the wind and difficult to approach. And there I sat. And before an hour had passed, I had fallen asleep.' He stopped talking for a long moment, his sharp face unreadable.

'It was a scream woke me up; someone falling. Then I heard another shout, someone in pain. But I could see no one, though it seemed close by. I looked about me, and what was it I did not see? I saw a small valley below, no place in Minginish; and houses such as I had not seen before sitting there. And before me, wrapped round the rock, was a bright rope and when I drew it up the end was severed.

'*Michael*, the woman's voice had screamed as it fell. That I remembered afterwards. At the time I thought the sun had turned my head, but I could not forget that.

'I closed my eyes, and when I opened them I was on the Red Mountain in my own land again. But there was a great stillness in the air. The wind had died and the land was hushed. Not a bird or a bee stirred, and the people in the valley below had stopped their work in the fields and were looking at the sky, for there was a light in it like the shine of blood, and the sun was dimmed. I scrambled down from my high perch with the silence deafening me, and made the best time I could through the mountain passes—but before that first day had gone into night, a cloud that was black as pitch had covered the sky and the wind had taken up again, waxing into a storm the like of which no one had ever seen. Some called it the end of the world. The barley was flattened in the fields, and the lightning struck cattle and people dead where they stood. And then the rain came lashing down like ice, roaring the rivers into flooding the land.' Bicker's eyes were far away, narrowed with memory. His hand touched the sword hilt at his side.

'And that was the beginning of it, the start of the Bad Time when the summer died and the snows stalked the land before autumn had even rightly begun; and the beasts came ravening out of the mountains. And the Giants that no man had seen for a score of years—they came down from the snows to spread terror through the Rorims. And the wolves bayed at the very gates of Talisker itself. Minginish began to die.

'I went south, to my home—to Ralarth Rorim, and found the Dales under siege and swamped with snow. A bitter winter had come upon the land and none could find any reason for it.' He paused again. 'Except me. I thought I knew. I told my father—the Warbutt—and took the northern road again, and Murtach joined me. We fought our way through the hills and followed the Great River north, and then had a lean time forcing the passage of the mountains. And we went through the door. We found ourselves on the mountain you name Sgurr Dearg, in the Isle of Mists, and we breathed for the first time the tainted air of your world...'

He trailed off, looking suddenly weary.

'A thin time of it we had, at first. Strange to say, we spoke the same tongue as the folk of the Isle— the same you write in your books. We sounded different, but we could make ourselves understood. Murtach was better than I at aping the accents of the people there.

'We lived like beggars or thieves, stealing enough to live on, finding ourselves more fitting clothes. Murtach's little pets were a problem. Much of the time they had to remain hidden.'

'Pets?' Riven asked.

'Wolves, Michael Riven. Murtach has a pair of wolves for his constant companions—Fife and Drum.'

'Wait a minute—'

But Bicker shook his head. 'Let me finish this in one go, or it will never be told.

'At any rate, we frequented a string of drinking houses on the Isle, and after a long, weary time, we found out what had occurred that summer's day on the slopes of the Red Mountain. A woman had died, and a man had been crippled. We learned your name. The trail was easier to follow, then. Murtach did that: with Minginish gold, he pawned his way south. I remained in the north searching for another door to take us home whilst he was looking for you.'

'He found me.' A vision of wolves crouched under the willows in the night. He had not been imagining them.

'Yes. When he was sure you would be returning to the Isle, he returned himself. It is a long tale, that of his journey: part on foot, part in the machines your people use to move in. And Fife and Drum complicating matters all the way.' Bicker chuckled. 'Fine scrapes they got in and out of, I can tell you. But they did it. They came back with the news that you would be returning within weeks or days.

'And Murtach brought two other things north with him, Michael Riven. He brought your books, which we could read as easily as we could speak your tongue. And when we read them, we were dumbfounded. We knew then that your accident, your loss, was somehow tied up with the happenings in our own land. Somehow you are connected with Minginish. Somehow—and this is much worse—you may even be directing what is happening here. That is something which must be thought about.'

Riven started angrily, but yet again Bicker halted him.

'There is more. I found the door that would take us into Minginish down by the sea not far from Sgurr Dearg in your world.'

'How?' Riven asked curtly. He was sure the answer was important. Bicker did not look at him.

'I stumbled upon a dark-haired girl wandering in the mountains of the Isle. I followed her, and watched her disappear through the door. It may be she is here now, in Minginish.'

'You bastard!' Riven spat, his gaze swimming with anger. 'You knew about her all the time. You knew who she must be.'

'I am sorry,' Bicker said stiffly. 'I had little choice.'

'She's my wife! She's supposed to be dead.'

'I know. I know how this must be paining you. You must try to accept it. It will make it easier. There may be many lives hanging on your deeds, my friend—perhaps the fate of a whole world.'

'Spare me the sermon, Bicker.'

So Jenny was here, also. Wandering these hills, perhaps, alone with the beasts.

Grief and bitterness rose in his throat like vomit. But why had she run away from him? And how could she have gone through the door *before* the night she had been in the bothy?

He spat into the fresh grass as he walked. It was mad—crazy and insane. He was treading a nonexistent world with a character from one of his own books. And his dead wife was somehow alive again.

Jesus Christ!

He had to stop. His legs were quivering like reeds.

'I can't—can't take it. Bicker, this is too much. It is wrong.'

'It is,' the dark man agreed. 'But it is nonetheless real.'

'It's not right. She died. My God, is nothing sacred? She was my *wife*.'

'And this is my country.'

Riven blinked furiously. 'Where's the snow and ice, then? Where are the Giants and the wolves? It looks pretty much fine here to me—or am I missing something?'

For the first time Bicker seemed at a loss. 'I know,' he said. 'That I cannot explain. When I last was here the whole land was in the grip of a savage winter. But you like this place, do you not, Michael Riven? You have enjoyed walking through it?'

'Yes. So?'

'Then perhaps that is something to do with it. Perhaps.'

'Bloody hell! What am I then—some sort of weatherman?'

'Maybe you are,' Bicker said mildly, and continued walking. After a moment Riven followed, swearing silently.

'Where are we going?' he asked at last.

'To Ralarth Rorim—where else? And it is still a good two days from here. So walk on, Michael Riven, and pray this weather holds. We want a way yet under our belts before dark.'

So Riven kept walking, because there was nothing else for him to do.

THERE WAS A soft rain that night, like a whisper at a funeral. It lay like a silver mist in their hair as the light went and they sat beside another fire. Bicker had lit this one with flint and steel, and it took a long time to catch in the moist air. They ate some of Riven's tinned food and buried their litter, then sat cloak-wrapped staring into the fire in silence. The rain continued. A soft night, Riven thought, and the mourning rose in him to clench his throat as he wondered whether this land was mourning with him.

'Bicker,' he said, the quiet patter of the rain in his words. 'Tell me a story.'

His companion looked up, his face a maze of shadows and beard, but the eyes reflected the firelight. 'You are the storyteller,' he said. Riven shook his head helplessly, and buried his stare in the embers. There was a fantail of sparks as Bicker threw another faggot on the fire, then he leaned back into the heavy folds of his cloak.

'I can't tell you many tales; we have few here in Minginish. I know an old story that concerns the Myrcans, though.'

'The Myrcans?' Riven remembered. 'They're soldiers, fighting men.'

Bicker made a face. 'No other word can be used about them. They are soldiers, and they are nothing else.' He frowned, and sucked his teeth.

'I was a soldier once.'

'You said. But Myrcans, they are born soldiers and die so. I will tell you the tale, so that you may know, for you will meet them soon.' He built up the fire, edging a larger log into its bright heart. Then he began.

'There were Giants in the north of the land once, tall as hills.

'Some were good, some were not, for that is the way of things. But, being Giants, when they were good they were very good, and when they were bad—' He shrugged. 'At any rate, there was one of them who lived in the mountains beyond Dun Drinan, and he was bad, bad right through. He enslaved the people of the valley and made them pay tribute. He took their cattle and their women for his amusement, he razed the walls that they had built, he slew their menfolk for sport. And the long and short of it was that the people beyond Dun Drinan were not happy. But who argues with Giants?

'Well, this Giant—Myrca was the name he called himself by, though he was called by many another— grew so full of pride and arrogance that he wanted to have his face stamped for ever into the faces of the folk in the valley. So he made them build a statue of him, and it was the same size as himself. The Dwarves of the mountains he forced into labour as well, for they were handier with stone, and hardier—but he forgot that they are also stronger in heart than most folk, and most likely to avenge an insult. So they built the statue, and a wondrous sight it was, towering over the Dale and darkening the houses of the people with its shadow—but what do you think, when he looked at it closer, did he see? He saw that the stone was shaped in his likeness, down to the very club he carried, and he was well pleased by that; but when he looked at the face he saw that it was hewn in the likeness of a great pig, with little eyes and drooling chops and a long snout. Then he was not pleased, and his roars flew down the valley to terrify the people. And what did he do? Well, he raised his club, long as a fair-sized tree, and he smote the statue so it crumbled into fragments— but did the fragments not then stand up and start to move around his feet? And did he not see then that everyone was a stern-eyed soldier with hands of stone? And they slew him there and then, and his bones enriched the soil, so that the Dale was ever afterwards one of the richest in the land. But the soldiers who slew him: they called themselves the Myrcans, and their great host split up among all the Dales of Minginish to guard the folk of the world from Giants. And so it is today that the Myrcans, a few to every people in the land, hold the Dales safe from the beasts that come out of the mountains.'

The fire rustled, and Bicker yawned. 'Not much of a story, but it passes the time.' He looked at the sky. 'We'll be wetter before the morning. Get some sleep, and I'll do the watching for a while.'

But Riven woke up in the dead hour before dawn to find Bicker standing beside him with a drawn sword, and his head up like a hound's on a scent.

'What is it? What's wrong?'

'Nothing, I think. An odd smell on the wind. Nothing.' He sheathed his sword. 'But we'll move out now, nonetheless, break our fast in some other place.' And he helped Riven's chilled fingers to pack in the pre-dawn gloom.

THE SUN ROSE in a clear sky, drying out their damp clothes and warming Riven's aching legs.

I'll get metal fatigue if this goes on much longer.

He wondered how far they had walked in the past couple of days, and preferred to give up calculating when he found he was adding together miles walked on Skye and here, in this place, Minginish.

Just take it as it comes.

'There's smoke ahead,' he said, noticing. He glanced at Bicker, who seemed pleased.

'I see it. But don't worry. We are expected.' One raised finger halted his companion's questions. Riven threw a few choice words around in his head, but held his peace.

Another mile, and they had reached a small camp fire with a group of figures gathered around it. Two were animals, built like large grey dogs, who sat on their haunches and eyed the newcomers warily, sniffing the wind. The other two were human. They stood up as Bicker and Riven approached, one huge and broad, the other slight—smaller than Bicker. They both wore grins on their faces as the travellers reached them.

'Out of the misty island and looking twice as ugly as the day he was born,' the smaller one said. He was dressed in a linen shirt with a coat of sheepskin and breeches of leather. A sword hilt rose up behind one shoulder, and in his brown face gleamed eyes blue as a lochan under a clear sky. The two wolves took their place at his side.

Riven frowned as he saw him.

'Murtach, you smell like a dead sheep in high summer,' Bicker rejoined, slapping him on the shoulder and sparing a hand for the two wolves to lick. They sidled round him and Riven, sniffing at the strange smells, their yellow eyes deep and eager. Riven froze as a wet nose was pushed into the palm of his hand.

'And what about me, you spawn of a hill fox? Have you no word for Ratagan?' The big man was also clad in sheepskins, but he wore a blue sash around his waist with the haft of an axe tucked through it. His face was blunt as a crag, written over with lines of mirth, and a red beard jutted out from it, the sunshine setting it alight. He picked Bicker up as though he were a child and shook him until his teeth rattled.

'Hair of the dog!' Bicker cried. 'I would have spoken sooner if I'd known you were sober—' and he was flung on the ground. He landed catlike, and the attention of the other two fell on Riven, so that he wondered if he were to be thrown around like a rag as well.

'And you have brought the Teller of Tales with you,' Murtach said. 'He looks a mite healthier than when I last saw him.' The small man came forward and bent in a low bow. 'Murtach Mole at your service, Michael Riven. It is a while I have waited to see you in Minginish.'

'Molesy!' Riven cried.

Murtach grinned, showing teeth startlingly white against his brown face. 'The very same.' Then he bent like an old man, and said in a Highland accent: 'So how are ye today, Mister Riven?'

Riven could only gape, astonished.

'Are you on your own, or are there others out?' Bicker asked Murtach.

'Two Myrcans watch over us even as we speak,' he replied. 'Their woodcraft is woeful, but they are roving the hills around us to discourage pursuit.'

Bicker raised his eyebrows. 'Myrcans. You must have had a well-oiled tongue to persuade them to join a party such as this.'

Murtach sobered. 'Much has changed while you were away, Bicker. The snows have gone for the moment, but even so few venture into the hills at any time now. The easing of the weather has not lessened the attacks of the mountain creatures.'

Bicker grimaced. 'We'll talk of it later when we have a roof over our heads. I have much to tell the Warbutt.'

'That will be no one-sided talk, I fear,' Ratagan said, kicking out the fire. 'He's not been holding his toes since you left. There are changes at the Rorim, also.'

'That can wait, though,' Murtach put in. 'We'd best be moving; there are miles ahead of us yet, though the day is not old.'

Bicker nodded. Ratagan and Murtach slung their packs, and the company set off briskly, the two wolves loping ahead. They made great speed, for the ground was good and the morning was still cool. Riven stumbled along in their midst, his mind reeling with questions which he knew better than to ask.

It's Thursday. And yesterday it was Wednesday, and the day before that I was on Skye. I had bacon and eggs for breakfast. It was a nice morning. A nice morning.

These are the labours of your imagining.

But what is going on here? How can this happen? What is happening to me?

CHAPTER SEVEN

THEY WALKED ALL day at a pace that was punishing for Riven, and he began to feel like a hounded prisoner. He was glad to see the approach of dusk, but with it came the sight of a dark line across the horizon ahead.

'Scarall Wood,' said Bicker. 'We have made good time. We will camp there tonight and be in Ralarth Rorim by evening tomorrow.' He looked at Murtach. 'What of the Myrcans?'

'They rejoin us at dusk. If we camp on the southern edge of the wood, they should find us easily enough.'

They reached the eaves of the wood an hour later, and Ratagan immediately hefted his axe and stood guard whilst the others set up camp. Fife and Drum threw themselves on to the ground, panting like dogs. Their yellow eyes seemed to glow in the gloom.

Soon after they had the fire lit, there was a rustle of dead leaves, and two men stood in their midst as if they had sprung out of the ground. Riven bit back an exclamation of surprise and took a good look at his first Myrcans.

In his books they had been taciturn mercenaries who took service under the Dale lords. From what Bicker had told him, however, it seemed their role was more subtle than that. It was strange watching the characters of his imagination alive, walking and talking with him; almost like being on a vast film set. Both terrifying and exhilarating. Perhaps the weirdest thing was that these characters of his had a life of their own, sides to them that he had never imagined in his stories. They were, he supposed, necessarily more complex, as life was more complex than any man's art. Two questions gnawed at him, however: first, had he brought Minginish to life, somehow, or was he merely tapping into it for his stories? And second, how?

The Myrcans who stood there were somehow more brutal in appearance than he had ever envisaged. Riven had never seen men who looked more solid, more part of the earth. They were short, broad-shouldered and powerfully built, and they seemed to crouch as though ready to spring. Their hair was black and cropped almost to the scalp, and they were clean-shaven. They wore close-fitting leather breeches, stout knee-high boots, and heavy jerkins of hide which seemed to be reinforced with glinting mesh at the shoulders, the chest and the groin. Around their waists were blue sashes like Ratagan's. They bore in their blunt hands five-foot staves of dark wood which were bound all along their length with metal rings that glinted in the firelight.

Their faces were dark, their eyes like black stones. Both of them wore a stripe of white paint on their faces from ear to ear, running across the bridge of the nose. They might have been twins. No one spoke as they took their places by the fire. Eventually Ratagan broke the silence with a rumble from where he stood at the edge of the light.

'What news, my friends?'

The metal-bound staff flashed as the Myrcan responded. 'Naught to the rear of us. The land is empty. We saw winter wolves, but they are far off now. The melting of the snows has sent the beasts retreating to the High Ground.'

The Myrcan was staring at Riven with uncomfortable intensity. He shifted uneasily, and whispered to Bicker: 'Tell him I'm friendly, will you?'

Bicker smiled. 'Ord, this is Michael Riven, the Teller of Tales. He is the one Murtach has spoken to you about, who comes from the Isle beyond the sea to help us.' Then Bicker turned to Riven. 'These are Ord and Unish. They are of the Myrcans.'

'I'm honoured,' said Riven, partly because he felt he should say something, and partly because he wished to allay any suspicions these formidable natives might harbour about him.

The Myrcans regarded him unsmilingly, and then their gaze left him. He was tired and irritated, and no one would tell him anything. He pulled out his sleeping bag—which made the Myrcans stare again—and wrapped himself in it whilst the others prepared food.

The ground under him quivered for a moment, then was still. He frowned and sat up, felt the place with his hands.

'What is it?' Bicker asked.

'Nothing. I thought I felt... something.'

'In the ground?'

'It was my imagination,' said Riven, feeling a fool.

But Bicker and Murtach were exchanging glances. 'Scarall is all right, isn't it?' Bicker was saying.

Murtach looked worried. 'I thought so.'

Then the ground underneath Riven gave a heave, and sagged. He jumped to his feet. 'Shit. There's something under there. Something moved.'

The company stood up, weapons hissing out of sheaths. Fife and Drum began growling low in their throats, eyes luminous in the firelight.

'What is it? What's wrong?' Riven demanded angrily. And the ground erupted beside him.

A great clay-black shape sprang from the soil and launched itself at him. Stone-hard paws smashed him to the ground, and outlined above him by the fire was the head of a huge dog or hound, eyeless, black-mawed. Then the Myrcan staves crashed into its back, and it leapt at them with a howl. Riven crawled backwards, mind white with shock, and saw a black hound six feet long throwing the Myrcans about as though they were dolls, whilst the two wolves snapped uselessly at its heels. Bicker's sword came whistling down on its flank with a crack, and bounced off, taking only a few chips out of the creature.

Chips?

It did not bleed, and where the sword had struck it was a shallow white scar the colour of new wood.

Wood? Something from a far memory hammered at the back of his mind. A subterranean, wooden hound—but there was no time to speculate.

Ratagan entered the fray with a roar, and his axe hissed down to thud into the creature's neck. It sank inches, and he wrenched it out again whilst the Myrcans belaboured it with their staves. Murtach called off Fife and Drum, and they retreated from the fight, snarling. The beast seemed unharmed, and the staves bounced off it ineffectually. The huge mouth clamped over Ratagan's lower leg, and he cried out, falling to the ground and thumping the head uselessly with his fists.

At once, the Myrcans dropped their weapons, and fell on the beast with their bare hands. They wrestled with it, prising it free of Ratagan and manhandling it towards the fire. The hound struggled madly, and succeeded in crushing one of its attackers against a tree. The Myrcan released his hold. The hound was too much for his comrade, and it bit and buffeted its way free of his grip. Then, to his horror, Riven saw that it was coming back towards him.

But Bicker and Murtach sprang on it with burning sticks from the fire. They shoved them into the beast's face, and for the first time it howled with pain and thrashed blindly away. The two Myrcans grabbed torches also, though one of them had an arm that hung useless at his side, and the four surrounded the hound, jabbing it with the flaming brands. It writhed and snapped at them, but recoiled from the fire. Finally it howled in anger, and Riven saw its rear end sink into the soil. It corkscrewed backwards into the ground, their last sight of it being its black, revolving muzzle. Then it had disappeared, and there was no mark in the grass to indicate its passing.

The company stood still, the flickering torches

throwing their shadows among the trees. The only sounds were the flames, Ratagan's hard breathing and the sniffing of the wolves as they padded round Murtach, verifying he was unhurt.

'It is gone,' Bicker said at last, and returned his torch to the fire. The others did the same. He went over to Ratagan, who lay with pain written on his face at the edge of the firelight, and bent to examine his leg. The unhurt Myrcan was tending to his injured comrade. Riven joined Murtach, who was watching over them with Ratagan's axe in his hand.

'That was a gogwolf,' he stated, shaking. Murtach's pets eyed him with suspicion.

Their master stared at him grimly. 'Indeed. Another of your pet monsters. It is a creature of the trees and the earth, and it moves through the ground as easily as we move on top of it, following the roots of the trees.'

'It really looked as though it were made of wood.'

Murtach seemed slightly impatient. 'It is, and its hide is as hard as the bark of the toughest oak.' Then he shrugged. 'We should have remembered that sooner; but it is a long time since any of us here has encountered a gogwolf, and we never thought they would have come this far south out of the high forests. This is ill news indeed.'

'What about Ratagan?'

Murtach's troubled expression eased. 'Him? He is as tough as tree roots himself. A bite on his leg will not hamper him much.'

They were silent. Bicker heated water in a copper pot and ripped up clothing to bind wounds.

'Will it come back?' Riven asked. He was still marvelling a little. I've seen a gogwolf.

Murtach shook his head. 'We hurt it, and it attacked on its own. If it had possessed comrades, then we would have had to leave the wood; but we will be all right here now, I think. Which is just as well, since I don't think these two had better be moved, for tonight, at least.'

'It was after me,' Riven realised, unable to get the picture of that black maw out of his mind.

'Maybe,' Murtach replied. 'That is something we can discuss in Ralarth Rorim, along with other things.' He did not seem disposed to say more, and played with Fife's ears absently.

Bicker called them over, wanting more water heated. Ratagan's wound was full of clay, and needed careful washing. It was ragged and bloody, making a mess out of his calf. The big man cursed furiously as he watched Bicker treat it.

'Whoreson animal. This'll lay me up for days, once we get home.'

'But the women will love you for it,' Bicker replied, grinning. Ratagan laughed, then looked about him. 'Mole, you evil-smelling midget, where's my fine weapon?'

'In equally fine hands, clumsy one. She's wondering if her master was drunk when he made that swing at the beast.'

'Drunk or sober, she made a bigger impression than that pig-sticker of yours.'

Riven turned his attention to the Myrcans. They were sitting quietly by the fire, the injured one—he could still not tell them apart—with his arm splinted and bound. He shook his head. Unreal, those two.

Bicker stood up, wiping his hands. 'It would be

better to leave the wood, but we'd best stay here until morning, with the hurts we have suffered.' He cut off Ratagan's protest with a curt gesture. 'We will set watches and keep the fire high. We cannot afford to be caught like that again. If there are gogwolves in Scarall, there may be all sorts of other things as well.' He bent down and fumbled with his pack, grunting as he found what he was looking for. His hand flicked, and a flash spun through the air to become a dagger embedded in the grass at Riven's feet.

'That is for the Teller of Tales,' he said, meeting Riven's eye with a wry smile. 'So that his tales may not get the better of him.'

Riven pulled the weapon out of the ground. It was heavy, a broad double-edged knife with a twelve-inch blade. He whistled softly as he thumbed the edge. 'You people don't muck about.'

'We can't afford to,' Bicker responded shortly. 'Now you know why.' He retied his bag. 'You and I will take first watch. There will be little sleep tonight, but this time tomorrow we will be in the Rorim.'

'Ralarth Rorim.'

'Yes. That much at least you will be familiar with. But there is more to Minginish than in your stories.'

'That I believe.'

THE OTHERS WERE asleep, and Riven was nodding, the knife cold in his hands. He rubbed his eyes. 'Bicker?'

'Yes?'

'Talk to me. I'm falling asleep.'

Bicker was cleaning his sword with a scrap of hard

leather. 'Another story? You will make a Teller of me yet.'

'What about telling me how Murtach found me. He was at Beechfield, but he was an old man. How was that done? How many of your people know about me?'

Bicker clicked his tongue. 'We are a conspiracy, we are—' He gestured towards the others who lay asleep. 'We wanted to stop what was happening to Minginish. Murtach and Ratagan are my foster brothers, just as you imagined. Ord and Unish are two of the Myrcan Hearthwares of Ralarth Rorim. I am the Warbutt's heir, though hardly a prince.' He smiled crookedly. 'The Warbutt does not take kindly to my... wanderings.'

'Does he know what is going on here?'

'Of course. Myrcan Hearthwares do not wander off without their lord's permission.'

'Tell me of Ralarth Rorim. Tell me of your family.' Riven was biting back some of the questions he most wanted to ask, especially those concerning Jenny. They gave him a hollow feeling in the pit of his stomach.

Bicker scratched his beard. 'There is not much to tell that you do not know already. The Rorim is old, as much is in Minginish. It was built long before the first beasts ventured out of the mountains; but it was built at a time when the Dales were at odds with one another, and there was more raiding—for cattle and weapons, mostly. Sometimes for women. So it is truly a fort as well as a dwelling place, and though many live there many more can gather there in time of need. Its walls are not high; but they are long, and there is grazing within them and a spring that never fails.'

Riven digested this for a moment. 'And your family?' he asked.

'My mother is dead,' Bicker answered succinctly. 'The Warbutt—my father—you will meet. Murtach and Ratagan are sons of my father's captains. There are no more.'

'What about the people? What are they like? Are they... as I drew them?'

Bicker smiled. 'For the most part. There are just over two dozen Hearthwares, trained fighters who have been taught by the Myrcans. Their captain is Udaim, Ratagan's father. Murtach's father, Guillamon, is the wisest man in Minginish—or so Murtach likes to say. He is Warden of Ralarth. Some say he is a wizard of sorts.' Bicker shot a quick glance at Riven. 'Your story has a wizard.' Riven nodded impatiently.

'No one counts our people, but there are many of them. Shepherds, most of them, and farmers who till the earth around the Rorim. Now they and the sheep herders are at odds, for the flocks have been forced out of the hills by the beasts and there is competition for space. There has been trouble, and the Hearthwares have never been so busy.'

'What are these beasts like, that come out of the mountains?'

Bicker ran a finger down his sword blade. 'You know now the gogwolf—though that is the first one we have seen this far south. A bad omen. There are normal wolves also, but bolder than we have ever seen them before. And then there are things such as the grypesh, the rat-boars, and the Rime Giants and the ice worms. All these we have known to have existed for a long time, but they stayed in their highland haunts and only hunters and wanderers encountered them, making for a good tale in the winter. But now they terrorise the very folk of the Dales and stalk the hills in between at will, cutting one village off from another; only the hardiest travel far these days, and then only at great need.'

'I know the Rime Giants,' Riven said. He stabbed his new knife into the turf. 'I dreamt of you and Ratagan while I was in hospital. We were fighting a giant.' He did not say that it had spoken with Jenny's voice. That part of this world still frightened him too much. The thought of Jenny, here, frightened him, when it was not breaking his heart.

'Guillamon—Murtach's father—has seen you in dreams also,' Bicker said soberly. 'It was he who urged me to return to the Staer, though my father was against it. Murtach came for an adventure, and because his abilities made him useful.'

'In the book he is a... shapeshifter,' Riven said, choosing the word with care.

The dark man nodded. 'There is no magic in your world, but we have a brand of it here in Minginish.'

'He was a werewolf,' Riven said, his gaze flickering to the two wolves who lay dozing just outside the firelight. He felt a chill scale his backbone.

'Murtach can take many guises,' Bicker conceded. 'He is a man with a gift, as is his father. He is a boon to us all.'

But Riven was remembering a scene he had written once, where a transformed Murtach had roamed the high moors under the moon with his two fellow wolves for company. He shook his head. 'Unreal,' he muttered. And he suddenly recalled getting drunk with Doody, and glimpsing through the haze the prick-eared shape at the window, looking in at them from the darkness outside.

What sort of people are these?

'All this—all these troubles. This winter which you say has come and gone here, the monsters from the mountains. All this has happened in the past year since—since Sgurr Dearg?'

'Yes.'

'And you think that, somehow, I'm responsible for it, don't you?'

Bicker did not reply.

THEY CONTINUED ON their way the next morning without incident. Murtach and the wolves took the lead, and after them came Bicker, supporting an evil-tempered Ratagan, who leaned heavily on the haft of his axe. Riven came next, his new knife thrust through his belt, and then the two Myrcans, one with his arm slung.

The land changed as they walked. They had been travelling across undulating hills that were almost moor; but now the folds of the hills dipped and more and more downward slopes began appearing, whilst before them bloomed a long view of flatter land that glittered with rivers and was scattered with small woods. It stretched off into blue distance, becoming a guess of more highland in the north. Riven stared at it. Valleys within valleys. Minginish was vaster than his glimpse of it on the hill of the door had allowed him to estimate. There were skylarks here, and corncrakes. The grass was less yellow, and the heather petered out. Just like the book. He did not know if that was disturbing or comforting.

He could make out fields now, tawny with sun, and the grey dots of houses with their wisps of woodsmoke. Ponds of what seemed to be meltwater had gathered in hollows and there were ragged remnants of snow in the shadows of the steeper slopes.

'Ralarth,' said Bicker with gladness in his voice. 'A long time, it seems, since last my eyes were on it.'

'It's still there,' Ratagan growled, 'though the Warbutt may have a word or two for your ear when we get to the Rorim.'

'Hasn't he always?'

There was a low rumble on the air, and then two horsemen burst into view on the rise ahead, the turfs flying from their mounts' hoofs like startled birds. They were in full armour, the steel plate glinting in the sun, the light shining off their helms and their harnesses jingling. To Riven, it seemed one of the most beautiful sights he had ever seen. They cantered over to the company and reined in their steeds ten feet away, throwing up their hands in salute.

'Well met, Bicker! Has Ratagan stumbled and hurt himself?'

Bicker grinned back. 'Indeed! And this time he was sober.'

'You whelp, Dunan!' Ratagan roared. 'While your backside has been warming a chair, we've been battling the beasts of the hills and brought a Teller from the Isle of Mists.'

The Hearthware's eyes widened. 'That is news. Do you need help to the Rorim?'

Bicker shook his head. 'Our feet will serve us, even Ratagan here. But tell the household of our arrival.'

Dunan threw up his hand again. 'That I will. My sister Mira will be more than a little glad to see your face again, I'm thinking, Bicker.' Then the pair were off, thundering away across the hillside.

They had their first sight of the Rorim almost an hour later, when they made their way over the last rise before the Dale of Ralarth and the valley spread like a cloak under their eyes.

A seven-foot drystone wall ran like a snake across the undulating floor of the Dale. There were several gates set in its length, each guarded by a tall tower and an accompanying longhouse. It must have enclosed nearly three square miles, Riven reckoned. He could see herds of cattle grazing within, and scattered clumps of houses.

In the centre of the enclosed pastures there was a circle, a rampart of turf with an accompanying ditch, and on the rampart another circular wall higher than the outer. Inside its confines was a cluster of large buildings: longhouses and smaller structures, built out of wood and stone, some roofed with turf. They were built so close together that their walls touched, and indeed Riven could make out connecting corridors and annexes. The biggest structure was a stone building with three storeys, and glass shining in its windows. Even it had only slits for windows on the ground floor, however, and a stout double door. At its rear was a square tower with larger windows that overlooked the whole Rorim, and from whose pinnacle a blue pennant flew. Smoke drifted up from half a dozen smoke holes and chimneys. The place seemed sleepy, though someone was leading horses across the open yard before the biggest building.

'The Warbutt will no doubt be watching our approach,' Bicker said, and waved at the Rorim with his free hand.

'As long as they have some beer foaming in the Manse, he could be sucking his toes, for all I care,' said Ratagan, too tired now to keep the pain out of his voice. He was leaning heavily on Bicker, a scowl biting his brow.

'It gets worse?' Bicker asked him, concerned.

'It gets no better, dark one, but I'd not have me carried into our Circle like a woman in labour, so save your breath and let's be on our merry way.'

Dunan awaited them at a gate in the outer wall. He wore his shining metal armour, and there was a sash the twin of Ratagan's around his waist. The big man finally consented to ride a horse, and they made better time as they marched on through the Circle to the Rorim itself.

They forded a stream that had its source in the ramparted fort, the water clear as dew, and drew up to the Rorim's gates. The heavy portals were open, though other armoured and blue-sashed figures watched them from the catwalk, and there was the glitter of spear points in the sun. Their weapons were surrendered at the barbican, two squat stone towers and their accompanying longhouses, though Riven noticed that the Myrcans kept their staves. He handed over the knife that Bicker had given him to the Hearthware, and looked around.

They were in the courtyard before the biggest of the Rorim's buildings—the one Ratagan had named the Manse. It was cobbled, and there was a well near the middle. A group of women in dun clothes were drawing water from it in wooden buckets, but they stopped their work to stare at the company—and especially at Riven. He felt out of place in his hiking clothes and with his rucksack on one shoulder. He was also, to his immense surprise and chagrin, absurdly conscious of the scars on his face, and he turned away from the inquiring eyes with a silent curse.

The doors of the Manse opened soundlessly and two men came out together, closely followed by two Myrcans. One was armoured and sashed like the Hearthwares and was broad as a door, with a golden beard spilling down his chest. The other was slighter, with grey hair, beardless, and with electric blue eyes. He wore a nondescript robe and breeches, but there was a torc of gold about his neck. The Myrcans, unsurprisingly, were Ord and Unish's twins.

Ratagan dismounted with a grunt of pain and steadied himself on Murtach's shoulder. 'Greetings, my father,' he said.

The gold-bearded man gripped his sash with both large hands.

'Trouble, eh? Your mother has been worrying as always, Ratagan. With good cause, this time, it seems.' He smiled almost apologetically, but Ratagan only grimaced in reply.

The company moved towards the Manse, and the newcomers walked with them. Riven seemed to pass unnoticed, but then he caught the keen eyes of the greyer man upon him, and had to look away.

'The Warbutt is awaiting you all,' the grey man said, in a voice dry as an autumn leaf. 'I can ease your hurts as you talk to him, for he is impatient for news. Especially from you, Bicker.'

Bicker sighed. 'I guessed that, Guillamon. I have been overlong away.'

'But you have accomplished what you set out to do.' It was a statement.

'Yes.' Bicker jerked his head towards Riven, and again those sea-blue eyes were on him for a moment before flickering away.

They entered a small hall that was all dark wood and flagged floor. Here the Myrcans left them. Then they followed Guillamon and Ratagan's father through a double door, and found themselves in a vast hall whose massive roof beams crossed high above their heads. Light dropped in broad yellow shafts from high windows set in the walls. Dust danced in the sunbeams, which shone off old weapons hung near the ceiling and glinted on the gilt thread of tapestries along the walls. The firepit was empty, but a solitary brazier glowed at the end of the hall near a pair of high-backed chairs that were not unlike thrones. There was a figure seated quietly on the right-hand chair. He stood up as they approached, their footsteps raising echoes around them.

'Bicker. My son is back.'

He was old, very old, but with a shock of white hair and an aquiline profile. He looked like an eagle perching alone in moult.

'Father.' Bicker embraced the old man, and he sat down again.

'I see Ratagan has had some misfortune. You must

have much to tell me. Guillamon, would you see that basins of water and food and drink are brought in? I would call an attendant, but the fewer ears around here, the better.'

Guillamon nodded wordlessly and left via a small door to the left of the high seats.

There was a silence, during which Riven fidgeted uneasily and Bicker occupied himself with unbinding Ratagan's leg. Murtach frowned at the stone floor, where his wolves stretched themselves with a sigh of contentment.

After a few minutes, attendants came in with laden trays, and left quickly, ushered out by Guillamon. He bowed deeply to the Warbutt and then took a seat on the platform beside the fire pit, next to the company. There was a basin of faintly steaming water, silver sand and a thick towel for each of them, as well as mugs of cold beer, cheese, apples, beef, honey and bread. They washed, scrubbing themselves with the silver sand, and ate as the Warbutt regarded them, his face expressionless. Fife and Drum cracked at marrow bones, loud in the quiet. Riven could hear voices outside, far laughter and the lowing of distant cattle. Ratagan put down his empty mug and wiped his mouth with the back of his hand.

'Ah,' he said. 'That's better medicine than any the leeches hand out.' Guillamon chuckled, but Udairn, Ratagan's father, looked serious.

'What did this?' he asked, peering at his son's lower leg.

Ratagan shrugged. 'Gogwolf, in Scarall Wood.' The two older men looked at one another, but the Warbutt raised his hands.

'All in its proper place,' he said, seemingly unperturbed, but his eyes flashed.

When Ratagan's leg had been rebound, the Warbutt asked Bicker to begin with an account of his sojourn in the Isle of Mists. The dark man glanced at Riven, who felt much better for the wash and the beer, and began.

'It seems a long time I have been away. Eight months, since Murtach and I set out on the road to the Staer, through the blizzards that were destroying the land in the middle of the summer. Eight long months—and most of it spent in a strange land, a strange world. And on my own, too, much of the time. There were occasions when I thought that the Warbutt's son had been too clever for his own good.'

He grinned weakly. 'Murtach will have told you of the events that chanced from when he left the south, to where he had tracked Michael Riven, until he went through the door after meeting me to tell me of what had befallen. All I knew was that I was still on the Isle, for good or ill, and there I was bound to remain until the Teller of Tales came back north. I knew where he lived—this, and much more, we had gleaned in many drinking sessions with the natives of the Isle. I stayed in a rough hut to the back of his house, and a long, tiresome time I had of it. I still had some of the gold Murtach and I had been pawning for the money of the other world, but for the most part I lived by hunting and stealing from gardens like a wild animal.' Bicker paused and swigged at his beer thoughtfully.

'I had first discovered this other door by following a dark girl whom I had seen wandering the Isle. I watched her disappear through it. She was not one of the folk of that world—of that I am sure. She was as wild as a seal, and would not let me approach. I thought perhaps she was one of our people who had stumbled into the world of the Isle by accident and had lost her wits, but there was something about her that left me undecided. She seemed to be seeking something—or someone, maybe. Her eyebrows met in the middle.

'The strange thing is that I saw her again, soon after. Scant days after she had gone, she appeared once more. I glimpsed her hovering near an old, derelict dwelling place in a valley of the Isle the inhabitants call Glenbrittle. She could not have walked from the one door to the other in Minginish in that time, so either she knows of other doors or she can traverse them both ways—not just in the one direction, as we can. That was the last time I saw her.

'From then, it was not in truth such a long wait until Michael Riven returned to his home, and when he did I lured him here by guile, and so he is as you see him now—not totally unwilling, I hope.' Bicker stopped and looked at Riven, but Riven never saw him.

Glenbrittle. She was at her old home, where she first met me. But there's no one there to recognise her any more.

Guillamon nodded. 'You did right, Bicker, if half of what you and Murtach have hinted at concerning this man is true. But tell us: what happened on your return to Minginish? What of the wounds of Unish and Ratagan?'

'That I can tell, and more besides,' said Murtach suddenly, his blue eyes mirrors of his father's. 'Ratagan and I, along with Ord and Unish, set out two weeks ago to make our way to the door and be there ready to meet Bicker when he came through. I had thought to be at the site of the door itself, but Bicker had prevailed upon me before I left to meet him one day's journey away, so that he might have some time to talk to Michael Riven and apprise him of what had happened to him before the Teller was introduced to us and his head made to swim with faces.' Here he smiled crookedly, but Riven only scowled.

'You see, to Riven I am both a stranger and known to him. He has met me in the south as an old man low on wits; such was the shape I took to allow me to linger around the place of healing where he dwelt. But Michael Riven knows me from another source also—as he knows of all of us, perhaps, and all of Minginish.'

'Enough of that for now,' Guillamon said, and his son gave a small bow.

'The story of the rest of my sojourn in the Other Place you know,' he said. 'It was not pleasant. There the air is tainted and the water stale, and the very earth fettered with tar and moulded stone. Over the cities hang clouds of filth, and the rivers are choked with it. It is not a place I would visit again. Fife and Drum and I—' The two wolves lifted their heads and regarded their master quizzically. 'We had a hard time of it surviving, despite the gold I took with me. Even hospitality has a price in that world, and travellers are regarded with mistrust. Several times I was almost apprehended by what passes for that world's Hearthwares. Each time I changed my looks and slipped away. There is no magic in the world beyond the door, it would seem. Only in the stories that are told there.

'And that is my brief tale.' He shrugged and gulped at his beer, nudging Ratagan, who seemed to be in a light doze.

The big man woke with a start. 'I suppose it is on me to tell you of our latest adventures.' He blinked and eyed his empty flagon with a moment's regret. 'There is little enough to tell, except that we were right to have the company of Ord and Unish. On our way into the hills, we saw many wolves, but were not approached. And there were grypesh also, though not in large numbers. We slew half of one small pack that trailed us through the snows from the first heights of the hills. The rest fled. With the thaw that then came, we made better progress. We could have used horses. We waited at the appointed place for Bicker, and for once in his idle life the wretch was more or less on time. We headed north again—easy travelling in fine weather—but encountered a gogwolf in Scarall; it gave me my limp and cracked Unish's arm for him before we saw it off. The rest you know.'

Udairn shook his head. 'Gogwolves so close to Ralarth! That's new. I do not like it. The Hearthwares will have to be alerted.'

'What has been happening while I have been away?' Bicker asked. He looked at his father, but there was no response.

'Nothing good,' said Guillamon lightly. 'As Ratagan has noted, there are grypesh in Ralarth; flocks are no longer safe on their own. The Hearthwares are under a tide of problems.' He nodded to Udairn, who sighed heavily.

'Twenty-six men and eight Myrcans, most of whom are stationed at the Rorim itself, cannot police the whole Dale and the hills beyond. This weird winter has destroyed every crop we have. The thaw came too late. The people are being trained in the use of weapons, since they have no fields to tend. Dunan sees to it. I intend to increase the numbers of the Hearthwares, and I have put both Luib and Druim of the Myrcans on to the training now, but we will not reap the results of that for another season at least. Trained fighters do not spring out of the ground, though these things that are closing in on the Dale seem to.'

Then the Warbutt spoke, addressing Bicker. 'While you have been away, dozens of our people have lost their lives to the beasts, and their herds have been scattered. And shepherd has fought farmer within the Dale, bickering over the use of the land. Wolves have roamed up to the very walls of the Circle. We are becoming an island. We face famine in a few months. This place needs you more than any place beyond the door.'

Bicker flushed at once. 'Do you doubt the importance of my errand?'

'I have yet to see its value,' the old man responded mildly, looking at Riven.

It was Riven's turn to flush. He glared at the elderly figure on the high seat. Up to now, he had been transfixed by the narratives of Bicker, Murtach and Ratagan, lost in pondering imponderables, and with horror slowly dawning on him as he saw more clearly what kind of situation Bicker had brought him into—and what his own role in it might be. And gnawing under it was the knowledge that Jenny was alive, and more than likely here in Minginish. That knowledge made him want to run out of the hall, out of the Rorim and into the wolf-ridden hills to find his wife. And then he saw her eyes on him at the bothy again—empty and afraid. He could have howled with despair.

And now an elderly man whom he had created in his own book to be a pompous reactionary was regarding him with disdain.

'Well that just fucking tears it,' he barked. 'Who the hell do you think you people are? You take me from my world, my own life, and you haul me into some kind of rural Disneyland, spinning tales of death and destruction—then you nearly get me killed by a dog made of wood, for Christ's sake, and you sit down in front of me and talk about me as though I weren't there. Well, I am here—here in your marvellous bloody world—and if I'm supposed to help you then that's well and good, but before I do, by God, you're going to stop treating me like a bloody child who can't understand what's going on. I created you people!' He stopped.

'I created you...' he repeated hoarsely.

There was silence. Fife and Drum pricked up their ears attentively. Finally the Warbutt broke the silence.

'So,' he said, still in the same mild tone, 'he has a tongue in his head, after all. I am glad to see it.' The old, bright eyes met Riven's. 'If we have offended, you then we apologise, truly. Welcomes and courtesy are not what they used to be in Ralarth Rorim, I fear. I see you are a man, even if you are not of Minginish. Our counsels are open to you; our home is yours.'

Riven nodded, slightly.

'But your words confirm what Bicker and Murtach have already told us.'

'And what is that?' Riven snapped, not yet appeased. The Warbutt inclined his head towards Bicker, and the dark man drained his flagon.

'I'm going to talk about you as though you weren't here again,' Bicker said with a wry smile. Then he turned from Riven and stared at the floor, toying with his empty flagon.

'As all here know, Riven is a Teller of Tales. In his world, he writes down stories that he has made up so that others can read them. There are so many people in his world that he cannot travel as our Tellers do, reciting their tales for a meal or a night's lodging, or for the favour of the lord. He writes them on paper, and they travel about the land in that form— for paper is common and cheap over there—so that all can learn them whilst he stays where he would, making up more tales.'

Bicker looked up at his father. 'Murtach and I have read these two volumes of tales, and they are about Minginish. He describes the land—the mountains and the Dales, the cities and the sea. He knows of Rime Giants and grypesh, Hearthwares and Myrcans. And he knows the people, also. We sitting here are in Riven's stories. He tells of Murtach's shapechanging, Ratagan's drunken debauches—' Here the big man bellowed with laughter and everyone smiled.

'But Riven had never been to Minginish when he wrote these stories. They came out of his head.' Bicker shook his own head, grave again. 'And there is more. You know how the first door opened, and when; how it is connected with the events of the

Teller's life. And you know also of the fate that befell Minginish after—the snow and the mountain beasts.

'Now think on this. There has been a thaw. When, Ratagan?'

The bearded giant raised his eyebrows. 'It began two days before you met us south of Scarall. And uncommon swift it was, too. The snow fled as quickly as it had arrived—the space of an afternoon, almost.'

Bicker nodded grimly. 'The same time we left Riven's home on the Isle and began to make our way around the coast.'

'What are you saying?' Riven demanded.

'Only this: that Minginish's winter ended when you left the home you had shared with your wife— the first respite this land has had since she died eight months ago. It is you, Michael Riven; it is your mind, your emotions, that are directing the fate of our world.'

A blaze of argument broke out amongst them, with even the Warbutt pitching in. It was absurd, they protested. A coincidence. How could such a thing happen? It was Riven who cut through the talk.

'What about my wife?' he shouted.

The noise fell.

'She's dead. I watched her die. And now she's walking around again. Explain that, Bicker!'

The dark man spread his hands. 'I can't,' he said.

'I don't believe in ghosts,' Riven said savagely.

'Do you believe in magic?' Murtach asked in an odd voice, and when Riven looked at him he saw that the little man's eyes were a lambent yellow, glowing in the last light of day that filtered down from the hall's high windows.

'Enough,' Guillamon said. He seemed annoyed. 'Talk goes around biting its own tail after a while.'

'Indeed,' the Warbutt assented. He looked tired, haggard. The shadows had begun to creep into the hollows of his face. Outside, the day was dying. Night was pouring down out of the eastern hills.

'I want my captains and my son about me for a time,' he said. 'The rest may leave. The Steward will accommodate you. You will all sleep in the Manse tonight.'

They stood up in silence. Riven felt unwanted and out of place, Bicker's words echoing in his head. Murtach took Ratagan's arm and helped him out, whilst Riven trailed behind. He wanted to stay and talk some more, hammer out some logic from the madness; but he was an outsider here, without rights. And if Bicker was correct, then he was killing this world.

CHAPTER EIGHT

GWION THE STEWARD was a small, stout man with a good-natured face. He had been the innkeeper of Riven's daydreams in Beechfield, a minor character in one of his books. In this world, however, he had a wife called Ygelda, a tall, bronzed woman with masses of coppery hair bound up at the back of her head and a wide, matronly figure. She took one look at Riven with her hands on her hips, making him feel like a schoolboy caught in mischief, and ordered her husband to escort him to the quietest room he could find, since 'the poor man looks about done.' Gwion obeyed without demur, a sheepish smile on his face—a smile Riven had seen him wear in his dreams. He was staring at the steward almost as intently as he was being stared at as he was led to his room.

He found he had been given a small guest room on the first floor that faced north. The walls were a mixture of stone and dark wood panelling. There was a bed spread with soft, gaudy rugs, and a table laden with a washing basin, a large jug of beer and a plate of fresh fruit. On the bed also there was a change of clothes. It was luxury itself after the nights sleeping out.

Riven poured himself some of the malty beer and stood sipping it, looking out of the window at the Circle and the Dale beyond. The sunset was flushing the sky pink and orange, and the room was becoming gloomy. Riven wondered absently if he was supposed to sleep with the sun when the door was knocked and Gwion came in with two wooden candlesticks and a handful of pale candles.

'Been so much on my mind today I nearly forgot,' he said breathlessly. 'I am sorry; what is it coming to? Letting guests sit alone in the dark. What will you think of us?' He set the candles in their holders and produced a flint and steel and a small iron box. 'There.' He looked at Riven, who was sipping his beer moodily. 'Now, sir, is there anything else you want or need? I'm at a loss as to what a foreign knight would be needing for himself.'

Riven smiled despite himself. 'No, everything is fine. It couldn't be better.'

'Well, we do our best,' Gwion said, obviously pleased. He went out again. 'A pleasant night to you, sir,' and was gone.

Riven continued to smile to himself as the gloom deepened in the room and he could watch the lights start up in the Dale, twinkling like gems in a mine. He poured himself some more beer, feeling in need of a good wash and a change of socks, but delayed getting them, knowing that they were possible now. There were too many things in his head, like silt in a stirred stream, and he wanted some of them to settle in the quiet of the room.

He finished his flagon, checking that the jug was not empty, and then undressed, his legs complaining to him now they could make themselves heard over the impossibilities. But he was glad to bother only about physical ache, beer in the belly, the prospect of a soft bed under him, the encroaching darkness; glad to switch off his mind for a while.

The water in the basin was lukewarm as he splashed in it, and scrubbed himself from head to foot. Then, hair dripping in his eyes, he examined the clothes that had been set out for him. He had a suspicion that they were Bicker's, for he and the dark man were not unalike in size. A pair of breeches which seemed to be made of suede, and a linen shirt with no collar and wide sleeves. He donned them, and hummed as he set to lighting the candles. The box contained shredded rags that smelt vaguely inflammable, and he clicked a few sparks on to them warily. They caught at once and he lit a candle, snuffing out the tinder by closing the box.

Immediately the world outside became invisible, and there was only the candlelit room and himself. He lit three candles, positioning them around the room, and then lay back on the bed with the beer at his side.

The candles had hardly burned down an inch when he was woken from a doze by a heavy knock on the door. He started, jumped up, and opened it to find Murtach and Ratagan standing there clutching bottles and glasses.

'We thought we could hardly leave you alone on your first night in Ralarth Rorim,' Murtach said as he let them in. There was a dark movement as Fife and Drum entered behind him, the candlelight kindling their eyes briefly.

'And we've not come empty-handed,' Ratagan added. His face was flushed and he leaned heavily on a stick, but his eyes were bright.

The bottles and glasses were placed on the table, and Murtach set about opening the wine.

'Let the great ones discuss matters of import downstairs,' he said. 'We have better things to do, like tasting this twenty-year-old Drinan which Gwion will probably not even notice is missing.' The cork popped, and he sniffed the neck of the bottle and closed his eyes. 'Nectar.' Then he poured three glasses of the deep, red liquid, ruby in the candlelight.

'Some say a wine should be left to breathe,' he said, handing round the glasses. 'Myself, I think that the poor thing has waited long enough and deserves to have its suspense ended at once. To the fire in your loins! May it never burn your fingers.' And he tossed down a gulp of wine.

Riven did likewise. It was sweet, fruity, but very strong. It made the candles in the room sparkle and his throat glow.

'Well, Michael Riven,' Murtach said with sudden gravity. 'What do you think of Ralarth Rorim—and, indeed, of all Minginish?'

'There's a question.' Riven took another drink of his wine. He was not sure he wanted to talk to Murtach on this subject, but the shapeshifter spoke first, leaning forward with his elbows on his knees.

'When I was in your world, acting my part, I saw your books displayed in windows. I bought them, and read them—even your world's writing is not a problem for the people of this land, once they have crossed over—and I was shaken. I was frightened, Mr Riven, because I was in them, and so was Ratagan here, and Bicker, and the Warbutt and Ralarth Rorim itself. And do you know—can you remember what the story of your books was?'

Riven did not meet his eyes. 'I remember.'

Murtach nodded. 'Of course you do. You are the creator of the story. You are the Teller of the tale.'

'What does the story say?' Ratagan interrupted brusquely. He sounded impatient.

Murtach smiled. 'The story chronicled the history of this land, through wars and intrigue, battle and strife—and into winter. The story takes place in winter, a winter that destroys the land, bringing the beasts down out of the mountains until three heroes go on a quest to save their world, travelling north into the teeth of the blizzards.'

'And?' Ratagan asked, cocking one thick eyebrow.

'And nothing, my beer-swilling friend. The story remains unfinished. It awaits a third volume to chronicle the redemption—or destruction, I suppose—of the world.' Murtach paused, a diabolical grin illuminating his face. 'We are the three heroes, Ratagan: Bicker, you and I.'

Ratagan's glass paused in midair. He gazed at Riven. 'I see,' he said mildly.

Riven knocked back his wine, feeling it leap to his brain, but he held out the glass for a refill and Ratagan obliged him. The big man's face was troubled, but he said nothing more.

'So,' Murtach went on, 'maybe now you can

appreciate why we brought you to Minginish, Michael Riven. We must work out how exactly you and your stories interact with this land. In the hall you said you had created us. Maybe that is even true.'

'Don't be absurd,' Riven snapped.

The smaller man merely looked at him. 'You sit here in the company of characters you had thought you had drawn out of your imagination, in a world which the laws of your own place say cannot exist. The word "absurd" had best not be bandied about too lightly.' Murtach smiled again, but the smile did not reach his eyes.

'I agree with Bicker when he believes that the turning point in this was your wife's death. That triggered off the changes in Minginish which correspond to your story. It opened the first door, tearing a hole in the fabric between your world and ours.'

'What about before?' Riven asked. 'What about your history?'

'The same as you have drawn it,' Murtach admitted. 'Some things are different—the name Minginish itself, for instance—but for the most part your portrayal of this place, its people, its politics, is accurate.'

'Whoopee,' Riven muttered.

'What was your wife like, Michael Riven?'

He seemed to have heard the question before, somewhere else. He shook his head. That was one train of thought he was not going to follow. Not tonight.

'Forget it.'

Murtach gazed at him soberly. 'She may be here.'

'She's dead!' Riven rasped in reply. He gulped more wine. The candles burned like yellow stars in the room, the night looming like a cloud outside the window. Jenny was out there now, in the darkness. He felt the familiar bite of grief and anger. A Jenny who had not recognised him, who had run from him at the bothy. But his wife, nonetheless.

'I agree also with Bicker, when he observes that our unnatural winter here ceased as soon as you had left your old home—as soon as you were leaving your memories behind, and who knows? Perhaps even gaining some contentment. So there we are. Your mood improves, and suddenly we have sunshine. But our crops are still ruined. We still face famine this winter. And the beasts still harry the land, killing where they will. When the cold weather arrives in its proper place—if it does—then the old and young will be the first to die. For the Dales, at least, the damage is already irreparable.'

Riven's face twisted. 'What do you expect me to do? All I did was write some stories, and then my wife was killed. I can't help the way I feel. I can't stop any of this... it's just so hard to believe,' he ended plaintively.

'Hard to believe!' Murtach repeated. 'You're sitting here in the middle of it! How can you not believe?'

'Because it's like something out of a book.'

'It *is* something out of a book—your book! And when you tell stories, our people die!'

They glared at each other, Murtach's wolves tensed and expectant on the floor between them, ears stiff. Then Ratagan's deep voice broke the silence.

'Ye gods, my belly feels as though it's a butter churn in full swing. Strong stuff, this little vintage. Maybe I should stick to beer.' They both switched their eyes to him with something like relief. He patted his broad stomach and frowned. 'I'll survive, though.' He looked at Murtach and Riven and grinned. 'Interrupt something, did I?'

Murtach laughed, and thumped him on the shoulder. 'You are more shrewd drunk than sober, you great bear.' Then he stood up and bowed formally to Riven. 'As the Warbutt said, manners and courtesy are sadly lacking these days. You are a guest here. Forgive me. I am an ill-mannered sot for trying you so. I will say no more on weighty subjects—it will ruin the wine.' He sat down again and emptied the first bottle. 'Ask me any question you will, and I will try to answer it. I am sure there is much you would yet like to know about the Rorim, and about Minginish.'

Riven was suspicious for a second, but the small man seemed sincere. He sipped his wine.

'The Rorim—there are others like it, aren't there?'

Murtach nodded. 'Our closest neighbours are Carnach Rorim to the east, under Mugeary, and Garrafad to the north, under Bragad. Carnach is higher up in the hills, and has suffered even more than we from the depredations of the beasts—the Giants, especially. Garrafad has been more fortunate. Bragad has mobilised its people into militias and organised regular patrols of his entire Dale. He has fought pitched battles against veritable armies of wolves and grypesh, the rat-boars; but we do not have many dealings with him. He is a deep man, a man with many hidden corners to his mind. And he speaks well. I do not trust him.

'There are other Rorim, of course, farther to the east and west. Tulm and Gruamach, Pollagan and

Moonen. All face the same problems. We have not enough trained warriors to safeguard the Dales and the surrounding hills.'

'I'm not surprised. You can't do much with two dozen men.'

'Hearthwares are Myrcan-trained,' Ratagan broke in, touching for a moment the sash around his middle. 'And then we have the Myrcans themselves, eight of them here in Ralarth. Each one is worth a company of any other soldiers. Formerly, in times of need, we would have enlisted the services of the Free Companies—Sellswords who auction their skills to the highest bidder. But none has been seen here in the south for almost a year. It must be that the cities have taken them all into employ, to protect the fiefs beyond their walls. Bragad has been trying to persuade the Rorim to combine their forces and launch a campaign of sorts into the mountains to exterminate as many of the Dale's attackers as is possible, but that is not the answer.'

'Why not?' Riven asked. 'Seems like a good idea to me.'

'It is not, for several reasons,' Murtach said. 'Firstly, these animals cannot be brought to bay as though they were an organised army, even if at times they act like one. Secondly, Bragad insists that such a combined force should be under his own command, since he is experienced in dealing with large numbers of men through his militias. And thirdly, our friend the Lord of Garrafad has always wanted to wear a pair of boots several sizes bigger than those he presently owns.'

'What are you going to do, then?'

Murtach fondled Fife's ears. 'Organise our own people, after a fashion. Increase the numbers of the Hearthwares, as the Warbutt said earlier. There is nothing much else we can do.'

Except speculate about me, Riven thought. He wondered if he was to be nothing more than a pawn in this, his own story.

Not if I can help it.

But it was so odd. So damned weird to be here, doing this. Drinking this wine with the candles glowing and a pair of wolves dozing on the floor at his feet. To be dressed in tunic and breeches, to watch the night gather over the far hills that had nothing to do with the world he called his own. He felt a twisting regret that his grief had to overshadow everything, and immediately loathed himself for it. How could he sit here enjoying this, submitting himself to it, whilst—

No. Enough.

They drank on for a while, until the first words began to slur and the candles had burned low. But the wine ended. It was Ratagan who poured the last drop of it into his glass and then kissed it away.

'Time to leave,' Murtach said, standing up and swaying. Then he grimaced. 'I could do with some air.'

The three made their way to the window, Ratagan humming happily and supporting himself on Riven's shoulder. The window swung open on protesting hinges and cold night air seeped into them, clearing their heads.

Below them, Ralarth spread out in the darkness of a starlit night, lights peppering the Dale here and there, the darker shapes of the hills rearing up beyond them. An owl hooted nearby, and they could hear the stream babbling to itself in the quiet. Sheep bleated, far off, and a dog barked, then was silent.

Ratagan breathed in deeply, and Murtach leaned on the sill, his eyes lost in the night. Softly, he said:

'I love this place.'

Then they turned away, wished Riven a good night and a better morning, and left, closing the door soundlessly behind them.

IT WAS RAINING when Riven awoke, and the room was full of a fine spray from the open window. He lay still for a moment, wondering where the hell he was, then got up, hopping with cold, and closed the window. He clambered into bed again, wondering what time breakfast was. To his relief, his head was clear. He drank some water from a pitcher by the bed, and listened to the weather. His hands bunched into fists, crumpling the rough linen of the bed, and he felt the texture rub on his palms, on his back, the side of his face. He felt the cold air from the window, and his feet tingled from the remembered contact with the stone floor.

This is all real, as real as me. I am inside it, breathing, touching, tasting it.

But how?

Brief snatches of physics he drew before his wandering mind, but nothing resembled an explanation. He was not in some well-disguised pantomime. The people were real.

For some reason he remembered Gwion, the Steward, and felt an absurd pleasure at recalling the character from his books. The same. The same, by God, down to the fussy manner and the beaming smile.

I know these people.

Something like logic hovered just out of his grasp as he recalled the night before, the faces of Ratagan and Murtach vivid with wine and candlelight. He had the sense of recognition, almost of deja vu; but it was hopeless for his conscious mind to try and batten it down, to draw lines around it.

He lay in the bed. His feet became warm and he breathed in the beautiful, impossible air; and something like a smile appeared on his face, so that for a moment he looked like a boy.

Soon after there was a tap at the door, and a young girl entered carrying a tray. She kept her eyes on her burden as she came in, but darted a quick glance at him to wish him a good morning. Riven wished her one back, again conscious of his scarred face.

She set the tray on the table and began arranging the breakfast things. 'My name is Madra,' she said shyly. 'Ratagan told me to bring you your breakfast, sir, and ask if'—she smiled involuntarily—'if your head is on speaking terms with your stomach. He says you will find him in the hall later, if you have a mind to go there.' She straightened. 'You had better eat before it gets cold.' Then she went out, closing the door behind her.

Riven got up and dressed swiftly, bolting the steaming porridge and buttermilk that was breakfast, and leaving his room straight afterwards. He wondered what Bicker was doing, then remembered Murtach's hot eyes from the night before.

'It is *something out of a book—your book.*'

My book. Maybe. But there's more to it than that.

The Manse was a maze of panelled corridors and sudden windows, stairs and arches, doors and alcoves. Riven met several of the attendants on his way to the hall—or, at least, he assumed they were attendants. And once he passed a blue-sashed Hearthware who was so lost in thought he did not even notice him.

A shout of welcome told him that he was at last in the right place. The hall was empty except for Ratagan and a short, spider-thin woman who stood beside him, dressed in rich, dark wool and with many rings on her fingers. The big man sat by the firepit with a jug at his side, whittling a stick. The only sound was the rain on the high windows.

'Michael Riven! Madra tells me that you are alive and well this wet morning. I thought you might like to provide an injured man with company.'

The eyes of the woman switched to Riven then. They were dark and bright as a bird's, uncomfortably sharp, but the deep worry lines around them dimmed their effect.

'Indeed,' the woman said. 'So this is the Teller from the foreign land beyond the sea.' Her voice was as reedy as a young girl's. 'Will you not introduce us, Ratagan?'

The big man seemed chagrined. 'Of course. Mother, you know who Michael Riven is.' He flapped one large hand, his whittling knife flashing as he did. 'This is the Lady Ethyrra, my mother.'

Riven bowed awkwardly, unsure what to say or do. The woman nodded primly, the grey in her hair plain against the darkness of it.

'I will leave you both, then,' she said. 'I am sure you and my son can do without me leaning over your shoulders. Perhaps, Michael Riven'—she laboured over the unfamiliar name—'you can persuade my son to be more careful with himself when he goes out roaming the country with the beasts.' Then she left them, her skirts a long whisper on the flagged floor. Ratagan looked unmistakably relieved, and there was a pause in the silence she left behind her.

Riven sat down, and Ratagan's knife scraped thinly at his stick.

'Where is everybody?' Riven asked the big man at last.

Ratagan tapped the stick on one hand, his brow clearing. 'There's a question. Today all is a hurry and a scurry, for they are out after a large pack of grypesh that raided the flocks last night, and it is said it was led by a Rime Giant. I believe it to be farmer's fears, myself—but they are on the hunt, nonetheless: Bicker, Murtach, Dunan and six other Hearthwares, plus Luib and Ord of the Myrcans. My father is doing his harried best to calm down the other herdsmen.' He made a sudden, vicious swipe at the floor with the stick. 'Whilst I, and you, are stuck here.' He threw up his hands. 'So we forgo the fun, it seems. The only consolation'— he peered at the windows—'is that they are getting wet. Guillamon has threatened to stop supplying me with beer if I so much as poke an unwashed toe outside and everyone in the Manse is busy with something or other, so we are left, ourselves to amuse ourselves.'

Riven was disappointed. He had hoped to talk to

Bicker this morning, and perhaps see some more of Ralarth.

'Murtach doesn't like me,' he said by way of conversation.

Ratagan barked a laugh. 'Ably put. But you are wrong, Michael Riven. It is not that he does not like you; he does not like the world you come from, and he does not like his land to be at the mercy of someone who is from that world. It makes him unsure. Murtach resembles a cat: he likes to know where he is putting his feet, and you have strewn his path with pitfalls. Is it any wonder the poor lad does not take kindly to you?'

'What about you, then—and everybody else, come to that? Is the whole Rorim secretly after my blood?'

'You do us a grave disservice,' Ratagan answered. 'Myself, I will place my shoulder next to anyone I like, whether they have the fate of worlds on their shoulders or they shovel dung for a living. A man is a man, whatever he does. That is how I judge.

'As for the rest of the Rorim... my dear fellow, the serving maids are in mortal awe of you, the Knight from the Isle of Mists. Murtach and I had to give you some sort of title, so we settled on that one. At any rate, they were arguing this morning over who would bring you breakfast, so I told Madra to take it, for she is prettier than most and has more than thistledown between her ears.'

They both laughed, though Riven could not recall what the girl that morning had looked like. He remembered her voice, though. Low. And the smile.

'Besides,' Ratagan went on, scraping again at his stick, 'you are a guest here, invited by the heir of the Warbutt. Hospitality is an unwritten law in this land, though from what Murtach tells me, it is not in yours. For the time being, at least, you are a member of this household as much as I am.' He began to whistle through his teeth as the slivers of white wood fell to the floor and the rain drummed away on the window panes.

Then he stood up surprisingly swiftly, though he still leaned on the stick. 'Come,' he said. 'I can see you are in no mood to pass the time in light banter, Teller of Tales. And me, I have yet to eat this morning, so we'll make our way to the kitchens and annoy Colban, then find a window to watch Ralarth in the rain. What say you?'

Riven agreed readily, and followed him out of the hall. He disliked sitting in the great emptiness; he half expected to find the Warbutt in their midst at any moment.

The kitchens were a cluster of large and small rooms at the back of the Manse, littered with wooden chopping tables and freestanding hearths, supporting several huge pots. There were iron-doored ovens set in the walls, joints of meat hanging from the rafters, and shelves around the walls piled high with every conceivable form of vegetable, herb, spice, fruit and seed. Dishes of wood and clay were scattered around, along with utensils of every shape and size. The air was pungent with the smell of cooking meat, underlain by a hint of cinnamon. A bald, fat man was working over a steaming pot, whilst others were chopping, washing, stirring or mopping, talking amongst themselves as they did so. It was a warm, busy place, far from the lofty emptiness of the hall.

'Colban!' Ratagan cried as they entered. 'I am here to make your life difficult.'

The fat man did not look up from his work. 'I swear, Ratagan, if you had been born solely for such a purpose, you could be no better at it. No more beer, for the sake of decency, your health and my peace of mind.'

'You misjudge me, Colban. I've brought the Knight from the Isle here to see where his breakfast came from, and to procure some more of the same for myself.'

Colban did look up then, as did many of the others in the kitchen. 'Well, why didn't you say so, you great bear?' He came forward, cleaning his hands on a cloth. 'Greep!' he barked. 'Keep an eye on that broth, will you?' An aproned figure ran to take over where Colban had left off.

'The Knight is a prince in his own land, a great leader of men,' Ratagan went on, nudging Riven. 'He has come to examine the layout of your kitchen, as the cook in his own keep is sadly lacking in inspiration.'

Colban wiped his brow. 'We are in a bit of a mess at the moment, you must realise; these raids are so unsettling, and the whole thing has interrupted supplies. What fresh vegetables we have at the moment are grown within the Circle, and the recent snows have ruined much of them. We are not smoking as much beef as we have in past years, for the herdsmen are all but driven from the higher pastures, you know.'

Ratagan was scooping himself a bowl of broth, nodding wisely. Riven was dumb, but fortunately Colban seemed eager to talk about his responsibilities. He took Riven's arm and propelled him through the kitchen.

'We have our plots of barley and wheat within the Circle, of course, though they will not be harvested this autumn, what with the weather. But we have a good store set by, and bake our bread here to supply the whole Rorim. Sometimes we even have enough left over to sell to the herders of the hills.' He gestured to a long row of heavy glass jars. 'Enough spices here to last a year, which is just as well; the caravan route from Nalbeni is just about closed. Our herbs, we grow ourselves; the garden is one of my successes, even if it is I who say it. Goats and the milch cows are in the west of the Circle, and we trade game for the occasional cheese with the hunters. All in all, we try to be self-supporting.' His face darkened. 'Which is as well, in times like these.'

Madra walked into the kitchen with a stack of wooden plates. Riven waved at her, but she did not see him.

'The storerooms are built on to the back of the kitchens, and there is living space there also for the maids and the servers. We all pull on the one rope here.' He smiled broadly at Riven. 'What exactly is your cook's problem, if you don't mind me asking, Lord? I could perhaps advise you on that score.'

Ratagan was grinning, but Riven ignored him. 'Oh, that's all right. I have seen enough here to set him straight. I'll show him the error of his ways.'

The fat man beamed. 'You are too kind, my lord. We do only our humble best here. I shall inform Gwion of your approval.'

'You do that, Colban; he'll appreciate it, I'm sure,' Ratagan interrupted. 'But for now, the Knight and I must leave you. Matters of import call.'

They left the kitchen with Colban's invitation to visit him at any time ringing in their ears. Ratagan chuckled.

'You have made a friend there at any rate, Lord Riven.'

'You'll get me into trouble with all this "Lord" and "Knight" business, you know.'

Ratagan shrugged. 'Who in Minginish is to say what you really are, Michael Riven? If what Bicker and Murtach believe is true, then you are more important to this land than any lord who ever walked.'

'And what do you believe?'

The big man looked at him gravely. 'I believe in a full belly, a warm hearth and a willing horse. Those, and the edge of my axe. I choose not to concern myself with the whys and wherefores of this life, for there are always plenty of others willing to do so.' Then he smiled once more. 'But see here: I have brought a counsellor out of the kitchen with me.' He pulled aside the neck of his tunic to reveal the dark, slim neck of a wine bottle. 'So let us find a quiet spot and consult with him.'

They found a window seat that looked south to the hills of Ralarth. In front of them the land within the Circle was barred by the silver of the brimming stream and patched with distant flocks of sheep and herds of cattle. There were the wrecked expanses of flattened crops also, and men at work in the quietly falling rain.

'They're building something there, inside the Circle.' Riven pointed. He could see men rearing thick timbers and moving heavy stones in the middle distance.

'Ah,' Ratagan rumbled, swigging wine from the bottle. 'Those are the new longhouses for the herders who have fled the hills. The Warbutt is building them homes within the Circle, and in turn, Luib trains them to fight in its defence. A few of them may even become Hearthwares.'

'They do training with weapons?'

'Yes, staves and spears, mostly. Few have swords, though there are some bowmen.'

'I'd like to do that. Could I join in?'

Ratagan stared at him. 'I see no reason why not. But for what reason?'

Riven shrugged. 'I was a soldier once, in my own world. I'd like to know something about soldiering in this one. Besides, it may come in useful one day.'

'Very well,' Ratagan said. 'I will have a word with Luib as soon as he gets back. If you show promise, we can always get one of the Myrcans to teach you along with the other would-be Hearthwares. Do you have a weapon?'

'I have a knife, and I can cut myself a staff if I have to.'

'Then it is settled. I would teach you myself, but this forbids.' He held up his bound leg. 'Besides, I was never one of Luib's most apt pupils.'

'What is the rest of Minginish like?' Riven asked.

'Not all like this. To the north are the cities of Minginish: Idrig-ill, Talisker and Avernish. Up there, the land is flatter, and it is possible to see that the country is truly but one great valley. Ralarth is but a dip in its slope. The Great River wanders about the land, and the soil is rich—the people are richer, too. Farther north, beyond Avernish, the land of Minginish ends in the steep hills that the northerners call Ullinish. Farther north still are the mountains proper: the Greshorns, and in their midst is the Red Mountain which we call the Staer, the Dwarves called Arat Gor and you call Sgurr Dearg.'

'Tell me of the cities. How big are they?'

Ratagan made a face. 'Talisker is the biggest. The Rorim could fit into it thirty times without being noticed. It does a great trade in hides and stock. The people of Drinan mine iron and copper in the hills nearby, and barter for what they have not the time to grow themselves. They are great ones for the mining, the Drinan, and their swords are the best in the land. Drinan smiths often wander Minginish offering their services to the lords.

'The eastern caravans pass into Talisker, so there is spice to be had there, and silk, and fine horses which can gallop for ever. They are from Nalbeni, the land of the Khans, away across the eastern desert. Only a few know the secret paths across the waterless places to Nalben itself, and the Guild of Merchants in Talisker guards its secrets jealously.'

Ratagan sighed. 'It is a long way from our rainy Dale. And now the roads are made unsafe by the beasts that maraud the land. Only a strongly armed band would travel with impunity these days.'

The rain grew heavier, rattling off the window. Outside, those who had been building the new longhouses gave up and sought shelter, and the animals stood patiently, rumps to the wind.

Is she in the rain, or has she found her way into the bothy again? Which world is she in—this, or the other?

He shivered at the thought of that dark girl huddling in the downpour, and was filled with restlessness. It was important—she was important. His Jenny was the alpha and the omega to this, he felt; but he wished he knew why.

To hold her, just once more.

IN THE AFTERNOON, the hunters returned, walking their horses patiently through the mud to the Rorim. Leatherclad attendants ran into the rain to take their mounts, and Bicker led his people inside, dripping. There were no injuries, and the tired group went straight to their rooms to wash and change. Gwion fussed over them like a woman, but Guillamon, after a few brief words with Bicker, retired grim-faced.

Ratagan and Riven went to the hall, which was already bustling with maids and servers who set up trestles, lit the fire, and began carrying in plates of food and jugs of drink. They sat down, and Ratagan automatically poured himself some beer.

'There'll be much talk tonight,' he forecast, 'if I know that look on Guillamon's face. But why, I wonder? None of our people is hurt, as far as I can see.'

Bicker came and took a seat beside them, leaning back with a sigh.

'A long day, that was.' He accepted a beer gratefully. 'Greetings, my lord Knight of the Isle of Mists. How has your day been?' he asked Riven with a smile and a raised eyebrow.

Ratagan laughed. 'News travels fast from the kitchen. I thought it no bad idea to bestow a title on our guest, so blame it on me if the Warbutt disapproves.'

Bicker shrugged. 'As you say, it is no bad thing.'

Then he looked at Ratagan, his face suddenly pained. 'And you—you've been raiding the kitchen for wine again!'

Ratagan took another gulp of his beer, and wiped his mouth. 'I have, and I am unrepentant.'

Murtach entered, followed by two Myrcans and half a dozen Hearthwares in leather jerkins. They took their seats and began to eat whilst a buzz of talk rose up and the servers brought in more food and refilled mugs.

'Well,' Ratagan said impatiently, 'are you going to tell us what happened, or aren't you?'

'We're eating,' Murtach protested, his teeth around a chicken leg.

'So talk with your mouth full.'

'We found no grypesh,' Bicker said. 'Some cattle were killed, but their herders were unharmed. We left them just outside the Circle.' He swallowed. 'But we found Rime Giant tracks leading clear into the Dale: three sets of them. We followed them, but they took to rock and the rain washed away all signs. We quartered the land to the west of the Dale, but no tracks left Ralarth.'

'So they are still here,' said Riven.

'Yes. Tonight, most of the Hearthwares will be out patrolling the Dale. We have been telling people to stay indoors. At least with weather like this, they are likely to do as they are told.'

Ratagan whistled softly. 'No wonder Guillamon looked so grim. They could wreak havoc with the flocks tonight.'

'Or every night,' said Murtach quietly. 'Until they are forced to leave.'

'Who argues with Giants?' Bicker asked, biting into an apple.

'Let me go out with the Hearthwares tonight,' Riven said on impulse. 'You can't forget that I thought up the Rime Giants. They are one of the monsters of my story.'

'This is not a story,' Murtach told him. 'Those things out there could kill you.'

Bicker held up his hand. 'Enough. But Murtach has a point. You cannot yet handle our weapons, Sir Knight, and we cannot afford to have you battered to bits by a Giant—not until we have puzzled out what you can do here. I am sorry.'

Riven was silent. It had only been a sudden whim, and he was secretly glad that Bicker had refused it. But if the Rime Giants of Minginish were the same as those in his story, they would have been worth seeing.

'And I suppose that I must stay behind also,' said Ratagan in a disgruntled tone. Bicker nodded, mouth full, and the big man swore.

Guillamon and Udairn came into the hall and joined them. Guillamon set one slender hand on Bicker's shoulder.

'We have settled it, then. You have twenty Hearthwares and four Myrcans. Dunan will command those left behind. Unish will stay, since his arm is no good to him, and Isay.'

'And I have talked to the men in training,' Udairn said in his deep voice, hands tucked into his sash. 'Twenty of the most promising will accompany you. We'll split up into groups: one Myrcan, five Hearthwares and five of the trainees to each group.'

'That's only four groups,' said Murtach. 'Will it be enough?'

'It will have to be,' Guillamon said to his son. 'If the groups are any smaller and they run into their prey, then they will be no match for them. As it is, eleven men against three Rime Giants are tough odds. The groups must not stray too far apart in case one of them finds itself in real difficulty.'

Bicker wiped his mouth, and looked at Udairn. 'Who are the group captains?'

'You, Murtach, myself and Ord.'

'Excellent. I think it is a good plan. I think it will succeed.'

Guillamon smiled wryly. 'Three Rime Giants should be easy to track down, even in the dark. They are not the smallest creatures in the world.'

'Nor are they the most quick-witted,' Bicker added. 'But they have an animal's cunning, and their strength is immense. I'm wondering whether we will be able to subdue them if and when we find them.' He frowned. 'We should go afoot, for horses are terrified of them. The Myrcans prefer to fight that way, at any rate.'

'Agreed,' said Udairn. 'We leave in three hours, when it's almost fully dark. I'll go and finalise things with the Warbutt.'

Ratagan shook his head. 'What a party to miss,' he growled.

THE RAIN CONTINUED into the night. The patrols had left and Riven was at the window of his room, staring out into the darkness and the light-glimmers of the Dale. He was glad to be alone for a while.

Sitting on the bed, he set to shaping the long

branch of dark wood that Gwion had given him to make into a staff. He had his knife in his room now. It was too large for the work, but he scraped on patiently, content to work with his hands and leave his thoughts behind.

He thought he heard muffled shouts in the night, and stopped for a moment to listen. Nothing.

The wind. He whistled quietly as the knife blade winked in the light of the candles. He was thinking of the quiet nights at the bothy, with the sound of the wind as it was now, and the sea behind it; Jenny reading at the fire. And the sudden tears blinded him, so for a second the knife blade was a bright blur. He shook his head angrily.

The window exploded inwards, glass and wood shattering into the room. He sprang away from it instinctively, falling to the floor. The candles guttered in the wind and rain that poured in. A huge arm, as long as he was high and covered in coarse grey fur, reached in through the smashed window, groping inside the room. Foot-long fingers scrabbled at the floor, and there was a bellow of rage. Riven could see two ice-blue eyes glowing just beyond the window sill, a glimpse of a great shaggy head and enormously powerful shoulders. He was paralysed for a moment, and in that moment the blue fires outside flared with recognition and the arm reached farther inside, one shoulder dislodging masonry as it followed. The hand swung, and smashed him clear across the wrecked room.

His door burst open and a Myrcan rushed in, followed by two unarmoured Hearthwares. The ironbound stave cracked down on the giant hand

and the monster roared with pain, striving to reach its attackers. The outside wall burst inwards, and then it was half inside, in a shower of stones and shattered wood panelling. One arm lunged out and crushed a Hearthware against the wall with a cracking sound. His eyes whitened and blood burst from his mouth. The other arm reached for Riven, but he scrambled out of its way. The Myrcan stood his ground and fended off the swings of the mighty arms with terrible blows of his stave. Blood appeared on the grey fur, and the inner walls of the room shook and groaned as the giant tried to force its way farther inside to seize its foe.

Riven's mouth was full of blood and bile and his head was ringing, but the other Hearthware hauled him to his feet.

'Come on. Get out of here.' He half-pushed, half-dragged Riven to the door, and threw him out into the corridor beyond. Then he drew his sword and stepped back into the fray with a loud cry.

Someone dragged Riven down the corridor; someone else jumped over him and ran on past. His ears were full of shouting and the sounds of wood and stone being demolished. He closed his eyes, for he was unable to see straight, and the blood in his mouth was making him feel sick. He spat it out, but the taste remained. He lay cushioned in someone's lap, and that someone was pressing a cloth to where his head dribbled blood. A hand took his hand and pressed it to the cloth.

'Hold that tight, there to your head.' He did so automatically, and listened to the sounds of battle coming from his room.

So I finally got to see a Rime Giant.

Then he remembered the Hearthware and the sound of the bones breaking, and his stomach turned.

There was a final crash, a bellow that trailed off into distance, and then silence. After a moment the Myrcan swayed out of what was left of Riven's room, his broken staff in one hand. There was a great wound in his temple and the blood was streaming down his face, but his eyes were clear.

'Madra, does he live?'

A girl's voice behind Riven's head said: 'Yes, Isay. He is hurt, but not badly.'

The Myrcan nodded unsmilingly. 'Feorlig and Gobhan are dead. The beast fell, but I think it is still alive. Watch over him.' Then he ran off, the blood spattering the walls in his passing.

Riven sat up, pushing away the hands that tried to help him. He staggered over to the door and looked in.

The entire outside wall of his room was gone, and all the furniture and panelling was in matchwood. One Hearthware lay by the wall with his chest flattened to a bloody mess of flesh and splintered bones; the other lay face down by the door with most of his arm and shoulder gone. Riven vomited.

Whilst the whine of the Quick Reaction Force's Land Rovers filled up the street behind him.

Then he picked up a dead man's sword and, ignoring Madra's protests, ran off in the direction he had seen the Myrcan take. He made for the sounds of shouts and screams ahead, and finally found himself running through the hall and out to the square in front of the Manse.

There was an unequal battle being waged there.

Four Hearthwares and two Myrcans, one with a slung arm, were fighting a pair of Rime Giants. Many other people were pouring into the square with pitchforks and staves and lit torches. The sounds of fighting came from beyond the yard also, mingling with the flicker of torchlight and distant shouts.

It seemed impossible that those fighting the Giants could still be alive. Their adversaries were ten or twelve feet tall, with arms that scraped the ground and small brutish faces lit by the icy flicker of their eyes. Long, dark, matted hair coursed from their skulls, lying over shoulders broader than the double doors of the Manse. They were slow-moving, but when their great fists crashed into the ground where a Hearthware had been a moment before, the cobbles split and flew into the air.

Riven quailed for a moment, but stronger in him than courage or fear was stubbornness. He caught a glimpse of Guillamon herding the people away from the yard, his blue eyes flashing with urgency; then he joined the fight, hefting the dead Hearthware's sword.

He surprised the nearest Giant, and swung the blade with all his strength at the rear of the great knee. He felt the flesh and sinews give way and saw blood gush black in the torchlight. There was a deafening cry, and the monster fell to one knee, but spun round on him with incredible speed. He darted back, the breath sawing in his throat, and evaded the wild fist that snaked out towards him. Behind the beast, the injured Myrcan called Isay brought a staff down on its head with a sodden crunch. It went silent, and crashed over the cobbles with its skull crushed.

The other Giant gave vent to a long mournful wail, and swung its fists furiously at the defenders.

A Hearthware was sent flying twenty feet across the yard and lay still.

There was another wail behind them, and a third Giant with bloody arms lumbered forward with a group of men in pursuit. Riven saw the huge axe-bearing silhouette of Ratagan clearly for an instant, then turned his attention to the fight. The two surviving Giants rushed the defenders, who backed away, the Myrcan staves slowing their attackers down. Then Ratagan and his group took them in the rear, and the axe flashed before it buried itself in a Giant. It squealed in rage and spun round, wrenching the axe out of Ratagan's hand and knocking him to the ground. Riven ran forward and hacked at it, and it turned on him, snarling in frustration. He saw one great fist speed towards him like a train, then was struck, the breath forced out of his lungs, the sounds of his own bones breaking vivid in his ears. He landed heavily on the cobbles, and, barely conscious, saw the Giant loom over him.

Killed by a twelve-foot Neanderthal. Who'll believe me?

But then he saw Ratagan perched impossibly on the creature's shoulders, a long dagger in his hand. His arm went up in the air, and then the dagger was buried to the hilt in one of the Giant's eyes, putting out its light. It fell like a hacked tree with the big man still clinging to it, crashing to the ground in front of a prostrate Riven.

The other Giant turned to flee, and the Hearthwares' swords opened up its back but could not stop it. It blundered into buildings with loud splinterings, hurling aside those in its way, and disappeared, with the Myrcans and the surviving Hearthwares in pursuit. For a long moment the square was silent, the cobbles shining in the rain.

One Rime Giant corpse heaved up, and Ratagan pulled himself out from under it, swearing. He sat on the ground and looked about himself groggily.

'Ratagan,' Riven croaked, the effort of making the word an agony. The big man scrambled to his feet and stumbled over. His nose was broken, and his face was dark with blood, but he managed a hoarse laugh.

'Well met, Michael Riven. I cannot tell you how glad I am that you have breath in you.' His hands felt Riven over gently. 'I think the cage of your ribs must be broken. And your collarbone. Your foe must have had something against you.'

Riven smiled weakly. 'Who argues with Giants?'

Ratagan laughed again, and then grimaced, touching his mangled nose. 'I have a hideous idea I will not be my pretty self after this.'

The doors of the Manse opened and Guillamon came out, closely followed by Gwion and other members of the household. When he saw the bodies littering the square his eyes burned.

'Make litters. Have them taken inside,' Guillamon barked. 'Some of the women heat water and rip bandages.' People scurried about at his bidding, tearing their eyes away from the carnage. He came over to Ratagan and Riven.

'Are you much hurt?'

'I am not, but the Teller here will be dancing no jigs for a while.' Then Ratagan leaned close. 'We are brothers now, you and I,' he said to Riven. 'I saved your life, and you saved mine.'

The two Myrcans and three Hearthwares trooped wearily into the square with bloody weapons in their hands. Guillamon straightened.

'Isay, have all the beasts been killed?'

'We caught the last one just outside the ramparts,' Isay said through his mask of blood. 'It lives no more. Three Hearthwares and six others are dead. The wall is breached in three places and there is some damage to the Manse itself. Of the Circle, I cannot yet speak; it will have to wait until the morning.'

The litters arrived, and the dead Hearthware was borne away on one. Riven was lifted gently on to another. Already the Giant corpses were being hauled off, and the blood was being washed from the square.

'Isay,' Guillamon said, as Riven was carried into the Manse, 'take a horse and find the patrols. Tell them to come in. Tell them what has happened here.'

Isay paused long enough for someone to bind up his head, and then ran off. Riven closed his eyes. It had been a long night.

By MORNING, THE patrols were in, and Riven was in a new room with an early sun flooding through the windows, his collarbone set and bound, his ribs doing their best to stop him breathing. It brought back memories of Beechfield in the early days, except for the view of blue hills out of the window.

Bicker, Ratagan and Guillamon were in the room also. Ratagan's face was one massive bruise, and his exertions of the night had burst the wound in his leg, which was rebound and propped up on a stool in front of him.

Bicker was standing with his face towards the window.

'They must have been lurking outside the Circle, waiting for us to go past before they moved. And then they went clear through the outer wall so the guards at the gates would not be alerted.' He shook his head. 'Are Rime Giants developing brains?'

Guillamon was inspecting the bandages that encircled Riven's shoulders in a figure of eight. 'They knew what they were doing.' Bicker turned around and stared at him.

'They knew where the Knight of the Isle slept, and one of their number scaled the Manse to try and get there. He demolished a wall in his trying.'

'More riddles,' said Ratagan, his voice thickened by his broken nose.

'Do you think that someone or something is directing these things?' Riven asked. He found talking painful.

The older man was thoughtful. He stood with his back to the fireplace. 'I have a theory, Michael Riven. It is this: that you are Minginish. That would explain much—the weather, the attacks of the beasts. But I also think that you do not belong here. It is not right that you should be sitting inside the world of your own imagination.' He smiled slightly. 'For such we are, in your belief. I believe the attack of the Giants—and of the gogwolf—was no mere chance. You are drawing all the destructive power you have unleashed upon yourself, such is the guilt and despair which yet governs you. Now you are in this world, it may be that everything in it will focus upon you and mayhap give the rest of the land a respite. I don't know. I am only speculating. Perhaps if Minginish kills you, it will live on. Or perhaps it will go down with you, locked in snow and beset by wolves. Or with your death, perhaps we would all simply blink out of existence.' He shrugged. 'But that I doubt. This land has existed for longer than you have lived. No, I believe it is in your own heart that the key to this lies.' He spread his hands to the fire behind him and swayed on the balls of his feet, his blue eyes shrouded.

Riven could not answer Guillamon's claims. He lay and studied the dark wooden beams of the ceiling. Bicker seemed irritated, and also very tired. He held himself accountable for the deaths of the night before, they knew.

'Go on, Guillamon,' he said wearily. 'There is more. I know by the look in your eyes.'

'I don't mean to try you, Bicker. We each have our cares at the moment. I am Warden of Ralarth, remember.' He stared at Bicker until the younger man sat down with a cracked laugh. 'On with it, then, you old goat; give us the benefit of your wisdom.'

Guillamon pursed his lips for a moment. 'There is one thing I have not thought of: Riven's dead wife, whom he—and you, Bicker—say is alive again, probably here in Minginish at this moment. How did this happen? How does someone return from the dead? In my own mind, I believe that no one does. Death is final. But if the characters of Riven's books—such as we are—are walking a world somewhere, why should his wife not, who has probably figured in his dreams and imaginations more than any of us?'

'That's crazy,' Riven broke in. 'I don't believe I've created anything. You're older than my books. Maybe I've gone through some sort of door, yes, and maybe somehow my imagination has found a way to tap into this place, but I'm not some god who sits and creates people and places.'

'Nevertheless, your wife—or a facsimile of her—is alive at this very moment,' Guillamon said gently. 'It may be that on her death, her spirit—or your imagination; it could be either—escaped through the door that had been torn open into Minginish. And thus she finds herself here, a creature of two worlds, who can move from one to the other without difficulty, unlike us, who can only move one way through a door.'

'She didn't recognise me,' Riven grated. 'I saw her at the bothy, and she didn't know me.'

'She cannot be your wife,' Guillamon said. 'Not truly. As I have said, death is final. But part of her is the woman you knew—perhaps. Perhaps.'

'Talk bites its own tail after a while,' Ratagan rumbled, and Guillamon smiled.

'You have the truth of it, there. But some talk is necessary. I am only sorry that it must by necessity be on painful subjects.' And here he bowed to Riven. 'There will be yet more talk, and discussions, and debate, and all of it will be on matters you had thought to hold private. For this I make my apologies in advance, Michael Riven. If there were any other way we would try it—but you are the clue to our ruin and our survival, and thus must become the property of us all. In the meantime, this Rorim is your home.'

Riven nodded. Somehow these people always managed to humble him. There was silence in the room for a few moments. Dust danced in the sun from the windows. They could hear cattle lowing in the Dale.

'If what you have said this morning is true, then we had best be on our guard, Guillamon,' Bicker said quietly. 'Minginish will keep on trying to kill the Teller here.'

'And the Rorim is between them,' Ratagan added ominously, scratching his beard. 'I foresee a busy time ahead.' Then he grinned. 'For those of us who are not invalids, that is.'

'Maybe you should send me back home, to my own world,' Riven suggested.

Bicker shook his head. 'We will keep you alive, never fear, but we will have to decide what it is we must do about this. Besides, you will not be fit to travel for several weeks.'

Guillamon came away from the fireplace, suddenly brisk. 'We have indeed a busy few days in front of us,' he said. 'There is the rebuilding and the burying. We cannot make good our losses until Luib and Druim are satisfied with their trainees.' He looked at Bicker. 'I am putting Unish on to the training, to try and speed things up. And'—he glanced at Riven—'our guest here will now be guarded by a Myrcan at all times. Isay has said he will do it. I think he was impressed by your actions in the square last night, Knight of the Isle; though he will never say so, being a Myrcan. I must go. There are duties waiting me.' And he left quietly.

'I think I'll get drunk,' said Ratagan. He sounded subdued.

'I think you won't,' Bicker retorted. 'Even a laggard like you can be put to use on this morning.' He smiled to take the sting out of the comment. 'Murtach has a Myrcan and six Hearthwares out with him, patrolling the Dale. When he gets back, I want you to get his news, and then pick six others to send out immediately after. Ord can take them.' He went to Ratagan and examined his face. 'Can you manage to do that, old friend? It must have been quite a battle.'

'I have fought easier foes,' Ratagan admitted. 'And Riven proved himself to be a soldier of our world as well as of his own. He has a sword, now; I think he should be allowed to keep it.'

Bicker moved to where Riven lay silent on the bed. 'Well, Knight of the Isle: would you bear a Drinan-forged sword and lift it in defence of this land that is trying to kill you?'

'There are worse causes,' said Riven, and he grasped Bicker's proffered hand.

What the hell.

CHAPTER NINE

BROKEN BONES. RIVEN had vast experience of them. He knew the fracturing of his limbs and joints as well as he could trace the contours of his own face. They ran through him like fault lines, cracking the strata of his memories so that under their pressure images slipped, slid, flaked away.

He was an invalid again, the broken parts of his body imprisoning him within his bed. From it he could see the blue sky beyond the wide windows in his room, empty of everything except cloud and the occasional far-off bird circling the distant hills—eagles, Ratagan had told him. They spun in the sky here as they did back at Camasunary.

He argued to have the bed moved to below the window after a few days, dismissing Bicker's worries that he would find a Rime Giant in his lap one of these nights, and from then on he could see the southern half of the Rorim and the Circle, and watch the people of this world come and go about their business. He spent untold hours lying there, whilst his collarbone and ribs knitted wearily together again, and he watched the rain come out of the southern sea and roll across the hills in great banners and stacks of cloud, the sun chasing after. Impossible that he was here, that he saw everyday scenes and faces he half recognised or felt he knew. Impossible that they could exist as he had pictured them—impossible that they could not, for now he touched, greeted, smelled and ate with them. Magnificent make-believe characters now dressed in linen and leather, wishing him good morning, riding past his window, returning from the hunt with deer draped across their saddles, sitting cleaning their armour outside the gatehouse or getting drunk in the hall. He had been given a glimpse of the nightmare in the eyes of the Rime Giant as they met his own and *recognised* him. Now he was allowed to live in the dream for a while—to wear a sword, perhaps, to ride a horse, to be the kind of soldier he had always wanted to be. Perhaps. But the best things are better not savoured too long.

IN THE WEEK following the attack, the Rorim buried its dead and rebuilt its walls. Bicker and Murtach led patrols of Myrcans and Hearthwares up and down the Dale and the surrounding hills, visiting the villages and hamlets of Ralarth in turn and reassuring their inhabitants. Even so, each time they returned to the Rorim they had a straggling band of people following them on foot—refugees of a sort, fleeing their farms on the higher hills and seeking safety within the long walls of the Circle. They told tales of massed attacks by wolves, or the marauding of solitary Giants. The snow had gone, but the beasts remained. And the harvest had been destroyed. It would not be long before the Dales began to feel the nip of hunger.

Within the Circle, Guillamon soon began to find himself pressed for space as more people sought sanctuary. Those farmers who had always lived there presented him with complaint after complaint. The Circle was common land, in that all men used it freely with the permission of the Warbutt, but daily the herds using it grew. Huts were thrown up by the newcomers, and the Rorim began to resemble a vast, ungainly camp. Eventually, many of the newcomers were moved out by the Hearthwares and settled on the lower slopes of the surrounding hills, not always willingly. Those who stayed were expected to provide more men for the militia that the Myrcans were training in the practice fields to the west of the Rorim. All this Riven learned as he lay helpless in his bed and waited for his bones to knit together. As the slow days passed, he was told of the other attacks which peppered the Dale, the constant raiding of the flocks, the sighting of grypesh—another of his pet monsters— within sight of the Rorim itself. He saw Bicker seldom, for since he had returned to his own world, the dark man had found more and more responsibilities loading themselves on his shoulders as the Warbutt left the daily running of the Rorim to him. And then there was Mira, Dunan's sister. In the evenings that were left to Bicker, she seemed to occupy much of his time. She was a petite, black-haired girl with pale green eyes who spoke seldom, but whose sharp-featured face lit up when the dark man was with her. And he in turn seemed to shed some of his cares when he was in her company. Riven thought of her as a girl, but in fact had learned that she was older than Bicker. The pair ought to have married years ago, Ratagan maintained, but Bicker had some itches to work out of the soles of his feet first, and she seemed content enough to wait.

The dark man was helped by the warden, Guillamon, and by Ratagan's father Udairn, but he had little enough time to spare, all the same. He came to Riven's room sometimes in the evenings, often accompanied by Guillamon, and they spent hours discussing and speculating, until Riven's head ached and the bed seemed like a prison.

It was Ratagan, the other invalid, who spent most of his time with him. There were others, also. The girl, Madra, seemed to have taken it upon herself to become Riven's nurse while he recovered, much to Ratagan's amusement, and she was in and out every day until her face was as familiar to him as the big man's. It was heart-shaped, framed by long tresses of feathery brown hair, with thoughtful eyes almost the same colour and heavy eyebrows that made her look as if she were frowning half the time. Riven both liked and hated having her near him.

Finally there was Isay, the Myrcan. Being what he was, his conversation was not plentiful, and he tended to stand solidly at the door of Riven's room, for all the world like a statue of a sentinel. He was younger than most of the other Myrcans, though, and Madra was good at raising sudden, almost shy smiles from him. He was Riven's bodyguard, and never left his side.

There were politics in the air, Riven discovered in his evening talks with Bicker, Guillamon and Ratagan. The Lords of Ralarth, who owed allegiance to the Warbutt, were unsettled on two counts. Firstly there was the obvious disaster facing them with the total destruction of the harvest, but there was also the fact that they saw the people of their own fiefs deserting them in droves and heading for the safety of the Rorim itself, with its walls and Hearthwares. They could not give the same protection that the Warbutt offered, having only a few retainers apiece to defend their own interests, and they eyed with dismay and apprehension the militia that was being trained in the shadow of the Rorim.

'The fools think we're trying to use the opportunity to leech power from them and centralise it here, in the Rorim. They cannot see that what we are doing is best for the whole Dale,' Bicker said hotly one dark evening, when he had come in from a round of patrols that had taken in the residences of the five most powerful lords of Ralarth.

Ratagan laughed deeply, his flagon dancing on his good knee. 'Though you will have to admit this is a golden opportunity to cut down some of the Warbutt's more troublesome vassals once and for all.'

Bicker smiled unwillingly. 'I shall have to resist the temptation. As it is, it would seem that they want some kind of meeting with the Warbutt to thrash things out. Our burgeoning militia has them scared stupid.'

The big man chuckled once again. 'If they could but see what left-footed, addle-headed idiots Druim and his comrades are working with, they would not be so afraid.'

'They are fools,' Guillamon put in darkly, and his blue eyes flashed. 'Do they think they must fear us more than the very beasts out of the mountains?'

'Turn them into toads, Guillamon. That'll show them,' Ratagan said, his humour unquenchable, and everyone laughed.

Riven's arm was still in a sling, and his ribs did their best to cut off his breath every once in a while, but he was healing. He was looking forward to feeling the wind on his face again, even if he could go no farther than the ramparts of the fortress. He wanted to taste the keen air he could feel outside the windows. It no longer seemed so odd that he was breathing the air of a world that could not possibly exist. He was glad now he was being given this thing—for the moment. He preferred not to think of the darker side of it.

'It is Marsco who is the real instigator,' Bicker was saying. 'He is a good man, but stubborn as a goat. He sits up in that crag of his at Ringill and reckons he can go his own way, but as soon as he thinks we're infringing on his rights, he's gathering together the other lords like hens under a hawk's shadow, putting all sorts of ideas in their heads. If it weren't for the fact that Ringill is so damned strong and in such a ticklish place, I'd have manoeuvred him out of it years ago.'

'You would?' Guillamon asked with a raised eyebrow.

'Well—I'd have got you to do it,' Bicker said, grinning wickedly.

'Why is Ringill so strong?' Riven asked. He knew the name, but it had had only a mention in his books. It conjured up an image of a black, sheer rock topped by stone walls.

'Ringill is the northernmost of the Ralarth fiefs,' Bicker explained. 'Hence its seat was chosen with care to be the best fortress, since it borders on the territory of Garrafad Rorim—Bragad's lands. And we have never been overfond of our northern neighbour. It is the poorest of the fiefs, but also, by tradition, the most independent.'

'Too blasted independent by half,' Ratagan muttered.

'All the Dale lords have private forces of their own,' Bicker went on, 'but they scarcely amount to much— maybe a dozen men apiece, and nowhere near as well trained as our Hearthwares. But Ringill has always had more, partly because of its strategic importance—'

'—And partly because the lords of Ringill have always tended to think a mite too highly of themselves,' Ratagan finished, and he drained his flagon.

Guillamon smiled. 'You are a Hearthware, Ratagan, and so see things like the soldier you are, but from where I see it it is no bad thing to have a man as able as Marsco in a place like Ringill. If the worst happened, he has at least the ability and the pride to defend the place to the last. That knowledge is worth the nuisance he makes of himself from time to time.' Here he looked pointedly at Bicker. 'The Warbutt's heir might also be expected to take the longer view of things.'

Bicker shook his head ruefully. 'Politics. I need more practice.'

'You'll get it soon enough,' Guillamon told him. 'The lords should be here any day now, to air their grievances. No doubt the Warbutt will be wanting you to do most of the listening for him.'

'As usual,' said Bicker, a little bitterly.

Guillamon ignored his tone. 'And there are things in the offing from north of Ringill, also,' he said.

'Bragad?'

'The very same. Murtach has run into two of his patrols whilst quartering the hills up there—twenty strong apiece, and only two of them Hearthwares.'

'So Bragad builds himself an army of sorts,' Bicker remarked.

Guillamon nodded grimly. 'It would be no bad thing to remind Marsco of that when he comes here complaining of our militia.'

'Nothing like an outside threat to cut short the squabbling,' Ratagan said with satisfaction.

'Bragad is good at talking, and the fiefs are in dire need of strong reinforcing. If he comes here preaching about combining Rorims the squabbling may get worse, not better,' said Bicker, frowning.

'Politics,' said Guillamon, shaking his head. But his eyes were bright.

THREE DAYS LATER, Riven left his bed for the first time since the Rime Giant attack. Madra and Isay helped him vertical, with Ratagan sitting on a nearby stool venturing helpful advice.

'Take his waist, Madra,' he was saying, with a grin in his beard. 'He won't bite you. And you, Michael Riven, lean your weight on her. She's a strong, sturdy girl, and your bulk will hardly make her knees buckle.'

Riven was pelted with images of Beechfield. Corridors and walking frames, and Doody telling him Rome wasn't built in a day. His life seemed to be going in crazy circles of injury and recovery. He wondered why Madra's face seemed so familiar to him. She was not one of his characters.

They draped a heavy cloak around his shoulders and supported him as he stood by the open window. He looked out on to the green-gold land, with its silver glitter of river and the crawling patches of grazing herds, the clumps of buildings far off with their ribbons of woodsmoke, and the long snake of the Rorim outer wall in the distance with the two towers of the south gate like stubby megaliths, dark against the grass. There was a tang in the air— greenness and growing things, the smell of dung. And punctuating the quiet was the rhythmic ring of a smith's hammer, clear as a bell in the wideness of the Dale, evocative as a call to prayer.

Riven breathed in the air as though it were wine. He felt as though it could lift him off his toes and knit his bones for him at a draught. His two helpers supported him wordlessly, one to each side. He had come to realise that neither Isay nor Madra was overfond of needless talk, whilst to Ratagan conversation was a game and an art, as necessary to life as bread and beer.

'It's all right,' he said at last. 'I can stand on my own.' And their arms fell from him at once. He swayed slightly on the balls of his feet and heard Ratagan shuffle up behind him. The big man was still lame, but surprisingly mobile.

'I'm thinking we should find you attire suitable to your standing,' he was saying. 'With the Ralarth lords clustering here like bees around a foxglove, you should look the part.'

'I will see to it,' Madra put in. 'Bicker is something of the same build as my lord here.'

Riven caught Ratagan's eye. *My lord?*

'Your reputation precedes you, Sir Knight,' the redbeard said, humour lighting his eyes. But Riven scowled. If there was a thing he did not need it was the titles Ratagan and the others had bestowed on him. They were something he could never hope to live up to.

There was a knock at the door, which Isay immediately answered. Riven took a seat on the edge of his bed as Murtach slipped into the room, Fife and Drum at his heels. The two wolves immediately began nuzzling Madra's palms, and she gave one of her rare smiles, the dark brows lifting.

The shapeshifter was clad in grey sheepskins, and his eyes were bright as buttons.

'Greetings, O wounded ones,' he said, and dodged a swing from Ratagan's crutch.

'What news?' the big man asked.

'I hardly know what to tell you,' Murtach replied, lifting his hands. 'We have the lords gathering in ones and twos, their retainers eating up Colban's meagre stores; we have news of a possible embassy from Bragad, and there are rumours of a battle to the north concerning Mugeary's son.'

Ratagan's face hardened. 'The outcome?'

Murtach shrugged. 'Ill. He is said to be slain, and a score of his men with him. Rime Giants overran them.'

'So much for the sudden spring,' Ratagan said quietly.

'Aye. Carnach Rorim is in mourning tonight.'

They were silent for a few seconds, the only sound that of the insistent smith's hammer beating out time on an anvil in the Dale beyond. Riven sat mute and tugged his invalid's shift down below his knees with his sound arm. He stared at them—Isay as expressionless as always, Ratagan with his humour quenched for once, Murtach with his eyes darting over the room, and Madra, her hair tumbled on her shoulders and shining in the light from the window, the two wolves striving to edge their heads into her lap. Riven had a sudden, irrational urge to place his own there.

'But the rub,' Murtach said, 'is that you, my fur-faced friend, are needed in the hall. Matters of import call, don't you know.'

Ratagan groaned. 'Cannot they leave a cripple alone for a while?'

'There's beer,' Murtach remarked.

Ratagan brightened. 'Duty is a burdensome thing, but it cannot be shirked... Come on, it'll get warm.' And the pair trooped outside, Murtach sparing a wink for Madra as he left. Fife and Drum cast her a regretful glance and then followed. The room seemed very quiet when they had gone, and Isay had taken up his role outside as sentry once more.

Beyond the window, the hammering smith had stopped, and all they could hear was the faint, far-off buzzing of humanity that might have come from the market place. Madra rose and picked up Riven's rucksack.

'What are you going to do with it?' he asked her, reluctant to see it taken away. It was all he had left that bound him to his own world.

'Sort through it and pack it neatly,' she said. 'You won't be needing these clothes for a while at least, and there are a few tears I might mend.' She pulled out his trousers and fingered a rent in them. It was an old one, and had been stitched before; once, clumsily, by himself, and then by Jenny. But her neat stitches had come undone. He felt a pang at the thought of Madra unpicking what was left of them.

'What can I do?' he asked her, and was angered by the plaintive note in his voice.

A faint smile hovered on her lips. Was she seventeen, eighteen? There was something about her that seemed ageless. 'I could mend them here, if you wish,' she said, and suddenly she looked like a hopeful child.

'All right,' he said roughly, and felt an odd relief which disturbed him.

The day wore round. He occupied himself with cleaning his boots whilst Madra bent over her needlework at his side. As the afternoon waned, she laid a fire, and the world outside the window became blue with dusk even as the flames cast a saffron glow about the room. The needle winked like a glede in the firelight, weaving in and out of his clothes in the grip of her deft fingers.

Only the sound of the sea missing.

He could imagine it now, the long breakers shooshing on the shingle before the bothy, the smell of peat smoke in the air, the twilight looming up out of the glen and reaching the first stars.

His eyes closed.

HE WAS WITH Jenny again, and they were riding together through a wide, unspoilt land of valleys and stone-strewn hills, with the sky a vast blue bowl above them and the mountains mere guesses of blue on the far horizon. They rode two fine horses with deep saddles and mild eyes, and the long grass of the open country swished at their stirrups as they travelled.

But she was dressed strangely, in garb he had never before seen her wear: a black riding habit of supple suede and a dun woollen skirt with a myriad of pleats that fell in folds around her thighs. There were high riding boots in her stirrups, and the hands that held the reins were encased in gloves of dark leather.

And her face... It was the Jenny he knew, but the wild wind-skein of her hair had been plaited and tied in rings around the back of her head. He ached to see it swing loose in the breeze.

And there was something in the eyes; in the bearing, perhaps. As if some of her wild-deer grace had been lost and replaced by artifice.

The wide, empty land unfolded around them as they rode steadily onwards, and he almost thought he could see the mountains become clearer as they went. There were snow fields, tiny with distance, on their flanks and the black of wind-scoured rock. They were riding north. North to the Greshorns.

'A thousand miles to the Greshorns,' Jenny said beside him, and he was somehow unsurprised to hear an accent in her voice that was not of Skye. 'Some say that the mountains to the north mark the end of the world, that after them there is nothing but the great gulf where the stars wheel. No one has ever gone beyond them, except perhaps the Dwarves, and they tell us no tales of their journeying, their earth-delving. So maybe the Greshorns are indeed the world's end.' And she looked at him, her eyes dark as well-water in a pale face. They were not his wife's eyes.

'You do not belong here,' she said flatly.

'You're my wife,' he croaked, the words like dust in his mouth.

'I am not,' she said, and terror crawled its way up his backbone.

His horse stopped.

She smiled at him, nothing of the woman he had known in the smile.

'What are you?' he whispered.

'I am you,' she replied calmly, and then her laughter hurt his ears, grating on the threads of his nerves. It was wild, full of grief, and it ended in a sound that was neither sob nor snarl. 'I am a bad dream you once sweated through. I am a darkened room you were afraid to enter. I am a dead hearth high with ash. I am the stone of a mountain. I am the story you cannot tell. And yet you must. Your life is the history of this world, your stories its life's blood. The magic that sustains it runs in your veins. Find it.'

'It's not that easy,' he said.

'Nothing is easy.' She grinned.

Fury flared up in him like a sudden coal. 'Leave me the hell alone, you bitch!'

She shrugged. 'Not possible. You need me, Michael.'

'Why?'

She leaned forward in the saddle. 'I am the life of your stories. Without me, your part of the tale is at an end, and there can be no new beginning.'

'The tale died with you,' Riven grated. 'There are no more stories.'

'There is always a story. Maybe the people within it are different—maybe it is even someone else's to tell. But it continues. Your part in it must continue also. It is not finished with you yet.'

'I'm finished with it.'

She shook her head sadly, and for a second that took the breath out of his mouth she was his wife entirely.

'Michael, the choice is not yours—or mine. We merely do what is given to us to do. You have this thing to put right.'

Tears choked him, clenching his face into a grimace of pain. 'Jenny—'

'She's gone. She is here no longer. There is only what your mind took and made out of her, and what this land made out of her.' And yet her face was before him, pale as death.

'Leave me alone,' he ground out, bowed over the pommel as though in bitter pain. He could not look at her.

'Do not forget, Michael,' she said, her voice becoming distant.

He hugged his chest as though it were bursting and would not look up.

BUT OPENED HIS eyes to muffled darkness, and felt warmth in his clawed embrace, someone yielding to his grasp. A hand caressed the hair on his head and the sob in his throat caught and strangled itself.

'Hush now,' a voice was saying, a low voice, and he went limp. 'You've been dreaming, crying in your sleep,' the voice said, and he thought for a second that a cheek rested on his head, light as thistledown.

Is this regular nursing procedure, he wondered? But no—that was another time, another world away. He gazed up into Madra's eyes, grave under the heavy brows.

'I'm sorry,' he said, cursing himself for the crack in his voice. She shook her head slightly and with a forefinger wiped the tears from his cheekbones. He flushed, but did not move, curiously content to remain in her arms.

A dream. Nothing more. But what is a dream in this land, and what is not? What is real, here?

Ah, Jenny.

And once more he buried his face in the breast of the young girl, who held him without asking questions.

THE NEXT MORNING found Riven on the ramparts of the Rorim with Isay and Madra for company. There was a keen wind blowing, like a remnant of the weird winter that had preceded Riven's entry into Minginish, but the sky was as clear as ever, the slopes of the nearby hills ablaze with buttercups.

Once again, Riven smoothed down the cloak which hung round his shoulders. He had not quite accustomed himself to its idiosyncrasies and it constantly fell off his shoulder to baffle his free arm. The other was in a sling. Madra hitched it up for him again without a word.

He was wearing a thigh-length tunic of leather, and breeches of close-knit dark blue wool, reinforced on the inside of the legs with leather patches. Beneath the tunic was a linen shirt, and on his feet were his hiking boots. There was a belt around his waist supporting a scabbarded sword with a two-foot blade. The belt was buckled around a sash of sky blue. Over all hung the cloak, blue as a twilit evening, pinned at one shoulder with a heavy bronze brooch that Madra had set in place for him. Strangely, instead of feeling inconspicuous at being dressed like the people around him, he felt self-conscious and ill at ease. And there was a bad-tasting dream running at the back of his mind.

'The cavalcade approaches,' Isay said beside him, with a trace of irony. Riven peered out towards the north gate, and thought he could indeed make out a dark line of horse and foot coming nearer. There were banners waving above their heads, something he had not yet seen in Minginish. The Myrcans, it seemed, disapproved of such fripperies.

Looking down, he could see an honour guard of fully armoured Hearthwares lined out from the Rorim gate like a row of steel statues. The Warbutt waited there, his silver hair flickering in the wind. With him were Bicker and Guillamon, Murtach, Udairn and Ratagan. The day was not particularly warm, and Riven wondered why Bicker had insisted he be present at the entry of Marsco and another two lords, Lionan and Mullach, into the Rorim, Two others, Malig and Keppoch, had been admitted earlier in the week with, so he had been told, none of this ceremony.

The cavalcade, as Isay had labelled it, came nearer, and Riven felt both his companions stiffen beside him.

'What is it?' he asked impatiently, but they did not answer him. Fuming, he focused his attention on the long line of horsemen and infantry now closing on the ramparts. There were five banners billowing in the air. Three were edged with the sky blue of the sash that encircled his own waist, whilst one had a scarlet border and the last was trimmed with green. Riven frowned, wondering if this was important.

'The three blue-edged banners are those of our own lords,' Madra said. 'But the scarlet one—that is the flag of Bragad, and the green is the badge of Mugeary, the two lords of the Rorim to the north and north-east of Ralarth.' Mugeary—he was the man who had lost his son. And Bragad was the would-be general of the Dales.

'Strange travelling companions,' Isay said sombrely, and Riven thought his grip on the metal-bound staff tightened.

The column halted before the gates, and the riders dismounted between two files of Ralarth Hearthwares. Armour flashed in the sun, the light chinking off chain mail and horse harness, helm and sword hilt. The visitors looked for all the world as if they were riding to war.

'It is an embassy,' Madra said. 'Bragad is here as his own herald. I see his wife, too. And Mugeary has sent his nephew, Daman.' She pointed. 'And, look, there is Marsco, on the big grey gelding.'

Riven saw a tall, lean man with a brown face who had dismounted to lay his hands in those of the Warbutt. Snatches of talk floated upwards, but the wind took them away before he could make sense out of them. He felt irrelevant and irritable, and his cracked bones were complaining to him. He paid little attention to the other newcomers below.

Grooms ran from the Rorim to take the company's horses, whilst a pair of Hearthwares received their weapons at the barbican. Riven turned and stared into the fortress as the procession moved into the courtyard beyond, hoofs clattering off cobbles. The banners were dipped as they entered the shadowy gateway, then furled, and the dignitaries moved off towards the great double doors of the Manse, whilst the men-at-arms and Hearthwares trooped off to their barracks.

Beside them on the ramparts, a Hearthware sentry spat casually over the wall and raised his eyebrows at Isay.

'There'll be much talking tomorrow, and much beer tonight, if I'm not mistaken. The captains will have a hatful of things to mull over.'

The Myrcan nodded. 'Sometimes it is good to be merely a soldier,' he said.

IN THE EARLY evening, with the sun beginning its slow slide beyond the western hills, Bicker and Ratagan came to Riven's room.

'Greetings,' the dark man said, his mouth curving into one of his quick smiles. 'I am afraid it has been a while since I have said hello, Michael Riven, and I apologise for my neglect, but—'

'He's been running round like a cat with a bee up its arse,' Ratagan finished, and his sobriety fell from him.

'Something like that,' Bicker said ruefully. 'It has been a busy time.'

'Especially today,' Riven pointed out.

'Aye. You will have seen the arrival of our... guests. It is all over the Rorim, of course, and there will be a banquet tonight after the official reception.'

'What's going on?' Riven asked. 'I've a feeling you haven't been telling me everything.'

'He hasn't been telling anybody everything,' Ratagan snorted.

Bicker looked pained. 'All right,' he conceded. 'It is not by chance that Marsco and his fellow lords arrived today in the company of Bragad, and Mugeary's herald. They have been treating with each other in the past few weeks, and come now as virtual allies to try and convince the Warbutt of their cause.'

Riven whistled softly.

'The best part is still to come,' Ratagan told him.

Bicker shrugged. 'Bragad and Mugeary have combined. Their two Rorims operate as one. Bragad has arrived in person for a parley, whilst Mugeary has sent Daman, his nephew. I have a feeling that Bragad is the senior partner in this combine.'

'The death of Mugeary's son brought that on,' Ratagan interrupted. 'He is an old man, tired of ruling. I believe he cares little now for power or politics...'

'A timely disaster, his son's demise,' Bicker speculated, and there was a hard set to his mouth.

'This isn't good,' said Riven.

'It is not,' the dark man agreed. 'Nothing like this happens in your stories. We have been meaning to ask you whether Bragad figured in the plans of your tales, or even in your imagination.'

'No,' Riven said. 'In my books, the Dales were all independent. There was no... overlord. They were too busy fighting the outside enemies.'

'That is Bragad's idea—a combine to fight off the monsters that beset us, and cooperation in the matters of food distribution with the ruin of the harvest.'

'Is that such a bad thing?' Riven asked.

'You do not know Bragad,' Bicker said. 'He cares little for the welfare of his vassals, so long as they are in a condition to serve his own ends. So to that end he needs more men, more territory. And Ralarth is the greatest of the western Rorim.'

'We'll know for sure this evening, at any rate,' said Ratagan. 'Before the feasting begins, Bragad will put a formal proposal to the Warbutt in the presence of the whole Rorim.'

'And what will the Warbutt say?'

Ratagan grinned, but did not reply.

THE GREAT HALL was crowded with people. A veritable sea of faces ran down its sides, with a narrow clear space left in the middle where heavy boards had been placed over the fire pits. It was like a gauntlet to be run, with all the folk of the Dale sitting in judgement, punctuated by the stern, upright figures of Hearthwares in full armour. They stood like graven statues of steel, their protecting plates edged with blue and the inevitable sashes belted around breastplated torsos. Riven was impressed despite himself, and realised why so few of them were needed to protect the Dale. An unarmed man would have little chance of harming them—unless he were a Myrcan. Almost unarmoured by comparison, the Myrcans somehow contrived to appear more fearsome still.

Riven took his place beside Ratagan in the upper end of the crowded hall, and met Bicker's welcoming smile from where the dark man sat on one of the high seats. The Warbutt occupied the other; his robe was the mirror of Ralarth Rorim's pennant in colour, and was trimmed with gold. The old man's head was bare, but there was a golden torc about his neck and he held in his blue-veined hands a rod of white, silver-trimmed wood. On the Ralarth side of the hall, Riven could just make out Udairn standing with the dark, diminutive form of Ethyrra, Ratagan's mother, beside him. And Dunan the Hearthware lieutenant was there also, his sister Mira at his side, with her eyes fixed on Bicker. Nearby was Gwion, looking harassed and no doubt wishing he were somewhere else, overseeing the preparations for the feast that was to follow; but Ygelda towered impassive and serene beside him, her copper hair ensnaring the light of the torches.

Someone squeezed his hand, and he knew it was Madra. She did that, to gain his attention. She was on his other side.

'You look like a Ralarth lord,' she whispered.

He shrugged, smiling back absently. Perhaps he did, but he did not feel comfortable with the illusion, for reasons too innumerable and tenuous to voice.

Riven made a game of trying to recognise Ralarth's lords from the descriptions his companions had given of them. Marsco was easy to pick out, half a head taller than anyone in the hall save Ratagan, his eyes like icy fires in his weathered face. His cheeks were hollow and ruddy, speaking of much hard exercise in the open air. He was clad in a doublet of black, close-fitting moleskin so smooth it looked like velvet. His sword hung at his side, slim-bladed and basket-hilted, unlike the heavy long swords Riven had seen most other warriors in Minginish carry. A circlet of silver glittered at his temples. Riven met his blue eyes and saw them widen slightly, speculating. Then he had to look away, cursing himself.

Behind Marsco were Lionan and Mullach, the two lords who had accompanied him into the Rorim that morning. Mullach was a low-browed dwarf of a man with a vast nose and a black moustache that curved in black tusks past his chin. His eyes glinted like flints lodged under an overhanging crag, and there was a battle hammer tucked like a pistol into his belt sash. Someone to watch, Bicker had said—someone who would abandon a year of intrigue in a moment of mindless violence. Riven could believe it. There was strength in his knotted shoulders and corded forearms. He thought that even Ratagan would have difficulty there.

And Lionan, beside him. Mullach was the hammer, and Lionan was the rapier. He was tall and thin as a young willow, with a spray of red-gold hair wreathing his head like a halo in the light of the torches. His skin was as fair as a girl's, his Adam's apple bobbing like a cork in his throat. Had he been a woman, he would have been pretty. As it was, he was disturbing, his fine hazel eyes hooded over by heavy lids, the eyebrows almost invisible. He was new to power, his father having died a year previously. He was latching on to the rising star he saw in Marsco, gleaning glory from his coattails. How had Ratagan described him? A white-fingered lady's maid. But Bicker had told him that Lionan was one of the finest swordsmen in the Dale. His weapon, a reed-thin rapier, had claimed more than one life in duels.

Yet again, Riven marvelled at the things and the people he was witness to. He could stand here and pick out a dozen of his characters without turning his head. Mullach had been a brigand, a bandit who robbed travellers of valuables and women. And Lionan had been a court dandy, sweet-smelling and murderous. Strange to see them transmuted into other roles. But not unfitting ones, he thought.

And then he saw the woman.

She was raven-haired, grey-eyed, dressed in black. A silver fillet adorned her flawless brows, and she took a place beside Marsco like a brittle flower.

She was the woman of Riven's dream, his dead wife's double.

Oh, Christ.

He poked Ratagan with a frantic elbow, and the big man turned quickly.

'Who is she?'

'Who?' Ratagan peered into the buzzing throng, puzzled.

'Her—the woman beside Marsco.'

Ratagan clicked his tongue in chagrin. 'Aha. You have seen her. That, my friend, is—'

'Jinneth.' He remembered. God help him, he remembered. It had been a joke at the time, a high-hearted prank to put his wife into one of his stories, to make a great lady of her. And so she was here, in this hall with him. Jennifer who had become Jinneth.

Mother of God!

But in his books she had been unmarried, unattached.

'She's married to Marsco,' he said dully. But Ratagan shook his head.

'She is the wife of Bragad, here out of courtesy; and to prove the peaceful intent of his mission.'

'No one told me,' Riven choked.

Ratagan frowned, and looked at him closely. 'You are troubled, Michael Riven. What is amiss?'

Riven could feel Madra's concern at his other side, her hand on his shoulder. He gritted his teeth.

'Nothing. Forget it.' Forget it.

So she was Bragad's wife. Somewhere there had to be a logic to the way this world was unfolding.

There must be a reason.

But he was damned if he could fathom what it was.

He stared at her like a hunted animal, unable to tear his eyes away. She felt his gaze, and her brows drew together slightly. They met in the middle. When their eyes locked, she stiffened momentarily, then half smiled and looked away, dismissing him. He felt a surge of irrational rage, his fists bunching helplessly. But then it flickered out, leaving him sick and empty.

Nothing is sacred.

The double doors at the end of the hall opened with a bass groaning of wood, and the hubbub in the hall fell to a church-like whisper. The hundreds within turned as one to watch the entry of a group of men sashed in scarlet and green as they made their way up the aisle to where the high seats dominated the end wall.

They were led by a stocky black-haired man who walked easily with one hand on his sword hilt. He was clean-shaven, short-haired, and had the bearing of a blacksmith or a sergeant major. Or a war leader. His scarlet tunic sat well on his broad shoulders.

'Bragad,' Ratagan whispered. Riven gaped.

'Hugh!' he breathed.

His editor; the man who had been midwife to his stories when the world was young. He belonged in a

London office, dressed in a suit that never looked at ease on him, smoking foul-smelling cigarettes.

He walked past, never giving Riven a glance, but drawing a wide smile from Jinneth, his wife.

Riven thought he might be going insane. He swayed where he stood, and only Madra's support kept him from stumbling backwards.

'Are you all right?' she demanded urgently, but he could not answer. He could only stare at Hugh-Bragad's back with fury and despair running circles in his brain. He seemed to hear Hugh's voice from a long time ago: '*You know how I felt about her, Mike. I adored her. She was a bewitching woman.*'

She was my *wife*, damn it!

But he stood still, shaking Madra's hand from him, ignoring Ratagan's anxious glance. His sword pommel was a cold globe in his palm.

The embassy had reached the foot of the dais on which the high seats rested. The men halted, their boots booming on the boards of the floor, and bowed. Bicker and his father inclined their heads in answer.

It was Bragad who spoke first, irritably. The Warbutt had greeted him as a suppliant, not an equal.

'To the Warbutt and the lords of Ralarth and its Rorim, greetings.' His sweeping arm took in the occupants of the high seats, Guillamon and Udairn, who stood beside them, and the rest of the lords who clustered near the head of the hall. 'My lords, I am Bragad, ruler of Garrafad Rorim. Here with me is Daman, sister's-son of Mugeary, lord of Carnach Rorim. I speak for both of us here, for we are of one mind in this matter, and our strength counts as one strength this day.' He paused, emphasising his last words. 'I bear a message from our two Rorims, to be heard by all who are willing to listen in Ralarth. Have I leave to deliver it?' There was irony in his smile. Bicker was frowning, but the Warbutt remained impassive.

'Deliver your... offer,' he said mildly.

Bragad turned to address the crowd running down both sides of the huge hall; and there was complete silence.

'I say this,' he declared loudly. 'We of Garrafad and Carnach have seen our people slain, our flocks slaughtered or driven off, our crops ruined by a witch's winter, our homes levelled by the marauding beasts. Carnach's very heir has been slain. This cannot go on. Since the seasons have returned to their proper order, the summer has followed on with unnatural speed. Autumn will soon be upon us, with no richness of harvest to stave off the arrival of the winter that will follow—the second winter in half a year. There is sorcery abroad in the land. Evil magic has brought us to the verge of famine.'

Riven saw Murtach's face darken with anger, and he exchanged a look with Guillamon, his father.

'This cannot be allowed to continue, or the land and its people will be ruined,' Bragad went on, his voice ringing in the silent hall. 'Garrafad and Carnach have combined, because two fists strike harder than one, and friends may give each other what aid they can in a time of need such as this. The Dales must stand together through this thing, help each other and bring succour to their peoples. We must root out the source of this ruinous magic, and destroy it. We must drive the spawn of the mountains back to their old haunts so we may live in peace again.

'I come here asking this: I ask whether the Warbutt may consider joining Mugeary and myself on this crusade, so that the western Rorim may act as one. United, they will prevail against these present troubles; divided, they are sure to falter. Let comrades fight shoulder to shoulder to rid the land of evil, and when it is conquered, let them remain comrades, united by the cause they fought for. Thus may the Dales Rorim survive and prosper.'

Bragad bowed to the assembled people, and then to the high seats.

The Warbutt stood up. 'You have conveyed your intent admirably, my lord Bragad. It will require much thought and discussion to answer your offer. I trust that you will remain to expound it in more detail, and while you do, you will avail yourself of the hospitality of this Rorim. You—lord Daman of Carnach, and your Hearthwares—are welcome here as guests for as long as it takes Ralarth and her lords to consider what you have said. And I trust that, this evening, you and your party will join our folk in a celebration to mark your visit.'

Bragad bowed deeply and said he would be honoured, then turned and left the hall with the rest of his party behind him, their empty sword scabbards slapping their calves. Only lords and Ralarth's 'Wares wore their weapons in the Warbutt's presence: another reason for the scrutiny Riven was now being subjected to from various corners of the hall. He was obviously not a Hearthware, since he wore no armour, and yet he had a 'Ware's sash about his middle and bore a sword.

Was he a lord, then? He could feel the questions in the eyes of Ralarth's other lords, and he could feel the eyes of Jinneth, also, which he could no longer bring himself to meet. He was sick of surprises, sick of being stared at. He wanted to be left alone for a while.

The crowd milled about the hall, a steady stream leaving through the end doors as attendants came in and lifted the timbers from the fire pit, readying the place for the feasting that evening. It was very warm with the press of people there, and Riven thought of the bothy with an instant's wistfulness, corrected the next instant.

Bicker came over to them with a frowning Murtach in tow.

'A pretty piece of rhetoric,' he said. 'Those lords he has not already won over will see him as the very soul of reason. I foresee a difficult few days.'

'I liked the part about sorcery and magic,' Murtach said lightly, but his eyes were glowing amber in the torchlight. 'Perhaps friend Bragad would like to taste some magic himself.'

Ratagan laid a hand on the little man's shoulder. 'Don't trouble yourself. He casts about for scapegoats, is all. Bragad is the kind of man who likes to show results, even if they are the wrong ones. There'll be no witch hunt in Ralarth, whatever may happen.'

'And no combining of Rorims, whatever Marsco and his friends may have to say,' Bicker went on. 'That black-garbed temptress has him in her pocket, it's plain.'

'Swords and magic are not the only weapons,' Ratagan rumbled.

He glanced at Riven. 'Maybe it was not such a

good idea to have the Teller here in his finery. I saw more than one set of eyes stray to him.'

'Bragad's lady will have her hands full servicing the needs of her lord and his allies,' Murtach said, flickering with dark laughter. 'The Teller at least should be safe enough from her wiles.' And he looked at Madra with something surprisingly like bitterness.

But Riven suddenly seized a fistful of the shapeshifter's tunic with his good arm, yanking him forward. His eyes blazed into Murtach's astonished face. Then, as quickly as it had come, the anger left him. He let go, shutting his eyes.

'I'm sorry,' he said. 'I'm sorry.' There was no way to explain.

The four stood looking at him for a few seconds amid the hubbub of the hall.

'There is something behind this you are not telling us,' Bicker said quietly.

Riven shook his head. 'Not now, Bicker. I need some air.'

'Later, then,' the dark man said. 'After the talks there will be this afternoon. Before the feast.'

'I want a horse. I want to get away from the Rorim for a while. Can it be arranged?' Riven asked.

Bicker raised an eyebrow in surprise. 'All right. Isay will—'

'No. Alone, Bicker. On my own. I won't go far.'

Bicker regarded him appraisingly. 'Very well, then. Do not leave the Circle alone, however.' He paused. 'Can you manage a horse with that arm?'

'I'll manage. I've had worse.' And he stalked away with their stares following him, their claims upon him pinned between his shoulder blades.

CHAPTER TEN

AUTUMN WAS COMING. He could feel it in the bite of the breeze, the faintly golden light of the afternoon. Summer seemed to have flitted by in a space of days. His shadow was strewn off to his right like a capering phantom as he kicked his steed northwards from the walls of the Rorim towards the ever-rising hills that surged out of the Dale into a heather-thick rampart of blue and purple heights beyond.

The Circle was almost empty of people. Most, it seemed, were in the Rorim itself or its environs—crowding the inns that squatted at its foot, making merry to mark Bragad's visit. Hugh's visit. Hugh and Jenny.

Christ.

He passed flocks of sheep and herds of cattle, and his mount nickered at other horses running free upon the common pastures. But the grass was stripped nearly bare now, and what was left was yellowing and cropped. There were houses of stone and thatch dotted in thorps and hamlets throughout the Circle, but there were also newer dwellings of hastily thrown up sod walls and heather roofs. And there were practice grounds where the Dalesmen were being taught to fight. He turned away from them, and rode onwards to where the Circle began to grow more empty to the north, and soon there was only the long bar of the outer wall between him and the hills.

Somewhere out there a facsimile of Jenny roamed, mute and afraid. And in here was her double—a black-garbed temptress, as Bicker had said.

What the hell was going on with this place? What is happening here? There were no answers, just agonising riddles he could not solve. Sourly, he wondered who would be next to pop up out of his former life. Doody, maybe—that would be a laugh. Or Anne Cohen—

He reined in the horse suddenly as an idea dawned on him. One that had gone even as he groped for it. Nurse Cohen...

No. Gone.

He cursed, and spurred his long-suffering mount onwards again.

WHEN HE REACHED the Outer Wall, he halted and dismounted, his cracked bones shouting at him. He grunted with annoyance and sat down in the sparse grass with his back to the worn stone and let the meagre sun warm him. It was quiet there; his horse grazed contentedly, its reins trailing on the ground. He pulled his awkward cloak about his shoulders and closed his eyes, emptying his head of preoccupations.

Autumn was not a bad season. There were gales, of course, but the bracken turned the mountainsides to copper, and there were mellow days scattered through it, like summer flotsam set adrift in the waning half of the year. The sea would start to roar at night, and the curlews would be hurled down the glen like dun-coloured bullets. That was a time for peat fires and firelit talk, with the wind a symphony to set stories to. Autumn on Skye.

'Hello, stranger.'

He opened his eyes to see Jenny there, with a horse at her side, and he smiled. The sun picked the deep brown tints out of her hair and made her skin like honey. She raised her eyebrows and returned his smile, but there was something about it, something—

He scrambled to his feet, throwing his cloak aside and hissing at the stiff pain of his collarbone.

'What are you doing out here?' he demanded, his voice shaking.

Her smile faded. 'I had thought to ask you the same thing. I felt like going for a ride, and when I saw you take horse, I followed, seeking companionship. It is not welcome, I see.'

He stared at her, mouth set in a bitter line. This world would not leave him alone, it seemed.

She went to remount her horse, but he stepped forward.

'No. Wait.'

And she halted, turning to him.

'Do you know me?'

She seemed puzzled. 'We have met before?'

His eyes bored into her, glittering, searching her face. But no. He bowed his head, teeth clenched.

'No. You don't know me.'

She came forward, arm outstretched, palm down. 'I am Jinneth, wife to Bragad of Garrafad...' He supposed he was meant to kiss her hand, but he did not move. He was frightened of touching her.

Her arm dropped and she frowned, the dark brows crowning her eyes. 'Wherever you are from, courtesy is not one of your virtues,' she said tartly.

'I don't belong here,' he answered at once, stung.

She stared at him. 'So you are not of Ralarth, then.' And she smiled again. 'And what are you? Lord... or Hearthware? You are no lord of Ralarth that I know of—and I know them all. But you are no Hearthware either, I think. You do not have the look of a warrior.'

Cheers.

She moved easily towards him, and he would have backed away but for the stone wall against his shoulders.

'You have not yet told me your name, stranger.'

'Michael Riven.' He thought for a second, just an instant, there was something there, something in her eyes like a flicker of uncertainty, but it was so brief he was unsure if he had imagined it.

'Michael,' she said, testing the word. Her accent was strange. It was not the way his wife spoke. Had spoken. 'A strange name. Are you from the north? From the cities, perhaps?'

He shook his head dumbly. He could smell the fragrance of her. Her nearness dizzied him. 'You're not my wife,' he whispered.

Her hands caressed his cheek, brushed his beard, and he froze. 'Why so stiff?' she asked. 'You are as tight as a bent blade. Are you afraid of the wife of a lord such as Bragad? Be not so. We have an understanding, he and I, and I am very discreet.'

'What do you want?' he croaked.

'Your eyes never left me in the hall. What have you been told of me?'

'Nothing. I know nothing about you.' Except what he had made into a story. Except for whatever part of her that might once have been Jenny.

'What do you do here in Ralarth?' Her fingers touched his neck, the knot there where the linen sling supported his arm. 'You have been hurt. How?'

'Fighting Giants.'

Her brow cocked. 'So. A warrior after all, perhaps.' The finger touched the scar on his forehead, making him flinch. 'You are much marked by injury, some of it not so recent. Are you a Sellsword, then?'

'A what?' He hardly heard what she was saying. He was losing himself in the grey surf of her eyes, his heart threatening to smother him with its frenzied pounding.

'A mercenary. A paid soldier.'

'I was, once.' Lieutenant Riven.

'Ah.' Her gaze sharpened. 'And you are not now?'

'No. No more.' There were warning bells tolling in his head. This woman was not his wife, and she had not come out here to seek conversation. Wheels within wheels were moving, and he wanted no part of them. 'I must go back,' he said. 'I'm expected.'

'By whom? The frowning girl who stood by your side in the hall? She is only a child, surely.'

He pushed her aside suddenly, roughly, and saw her face grow sallow with anger, but she did not protest. His collarbone throbbed. A groan burst from his lips as he mounted his horse, and for a second the world swam before his eyes. When he focused again, she was staring at him intently. But there was no concern upon her face—only curiosity.

'We'll meet again,' she called after him, but he dragged his mount's head around without replying and kicked it into a gallop back to the Rorim.

LATE THAT AFTERNOON, before the banquet was due to begin, he told Bicker, Ratagan and Murtach everything. They sat in his room whilst the wind whistled about the eaves of the Manse, and listened to him in silence. When he had finished, Bicker strode to the window and looked out at the tumbled clouds of the late day and the gathering darkness of the deserted hills.

'I know now why you did what you did in the hall,' Murtach said. He fondled Fife's ears until the wolf emitted a growling sing-song of pleasure deep in his throat. 'I am sorry.'

'It's nobody's fault,' Riven told him. 'Except maybe mine. I should have known that she'd be here. I put her here, after all. In the story.'

'But not in quite the same way, I take it,' Bicker said over his shoulder.

'No. Not quite.'

'I should have realised myself,' the dark man continued. 'There was a resemblance between her and the girl wandering the Isle of Mists.' He turned away from the window. 'But it is not perfect. They are different, somehow. Why? Why should this happen? Two images of your wife in this land, one a wanton, the other a waif. It beggars deciphering.'

'Guillamon's territory, I think,' Ratagan put in. There was a flagon of beer forgotten in his vast fist.

'And this man you knew in your own world—the one who helped you with your stories. He is Bragad.' Bicker shook his head. 'My friend, no wonder you wanted to be alone this afternoon. It is enough to drive a man to distraction.'

'Maybe Riven should not be seen at the feast tonight,' Murtach suggested. The dark man disagreed.

'That would raise more suspicions than it would allay. Bragad knows he is here now, that he is a stranger. There is no point in fuelling speculation.'

'We need an identity—a harmless counterfeit for our ex-Sellsword here to cling to,' said Ratagan. He sat a hand on Riven's good shoulder and rocked him slightly. 'How are you at playing a part?'

'I'm dressed for it,' Riven replied in a disgruntled tone, and the big man laughed. Some of the tension went out of the room.

Bicker smiled. 'What would you like to be, Michael Riven?'

'Well, she said I looked no warrior.' He was surprised at the bitterness in his voice.

I was a soldier once. Once upon a time. Maybe not in this world—but a soldier nonetheless.

'If she had seen you the night of the Giants, she might have thought differently,' Ratagan said gently.

'A merchant, then,' Murtach suggested.

'He does not know the reality of the country well enough,' Bicker returned. 'And besides, he wears a

Ralarth sash. Whatever he is, it must be of the Dale itself.'

'A Teller!' Ratagan said, thumping a fist down on to the table so that the two wolves started.

'What?' Riven was aghast.

'By all that's holy, why not use your true profession? A Teller from the west come to take service in Ralarth and learn a few more tales from the Dales people. Yes!'

Bicker nodded. 'The nail hit on the head. What say you, Michael Riven?'

'I can't do that. I can't tell bloody stories any more.'

'You won't have to, with luck.' Ratagan grinned. 'Just sit in a corner and appear thoughtful. If someone asks you for a tale, tell them you're learning the story of the Dwarf and the Firewood. It goes on for ever. They'll leave you alone, then, in case you decide to start telling it to them.'

Bicker chuckled. 'He speaks from experience, I fear. But, yes, I think that will suffice. I will tell Gwion to warn off our own people. Half of them think Riven is some sort of magical warrior from across the southern sea. They must be enjoined to remain silent. He is simply a Teller, come to seek new stories.'

And maybe that is not so very far from what is true.

Ratagan swigged at his beer and swallowed gratefully. Bicker rubbed his nose, deep in thought.

'It might not be a bad notion, though, to spirit the Teller out of the Rorim soon after the feasting is over. That way he will not be bumping into the Lady Jinneth again in such a hurry. Her husband had obviously told her to find out who and what he is.'

'None of us can accompany him without arousing suspicion,' Murtach pointed out.

'We could if it was a patrol,' the dark man said. 'You and Ratagan could take one out tomorrow, stay for a few days and have a look around at the western fiefs. You could visit home, my red-bearded friend.'

'Ivrigar, eh?' Ratagan took another long pull at his beer, an unaccustomed frown flitting on to his face. 'Home. I don't think that—'

'Aelin would be glad,' Bicker said gently, and Ratagan's frown deepened.

'She'd be glad,' he repeated. 'For a while.'

Bicker thumped him lightly on the shoulder. 'It is settled, then. After the feasting tonight, you three will leave the Rorim with an escort on a few days' patrolling. It is only prudent, with most of the Dale's 'Wares tied up here at the fortress. No suspicions will be aroused. Stay at Ivrigar for a time, or until I deem it safe to return.'

'Bragad will miss us from the negotiations,' said Murtach.

'Let him,' Bicker replied promptly. 'It will keep him on his toes. Besides, you will not be the only ones. Both Mullach and Lionan are departing directly after the banquet is over, leaving Marsco to plead their case for them—so thick, it seems, these three have become. They have the excuse of securing their northern borders. Apparently things are getting a little hot up there. We had a messenger from Drynoch this evening. There are grypesh out in force to the north.'

'A convenient point for Bragad to push home,' Murtach murmured.

The dark man nodded, exasperated. 'Marsco

emphasises his own side in this way, sending two lords back to secure their fiefs in the middle of a council. Dramatic, but effective.'

'And true, I take it?' Murtach asked.

Bicker shrugged. 'We have no way of knowing. But it is a good excuse for us to send out a patrol of our own. A strong one. And it explains your absences from the council quite nicely. That leaves us only tonight to get through.'

'I take it I can get drunk as a lord should on such an occasion?' Ratagan said, smiling; but Riven was sure he was only half in jest.

'Mind what you say, and who you say it to,' Bicker warned. 'The same goes for you, Michael Riven. If Bragad guesses at your real identity, it could cause us a world of difficulties with some of the lords.'

'Another stick to beat the Warbutt with,' Murtach said in disgust. 'You had best impress upon the household the need for discretion. There are a few feather-brains about who know too much as it is.'

'Not Madra,' Riven said, startled out of a reverie.

'No.' Murtach's face was oddly savage. 'Not Madra.'

THE RORIM WAS busy with scores of preparations. In the Manse, the household occupied themselves with the task of preparing a feast fit for the assembled lords. The kitchen was a chaotic babble of activity, with Colban issuing orders in all directions and striving to keep an eye on those attendants who were entrusted with the care of vital sauces and gravies. Several animals of various sizes were roasting entire on slow-spinning spits, basted by anxious boys, whilst a stream of young people ferried foodstuffs from the pantries to the Great Hall above until the trestles set up there creaked under their load. A rumbling filled the air also, as casks of beer were trundled from the depths of the cellar, the barrels thumping on the stones and resounding like the indigestion of Giants. Others brought to light with more care slim, dark bottles of wine with the dust and cobwebs thick upon them. In a corner quieter than most, a knot of musicians tuned their strings and tightened their drumskins. Through it all, Gwion paced with his pate shining in harassment and a gaggle of attendants in his wake seeking instructions, advice and permission. Some were sprinkled with pine needles, having just been engaged in decking out the hall with fresh sprays of evergreen. Others reeked of herbs or were powdered with flour. A few Hearthwares, stalking the corridors of the Manse, backed away hurriedly when they met them, for fear of grubbing their highly burnished armour. More than one was caught by a pair of squealing girls, who gleefully anointed them with kitchen grease and then fled with the warriors clanking in pursuit.

Walking through the Rorim was like living a medieval pageant. Riven was enchanted. He, Ratagan and Isay were wandering the fortress and taking in the holiday atmosphere for want of something else to do before the feast began. Ratagan had procured beer for them from somewhere with magical ease, and they were supping the malty liquid from brimming tankards as they went. The big man had a word for everyone he met, and produced blushes and laughs from the serving maids in equal measure. Even Isay unbent a little, and grinned at a raven-haired wench when she made a lewd pluck at his staff.

Riven received many odd looks, and was the subject of much behind-hand whispering, but it seemed in awe more than anything else. And the more beer he drank, the less he thought about it. He was content to give himself up to the occasion, similar to others he had described in his own books, but none of which had ever seemed to possess the colour, the noise, the smell, the sheer vibrancy that was before him now. He was seeing the Rorim as it should be, without the threat of ruin hanging over it—though tomorrow, these same people would be stinting themselves to eke out their supplies through the winter. But for now they were as careless as swallows. Riven realised with no surprise that he could love this world and its people, despite the heartbreak it had wrought on him. Which was fitting, since in one sense he had created it, had made these folk to people it. He had chosen this world, Minginish, out of all the others he could have thought up, because it had seemed good to him. And it was, despite the black-garbed temptresses and ambitious warlords who walked it. It was worth saving for its own sake, not just to give Jenny the peace she deserved.

He smiled at his own thoughts.

Maybe I'll write them down some day, if I get the chance.

They ran into Madra, nearly upsetting the jugs she held in her fists. Ratagan relieved her of one of them whilst she looked on with an eyebrow arched.

'For our health,' he explained, refilling their three tankards. 'It'll be a long night, with much talk, and we must fortify ourselves beforehand as best we may...' He winked at her, and her mouth twitched.

'Will you be at the feast tonight?' Riven asked her.

'I am to be your server,' she said.

'Mind you don't neglect him,' Ratagan told her with mock severity. But she did not take her eyes from Riven.

'I won't.' The rare, grave smile winged her face, then she reclaimed her empty jug with a reproachful glance at the red-beard, and continued on her way. They watched her go, silent for a second.

'She was not in your story, was she?' Ratagan asked.

Riven started. 'No. No, she wasn't.' But again, there was that odd feeling that they had met before. Ratagan gripped his good shoulder for a second, and then tipped back his tankard with a deft movement.

'Ah,' he sighed, wiping froth from his upper lip. 'Life is not wholly unattractive.'

ISAY HELPED HIM dress for the banquet that evening, showing no resentment at having to double as valet as well as bodyguard. Riven found that a set of finer clothes had been left out for him, probably by Madra. The sleeveless tunic looked to be made of doeskin, supple as linen, and worked into the left breast was a flame symbol, picked out in scarlet and yellow thread. He asked the Myrcan about it, and was told that it was the badge of a Teller. The fact that it lacked heraldry around it was a sign that he belonged to no particular lord, though the blue sash announced he was attached to the Household of Ralarth.

The tunic fitted over a loose linen shirt and was belted snugly by the sash that Riven was coming to see as his own. He did not put on his sword, for no weapons were permitted at such occasions, though Ratagan had told him a gory tale of a banquet where a certain disagreement had been settled with eating knives, which the victors had subsequently continued eating with.

Riven took a place halfway down the hall from the high seats where the lords clustered and the Lady Jinneth adorned her husband's elbow. Ratagan and Murtach were close by whilst Isay was at his side, as usual. Riven caught Bicker's eye as he had that afternoon, and the dark man threw him a rueful grin. He would no doubt be fending off the polite questioning of Ralarth's lords throughout the meal. Tragically, this meant he had to stay relatively sober. Ratagan had promised to quaff Bicker's portion of ale for him, to make sure none was wasted in these frugal times.

Jinneth was looking at him. Riven was caught by her eyes, grey as shingle. Her hair was down, making a black foam about her shoulders and setting off her silver circlet. Her gown was low cut, exposing creamy shoulders and the shadow between her breasts, and there was a slim chain about her white neck from which a single gem hung like a firelit star. Desire kindled in Riven like a coal, and he remembered times when he had held that body's twin in his arms and searched out all its secrets.

But the woman he had held was dust in a sea-girt grave, his love buried with her. He met Jinneth's gaze steadily, until her smile faltered and she turned away to speak into her husband's ear. He listened to her intently, even with deference, and Riven, remembering Hugh on the occasions when he had met Jenny, thought that perhaps there was a twisted sort of logic to this world after all.

Music began with the beating of a tabor and the whistle of pipes, and then the servers began trooping in in their dozens, with great platters of heaped food and jugs of ale. Riven blinked, and realised he had been staring at nothing for a long minute. Ratagan was leaning across the table and pouring him some of the dark, malty beer, but he could make no sense out of the big man's words. The beer he had already consumed that evening fogged his brain, and the brightness of the torches and the tall candles daggered his eyes. For a second he felt like retching. But then there was a calm hand on his shoulder, and Madra was leaning past him to set a tray on the table, her hair swinging over his arm. He could have buried his face in it, seeking darkness, but she set her cool fingers on the back of his neck and his head seemed to clear. And she left him with a quick glance from her eyes, dark as an otter's pelt, and a smile that was like a gift.

A cold nose nuzzled his knee, and he reached under the table with a scrap of venison for Fife— or Drum, he was not sure which. The wolf took it from his hand as delicately as a cat, and licked his palm. He met Murtach's eyes across the table, and the shapeshifter grinned like a gnome.

'Don't spoil him,' he said. 'Half the hall will be feeding my friends tonight.' He raised a tankard which condensation had jewelled. 'Here's to life, health and happiness, and the time to enjoy them.'

Half the board raised their own flagons in answer—most of them seemed to be Hearthwares— and they answered him thunderously, Ratagan loudest of all. Riven downed a great gulp of the cold beer and felt it alternately chill and warm his gullet. His brain cleared.

Slainte.

It grew warmer in the hall, and noisier as beer and wine loosened throats. The feasters attacked great joints of beef and mutton and venison, picked at pheasant and partridge, munched apples and pears and sweet onions, nibbled at cheese and rye bread, and washed it down with more beer. The few ladies present were given the privilege of drinking out of goblets, some of pewter, some of glass, some of wood. Wine bottles began to cluster at tables like sentries. Bones were flung to the floor and quarrelled over by the hounds, who gave way to Murtach's wolves when Fife and Drum desired some particularly meaty scrap. Hearthwares argued over past skirmishes and hunts, the lords over family history and precedence, the arguments becoming more fantastic as they put away more ale. Riven saw Bragad gesticulating at Bicker, who sipped wine reflectively. Marsco's cold gaze was fixed on Jinneth as she leaned forward to speak to him, her hand on his amid the clutter of the table. Lionan, the dandy, was talking behind his hand to the brutal Mullach, who was gulping his beer moodily and staring at the serving maids as they passed him in a bustling procession. He sucked one corner of his black moustache absently. Guillamon's eyes were icy fires in the haze. He smiled at Riven's roving stare and raised his goblet in salute. Riven did the same, unsmiling. He remembered a steel-eyed wizard from his second book, and wondered if Guillamon were he. It was hard to tell, sometimes, which of these people he had written about, now that they sat down yards from him.

He shook his head and sank more of the strong beer. He did not feel hungry, and the alcohol sent his imagination soaring into the smoky roof beams, so that he lost the thread of the story Ratagan was telling him—the one about the Dwarf and the Firewood, he thought muzzily. Instead he was thinking of Jenny. Jenny in his arms. And, oddly, that gave way to thoughts of Madra. When she bent to pour for him her breasts swung against the fabric of her robe and he could see the press of the nipples. He felt an urge to cup them in his hands, but gulped at his beer savagely and prised his eyes away.

Only a youngster, for Christ's sake. Besides, I'm married.

Married. Here in a world where she never existed, with people who do not exist in mine. Where her doppelgangers wander the hills or flirt in banqueting halls. He bent his head.

She's dead and buried in a grave in Portree. And where is that?

He swilled down the beer.

And where am I.

Madra's forehead shone in the heat, and with those dark eyebrows she looked as though she were concentrating hard on not spilling the wine. Spots of it stained the thighs of her robe.

Riven thrust aside his sling. It was picked up by Isay, who glanced at him. Riven wondered if he saw sympathy there, but laughed harshly. Myrcan sympathy, like milk from a bull.

The eating had ended, and the drinking was in full swing. The scene reminded Riven of many a drunken episode in a saga. Even Bicker seemed to have lost his wary watchfulness and was grinning with the rest. Someone was dancing crazily on the trestles, sending wooden plates flying. His blue sash marked him as a Hearthware, and his face was red with heat and wine. Laughter and clapping surrounded his antics. Watching him, Riven felt the return of bonhomie and contemplated touching Madra's hair next time she came round. His collarbone ached, and he dug at it with his good arm, massaging the stiffness with his fingers. He wanted her to do it for him, but she was busy across the hall. He met her eyes and for a second time; she smiled her shy smile at him, but his swimming head filled it with invitations. He remembered Nurse Cohen holding him, remembered Jenny underneath him, making soft noises at his ear in the dark.

Christ, I need air.

But he was not sure he could stand up. Isay would help him, capable soldier. For a moment he thought Isay was his corporal in Derry, and began smiling at him; but he was dead. In pieces, like the Hearthwares in his room. Like Jenny at the foot of Sgurr Dearg, the Red Mountain. Everywhere there was blood in his memories, and now he was drinking it himself. The blood of this world which he had created and which he was slowly killing. Hero. Soldier. Husband. Mourner.

He stood up, one hand on the table; his bad arm. He swore vaguely, pushed away from the board to see the enquiring looks. Big Ratagan and ferret Murtach, grey Guillamon and dark Bicker.

'Need some air.' He turned to Isay, and was lent a Myrcan shoulder. 'Get me out of here.'

The floor plunged at him, the faces at the feast blurring with noise; he made out Bragad watching him with sharp eyes. *Wondering who I am.* He almost tripped up over his own drunk feet, but Isay supported him. Out of the hall, lurching, swimming, swaying, feeling shamefully sick and gritting his teeth together to stop his stomach from heaving. And then the dark, the blessed dark, and the cold night air that iced him and ripped the mist from his brain, steadied his legs, poured pain into his shoulder.

Real pain. My pain.

He breathed in deeply, bent double. Felt a hand on his back and a quiet voice telling Isay he'd be all right.

I'll be all right. Leave me alone.

'Leave me alone.'

But the hand was still there, warm now on the nape of his neck; and the hand guided him as he lurched forward again, the firm body beside his, holding him upright; helping him up dark stairs and through a pitching doorway.

His room, moonlit by the silver-flooded windows. He stood with his back against a wall and closed his eyes. He could feel the sweat of the hall still on him, cold now; working up towards a shiver. His breathing became steady. He opened his eyes to the quiet darkness, the moonlight, the breeze from the window that his helper had opened. She stood worriedly in front of him, brows pulled together, feathery hair over her shoulders and clinging in fine threads to the sweat of her forehead. He reached out and caught her hand, pulled her close. Dark eyes, unreadable as mist. Then he hugged her to him, feeling her warmth and softness, the length of her thighs against his, the muscles of her back under his palms, the satin of her neck at his mouth. He kissed her there, gently, and she turned her head, offering him her mouth. He closed his own over it, but her questing tongue met only his teeth. He kissed her forehead, her chin, cupped her face in both hands and kissed shut her eyes, the tears falling from his own. In his mind he spoke another girl's name, a girl long dead, and asked her to forgive him.

HE SLEPT LATE, and when he awoke the wind was rising in the rafters. He lay curiously content in the warm bed for some minutes, then frowned. Abruptly he jumped up and tore away the bedclothes, searching the rug on which he had lain. There, dried in, the small patch of blood. He searched farther; long hairs on the pillow. But the room was empty. He closed his eyes and groaned. Not a dream.

You bastard.

He drank water from the pitcher, then staggered over to the basin on the table and thrust his head into it, the chill water making him gasp. He shook his head, spraying drops over the room, over his clothes discarded on the floor. He knuckled his eyes.

She's only a child.

'Oh, God,' he groaned aloud, then rubbed himself dry. He dressed and looked in the polished mirror, seeing a scarred, bearded face glaring out at him.

The door was knocked and opened, and Madra entered bearing his breakfast on a tray. She set it on the table, avoiding his stare, and made as if to leave, but stopped before she reached the door and looked in his eyes. Was it only his fancy, or were her eyes older?

'Do you want me to stay?' she asked simply, and he knew she was not just talking about leaving the room. He stared at her. Even now he hungered for her again, seeing the light in her hair, the length of her leg under the robe. It had been very sweet.

She's only a child.

He wanted to put flowers in her hair and make her laugh; but he would never be able to do that.

'I'll see you about, later,' he said, hating the clumsiness of the words. And she was gone.

'Well,' said Ratagan, 'for the next day or two, it seems hardly likely that I will be wetting my throat at all, so perhaps it is just as well I indulged in a draught or three last night.' He hardly limped now, and leaned only seldom on the haft of his axe. Riven did not reply. They were making their way round to the stables at the back of the Manse. He wore his sling again, for Isay had returned it to him wordlessly earlier that morning. The Myrcan followed them as they made their way towards the smell of horse piss and hay.

'Still, I am out of the council, at least,' Ratagan went on. 'Those meetings are about as bearable as a boil in the wrong place—though this one should be more interesting than most. Ralarth will not combine, but Marsco will not take that too well, and his Ringill is in a delicate position. A ticklish business altogether. I am glad it is Bicker's backside that is warming a council chair instead of mine.'

'We're going to your home,' Riven said absently. Ivrigar. The place had been a quiet country house in his books. Domestic bliss and all the rest.

But Ratagan frowned suddenly. 'Aye. We are.'

They reached the stables and found Murtach waiting for them, with his sword strapped to his back and a quiver of arrows at his hip. He gripped a pair of reins in his hand; behind him a blaze-faced chestnut nosed at the cobbles, whilst the two wolves sat by his feet.

'Tardy again, Master Ratagan, and now you have not even a real limp to excuse you.' Behind him were a crowd of men and horses; Hearthwares in full armour, their breaths steaming in the coolness of the morning, Myrcans standing impassively, indifferent to the cold, but nodding to Isay as he approached, and a pair of pack mules trying to bite each other's manes.

'It's my head, this time,' Ratagan confessed, the cheer restored. 'It berates me for the way I mistreated it last night.'

'And our knight—or resident Teller, I should say. How is his head this morning?' Riven searched his blue eyes for any hidden meanings, but they were closed to him. He did not answer, and Murtach raised his eyebrows, but made no further comment.

He found that a quiet bay gelding had been saddled for him, and mounted along with the others, the Hearthwares hissing with effort as they pulled the weight of their armour into the saddle. Riven's slung arm hampered him, and he pulled the sling off irritably and stuffed it down the front of his jerkin, moving his arm in circles. The collarbone complained, but it was bearable, and he was sick of bandages. Ratagan edged his mount over.

'Are you sure you are up to this?'

Riven nodded. 'It'll be good for me. I need the air.'

Ratagan grinned. 'This morning, we all need the air.'

There were fourteen of them. Riven, Ratagan and Murtach, then Isay and two other Myrcans—Luib, whose hair was peppery with age, and Belig. And then there were eight Hearthwares, seven of whom were in full armour. The eighth, a black-bearded, brown-faced man named Tagan, was the tracker. All except Riven and the Myrcans had sheathed shortbows and full quivers hanging from their knees, in addition to their personal weapons. They had food in their saddlebags for two days, and the pack mules carried grain and hay for the horses, there being little forage in the hills the patrol would traverse for the first two days. After that, they planned to pick up more provisions at Ivrigar, Ratagan's home, and return to the Rorim on the third or fourth day, by which time the council would be winding down, or even finished.

The wind was strengthening in their faces, and more than one man looked up at the sky in puzzlement. Autumn was here, on the heels of a mutilated summer, and it had arrived with preternatural speed. Almost from the moment he had seen Jinneth, Riven thought, and then scowled, putting the idea out of his head as though it were unlucky. There were too many things to think about this morning. Somewhere in the hills, perhaps, another Jenny walked with the beasts, no memory of him in her head. And in the Manse behind him was a girl, a child whom he had taken last night in a fit of lust and self-pity. He snarled at himself. I'm a real hero, I am.

But it had been... good. He had lost himself in her, and she had been willing to take him. And afterwards he had lain in her arms as though they were a world away, with the waves breaking on the shore outside. And he had known peace, for a little while.

Not now. Now it was a grey morning with the drizzle beginning to veil the hills. But he was looking forward to leaving the Rorim, to being in the open. Always, for him, problems had seemed much simpler in such places. As simple as lighting a fire or finding a dry place to sleep. Nothing ever followed him there.

Not in my own world, anyway.

The tracker, Tagan, took point, the rain beginning to mist his beard and the black mat of hair that covered his forehead, and they followed on, Fife and Drum looking wet and unenthusiastic already.

'What's the plan?' Ratagan asked no one in particular.

'West to the Skriaig first, to check the border,' Murtach told him. 'Then north to view Suardal and Corry. We'll see if we can't catch sight of Mullach and Lionan as they head back north. And then down to Ivrigar on the second night.'

Ratagan grunted.

They left the Rorim and set their faces towards the hills. Tagan rode to the rise in front as they left the Dale behind. After him came Murtach, who seemed to be leading the patrol; then Ratagan, Riven and Isay, and the other seven Hearthwares with the mules. Luib and Belig brought up the rear, and the two wolves loped alongside. They rode in single file, for the ground became broken as they climbed higher and the hoofs of their mounts dislodged loose stones that clattered down the hillside. Tagan's eyes were as much on the ground as on the land ahead. They were heading westwards, to where the land rose more precipitously and broke into a grey surf of scattered granite.

The rain remained a moist guess in the air, though they had to tug on their cloaks against the cold in the wind. It reddened their faces and made their mounts steam. There was nothing of summer left in it.

They halted on a rocky ridge, where heather poked up through gaps in the stones, and looked back to see Ralarth a green patch below them. Riven's legs were complaining about the unaccustomed riding, and the wind made his eyes water. He pulled the double thickness of the cloak tighter around him and wondered briefly why he had not worn his hiking clothes. But they would have looked ridiculous alongside the others. He smiled at himself. Vanity.

'This is the Skriaig,' said Murtach, standing up in his stirrups and staring west across the summits of the lesser hills. 'What you might call our border. Beyond it lives no man, and even the hunters cross the ridge only seldom. There is nothing beyond but the hills, and mountains in the far west; and the beasts.'

'Here be dragons,' Riven murmured, eyeing the empty spaces below. He felt the hilt of his sword.

'We are skylined here,' said Tagan after a few moments. 'Everything for miles around can see us.'

Murtach nodded. 'We will continue down along the eastern slope of the ridge.' He pointed with one gloved hand, then clicked his tongue and urged his mount forward. They continued on their way, the hiss of the wind and their horses' hoofs the only sounds.

The ridge ran north to south for miles, with an occasional saddle where a foaming river had scored its way through it. The country reminded Riven of Skye; it was harsher than Ralarth. The only life they saw were a few curlews, and once an eagle far off in the west, circling the heights. They continued riding through the afternoon, by which time the dull cloud above their heads had become unbroken, and it looked as though they were in for a wet night. They had seen no tracks and sighted nothing in the land below them, which Ratagan said was unusual, for deer were not uncommon here, as well as hill foxes and hares. But there was nothing in the emptiness, not even a field mouse.

It darkened, and they made camp. A fire was lit at the base of a broad crag, and they sat around it whilst a Hearthware took sentry and the night was blown in around them. Riven was stiff all over, hardly able to stretch himself flat. But once the horses were unsaddled, rubbed down and hobbled, he spread a blanket on the hard ground and took his place at the evening meal with the others. Thick slabs of bacon sizzled on a pan by the fire, and they mopped up the fat with grainy bread, washing it down with spring water.

A drizzle ran in streams down the rocks and dewed the horses, but the fire kept the worst of its effects from them. The burning heather curls gave off a bright, intense heat but burned quickly, and they each took their turn at collecting a pile, so the fire could be kept going, through part of the night at least. Then the watches were arranged. Riven drew the watch before Murtach, who, as leader, took the last watch before dawn. They talked quietly amongst themselves for a while of inconsequential things, content to watch the fire and feel the tiredness in their muscles; then rolled themselves in their cloaks and slept.

Riven was woken for his watch in the dead of night by a yawning Hearthware.

'All quiet,' said the man in a low voice. 'Murtach is on after you. You might build up the fire a little.' Then he left for the warmth of his blankets.

Shivering and sore, Riven stood up and buckled his sword. The fire was a mess of glowing embers that spat at the light rain. He searched around and found the pile of heather, and fed the fire until the flames licked up to warm him. He blew through his hands. The rain had soaked into his cloak as he slept, and it hung in heavy damp folds on his shoulders. He thought of his bed at the Rorim; then he thought of Madra in it, her warmth under him and her hands on his back, her hair in his mouth.

He checked the horses, but they were quiet, standing resting one leg at a time, with their eyes half-closed. The wind had dropped, he noticed. The rain fell silently and invisibly, kissing his scarred forehead. A soft night.

It was the click of rock beyond the firelight that made him turn. He stared out into the wet darkness, and heard it again. He wanted to wake up the sleepers, but it might merely be a rabbit, or a fox. He stood still, and heard then the sound of pebbles shifting under feet—more than one set of feet—and there was the rattle of loose scree. He drew his sword and held it in front of him, the pulse pounding in his temples, but he was not yet afraid enough to wake the others.

And then he saw them come into the amber flicker of the firelight with the flames lighting green lamps in their heads. Three wolves. Two were winter wolves, pale as ghosts in the night, but the third was a dark, short-haired animal, larger than the others. Its mouth was open and it seemed to be grinning at him.

The two smaller animals padded towards him and lay down beside the fire with contented sighs, hardly giving him a glance.

They were Fife and Drum.

The third sat on its haunches in that twilit area between the light of the fire and the rainy blue darkness of the empty hills. Riven stared at it, wonder widening his eyes. And even as he watched it blurred. The lights in its eyes faded and he saw the pricked ears descend. It whined deep in its throat, as though in pain, and he saw the body grow paler as the fur sloughed away into nothing. The forepaws grew thicker, the hind legs longer, the torso broader. And then Murtach was crouched there, naked in the night, watching him. Riven lowered his blade, hands shaking. The little man stood up and came over to join him at the fire.

'Well met, Michael Riven,' he said quietly, and the words were distorted in his mouth, as though it were not yet the right shape for them. He was shivering, and fumbled in his bedroll for a cloak, which he pulled about his shoulders before crouching beside the fire once more. Fife and Drum followed him with their eyes, showing no surprise.

'Christ,' said Riven at last. He sat down on the bare rock and shook his head.

Murtach grinned, showing canines that were still long and wolfish. 'Do you believe in magic now, my friend?'

Werewolves. Bloody hell.

'What were you doing?' he asked, not sure if he truly wanted to know. The little man shrugged, losing his gaze in the fire. His skin was goosepimpled.

'A wolf can travel faster in this country than a mounted man—and more silently, too. I thought we might take a tour round the surrounding hills and make sure there were no hidden surprises. And besides, it has been a while since I have wandered four-footed with my children.'

Your children.

'It's one thing to write about it...' Riven said dubiously. Werewolves. Bloody hell.

'We did find something,' Murtach went on. He looked at Riven closely. 'A few miles out to the east we glimpsed the dark girl you and Bicker described from the Isle of Mist. She was wandering the crags. When we approached, she took to the steep places where we could not follow, and so we left her.' He buried his eyes in the fire again. 'Wolves can smell fear, and she was not afraid. They can smell other things also: she is dying, Riven.'

'What do you mean?' A chill caught him in the stomach.

'I mean she is dying. She is bloodied and starved, though still swift on her feet. But how she is surviving out there, I cannot say...' He trailed off. 'Is she really your wife?'

'I don't know.' He saw dark eyes with no recognition in them. But Bicker had seen her wandering Glenbrittle, and she had been to the bothy. She had tried to come home.

I don't know.

'I don't know what she is,' he said, blinking hard. 'She doesn't know me. She hardly seems real. I don't know what she is.'

The little man pulled his cloak tighter about his shoulders. The drizzle was already soaking it darker.

'I'm half-inclined to pursue her tomorrow; perhaps if we had her, we would have a few more answers to all this. But I'm not sure we could catch her if we tried. I don't think it is meant to happen. She is not merely a girl.' He paused. 'Maybe she is suffering the same fate as Minginish,' he said obscurely. And then he stood up in one fluid movement. 'It is my watch. Dawn is not far off. I'll dress and let you get some sleep.'

But Riven did not think he would sleep again that night.

BY DAWN THE sky had cleared and was a hard, pale blue. They creaked awake and set to rousing the fire and cooking breakfast, the Hearthwares cursing the chill weight of their armour, hopping up and down to get the blood moving through their limbs. They ate breakfast standing, Riven wishing momentarily for coffee. But then Ratagan handed him a battered silver flask with a wink and he spluttered over strong barley spirit, the last of the cold burnt out of him. They rubbed down the horses roughly, saddled them, and then were on their way again, their fire circle buried under stones and heather tufts. They began to pick a path down out of the high land to where the towns and villages of Ralarth and its fiefs stretched green below them into the far distance, silent under the early sunlight.

They were heading northeast, the morning light in their right eyes and their shadows cast back towards the Skriaig and Ralarth's western border. If they strained their eyes they could make out the clusters of houses and farmyards that were Suardal to the north, the pencil-thin bars of smoke already rising from them and the meagre herds moving across the open country like ants.

The day passed with little talk. It seemed the silence of the hills was infectious. They rode steadily downwards until it was grass under their steeds' hoofs instead of rock, and there were trees and calm rivers meandering in the dips of hills. The sky clouded, grew overcast and heavy, and they waited patiently for the rain to start in on them again, knowing they would be in the warmth of Ivrigar by nightfall.

Riven kicked his mount ahead until he was level with Murtach at the front of the column, Fife and Drum trotting effortlessly off to one side. Oddly, they did not seem to bother the horses. Perhaps they had been in the Rorim long enough for the animals to become used to each other.

'Tell me about the shapeshifting. Tell me about magic,' Riven said.

Murtach looked at him with raised eyebrow. 'Your own stories go a long way towards doing that.'

'Tell me.'

The little man sucked his teeth for a moment. 'Magic. Now there's a thing. A strange thing. Do you know, Michael Riven, that I and my father are two of the lucky ones?' He turned to Riven. 'They had witch hunts here a generation ago, or more. They rooted out those folk who were not... ordinary, and banished them from Minginish. People are afraid of what they cannot understand.'

Werewolves and wheelchairs. Riven nodded.

'The Warbutt was my father's friend. He saved him from a mob. He could not save my mother.' There was no inflection in Murtach's voice. It had gone flat as flint. 'As time went on, Guillamon became a trusted adviser, and eventually what you see now. But to do that, he had to forswear his... abilities. He has hardly used them since. Perhaps he has lost them by now. It is of no matter. These days we can joke about it, ask him to turn people into toads. Myself—I do not forget. An entire society was uprooted and destroyed, vanishing into the high mountains, never to return. And why? Because people were afraid of differences. My father has told me. There were witches who healed children and cattle, wizards who worked great things for lords. They were all swept away. And the land was made the poorer for it. The weaker.' He smiled.

'Mayhap if we had a few more wizards among us we would not now be in the straits we are in.' Then the smile left him. 'But there are those who blame the present plight of Minginish on the misdeeds of the past. They believe that the wizards and warlocks are still up there, in the mountains, working this evil on the land in revenge. People like Bragad believe this. They would be content to see another purge of the suspects, such as myself. It is one reason why you are here now, my friend. To keep Bragad from seeing another wizard in you. Such things would give him the freedom of action he craves. There would be pyres up and down the Dales and himself lighting them, redeeming the people. And they would believe him. In times like these, they are frightened enough to believe anything.' He seemed to sniff the air. 'The year turns already. It winds down into winter, and yet by rights it should be barely midsummer. There is indeed magic walking the earth. Perhaps it is in you. Perhaps it is in the dark girl who looks like your dead wife. I do not know. I think you carry our ruin in your pocket, Riven, but I cannot say how. And Minginish itself—it has a hand in it also, I believe. Your books do not tell the whole story. One man never can.'

'Where did the magic come from?' Riven asked.

'You know the tale—you wrote it yourself. From the Dwarves, the Deep Ones of the Greshorns, the oldest folk of the earth. They gave the magic to a cripple named Birkinlig, and he took it to the lower land and in turn bestowed it upon his friends, his household. People came from far and near to see the wonders they wrought, and eventually, like the Myrcans, some of them accepted service with the lords of Minginish. Others went their own way, delving farther into the secrets that had been revealed to them, living in the deep woods of the high crags, visited by petitioners who sought aid. And so they scattered over Minginish, becoming the Hidden Folk. And now they are gone.'

'Why a wolf?' Riven asked him.

'I can be anything up to a bear if you like. Or any*one*. I found Fife and Drum as cubs, the dog-wolf slain by hunters, the she-wolf dying. And so I became a she-wolf myself, and rescued them and suckled them. And they became my children. Does that shock you, Michael Riven?'

'A little.'

Murtach chuckled. 'It is not in your book, at any rate. In it I am an unreliable type, with too much of the wolf within me—is that not so?'

'The stories are not always exact pictures. You know that.'

'Yes, but it is interesting all the same. And now we find that the people who are troubling the Dales most at the moment are out of your own world—Bragad and Jinneth. Is there anyone else we should know about?'

Riven shook his head wearily, though he thought there might be. Then he rejoined Ratagan down the column. Talking to Murtach was like fighting a duel, at times.

Jenny is out there now, in those jagged hills to where the magicians and witches of the world were banished.

He was beginning to see a glimmer of sense about this world.

THEY BEGAN TO meet people in their travelling, and actually came upon a gravelled road that some lord of Ralarth had laid down decades or centuries ago, the wagon ruts deep in it. The Hearthwares and Myrcans were greeted with friendliness and something like relief by the people they came upon— merchants in covered carts, farmers with flocks and herds, women bent under loads of firewood or water, children trailing behind them and eyeing the armoured figures on the big horses in wonder. Fife and Drum received a few wide-eyed stares, but for the most part the people seemed to recognise them and their owner. Murtach was greeted by name more than once, and one of the Hearthwares bent to receive a spray of honeysuckle from a dark-eyed girl who ogled him with adoration, to the amusement of his comrades.

At each village they came to, Murtach halted the company and paused to talk to the headman. Riven could not hear their speech, but there were always shakings of heads and grim looks. Some villages had wolf skins pinned to their doors, freshly flayed, and one they came to had the head of a Rime Giant set on a stake outside the headman's house. The eyes had sunken in and the skull was showing through the thinning hair of the pate. A crow perched on it while they watched, and poked hopefully at the sockets.

They moved on quickly, for they would have to retrace part of their way to make Ivrigar before nightfall. Murtach had learned of a great wolf pack that seemed to roam west of the Skriaig and had been seen by a few desperate hunters seeking deer beyond Ralarth's borders. It was as great as an army, they said, and Rime Giants walked with it like shepherds. It was heading east. And there were grypesh also—the rat-boars who haunted the forests at night and stole into the streets when the moon was dark. They had carried off children. And where had the Hearthwares been then? And where had been Lionan's fighting men, the retainers who were bound to protect Suardal as the Hearthwares were? No one had seen them for days. And the gates of Rim-Suardal were closed.

They rode on. One village had slain three men from the north who had tried to steal food, and they hung like scarecrows on a crude gibbet. Murtach ordered them cut down, white with anger. Hearthwares were the law in the land. He told those responsible their hamlet would burn if it happened again. They listened to him in stony silence—a dozen half-starved men with their womenfolk clustered behind them, infants whimpering at their skirts. The column gave them what food they had left, and rode on.

The farther west they went, the worse it became. They passed two prosperous-looking farmsteads that had been abandoned completely. One of them had the carcasses of wolves and grypesh, leathery and stinking, littering its yard. The mood of the party grew sombre. Even Ratagan seemed to have forgotten how to smile, and the sternness of the Myrcans deepened.

They turned south at last and began heading towards Ratagan's home as their shadows lengthened and the second day of the patrol drew to a close. None of them had any particular wish to be abroad after dark. It began to rain, a steady stream that blew in from the east and beat against the stony flanks of the western hills. The Hearthwares shifted uncomfortably as the water ran down inside their armour, and fumbled oilskin cloaks from their saddle bows. The Myrcans let it run down their faces unheeded.

Then Tagan, the tracker, stopped and stood in his stirrups, his head up and his eyes narrowed. Murtach joined him. The two wolves stood by his horse with their ears pricked, and suddenly they began growling deep in their throats. Tagan pointed into the darkening hills, and Riven followed his finger. There was movement there amid the tumbled rocks that the dusk was making into a maze of shadow.

A thin sound beside him, and Ratagan had unsheathed his axe from its case at his pommel. The rain dripped from it. It ran down his forehead and into the deepset eyes below, trickling into his beard.

'I believe we have company, my friend,' he said softly.

Down the line, swords hissed out of oiled scabbards. A mule began to bray in alarm and a Myrcan struck it at once with his staff until it fell silent, blood oozing from its nose.

'Grypesh!' Murtach exclaimed quietly. They were moving in a dark tide along the contours of the hills. Riven could not make out individual animals, only the shape of the pack.

'How many?' he asked.

'Three, four score,' Isay said from behind him. There was a dreadful eagerness in his voice. Riven tried to dredge up images of their foes from his books, but the reality of the rain, the darkness, and the approaching pack left him no time to think.

Murtach spun his horse around like a centaur. 'There are too many,' he said. 'We must ride—ride for Ivrigar. Luib, free the mules. Leave them. Tagan, lead on!'

And they sped forward with the squeals of the pack to their right as they were sighted, the clods and stones scattering from their horses' hoofs, into a full, tearing gallop in the twilight. The rain beat at their eyes and the lurch of the uneven ground rollercoasted beneath them, jostling them in their saddles despite the grip of their tired knees. Riven felt a thrill of fear in his stomach, like liquid ice poured into the bottom of his lungs; and then it was all he could do to steer his terrified horse in Murtach's wake, and stay aboard as it swerved past rocks and bushes, and leapt hollows with the thunder of the other horses like a storm in his ears, and the rain a freezing hail in his face that blinded him.

Behind them, they heard the death screams of the abandoned mules, and their steeds accelerated even more whilst the grey ghosts of Murtach's wolves darted beside them at an impossible speed. They clattered downhill as though they were chasing an enemy. But the enemy was behind them. They could hear the squealing roars of their pursuers over the tumult of their mounts' hoofs. The horses were terrified, the foam flying from their muzzles and their eyes circled with white. But they were nearly spent also.

Ahead, Murtach shouted and slowed. In a wide bowl there was the night glimmer of a stream which was churned to flashing silver as they thrashed through it, the spray soaking them to their thighs. And beyond it was the great black bulk of a building, rearing up against the night sky with lights flickering yellow and bright in its blankness.

They milled together and dismounted, the two Myrcans immediately running to the rear to intercept the pursuit. Riven saw something like a black tide sweep out of the stream, and then there was the green glow of eyes everywhere in the chaotic darkness, and the Myrcan staves were whistling and cracking down to break bones and shatter skulls. The air filled with a crescendo of screams in which the horses joined. Riven hung on to his mount's bridle grimly whilst it bucked and reared in a desperate effort to get away. Warm slobber hit him in the face. He heard Murtach shouting, someone banging on timber frantically. Armoured figures drew their swords and shouted incoherently, joining the fight to the rear. He saw Ratagan's axe flash like a star and bury itself in a hairy snout, splintering black blood.

Grypesh. They were like something out of a nightmare. They had the heads of rats; rats five feet long. But from the sides of their mouths projected the glistening tusks of boars, and they were crowned with great, bristling manes of stiff hair that ran down to the base of their spines. Their feet were clawed, but the legs were squat and powerful, the bodies ending in a hairless snake of tail. They squealed and roared alternately. Riven saw a Hearthware go down as one charged and sent him flying. He was immediately engulfed by three of its fellows. His ironclad limbs flailed in a scrum of fur and claws and wet teeth. But then Luib had stepped in, braining the beasts left, right and centre, hauling the stricken man back.

There was a rumble, and then torchlight spilled out over them as the gates of Ivrigar were opened. They laboured inside, trailing their horses by the reins, half of them fighting a ferocious rear guard battle whilst the grypesh massed within the gate and strove to win through to the courtyard beyond.

The rain grew heavier, slicking the ground. Riven drew his sword. The horses were free in the courtyard now, cantering about in terror whilst Ivrigar's people tried to control them. Others were fighting to shut the gate, pushing against the sheer weight of the beasts in the gateway.

They're trying to get to me.

The thought came to him in an instant as he stood, hesitating over whether to join the fight. The grypesh were clawing over their own dead to get through the gate whilst swords and staves and Ratagan's axe took a fearful toll. But why?

And then Ratagan went down with a grypesh at his throat, and Riven forgot about hesitating. He waded in with his sword swinging, and felt the jar down his arm as it almost decapitated an animal. He swung again and again, and felt the slow, red pain in his shoulder and ribs grow with each swing. The world flickered in his sight. He helped Ratagan away, the big man leaning on him for support and cursing his lameness.

And then it was over. The gates boomed shut, and the last grypesh in the yard was slain. The rain covered Riven's face, trickling off the armoured Hearthwares in streams. They were gasping like sprinters. Outside they could hear the rest of the pack throwing themselves against the timber of the gate and the outer wall. There was desperation and hate in their squeals. Riven felt sick.

'Well met, my friend,' Ratagan croaked. 'We are for ever saving each other's neck, you and I.' He halted, striving to get his breath. 'A fine tradition. Long may it—may it continue.' And his grin was a flash of teeth in the torchlight and the flame-kindled rain.

'Ratagan. My lord.'

A woman's voice in the crowd of warriors and attendants, and a slight figure appeared, hooded against the rain, the Ivrigar people making way for her. She threw the hood back, revealing gold hair that shone in the rain.

'Come inside. You are hurt, and I must welcome you back to your home.'

Ratagan's grin faded.

THERE WAS NO light in the room save that of the fire. It was a large fire, the mantle above it the height of Riven's shoulders, and it was as long as a bed. The flames licked up round thigh-thick logs and made the iron firedogs into burning icons. The fire filled the room with a tawny, saffron light and poured pools of impenetrable shadow in the far corners. Its light revealed a high-ceilinged room barred with black rafters, a flagged floor, and a long, heavy table set with unlit candles and piled with clothing and weapons of one sort or another. Before the fire, Ratagan and Riven sat on two high-backed wooden settles. The big man had a full flagon tilting in his fist and a tense cast to his face. They had both changed into dry clothes. Ratagan cocked his head to listen to the race of the wind outside that creaked the rafters.

A door opened, and Isay entered with a tray of platters of food. The woman followed him. There was a scrape as she brought a taper forth from a tin box and leaned towards the fire to light it. Ratagan took it from her wordlessly and held it in the flames till it had caught. She smiled at him, but he buried his nose in his beer.

The candles were lit and the room brightened, suddenly becoming bare as the high walls leapt into view.

'What news?' Ratagan asked the firedogs.

'The beasts have drawn off,' the woman said. She had a high voice, and there was something of a shake in it. 'Murtach and the others are going round some of the outlying tenants now, to ensure they came to no harm.'

'It was a fine fight,' Isay said, and his eyes were shining in the candlelight.

Ratagan grunted. 'Would have been finer still had the invalids but been allowed to stay in it. I'll have words with Murtach when he returns.'

'It was a running fight, at the last,' Isay said. 'Your leg—and the Teller's weakness—would not have let you stay with it.'

'The Myrcan speaks truly, Ratagan,' the woman said. She set a hand on one huge shoulder. 'Must you always be straining at the leash to bloody your blade?' She was small, slim, with the pale-gold hair plaited behind her head, and steady blue eyes. Aelin. Ratagan's wife.

'It is one of the few things in which I excel,' Ratagan said. 'Another is drinking.' He emptied his flagon, and after a minute's hesitation she took it over to the table to refill it.

Riven shifted uneasily. Aelin had brought them inside and the battle had restarted, Murtach attacking the grypesh still outside. But now it was over, and Isay had rejoined them, along with a trio of wounded Hearthwares who were being tended in the hall below with their armour stripped off beside them. And Murtach was out with the others, harrying the defeated pack on foot and doing the rounds of the surrounding farms.

And since then, Ratagan had hardly said a civil word to his wife, though she looked at him almost imploringly at times, and Riven had seen him gaze at her when her head was turned, brow creased in pain. It was a side of Ratagan that he had never guessed at. Riven was not sure he wanted to know the reason. He had had enough experience of strangers probing his own hurts without wanting to pry into those of others.

Aelin brought them food on wooden platters. It was good, wholesome fare: rye bread and cheese, apples and meat. But the apples were wrinkled from long storage, and the meat had been salted to preserve it.

'How are things?' Ratagan asked her quietly, slicing into his cheese.

She joined him on the settle. 'Fair enough, for the times. We have had losses, but not so many as some. The patrols pass here as regularly as always. We have had a few of Lionan's men here once or twice, some wounded. It is worse in the north, they say. Something will have to be done.' She flicked a quick look at Riven, taking in his scarred forehead and the Teller badge on his breast, its thread shining in the firelight.

'There are rumours of people in the mountains...'

'What people?' Ratagan asked sharply.

'The Hidden Folk. Some say it is they who are

bringing about these times that are upon us. Lionan's men said that the Dales needed to be purged and united. They said there was evil walking the hills in many guises—that there are witches in the high places, and warlocks who seek the fellowship of men.' Again, she looked at Riven.

Abruptly, Ratagan threw the chunk of bread he had been gnawing into the fire. 'Horseshit!' He hobbled upright and put his back to it. 'These are Lionan's people who say this, and Lionan consorts with Bragad now. These tales are to suit the aims of Garrafad and Carnach. Times are bad enough without men running up old horror tales of the Hidden Folk in the mountains.'

'Then what is doing it?' she asked, her face tilted up to him and her throat a fine line in the firelight.

'I...' he faltered. 'I don't know. No one does. Not even Guillamon.'

'He of all people should know, being what he is.' There was something of a sneer in her voice. Ratagan's brow contracted.

'I did not come here to wrangle with you.'

'Why did you come here, then—when I have not seen your face this six months?'

'Moon and stars, woman! Do you think I *want* to be here?' And then he shut his eyes. She stood up, and spun away.

'Aelin—no. Wait!'

But she had left the room on silent feet, and the door had closed without a sound behind her. Isay set to drying the weapons on the table, though they were already dry. Riven chewed bread which had turned to sand in his mouth.

The big man sat down again. 'I did not make a great job of that, did I?' he asked.

Riven handed him his flagon. 'Nope,' he replied.

'Always, Bicker and Murtach try to get me out here, and always it is the same.' Ratagan shook his head and smiled, but there was an odd brightness about the eyes. He knuckled them quickly, and addressed the beer again. Behind them, Isay left, bearing an armful of equipment, and banged the door behind him.

'Ratagan—' Riven began.

'I got her with child,' Ratagan said. 'When she was nothing but a child herself. The child died, and she never had another. All innocence and sweetness it was, when she became my lady. She is lovely still. But now there is that between us. And the fighting. And the drinking. There is no help for it.' He gulped at the beer again. 'A running fight indeed! I'll tan Murtach's hide when he creeps back.' He filled Riven's flagon for him. 'I'll tell you a tale,' he said. 'And a fine, funny one it is too, if you've the patience to take it in...'

The wind howled outside, battering the heights of the western mountains and bringing winter in its wake.

CHAPTER ELEVEN

THEY DID NOT linger in Ivrigar. Murtach and most of the company came in late that night, and by early the following afternoon, they were preparing to go on their way again. Over thirty grypesh had been slain, and the rest of the pack had dispersed in the western hills. Little damage had been done to the surrounding farms, since the beasts had concentrated their efforts on following the patrol and striving to enter Ivrigar. Riven, remembering the Rime Giant's attempt on his life in Ralarth Rorim, wondered how many more times he was to be the focus of a battle.

Aelin wished them goodbye, members of her household helping the injured Hearthwares to mount their steeds. She kissed her husband dutifully, and for a moment Riven saw her and Ratagan exchange a look which had in it something of despair. Then they were formal again, and the company was trooping out of the courtyard and into the cold breeze that billowed down from the distant mountains, their faces set towards the east.

They rode through the stink of pyres where local men were burning the bodies of the beasts killed the night before, and then the land dipped and they were back in the Dales proper, with the hills behind them and some of the chill wind cut off. Riven pulled his cloak up about his neck, his bones aching and stiff and his legs still complaining about the horse between them. But he would have a drink and a warm bed awaiting him when he got rid of it. And Madra there, also, he suddenly remembered, and groaned aloud as he thought of the complications ahead. This world was more complex than his stories had ever made it.

Because it is real. It is not a story. It never was.

Then why Jenny, and Hugh? Why the spillover from his own life? He thought of his books. If anyone knew the answers in this country, it was the Dwarves. But how to get hold of them? There were none in Ralarth, none in the south. The only place they lived was in the northern mountains, the Greshorns. He shivered, remembering a dream where he had been riding north into the mountains with a woman who was not his wife.

Time to move on, maybe, to search for some answers before the whole thing comes down around my ears.

'Riders ahead,' Tagan, the black-bearded scout, said up front. 'Half a dozen. 'Wares, I think.'

'Not Ralarth's 'Wares, though,' Murtach said, his blue eyes narrowed against the wind that watered them.

They rode on at an easy trot, eating up the ground, until finally Murtach said in disgust: 'Bragad's lady—out for a ride, it seems, with five of her husband's escort for company.' And he spat over his mount's shoulder.

The small group of riders spied them and altered their course to meet the patrol. In minutes, they stood facing each other across a few feet of upland grass, the fresher horses of Jinneth's escort stamping impatiently. She was dressed in black, as always, making Riven wonder sourly if she were mourning someone, but there was a bright smile on her face as she took in the battered condition of Murtach's patrol; the bandaged Hearthwares, the clawed mounts and the weary eyes of them all.

'My lords Murtach and Ratagan,' she said gaily. 'You have been sorely missed from the council chamber. My husband was eager to meet the axe man and the shapeshifter of Ralarth once more.'

Murtach scowled, but said nothing.

'Surely your errand was urgent, to take you away from such an important gathering in your own Rorim. And you have the foreign Teller with you also, I see.' Her gaze flicked over Riven cursorily, and he stiffened as though he had been struck. 'But here! I notice you have been fighting, so maybe your errand was not so slight. I trust you were the victors of whatever engagement you became embroiled in?'

'We were,' Murtach said succinctly. A low growl from Fife was silenced by his glare. 'It might be better, though, my lady, if you were not to wander the open Dale with such a small escort. There are evil beasts abroad in great numbers, and even a well-armed group such as ours has its difficulties.'

'My husband's Hearthwares are equal to any task he sets them,' she replied, her smile becoming frosty, like brittle icing on an old cake.

There was a low derisive murmur from the Ralarth 'Wares at this. Bragad's men in their red sashes set hands on sword hilts.

Jinneth ignored them. 'And we will be moving on now, if you don't mind. The day wanes, and if your words are to be believed, then I had best be back in the security of your Rorim before nightfall.' She gathered up her reins, but Murtach's voice stopped her.

'What of the council—is it yet over?'

She checked, irritated. 'No. It continues, and will for another day or so at least. Your Warbutt and his son prove intractable, though their own lords disagree with them.'

Murtach cocked a brow. 'Indeed? But then there are strange bedfellows about in these times, are there not?'

She whitened, and Riven saw the knuckles bunch on her riding whip. But then she jerked her horse around savagely, and wheeled off with her escort in pursuit. The Ralarth 'Wares grinned at her receding figure, but Murtach was sombre.

'The council goes on too long,' he said. 'There is something here that smells bad.' And he led them in a weary canter down to the Rorim.

THEY ENTERED THE Circle by the South Gate, the Hearthware lieutenant Dunan greeting them as they arrived, and walked the tired horses with their injured riders up alongside the Rorim's stream to the Inner Circle, and the Manse with its blue pennants snapping in the brisk wind. There were many people about working at the common land between the walls, and more than a few seated outside the few inns they passed. Everyone acknowledged the Ralarth 'Wares and Myrcans with nods or bows, and someone, recognising Ratagan, swung him a tankard of beer. He drained it at a draught and threw it back, the dark mood that had kept him silent from Ivrigar falling away.

They rode through the market, with its gaudy awnings and crammed stalls, its pens of bawling sheep. Many of the pens were empty, however, and the shepherds who lounged on the rails there had a hopeless look. The big horses shouldered passersby aside, for which Murtach courteously apologised, and the wounded 'Wares, bloodstained and tired, drew stares from everywhere. There were concerned looks from burly matrons, and longing admiration from boys.

They caught a brief glimpse of the struggling figures on the practice grounds, the clash of their weapons on the wind. Then they entered the barbican of the Rorim itself, and clattered on the cobbles of the Inner Court where Riven had battled Giants. They came to a halt before the doors of the Manse and grooms ran out to take their horses, unarmoured Hearthwares helping their comrades from the saddle. Bicker was there, looking as tired as if he, and not they, had been riding and fighting in the past three days. And Madra was with him, the worry clear on her face a hundred feet away. Her eyes ran over the company for a moment, and then she turned away to go inside again. Riven and Ratagan exchanged a look, and Riven realised that the big man knew everything. Ratagan thumped his shoulder lightly, a crooked smile playing in his beard.

'Women, eh?'

And they shared a laugh, dismounting together in the clatter of the crowded court.

LATER, AS NIGHT crept over the Rorim, they met in Riven's room and shared a few pitchers of ale. Guillamon and Bicker were there, as well as Ratagan and Murtach, and Isay took up his usual post at the door. Fife and Drum sprawled contentedly on the floor. There was no sign of Madra, Riven noticed with a pang, and the beer was brought up to them by a serving maid he did not know.

Well done, Riven; another good deed done.

They sat savouring the malty brew for a while, with the darkness silent outside the windows. Both Bicker and Guillamon were preoccupied and frowning, and Ratagan's attempts at jokes fell flat.

'How is Aelin?' Guillamon asked hopefully at last. Murtach shot his father a warning glance, but the big man merely shrugged, his deep eyes becoming shrouded by the overhanging brows.

'Much as she was before. And so am I. There is no profit to be made there, Guillamon, not any more. I wish my friends would take that to heart. And my mother, also.' He sipped at his beer. A savage look flitted across his face and was gone.

Guillamon grimaced. 'Fair enough.'

They fell silent again. Murtach had already told Bicker of the fight at Ivrigar, and a strong patrol was being sent out in the morning under Ord. There were reports of other attacks to the north and west, but still no word had come in of Lionan or Mullach, and Murtach's patrol had not sighted them. They and their forces seemed to have vanished from Ralarth.

'But these talks, Bicker,' Murtach was saying. 'Why do they continue so long? Why does Bragad not give in? What does he hope to gain?'

The dark man looked harassed. 'He has the support of three of Ralarth's lords—a fair foothold, I would say. Theoretically they should follow the lead of the Warbutt if he commands them; they are his vassals. But you know, Murtach, that in the past the Warbutt has waived a point when a majority of the lords were against it.'

'Not with this one, he won't,' Ratagan snorted.

'I know, but the precedent is there.'

'Well,' the big man declared, 'I see two lords sitting here who will not change their minds.'

'The axe man and the shapeshifter,' Murtach murmured. He appeared uneasy.

'Bragad wants the pair of you present at the council. It is one of the reasons he has been delaying us these three days, I think,' Guillamon put in.

'He thinks he can change our minds?' Ratagan asked derisively.

'I don't know. He wants to canvass every one of Ralarth's lords.'

'He is killing time,' Bicker grated, 'and I would like to know why.' No one answered him. Ratagan refilled their flagons from the pitcher on the table.

'One more day,' Guillamon said. 'Two, perhaps. Then we'll give him another feast and send him on his way.'

'And maybe have a word or two with the more bothersome of our lords,' Murtach said darkly. 'I'm thinking it's no bad thing that we've Druim training a militia and extra Hearthwares for us. A small show of strength might be called for, to teach men like Marsco who is overlord in Ralarth.'

Guillamon nodded. 'The very thing he feared he may well have brought upon himself anyway. We cannot have the lord of a place such as Ringill intriguing with the likes of Bragad.'

'Or Bragad's lady,' Bicker added, and he darted a look of apology at Riven. Riven said nothing. He was becoming used to the idea that Jinneth was not Jenny, that Bragad was not Hugh. But it reminded him of what he wanted to say.

'I've been here in Ralarth a fair while now,' he began, and the others stared at him. 'There are things and people here who were in my books—whom I created, in a manner of speaking. There are people here from my own world who have somehow been translated into Minginish. And there are people, places, history in this country I'd never even guessed at, though I sometimes feel I know them anyway.' He met their eyes steadily. Fife and Drum lifted their heads off their paws and seemed to sniff the air.

'It is here, in Ralarth, that the thing begins—here that the main characters come from, just as they did in the book. But it doesn't end here, and the answers will not be found here in the Dales. I'm sure of that now. Staying here, I'm just the target for further attacks, with the Rorim between me and what's trying to kill me. But the story has to move on.'

'The third book,' Bicker said quietly. 'The last one.'

'You know how the story goes,' Riven said. 'A trio of heroes set out in winter to save the land in a quest to the north.'

'To find the Dwarves of the Greshorns,' Murtach said.

'And Sgurr Dearg, the Staer, is in the middle of those mountains,' Riven told them. 'That's where it began. That's where it will end. I'm sure of it.'

'Had you planned the third book?' Bicker asked, his eyes like two black holes in his sharp face.

'Part of the way, yes. But I couldn't get to grips with it. I couldn't write it.' He remembered sitting at his desk in the bothy before Bicker arrived, trying to tear the story out of himself and filling pages with blizzards and killing. He wondered if that was what was before them, but did not say anything. Best not to know.

'The story has to be finished, and I must be the one to finish it.' The words were like stones in his mouth. He felt he had said them before, and thought he could sense death sniffing at his shoulder, as he had that day on the Red Mountain. But that did not matter now. There were more important things.

'I must leave Ralarth.'

He remembered the dream where he had been riding north with Jinneth into the mountains, and he was sure that something of that figure had been Jenny. Jenny telling him what to do, perhaps.

'It is a long way to the Greshorns,' Guillamon

said. He seemed suddenly old. 'And through a land that is every day stepping one pace closer to anarchy. Are you sure this is where you must go?'

'I am,' Riven said. He knew what he was asking these people to do and he did not like it, but there was no other way.

'A curious time you have picked to tell us of this, Michael Riven,' Murtach said, smiling wryly. 'You will turn Bicker grey before you are done.'

'The northern mountains,' Bicker said, ignoring Murtach's comment, 'are almost a thousand miles away. At least six weeks' travel. And as Guillamon said, these are arduous times...' He shook his head, doubt written all over his face.

'I'll go alone, if I have to,' Riven snapped with sudden irritation. 'I don't like this any more than you do.'

'But you are sure?'

He clenched back his own fears and doubts. 'Yes. It has to be done.'

Bicker sighed, and threw back half the beer in his mug. 'Strange times,' he said, wiping his mouth with the back of his hand.

'Indeed,' Guillamon agreed. 'Horses you will need, and an escort. Hearthwares we can ill afford. Supplies. A guide.'

'I know the Greshorns, the path to the Red Mountain,' Bicker said heavily. 'I, for one, must go.'

'Things here are not so settled that you can all of a sudden disappear,' Guillamon said.

The dark man nodded. 'First things first. We must wait until this thing with Bragad is resolved. The Rorim must be secure.'

'What will the Warbutt say?' Ratagan asked.

Bicker cursed. 'His son on his wanderings again. I will not be popular, but there is no help for it.'

'I always wanted to see what the Greshorns looked like,' Ratagan said.

'They are not so appealing that I relish the idea of seeing them again,' Murtach retorted.

'Three lords—two of them our most able captains—leaving us on such a quest.' Guillamon was grim. 'I don't like this. I do not know if you can all go.'

'Strange times,' Bicker repeated. 'But I agree with the Teller. Nothing is being accomplished by his remaining here. Half the Dale believes him to be some sort of wizard out of the western mountains, and folk such as Bragad will use the rumours. The clearances of thirty years ago are not forgotten. The Hidden Folk are still feared. If it is not those of Garrafad and Carnach we will soon have to face, it may be our own people. They are afraid.'

'We're all afraid,' Ratagan growled. 'Doesn't mean we have to start the burning and the exiling again.'

'No, but Bragad will use fear to help himself. He has our own lords turned to his way of thinking already.'

'Then we must turn them back,' Murtach said sharply, his blue eyes glinting. 'A purge of our own, perhaps. There used to be such a thing as loyalty in this Dale.'

'Maybe,' Bicker mused. 'Maybe.' He looked at Riven. 'All right. We will do it. We will aid you in your quest.' He smiled slightly, for a second becoming entirely the quicksilver character of Riven's stories. 'It is, after all, what we brought you here for—to resolve our problems for us.'

And my own, also.

'I suppose I had better go, to keep an eye on you,' Ratagan said absently, but he was grinning. Murtach did not speak. His face was closed.

'I also,' a voice said, and they looked up, surprised, to see Isay by the door, his beer gripped in one knotted fist. 'I am the Teller's bodyguard. I must go.'

'So you are set on it, then,' Guillamon said heavily. 'I suppose you are right. We are not accomplishing anything keeping the Teller here, except to fuel more rumours.' He paused. 'Who else do you suppose should go?'

'Tagan is our best tracker,' Ratagan said, 'and he has been to the Greshorns.'

'Luib will go,' Isay informed them. 'He becomes old, and would be glad for the chance to see the hills around Merkadale again before he dies.'

'All right.' Guillamon became brisk. 'Later we will organise this. It is enough to know for the moment that you are going... But do you know what you will do when you get there?'

'Find the Dwarves,' Riven answered him.

'They say that Birkinlig, the Father of Sorcerers, dwells still in the high mountains, perhaps with the Dwarves.'

'They say also that the Greshorns are the end of the world,' Murtach said shortly.

His father smiled at this. 'My son, for someone with your heritage, you are overfond of scepticism.' Ratagan chuckled.

'I believe in magic,' Riven said, meeting Murtach's eyes. 'Maybe that's what I'm looking for.'

'You may not have to look far,' Murtach said, obscurely.

Guillamon stood up. 'Indeed. But it is suppertime soon, and this old man needs his board, magic or no magic.' He turned to go, but stopped. 'Say no word of this to the household at present. We do not want the Rorim humming like a top with news like this, and Bragad here.' Then he left, nodding to Isay as he went.

Ratagan sat back in his chair till it creaked, and blew air out through pursed lips.

'Such tidings! My head spins. We live back in the time of fairy tales. A quest awaits us, no less, and who can say what it will bring?'

'Or how it will end,' said Bicker, watching Riven as he stared out at the darkness beyond the window.

THE NEXT MORNING saw a sky heavy with rain hanging over the hills. Murtach and Ratagan had joined the council, and Riven was left largely to his own devices. He sat and stared out at the drizzle-veiled Circle for a while, and then buckled on his sword and left his room. The Rorim was almost subdued this morning, though from the upper storeys of the Manse he could see Hearthwares busy with horses and harnesses in the yard outside their barracks. They were packing mule yokes also. He wondered if these were preparations for the journey he had suggested last night. The day's patrol had already left under Ord's leadership. They would be in the hills above Ivrigar by now.

Peering farther, beyond the ramparts, he could see the two longhouses in the Circle where the 'Wares of Bragad were billeted, but they held no sign of life.

Probably out riding with their lord's wife. Bragad had brought quite a few men with him—a dozen or so, though some, of course, were Mugeary's, if that made any difference. Riven felt momentarily uneasy thinking about them, and remembered Bicker's question of the night before. Was Bragad killing time here? And where were Mullach and Lionan?

Wheels within wheels. Not my business.

Or was it? He felt responsible for having Bragad here. He was, after all, a facsimile of someone from Riven's own world.

He wandered around for a while and ran into a few of the household busy with their duties. Then, afraid of meeting Madra, he decided to go outside, to where the trainee Hearthwares were at work in the practice fields. Isay followed him unquestioningly as always when he passed through the gates of the Rorim proper to the open space beyond. A large square had been beaten into the dirt there, muddy with rain. Jutting out of it were a line of tall posts, high as a man, a score of figures attacking them whilst thirty others looked on, wooden swords in their hands, and three Myrcans directing the whole group. Riven watched in fascination, for he had never seen the Myrcans more animated. They jumped about in the mud, correcting a swing here, a stance there; demonstrating how to stab with the bodyweight behind the thrust, how to parry, how to club with the pommel. Riven forgot why he had come, and stood in grudging admiration for their speed and sureness. Their pupils were covered with red mud from slips and falls, but the teachers were unmarked except for ochre spatters that streaked their mailed tunics.

When he finally stepped into the group and asked to join, there were murmurs from the trainees at the blue sash he wore. The leading Myrcan looked him up and down critically, then his gaze passed over Riven's shoulder to Isay. He seemed to see something there, and nodded.

'Remove your sword belt and take up a practice weapon. Join the large group there, and do as they do.'

So it was that Riven found himself attacking a wooden post with a wooden sword that was slippery with mud, and being lectured by the unsmiling Myrcans. It reminded him of Sandhurst, except that the instructors there had always bellowed their orders and called their charges by various unsanitary epithets. The Myrcans were quiet, darting here and there to adjust and correct. They never had to shout, and no one ever argued with them.

He trained on until dark, when it was just he, Isay and the three Myrcan instructors who were left on the practice field. He realised dimly that if he had volunteered to go on training all night, his teachers would not have objected. They radiated a fierce interest in their work that was at odds with their taciturn manner. And Riven was eager to learn. Even so, by the time he finally put down his wooden weapon and re buckled his sword belt, his recently healed collarbone was shouting at him and the older injuries over his body joined in. He was stiff with mud and thickheaded with tiredness as he and Isay trooped back through the gatehouse to the Manse. The first candles were being lit, and the stars were out. The night was clear, and arched up from the hills with a new moon rising over their crests.

Usually he ate with the others in the hall in the evenings, but this night he asked Isay to see Colban and have a tray brought up, and some hot water. He felt better than he had for a while, with hard work aching in his bones and the knowledge that he had decided what he must do at last.

Savour it, while you can.

The mirror showed that his face was smeared with mud, and it had stuck in his beard also. He grinned tiredly at himself, and wondered where the young officer had gone. Staring out at him were a pair of steady eyes that had lines of pain and care etched round them. There was a frown line bitten deep between the brows, and the forehead was intaglioed with scars. The mouth was harsh, downturned at one corner, though it rose when he smiled.

Sir Michael, Knight of the Isle. And now he has a quest.

He unbuckled his sword belt, then unlaced his jerkin and began to slip it over his head. There was a knock on the door, and when he grunted muffled assent it opened and someone came in. He managed to free his head, and threw the jerkin to the floor, to see Madra there with a heavy tray at the table.

Half a dozen stupid hellos passed through his mind, leaving him with nothing to say. She lit more candles without a word, and shut the tinderbox with a snap.

'You should wash before the water gets cold.'

He stared at her for a minute, then stripped to the waist and started to scrub the clay off in the basin of steaming water. He thought she would leave, but she did not. As he blinked the drops out of his eyes, she handed him a towel. He realised, looking at her then, that the line of her jaw could be formidable, that there was stubbornness under those brows. She seemed older. He pressed the towel to his face until the lights started behind his eyelids, then pulled on a fresh shirt. His boots were still caked with mud, but they could wait. He sat down at the table and began eating without tasting the food.

'You're going away up north, aren't you?'

He stopped chewing. 'How do you know?'

'Colban finds everything out, one way or another. The kitchen is always full of talk. There are Hearthwares preparing for the journey even now.'

'It was supposed to be a secret.'

She sat down. 'Keeping a secret in the Manse is like hiding a fire under straw. You are travelling to the Greshorns.'

Riven said nothing.

'Are you going back to your own world, to the Isle?'

He liked the steadiness of those eyes, the earnestness of the face; but they confused him. 'I don't know.'

Her hand darted out to his across the table. 'Take me with you.'

'What?'

'Let me go back with you. Let me stay with you.'

He pulled away his hand with a jerk. 'You're kidding!'

'You're alone back there. Ratagan told me, and Bicker says that the Isle of Mists is an empty place, full of mountains and deserted coasts. I cook well. I can work hard. I am not afraid. Please take me with you. I—'

'Shut up!' He knew what she was about to say; something he had never thought to have heard said to him again. The tears jumped into her eyes and she bent her head, hugging her arms to her breasts. A hurt child.

But she terrified him, because he wanted her and he liked having that grave face near him, and she was willing to have him even with the ghosts crowding at his shoulder.

He stood up at the same time as she did, and caught her as she made for the door. A brief struggle and she was still, her face set, but tears on her cheeks. He wiped them away, held her in his arms and buried his face in her hair. Bastard.

Her voice was muffled by his shoulder. 'I thought you wanted me. I thought—' And she pressed harder into his embrace. But she was seeking comfort, nothing else. Then she raised her head and looked at him, hair caught in her mouth. He could not keep her gaze. She left him and went to the table.

'You've hardly eaten anything.' She laughed through her tears. 'That is my fault, keeping you from your food.' She took up the basin, spilling muddy water on the floor. 'Colban will be wondering where I have got to.' Then she left.

He unsheathed his sword and grimaced at the blue steel. He swung it in a glittering arc, and it sliced through the table as though it were butter, carving its way through the heavy wood and jarring his arm, striking sparks off the stone floor.

Isay peered in. 'I heard a noise.' He saw the great slice that had been hacked out of the table. Riven met his eyes with a wild glare.

'Just practising,' he said, and the door was closed again.

* * *

THE NEXT MORNING found him on the practice fields as soon as the sun was up, battering his post as though it were a mortal enemy. The Myrcans looked on with what he could have sworn was approval. Old Luib, the chief instructor, took his arms and adjusted the swing.

'Put all your weight behind it, but move on the ball of your foot, ready to recover if the swing does not strike home.' The white stripe on his face glistened in the early light.

Riven halted, panting, as the other trainees trotted over. He nodded to them and asked Luib, partly because he was interested, partly because he needed to get his breath back: 'How many of them will make Hearthwares?'

Luib shrugged fractionally. He studied his charges as the other instructors put them through their paces.

'Five; maybe six.'

Riven whistled softly. 'What about the rest?'

'They are to remain in the Circle under arms and defend the Rorim, so that the Hearthwares can be freed for duties beyond the wall.'

'And what about the Myrcans? Where do you get your new recruits from?'

Luib met his eyes with a slight frown. 'Myrcans are born. They travel from their home Dale in the north, and take service with whoever needs them.'

Riven's interest quickened. 'Whereabouts in the north?'

'West of Drinan.'

There was a pause, Riven trying to remember Minginish's geography, but a few moments later

Luib put him back to work. With every crack of the wood he was seeing Madra's face, and the tears springing into it.

He would have stayed there until dark again, but Ratagan and Bicker came out to find him. By the time he noticed them, they had been watching for some minutes. Luib took the practice sword from him with a nod, and he joined them at the edge of the field. There was a wind blowing, clearing the sky of cloud wrack, and a pale moon was already inching its way above the brows of the hills. It would be another clear night.

'If you are not careful, someone will mistake you for a Hearthware,' said Ratagan, handing him his sword belt.

Riven pulled it on. 'It passes the time.' He slapped the scabbard. 'And, besides, if I am going to wear it, I may as well be able to use it.'

'You use it none so badly,' the big man retorted.

They moved off, toward the walls of the Rorim. Bicker seemed deep in thought, and he splashed through puddles without seeing them.

'What is it?' Riven asked.

'Oh, things. Too many little things are happening at the one time. There is something in the air.'

'Is the council over yet?'

'It finished this afternoon. Bragad was affable enough at the end—said that all things came to pass in good time, if they were meant to. Even Marsco seemed resigned to the fact that the Rorims will not combine.'

'But you are worried.'

Bicker nodded. 'He gave in too easily, at the last; too graciously after the time and prestige he has wasted here. And there is more. The Lady Jinneth went out riding alone this afternoon, and she has not yet come back. And her husband is not worried; he says she will return in her own time.'

'That she will,' Ratagan snorted.

Bicker shook his head. 'Too many people are wandering the Dales—important people. Lionan and Mullach, for instance. No one has heard from them for days. And both Rim-Suardal and Rim-Drynoch are well-nigh deserted—or so Ord says. He went round there yesterday on his patrol.'

'Bragad has the strength of two Rorims behind him now, plus maybe the men of three of your own lords,' Riven said quietly. 'Do you think he would attack Ralarth?'

Bicker was startled. 'Attack Ralarth? But he himself is inside the Rorim.'

'Ever heard of the Trojan horse, Bicker?'

'Tell me.'

'If Bragad wanted to take Ralarth Rorim, what better way to begin than to get some of his men inside beforehand?'

'There are twelve of his 'Wares billeted in the Circle,' Ratagan rumbled thoughtfully.

'Lionan and Mullach, and Jinneth, could be out there somewhere now, waiting for a signal to attack—or Jinneth could have brought the signal herself. Or the men in the longhouses could be tasked with sending it.'

'That is surmise,' Bicker said sharply.

'Better safe than sorry.'

The dark man fell silent. They walked through the barbican of the Rorim into the cobbled courtyard beyond. There was a smell of hay and horse urine from the stables, and a pair of serving maids, wrapped against the cold, were winding water up from the well.

'The household knows about the journey north,' Riven said.

Bicker nodded, and sighed. 'Young Hearthwares. They tell their lady friends, and then all secrecy is lost. Your reputation as a wizard is secured, my friend. Why else would you be seeking to travel to the Greshorns in such times?' He spat, and rubbed it into the cobbles with his boot. The three stood silent a moment, receiving stares from the girls at the well and a pair of passing Hearthwares.

Bicker swore suddenly. 'All right. You have a suspicious mind, Michael Riven, but my own goes along with it. I will try to set up a few... safeguards, in case our fears are proved true.'

'The captains will be at the feasting tonight,' Ratagan pointed out. 'If it is defenders we need, who will lead until we can join them?'

'There's Dunan,' Riven offered.

'And Luib,' Bicker added. 'He can lead the trainees. We will divide our people—some to the Rorim and the Circle, and some to the outer wall to give us advance warning.'

'The Warbutt will have to be told,' Ratagan said gently.

'Aye,' Bicker said. 'My task, I believe. He will take some convincing, but it will be done.' He looked up at the clearing sky, darkening now into dusk. 'This is Bragad's last night in the Rorim. If we are right, then it will be tonight. Whatever he has planned will be tonight. Some night for a feast.'

'I'm not going,' Riven said. He was thinking of Madra pouring beer for him at the last one.

'An extra man on the ramparts is no bad thing,' Bicker said absently. He turned and stared at the Manse. 'I must go, then. I have things to do...' And he walked off slowly with none of his usual sprightliness.

Ratagan followed him with his eyes. 'This is not Bicker's province,' he said. 'More Murtach's. Bicker was never one to be tied down with intrigue and politics.'

'Hence his wanderings in the mountains,' Riven noted.

'Aye.' Ratagan hesitated. 'You really believe Bragad is going to try and take our Rorim?'

'Yes.'

Ratagan thought. 'That would mean killing. 'Wares against 'Wares. Perhaps even—' He stopped. 'No, he'd never get Myrcan to fight Myrcan.' He frowned. 'Is this sort of thing common in your world?'

'Where I come from, there is always a war going on somewhere or other. That is why I was able to be a soldier; we keep armies at the ready all the time.'

Ratagan shook his head. 'Sounds like somewhere the Myrcans would love.'

Riven stared up at the Manse with its flapping pennants. 'No,' he said. 'I don't think they would. I think they would hate it.'

The big man gripped his shoulder. 'I had best put in an appearance at the feast. I am expected to be present where there is beer flowing.' He bit his bottom lip for a moment. 'Riven?'

'What?'

'Madra is... young. I know I am not such a blameless one as should be saying it, but try and find it in your heart to be good to her, for she is lovely.'

Then he turned away.

JINNETH HAD STILL not returned when the feast began. Riven walked the ramparts, watching the Dale under the young moon. He heard the sounds of merriment from the Manse, and he knew that Madra would be in there, pouring wine for Bragad and suffering the leers of drunk men.

And he watched the high hills to the west, and knew that out there, also, there were other women whose faces he knew. He continued his pacing, caught in contradictions. Better to turn over in his mind the arrangements he and Bicker had organised, to search for loose ends, gaps in the plan.

Steps behind him; light, not like those of the Hearthware sentries. They stopped at his side. He could faintly smell her sweat, and also the lavender of the garland she wore in her hair. She tugged it off and played with it in her hands as she watched the Dale with him, leaning on the stone of the wall.

You don't give up, do you? He smiled weakly.

There was torchlight in the longhouse where Bragad's men were billeted. They were making merry also. He wondered if the whole Rorim were drunk tonight. At least the Myrcans would be sober.

A wind stirred his hair, fanned Madra's out behind her. It looked black in the starlight.

'What is it you do in your world?' she asked him.

The question caught him by surprise. He realised that there were things he had done; but now, he did nothing.

'I was once a soldier, and then a storyteller.'

'You loved someone.'

He grimaced. 'She died.'

'But you still love her.'

'Yes.'

She squeezed his hand, and he looked at her.

'I'm sorry,' she said. 'I didn't know before.'

'Did Ratagan tell you?'

'Yes.'

It was cold in the clear night, with the wind running through the Dale. Her face seemed ageless in the dim light, and she was stifling shivers. He brought her inside his cloak, and wrapped it around the both of them. Her hands were chill, and she slipped them inside his shirt to warm them. He could feel them at the small of his back, feel the scratch of the lavender garland which she still held.

'How old are you?'

Her face turned up to him. 'I have seen sixteen summers.'

Sixteen. Jesus Christ.

'How old are you?' she asked.

'Old as the hills.'

'I do not believe you. You are not even as old as Bicker, and he has no grey in his hair.'

He laughed and hugged her closer, unthinkingly. He was responding to her presence. Warning bells sounded in his head.

I'm supposed to keep my wits about me, and an eye on those longhouses.

But he did not push her away. It was warm under the cloak. Her palms were no longer cold against the skin of his back. She rested her head on his chest.

'You are leaving after Bragad's visit, aren't you?'

'More news from the kitchens?'

'It is all over the Rorim.'

He cursed. Too many tongues wagged in this place. He wondered if Bragad knew, also.

An owl hooted nearby, and was answered by another farther away. A lone sentry stood watching on the ramparts some way off. The moon caught a glint of his metal armour as he turned in his walk.

'Shouldn't you be in at the feast?' Riven asked.

'Bragad asked the Warbutt if the captains and the lords could drink alone in the hall. The servers were sent out as well, as soon as the eating was done.'

'Talking about matters of import,' Riven said absently, though uneasiness buzzed at him like a fly. He watched the longhouses in the Circle. The torchlight still flickered at the windows, and there were faint bursts of song filtering out.

Doesn't look as though they'll be up to anything tonight.

Dunan and twenty Hearthwares were out in the Circle to keep an eye on them anyway. Luib was on the gates with his trainees. The Rorim itself was not so well defended, but they had enough men to neutralise Bragad and hold the gates—for a while.

So why the uneasiness?

He looked down from the ramparts to see Isay standing with his arms folded and his staff tucked into his belt. The sight reassured him.

'Why did you not go to the feast?' Madra asked.

'I wanted to be on my own.'

'Oh.' She drew away, but he pulled her close again. 'You are a strange man,' she said. 'You can get drunk and sing with the rest, and yet you like to be on your own. You never lifted a sword before, yet you use one as though you are born to it.'

'How do you know that?'

'Isay told me.'

'Isay!' The exclamation was soft, so the Myrcan would not hear him. He nuzzled Madra's hair. 'You get told everything, don't you?'

She did not reply, but her arms pulled him tight to her with surprising strength and she kissed him fiercely on the lips. Her thighs pushed his legs apart and she pressed herself against him.

'Let me stay with you tonight.'

And there was that formidable cast to her jaw, the steady sureness of her eyes.

'All right,' he replied hoarsely. The cloak fell away from her, and they walked along the ramparts to the catwalk stairs, the air cool on their hot faces. But Riven tripped on a shadow, and would have fallen if she had not caught his arm. He stared down.

'Oh, shit,' he whispered.

It was a dead Hearthware, lying in a dark pool of blood. He had been stabbed through the throat.

Riven straightened and glared over at the longhouses. The lights were still there, and he could hear the singing.

'Isay!' he yelled. The Myrcan was at the stairs in an instant, with his staff in his hands. His eyes fired as he saw the corpse of the Hearthware.

'Get to the hall—tell them what has happened,

and get them to secure the Manse. There are enemies in the Rorim, and probably more on the way.'

Isay nodded and pelted off.

'It is Phelim. He was only two summers older than me,' Madra said, with tears in her voice. She smoothed the hair back from the dead face. Riven pulled her to her feet.

'Go to the kitchens and warn them there. We are about to be attacked. Tell them to try and arm themselves.' He shook her. 'Tell them, Madra!' She looked at him wide-eyed for a second, then ran off in the same direction as Isay. Riven leant on the ramparts and drew a deep breath.

Think, Riven. What does this mean? What are they doing?

As he stood there, one of the Circle longhouses where Bragad's 'Wares had been billeted began to blossom with flame. Two figures were at its eaves with torches. Even as he watched, he saw lights flaming in the Dale in answer—and he saw Dunan and his men rush the longhouses with the moon glittering on their swords.

They are coming.

Luib's men were divided between the three gates in the outer wall. If their attackers were in any strength, it would not take them long to get through. Or they might just clamber over the wall at any point. The outer wall was a defence only against animals, not men. It was to protect the flocks and herds within, more than anything else. Not for the first time, Riven cursed the trust of these people in... other people.

The longhouses were ablaze from gable to gable now, and Dunan's Hearthwares milled about them.

Then Riven was jolted, as Isay nearly knocked him down.

'They have taken the hall,' he panted. 'Bragad's men hold it, and all in it; his 'Wares must have come over the ramparts in the night.'

And two left behind as a diversion. Clever. Was that a faint shouting he heard, away by the outer wall?

'Run to Dunan. Tell him to get his men into the Rorim, and to send a runner to Luib on the gates. We have to get everybody back to man these ramparts.' Isay turned to go, but Riven stopped him. 'What about our Myrcans? What are they doing?'

'Two guard the hall doors, with two 'Wares. Druim and Belig arm the household.'

'Good. Go on!' Isay leapt over the wall and disappeared into the depths of the ditch. A moment later he was up and running towards the blazing buildings in the Circle.

Riven stood alone on the eerily deserted ramparts, and chafed with impatience. Bragad's plan was clear now. Hold the leaders hostage in the hall whilst the larger force punch their way through the defences to take the Rorim from its leaderless and probably drunk defenders. His 'Wares had left their billets and accomplished the first part of the plan, leaving some of their number behind to allay suspicions. No doubt Jinneth and the two renegade lords of Ralarth were on their way, with God knew how many at their back.

Dunan's group began loping towards the Rorim, leaving two bodies behind them on the moonlit ground. They had half a mile to run. From the outer wall came the faint but definite sound of fighting.

Riven rubbed his sword hilt with a white thumb, thinking for a second of Madra pressing against him. He shook his head angrily, and heard a clatter of feet behind, coming up the catwalk stairs. He met them with a drawn sword, but it was Gwion and Colban and a score of others armed with staves, kitchen knives and clubs. Colban was sweating and breathless.

'Well met, Lord,' he gasped as his group trooped out along the ramparts. Then he leaned on the wall and rubbed his face with his free hand. 'I am too old for this sort of thing.'

Gwion was the only one of them who had a sword.

'Our people are helping the Myrcans guard the hall doors,' the Steward said. 'My wife commands them. There are many of Bragad's 'Wares in there, holding the captains. The doors have been barred. All the others I could find, I brought here.' He put his fist to his chest and coughed.

'You did well,' said Riven. Madra glided to his side with a knife in her hand. Their eyes met for a moment, then he looked away. 'Dunan and our Hearthwares will be here in minutes. More of Bragad's men are on the way. We have to hold the Rorim against them.'

There were frightened murmurs at this. In the clear night air, the sound of battle at the nearest of the gates was clearly audible. Gwion ushered them about like sheep and positioned them along the wall. Two-thirds of the ramparts were undefended.

There was a tumult at the gates, and in a few moments Dunan and the Hearthwares joined them.

'A fine night for a fight!' the Hearthware leader said, his teeth flashing and the blood shining on his sword. Isay took his place at Riven's side once more. As the 'Wares positioned themselves amongst the household, Dunan gazed out on the Circle. 'Luib is pulling his men out in feigned flight; when the foe attacks us, he and his men will take them in the rear.'

Riven nodded. And here it was. Four years in the army, and this is my first real battle—with a sword in my hand. He felt Madra's arm encircle his waist.

'Are you afraid?' she asked.

'You bet your life I am.' Then he frowned. 'You can't stay here. You can't stay in the middle of a battle.'

'There are other women on the ramparts.'

His face twisted as he glanced about him. 'I know, but—' He was conscious of the others there watching them. And he saw the stubbornness under her brows. 'Damn it.' And he turned away from her smile.

The sounds of battle on the outer wall ceased, and the night was quiet except for fidgeting on the catwalk. Madra was shivering again, her eyes fixed on the Circle beyond the burning longhouses. There was a distant crash as a roof collapsed in flames.

A figure appeared, running past the blaze and stumbling his way to the gate, which boomed open and then closed behind him. He lurched to the catwalk, the breath tearing in his throat and the sweat shiny on his face. A Hearthware.

'Where is Dunan?'

'Here, Fimir. What news?'

'Luib has lost nine men. He has pulled his lot away in flight.' Fimir seemed to choke on his words. 'It is Mullach and Lionan—our own lords! They lead the attackers.'

'How many are they?' Dunan asked sharply. The Hearthware gulped for breath.

'Luib tried to count. At least a score of 'Wares, and half a dozen Myrcans; maybe a hundred others, unarmoured like our trainees. Some of them are Suardale men—and Drynoch men!'

Dunan cursed softly. 'All right, Fimir; that was well done. Get your breath back. You'll be needing it soon.' Fimir nodded and tottered away.

'We have a fight on our hands,' Dunan said. He sucked his teeth. 'Our own Dales. And Myrcan fighting Myrcan. I'd like to know how the fox persuaded them to that.'

'Why would your people fight each other?' Riven asked Isay.

'I know not. But they will have had a good reason.' Doubt clouded his face, and he was troubled.

'Just kill their 'Wares for us, then, and we'll try and take care of your countrymen,' said Dunan dryly. He spat over the wall into the darkness of the ditch. 'I hope Luib's bunch bloodied their noses for them, or things are going to be rather tight around here in a few moments.'

They all heard the noise of feet at once, and instinctively leaned over the battlements, craning to see.

'There,' said Riven, pointing. 'Coming into the firelight.'

Then they were visible: a dark crowd of men with the light glinting off armour and sword blades, and two figures, one slim, one broad, leading them. They fanned out as they approached, and the Hearthwares on the catwalk produced bows from the sheaths at their backs and nocked them with pale-fletched arrows.

'Wait till the bastards get closer,' Dunan grated. The attackers halted and seemed to consult amongst themselves; then they gave a ragged cheer and charged, discharging a volley of arrows as they came. They hailed down and clinked on the ramparts. One of the household screamed and fell off the catwalk to the buildings below.

Then the Ralarth 'Wares fired, on Dunan's hoarse order. There was a hissing sound in the night, clear above the roar of the attackers, and men began to crumple below, hitting the ground with the feathered shafts decorating them. The charge hardly paused, however, and swarmed up to the gates in a rush. They milled there for seconds, a dark mass glinting like beetles in the light of the moon—and then there were thin, spiked shapes being raised against the walls. Slim tree trunks with the branches cut down to within a foot of the bole were placed against the battlements, and men began to climb up them.

The defenders pushed at the makeshift ladders, and at least one went crashing back down into the crowd below; but those who exposed themselves to do it were immediately the target of a dozen archers. Riven saw a Hearthware collapse with arrows in his face and neck. A cook from the kitchens took one in the eye and stumbled backwards with his hands pressed to his temples.

Dunan swore viciously. 'Those whoresons have twice as many archers as us. They'll pin us down and then swarm all over us.'

Enemy heads began appearing over the wall.

Many died there, with spear points in their mouths or sword blades splitting their skulls, but defenders were falling also. Riven hacked at the neck of one man who had a leg over the wall and saw the agonised face disappear. I've killed a man, he thought, but the realisation meant nothing to him in that mad moment.

Armoured Hearthwares with red sashes belting their middles laboured on to the battlements, with the defender's weapons pounding them like smith's hammers on an anvil. They reeled under the blows, but the heavy steel saved them and they recovered to push back unarmoured householders. Their comrades followed in a steady stream, like water widening a hole in a dyke—and then Riven saw Mullach top the battlements, with his hammer whirling about his head and the black moustache framing a snarl of a mouth.

The fighting became hand-to-hand all along the wall, blades flashing wickedly in the moonlight. Riven wanted to find Madra, for she was no longer at his side, but the man in front of him fell and he found himself confronting an enemy militiaman. His brain switched off, his limbs doing their job automatically. Their swords rang together, and Riven knew he was the weaker man. He was forced to back away, almost tripping over bodies and becoming enmeshed in other fights. He blocked blow after blow, but his healing bones were ready to collapse. The man grinned, seeing the defeat in Riven's eyes, and beat down his blade. He raised his own weapon again for the kill, and then fell forward on to his face with a knife buried to the hilt between his shoulders. Madra stood behind him, eyes wild, blood on her hands.

'Are you all right?'

He nodded, fighting for air. Isay staggered over with a crimson slash across his temple and gore clinging to his staff.

'I was held back!' he gasped, his face a maze of guilt and anger. 'I could not come in time!'

'It's all right. I'm all right, for God's sake.' The three stood in a momentary island of calm, whilst around them the fighting surged like surf beating up a beach. Wedges of red-sashed men were driving in up and down the catwalk, cutting the defenders off into pockets. Dunan was there, flailing like a maniac, whilst Mullach was laying about himself with something like ecstasy written all over his brutal face. And Lionan had arrived now also, poised like a cat on a merlon and watching the fight intently, the rapier a silver sliver in his hand. He wore a red sash. Riven wondered where Jinneth was—and the enemy Myrcans, also. He could see none on the wall.

The fight swayed towards them again, and Riven cursed, pushing Madra behind him. Chivalry, and the rest. He hated to see her with blood on her hands.

The fighting continued, spreading off the great curve of the ramparts down into the buildings below. Another fire started up somewhere, limning them all in orange and yellow. Ralarth Rorim was burning.

There were lights in the Dale now, as the men who lived there came forward to investigate the tumult. The night was a chiaroscuro of light and dark, moon and flame, steel and shadow, and the Rorim resounded with screams and shouts, the clash of metal, the crack of bone and thud of flesh. All order became lost as the battle opened out and a struggling press of men fought for the ramparts, the rooftops, the alleys between buildings. They slipped on the blood-slicked cobbles or tripped on the bodies that choked the ground. And above the flames of burning houses rose up to drown out the moonlight and rush hot air into their streaming faces.

Where were Luib and his men? Riven had time to wonder. Then he heard Madra's despairing cry, and turned to see the enemy Myrcans surging on to the ramparts, their staffs swinging, cutting down the defenders like corn.

Isay pushed Riven aside and stood holding his staff at the ready as his countrymen approached.

'Flee,' he said. 'The wall is lost. I will hold them.'

'Not on your life,' Riven spat, and he took his place at Isay's shoulder.

They saw Gwion fall with a smashed skull, a Ralarth 'Ware hurled down to the street below; and then the enemy Myrcans confronted Isay and Riven.

'Will you fight your own people? Have you fallen that far?' Isay yelled at them, eyes wild. The two leading Myrcans paused for a second. One of them pointed his bloody staff at Riven.

'You harbour in this place a lord of the Hidden Folk, an agent of this land's destruction. It is from his like, here and in the mountains, that the ruin of the Dales is come. Give him up and the fighting will end. You are of the same blood as us, sworn to protect Minginish. He would seek to destroy it. Your service has been twisted by shapeshifters and wizards.'

'Those are lies!' Isay cried. 'The lies of Bragad!' But the Myrcans were already upon them. Riven had no time to think before the Myrcan staff whistled around his ears, and smashed lights into his head.

Not again.

He fell, and was dimly conscious of Isay standing over him, swaying like a tree in a gale under the assault of his countrymen; then another figure joined him. Her hair swung as she bent to pick up his sword and he tried to move, to stop her, but could not. He saw the sword flash in his defence, and groaned.

Then there was shouting, and someone was crying: 'Luib! Luib has come!' And he could have sworn that he heard Ratagan's roar above the din of the battle. His head reeled. He smelled the burning in the air, saw the stars dimmed by smoke above him. The screaming would not stop, and he grimaced.

Dying in my own story. Bad luck, that.

Scenes flickered in front of his closing eyes. Lionan brought to bay like a wildcat, eyes blazing. Mullach falling with that rictus of hate still contorting his face. And Nurse Cohen above him, her head snapped back by a blow and the blood splintering from it. But it was not Nurse Cohen, it was Madra.

He groaned again, but could watch no longer. The dark took him, rushed on him like a cloud, and the noises stopped. The visions fled, the pain died.

CHAPTER TWELVE

ALL HE COULD make out was a blur of a face with dark hair framing it.

'Jenny?'

He said her name aloud, though it was someone else's voice that was cracked and whispering out of his throat. The white light that was the pain in his head receded as something cool was pressed to it. He could feel fingers on his brow. Then there was nothing again but the darkness; the darkness that he knew waited for him at the foot of the mountain.

THE HOT STILLNESS of the day made the water quiet. The waves lapped into the bay in a murmur, and the sun set the sea dazzlingly alight. Midges danced where the burn opened out into the bay; a haze shimmered off the rocks.

They were on a granite slab that had fallen

centuries ago, and lay by the shore with the water rippling at it. The remains of their meal were scattered around them, and some paper sheets, tugged by the slight breeze off the sea. He had his head in her lap and his eyes shut, listening to the sea and the faint call of gulls. She nudged him as the sleek dark head of a seal bobbed up scant yards from where they were. Two liquid brown eyes gazed on them with mild curiosity, rising and falling with the pull of the waves. They stayed quite still, smiling back at it, until it disappeared with a plop, leaving ripples of disturbance that were erased by the next wave.

He looked up at the face with the dark hair above him.

'Where am I?' he asked, rolling his eyes. 'What happened?'

She grinned down at him. 'You're near Glenbrittle. You fell off a mountain.' And she kissed him. 'Michael,' she said in a low voice, straightening.

'Mmm?'

She gestured to the papers that were anchored to the rock by a heavy stone. 'Don't put me in it.'

He blinked. 'Why not?'

'I don't know. It's a lovely place in there, all clean and shining and untouched.'

'They fight the odd war now and again,' he said dryly.

'Maybe—but the fighting in it is clear-cut and necessary, with less of the grey than there is in this world.'

He stirred. 'You're in it already. I can't take you out now.'

She made as if to poke him in the eye. 'Again? I knew it. And you never even asked.'

'Artistic licence. Besides, there has to be a heroine.'

She shook her head, half-smiling. Her eyes were looking out to sea. He could feel the warmth of her thighs under his head, her fingers in his hair.

'This third book had better be good,' she told him.

'It'll be a masterpiece. It'll make our fortune. We'll live in luxury for the rest of our lives.'

'This is luxury. Here. Now. We're on Skye, and it's summer. What more could you want?'

'You're distinctly odd, MacKinnon, you know that?'

She wrinkled her nose at him. 'How about some climbing this afternoon?'

'Where?'

She twisted and gazed back to where the Black Cuillins arced away in ridge after ridge of jagged stone, rearing up into a flawless sky.

'Sgurr Dearg. Let's climb the Red Mountain, and watch the world from the pinnacle.'

He was silent a moment, feeling the summer on his bones.

'All right,' he said at last.

AN ARM CUSHIONED his shoulders, and his face was close to the softness of one breast. He turned towards her, but the blankets entangled his legs and he fought his eyes open in irritation.

To see a strange room with a view of white hills out of the window, and a sheathed sword propped against the table.

He lay perfectly still, remembering, listening to Madra's quiet breathing. He reached out his hand and touched her face gently, traced the line of her lips with one fingertip, felt her hair. And then he let the tears come for a while, to trickle down his temples and wet his neck.

Forgive me.

The girl lying beside him stirred and woke. Her hand touched the compress on his head tentatively. When she saw he was awake, she made a sound that was half a sob, and buried her head in his shoulder. He stroked her hair.

'I'm not dead yet, you know.'

She laughed. 'It took you long enough to decide.'

He raised his hand to the cut at the side of her eye, the black and yellow bruise there. 'Was everything all right, in the end?'

'Luib came, and the captains overpowered their captors in the hall and joined us. We won.'

He wanted to hear nothing more for the present, and he put a finger to her lips. But looking out of the window, he saw the hills again.

'Madra—'

'You have been senseless for three days. It snowed for nearly all those days, and the Rorim stream has frozen over.'

He saw the ice at the corner of the window panes, the hard blueness of the sky was not a summer colour.

'Bicker and Ratagan want to see you as soon as you awake. And Isay is outside.'

'He's all right?'

She nodded.

'What happened?'

You're in Glenbrittle. You fell off a mountain.

'I will let Bicker tell you.'

'But you were there, with my sword. I remember.'

'The Myrcans struck me down. It is in my mind that they did not want to kill me, but Isay was left to face them alone. He kept shouting that they were wrong while he was fighting them, and in the end they listened. By then, Bragad's other men had surrendered, for they were surrounded and their lord was captive. The folk from the Circle came to our aid also, hundreds of them. They ringed the Rorim. The enemy could not escape.'

There was a knock at the door, and then Bicker, Ratagan and Guillamon walked in with Isay behind them. Bicker's face looked as though it had been ground out on a millstone, but Ratagan was beaming.

'You look worse than I feel,' Riven told the dark man.

He grinned ruefully. 'The strain of victory. I need another set of hands, and eyes in my backside. But I survive.'

'And I am getting used to picking you off battlefields,' Ratagan added. 'You have an unhappy knack, Michael Riven, of finding yourself in the thick of things. It is lucky your head is so hard.'

'Unhappy knack or no,' Bicker said, 'you have our thanks. You did a lot towards ensuring victory. Bragad took us by surprise. We had not bargained on being trapped in our own hall.'

'How did it happen?' Riven asked.

Bicker shrugged. 'It was so simple it shames me. Ten of his 'Wares crept over the ramparts in the night, and before we knew what we were at, they were holding swords to our throats as we sat at our wine. Had it not been for Unish and Belig and a few others, we would be there still. They broke through the upper windows and tumbled down in the middle of us. That was a time and a half, I can tell you. But we overpowered our captors and got out to find the battle in full cry and the northwest quarter of the Rorim in flames. By that time, Luib had gathered his men from the outer gates and was attacking the enemy rear. We joined in with a will. It must have seemed to Bragad's minions that we were falling on them out of thin air. Many died, Marsco among them—and Lionan, and Mullach. They will not be mourned. Murtach is at Ringill now, setting up a garrison of our own people.'

'Bragad and Jinneth?' Riven asked, a little afraid of what Bicker would tell him.

'Bragad is dead—slain by his own Myrcans,' Bicker said grimly. 'They do not like being deceived, the Soldier-folk. They have sworn allegiance to the Warbutt now. I have a feeling that it will not be long before Carnach's people do the same, for Mugeary is dead, killed by his nephew Daman. He is our prisoner at the moment.'

'So it looks as though the Rorims are under one leader after all,' Riven mused.

The dark man nodded. 'Of Jinneth there is no sign. There are rumours that she has fled the Dales—perhaps to the cities in the north. The snow will slow her flight somewhat, but we are not pursuing her. There has been enough killing. Enough fighting.'

'Your own lords...' Riven said softly. 'Do people still think I'm a wizard?'

Ratagan smiled. 'And a great warrior who stood steadfast under the attack of six Myrcans until he fell.'

'People talk too much,' Riven said.

'If there had been less talk these past few weeks, then perhaps the rumours that aided Bragad's cause would never have arisen. The household is rather more discreet, now, those that are left of them.'

'How many did we lose?' Riven asked.

Bicker looked away. 'Too many. Far too many.' He struggled to smile. 'We have made Ygelda the new Steward, and she says it will be nothing new to her, for Gwion was always running to her for help.'

There was a silence. Madra's fingers lingered briefly over Riven's head.

'It's snowing,' he said.

'There is almost a foot of it out there,' Guillamon told him, his blue eyes like ice. 'And midsummer is hardly past. Many of our people are out in the hills, bringing in the flocks, as are the Hearthwares— those we have left. The Giants have been sighted in great numbers to the west.'

It was speeding up. Riven felt incredibly mortal, but at the same time there was a rising restlessness in him. He felt that time was slipping through his fingers. The Greshorns were calling him. And so was Sgurr Dearg. He only wished he knew why. Perhaps the Dwarves would tell him.

'How bad is my head?'

Guillamon leaned forward and pulled down the lower lid of his eye. 'The skull was not cracked, I think. You need to rest for a few days, but you should be all right soon enough. As Ratagan has observed, your head is hard, Michael Riven.'

Riven lay back and stared at the ceiling. 'We must leave as soon as we can. Minginish has been trying to keep me here, in the Rorim. I don't know what we'll find in the mountains, but I know there are answers there.' He smiled slightly. 'In the book, that is where the quest finds an end. With the Dwarves. And on the Red Mountain.'

'We need time, here, to organise the Rorim,' Bicker said. 'That is for the captains to do. And we have to think about Carnach and Garrafad Rorim; they are leaderless and almost unreachable through the snow. With their garrisons at less than half-strength, and the Giants abroad, they are isolated and vulnerable.'

Riven sighed. 'I know. But if you want to tackle the problem at the source, then we must be on our way soon.'

Bicker made as if to speak, but Guillamon set one hand on his arm. 'Leave some of this with me. I can reorganise the Rorim, with Udairn and Dunan to help me. And Murtach has said he will lead a party to Carnach through the snows, once Ringill is secured.'

'That will be no soft journey,' said Ratagan.

'You've volunteered for a harder,' Bicker retorted. 'Or do you think we can grow wings and fly across the Greshorns?'

Ratagan laughed and bowed. 'I am chastened. But you are right, of course. I talked to Tagan before the battle. He knows the Greshorns, and has some pretty tales to tell of them—'

Guillamon rose. 'They can wait. The Teller here needs rest from your voice, Ratagan, and from our arguments. We will leave him to his nurse.' He gave a surprisingly bright smile to Madra.

They left, and Isay remained alone by the door. Riven caught his eye.

'Thanks, Isay.'

'I did my duty,' the Myrcan said, 'and reminded my people of theirs. Your life is in my care. Our world is in yours. Ward it well as I would ward you, and I shall be content.' He went to take his usual post outside the door.

Riven lay still, his head throbbing and Madra warm beside him. He heard the wind in the rafters and watched the snow whirl outside. Madra went to build up the fire. He watched her tuck an unruly lock of hair behind her ear as she knelt at the hearth, and was pelted with a score of remembered images. A dark-haired girl with firelight on her face, the smell of turf burning on a winter night, the sound of the sea raging at the shore in a fury of storm.

Winter. It was winter back on Skye; and now that winter was here, in Minginish. The curtain which divided them was wearing thin. Memory and imagination were grappling at each other's throats, and these people would lose if he lay here much longer. Of that he was sure.

'RATAGAN AND I will be coming with you, of course,' said Bicker, 'and Isay intends to watch over you. As we decided earlier, Tagan will join us, for his is the best woodcraft in the Dale; and Luib has agreed to come. He has given over the training to Druim and Unish. As Isay said, I think he wants to see the mountains around his homeland once again. I think also that three other Hearthwares shall come, in case we need to fight our way out of some tight spot. Rimir, Corrary and Darmid have volunteered. They were on the ramparts with you during the battle. That makes nine, which I reckon is enough. Don't you?'

'Seems fine,' Riven answered him noncommittally, though he was fidgeting with restlessness. 'What about mounts?'

'We shall have the best in the Dale, and two pack mules for extra food and gear, since we want to travel swiftly. Winter gear is being readied at the moment, but it will be hard, all the same, travelling in such weather.'

Riven nodded. The fire flickered about the walls of the room, but the wind was howling outside, lashing snow against the window and darkening the afternoon. Ratagan sprawled in a chair, his long legs crossed in front of him. His eyes were lost in the fire.

Bicker nudged him. 'You are very quiet, my hale and hearty friend.'

'I am already in mourning,' the big man replied. 'For the dearth of beer which I foresee on this trip.'

Bicker chuckled. 'Do not be so quick to grieve. There are towns and cities along our route which boast the best ale houses in the land, and whilst we cannot linger, we can, I am sure, find the time to slake a thirst or two that the ice and snow have worked up in us.'

Ratagan brightened immediately. 'I had forgotten that, in my ignorance. What it is to be well-travelled!' He stood up, his vast frame reaching to the ceiling. 'I shall miss warm hearths, warm beds and willing wenches before long, I do not doubt; but to deprive a man of his beer, that is true hardship.' He slapped

Bicker on the back, staggering him, then turned to Riven. 'The head is up to it, then?'

'It'll do.' Then Riven asked the question that had been gnawing at him for the last day: 'What about Murtach?'

Ratagan's face clouded. 'He stays in the Rorim, or at Carnach Rorim, where he is going after Ringill. He will not be coming with us.'

'Do I still make him unsure of where he is putting his feet?'

'Something like that,' Ratagan said. 'Murtach has always been a deep one, trusting no counsel but his own. He thinks you will find nothing in the mountains but stone and snow. He wants you sent back to your own world.'

'And you?'

The big man looked at him. 'I told you once before what I believe in, Michael Riven. I believe in friendship, also. If you believe that you can aid this world by standing on your head, then I will hold your ankles for you. It seems to me you have earned a little of our trust—while Murtach—'

'Trusts you about as far as he could spit,' Bicker finished.

'And he has always... liked... Madra,' Ratagan said.

Bicker got up. 'We will leave you to get some sleep. You will need all the strength you can muster on this journey.'

When he had gone out, Ratagan lingered a moment. 'Men do stupid things,' he said quietly, 'without ever considering them stupid. But often such things cannot be helped. We all fail in the end,

Riven. It's making a game of it before we go down that matters. I know. Regret is the bile of life.' And he smiled a wrecked smile. 'Murtach has never really failed, so he does not know such things happen.' Then he left, wishing Riven a good night, and a better morning.

TWO DAYS LATER they were ready to leave, and sat on their horses in the square before the Manse. There was still a smell of burning in the air, and around them the blackened shells of buildings were stark under a covering of snow. Groups of men had been working ceaselessly since the battle to tear them down and salvage what they could of their contents. The cobbles were littered with pieces of burnt wood.

My fault, Riven thought helplessly. Everywhere he went in this land, destruction followed. Perhaps Bragad had been right. Perhaps it was he who was truly destroying this place. But Bragad was dead. He wondered if Hugh was sitting in his office, watching the traffic outside and smoking his foul little cigarettes. And had he felt anything as his twin was slain here? Best not to dwell on it.

The snow had stopped falling and the skies were clear, but a bitter wind winnowed the Dale and they pulled their thick winter garments about their faces. The horses nosed patiently at the ground as they waited.

Riven searched for Madra. He had not seen her all day and badly wanted to say goodbye, but there was no sign of her in the crowd that had gathered to see them off. The Warbutt had not come down from his tower to wish his son farewell, and Bicker was grim and silent with his cloak held up around his mouth and ice crystals forming on it where his breath froze.

Ratagan was like a great bear, and he rode something approaching a cart horse. There was rime on his beard, making him appear grizzled and old.

The other members of the party, Myrcans and Hearthwares all, were similarly dressed, bundled in layers of wool and sheepskins, wrapped in cloaks of double thickness, with large saddlebags behind them. Two of the Hearthwares, Darmid and Corrary, led the two pack mules. Somewhere in those packs were the clothes Riven had entered Minginish with, though only Bicker knew that he had brought them along.

Guillamon stepped out of the Manse; he was grey and brittle in the cold, but his eyes were flashing brighter than the hard sky. Udairn was beside him, seeming younger than his son, and his wife Ethyrra was on his arm, looking like a frostbitten starling. Her eyes were red-rimmed, but the set of her mouth was as severe as that of a judge. Ratagan did not seek to meet her eyes.

Mira was there also, forlorn in the snowy courtyard as she contemplated Bicker leaving her yet again. The dark man had embraced her before he mounted, and whispered something no one else could hear. Now she stared at him as though she would never see him again.

'Better weather,' Guillamon was saying, eyeing the sky. He surveyed the company critically. 'Forgotten anything?'

'We have enough for three weeks' travel,' Bicker said. 'That will take us to the cities where we can buy more. We will make it easily, if the weather is kind to us.'

Guillamon turned to Riven and offered his hand. Riven took it without speaking.

'I hope you find peace,' was all the grey man said, before releasing his grip and stepping back. 'The blessings of the land be upon you. May the way be kind and journey's end what you hope it to be. Farewell.' He lifted one hand in salute, and the household copied him. Riven saw Colban there, smiling uncertainly; Dunan, Ord and others whose faces he knew. But Madra was not there. He kicked his horse with a small, angry sense of mourning and followed Bicker as they made their way out of the square to the gates of the Rorim; felt the wind rasp his face as they left behind the shelter of the buildings. Then they were in the Circle, and the Dale opened out before them in a vast, dazzling whiteness, powdery snow blowing in clouds off the summits of the hills. He stared at the icebound heights, remembering other mountains. He was following a shadow, but now he had an idea about where it was leading him.

Bicker was conferring with Tagan about the way to the north. They agreed over something, and Tagan rejoined his Hearthware comrades. Bicker led, and after him came Ratagan and Riven, Isay and Luib, then Tagan and Rimir and finally Darmid and Corrary leading the pack mules. The company buried their noses in their cloaks as their horses plodded through the hock-deep snow and the wind tore at their hair. They had soon left the Circle behind and were climbing steadily into the hills to the north, their horses' hoofs turning stones underneath the snow, straining on the steeper parts. Riven looked for a path, but could discern none through the snow and the frozen boulders.

The wind grew stronger as they rode higher. The rocks began to assume a mantle of translucent ice that dripped in grey icicles from overhangs. Drifts appeared, gathered up against sheer slopes and the larger boulders, and the snow blew across the hillside like smoke, coating themselves and their mounts with white and frosting their eyebrows. Riven wriggled his toes inside his boots in an effort to keep them from going numb.

The hills levelled out as they reached the crests, and they could see a vast, rolling country expanding blindingly far northwards; a sea of white, frozen breakers, tumbling into an unknown shore under a clear sky. The wind whipped at their cloaks and the horses kept their eyes half-shut against it. Riven was already thinking of bright hearths and warm beds as they made their way along the summits, following Bicker in single file now, their mounts' hoofs throwing up bobbles of snow that were swept away into the air as quickly as they were kicked up.

They halted for a short time near midafternoon to rest the horses. They had to break away encrusted ice from the beast's muzzles and try to rub warmth into them in the lee of a blunt hill. They ate meat and bread that was hardened by the cold, but Bicker would not allow them to eat snow. Their water was unfrozen, hung in skins from the saddle pommels where the warmth of the horses' bodies would keep it liquid. They could light no fire, and

Ratagan prophesied gloomily that their camp that night would be cheerless. They did not remain long, for the cold soon had them hopping about, and the journey was resumed. Riven wondered if it would be like this for the next six weeks, and wiped his nose, thinking of the dark girl barefoot in the snows. But when he tried to picture her face, all he could see was Madra, and the grave eyes under the dark brows.

The day drew on, and Tagan scouted ahead to look for a possible camping site. The tracker had ridden ahead more than once during the day, and to the rear and flanks also, though Riven could not imagine them being followed in cold such as this. They finally halted in a rough copse of thorn that had lopsided boulders scattered about it and was sheltered from the wind by the long shoulder of a hill. Ratagan set himself to starting a fire whilst the rest rubbed down the horses and searched for firewood. There was much swearing, but the big man finally had a leaf of flame springing up to lick around the dried heather curls from the tinder sack. When they had caught, the less-dry fuel was used, and the fire grew, much to the company's relief. They set out their bedrolls and crouched round the flames, except for the unfortunate Rimir, who had first watch.

'How far have we covered today?' Ratagan asked with a stiff-faced yawn.

'Not far,' Bicker replied, throwing more sticks on the fire. 'The country is less broken farther on, so we should make better time tomorrow and be out of the hills the day after that.'

'And then what?' Riven asked.

'And then the Great Vale, with the Great River, which we must follow north to Talisker.'

'A long way,' Ratagan said, and yawned again. 'Tagan thinks we are being followed.' They looked at him, then at the tracker where he squatted in his sheepskins, with his brown hand tugging at his beard.

'What, or who, by?' Corrary demanded, the fire catching glints in his red hair.

Tagan shrugged. 'I know not for sure. But there is something in the hills behind us, I am certain. I can feel the eyes in my back.'

'Maybe we should double back and ambush them,' Darmid suggested. His red hair mirrored his brother's.

Tagan shook his head. 'At the moment it is only a feeling of mine; a hunter's suspicion. Let me be more certain before we go trekking over ground we have already covered.'

'Sound wisdom,' Bicker said. 'I don't want to waste any more time if I can help it.' He nudged a steaming pot nearer the fire. 'But if all the Rime Giants ever spawned were after me, I would still sit here, for I need some hot food in me to fight the ice in my bones.'

They shared out the thick broth and dipped their bread in it, licking their fingers. Riven began to feel his ears and toes thaw out.

'And this is summer,' he muttered.

When they had finished eating, they lay unsleeping though well-wrapped before the fire and listened to the mournful wind. The horses stirred restlessly and the limbs of the thorns wriggled. The cold of the ground slowly seeped through Riven's bedroll to chill his back, and he edged closer to the fire, sick of the aches in his bones and counting out in his mind the hours before he had to go on watch. He was tired, but sleep refused to come. The cold held it at bay despite the glow of the flames on his face.

But sleep came unawares, for he was woken by Luib in the dark, and told by the peppery old Myrcan that it was his watch, and that Corrary was on after him. Riven struggled out of the blankets and the cold ate into him at once. He shivered as he buckled on his sword and took up his post, hating the chill darkness and the loneliness. But the wind had dropped, and he could see the stars.

He stamped up and down at the limit of the firelight and listened to the silence of the hills.

And heard the crunch of brittle snow, out in the darkness.

Not wolves, this time.

A figure approached him with its arms wrapped around its chest. It was bundled in furs and wore high boots. He drew his sword and watched it come closer. It moved stiffly, and yet there was something familiar there. He saw eyes, and then the cloak was thrown away from the face and he could see that it was her, blue-lipped with cold, reaching for him. She half-fell into his arms, and his sword slid to the ground.

'Mother of God! Madra, what are you doing here?'

She was shivering against him, and he helped her back to the fire and bundled her in his own bedroll; but she kept her arms about him.

'Hold me,' she whispered, and he tried to share his warmth, to stop her quivering. At last her clutch on him became less desperate and her shivers less violent. He looked at her in the light of the fire. No one else had woken.

'You followed us,' he whispered.

She nodded. 'I stole a horse and other things, and trailed you through the hills from a distance.'

'But why, damn it?'

'I wanted to come with you, to go with you to the mountains.'

'You crazy kid. We'll have to return to the Rorim with you now.'

'No.' Her eyes were blazing, but her voice was low. 'I'm not going back. I'd only set out again—and again—so you will have to let me come.'

'I think we must leave that up to Bicker. Have you any idea how long this journey is?'

'Have you? You know less about it than I do.'

He was silent in the face of her persistence, partly because he wanted to lose.

'Where is your horse?' he asked at last.

'Round the side of the hill. I'd best go and fetch him soon, for he is hobbled and there may be wolves about.'

'No. I will wake up Corrary in a minute. He can do it. You try and get warm.'

'I am warm,' she replied, with the hint of a smile.

IN THE MORNING, Bicker was ill-tempered when he was told of the latest addition to the company, but Ratagan was pleased. They argued for a while. Tagan was glad his suspicions had been vindicated. The Myrcans were inscrutable and the Hearthwares dubious, but when they finally set out again, there were ten in the company, and Riven had a new companion riding at his side. Bicker muttered to himself as he rode in front, but they made better time, for the wind had not risen and the sun was almost warm. They were able to let their cloaks drop from their faces and enjoy the view. The horses began to steam in the sunlit air.

Ratagan raised his face to the sun. 'This is more like travelling weather. If only it holds for a while.'

'We begin descending into the Vale tomorrow,' Bicker called from ahead. 'The weather should be milder there, with any luck, and the going will be easier.'

'And there may even be an ale house to brighten our way,' Ratagan added. He hummed to himself as they continued northwards.

The attack was so sudden that Riven had not even time to be afraid. His stomach jumped as grey shapes poured from behind the boulders ahead and loped towards them. Bicker's horse reared, and he shouted, 'Grypesh!' Then they were among them, milling about the horses, and the terrified animals were bucking and screaming and it was all Riven could do to stay mounted. Luib and Isay were the first to dismount, and Riven heard the familiar hiss and crack of Myrcan staves. He saw Madra fighting with her reins, hair wild; then a face out of a nightmare lunged up at him, and for the second time he confronted the tusked maw of a grypesh. With a twitch of its jaws it had ripped into his hide leggings. His horse spun wildly, but the grypesh held on, one of its claws digging into the leather of the saddle, the other curled round Riven's calf. He tried to reach for his sword, but could not. The beast's eyes shone at him and he felt the teeth touch his bare skin; then Isay appeared out of nowhere and brained it. The heavy grey body fell to the ground with a *scree* and was lost to view amid the plunging hoofs of Riven's horse. He saw that all the company had dismounted, and were fighting a desperate battle against the pack surrounding them. He swung himself off his horse and nearly fell, but managed to jerk his sword out of the scabbard. Isay was beside him, wreaking carnage with his staff. Riven held his reins in one hand and jabbed at the snarling grypesh with the other as they darted into his reach.

And then they fled. As quickly as they had arrived, the pack scattered and disappeared upslope into the maze of boulders and gullies, the odd stone rattling to mark their passing. They left the bodies of a dozen of their comrades lying lifeless on the ground behind them.

The company quietened the maddened horses, some of which were slashed along flanks or belly. Riven examined his leg and found that his boot had been ripped open like paper, but that his calf was only scratched. He felt sick at the memory of the beasts he had just seen.

Bicker mounted, and the Hearthwares hit the saddle a moment later.

'Come on,' Bicker shouted. 'They will be back, and in greater numbers. We must ride on at once and get out of the hills before dark.'

The rest clambered into their saddles, and followed him unquestioningly as he led them at a canter downslope to where the hills opened out, and patches of ground could be seen where the snow was melting. The horses were as eager to leave the scene of the attack as their riders, and the snow flew from their hoofs as they rattled along, blowing hard.

'Look to the heights on our left!' Corrary shouted, pointing. They stared and saw the grey flicker of movement there amongst the rocks, and kicked their horses on.

After a while, with their mounts winded, they halted. It had begun to snow, and small flakes were drifting down to settle on their eyelashes. They dismounted and walked the horses, Luib and Ratagan taking the rear. The land was flatter here, and there were fewer boulders strewn around. Bicker estimated that they had put some three miles between themselves and the scene of the attack. His steed was lame where one of the grypesh had gashed its forequarter, and he called a halt.

'We'll camp here,' he said wearily. 'We need to see to the horses if they are to bear us any farther. Tagan, you, Darmid and Corrary take a walk and see what you can see.' The bearded Hearthware nodded, and stalked off with his younger companions in tow. The rest of the company set to unsaddling the horses and building a fire. The wind began to pick up again, moaning round their ears. Riven occupied himself with trying to tie up what remained of his boot and leggings, whilst Luib and Rimir produced tarpaulins of waxed cloth from the packs and began constructing a crude lean-to to keep the snow from them. Bicker doctored the hurts of the horses with some strong-smelling salve, which he gouged from a small wooden box and smeared on their wounds.

The animals flinched as they felt it, but Isay held them firmly, talking to them in a quiet voice.

Madra helped Ratagan with the fire, and when Riven had done the best he could with his ripped clothing, he wandered about the campsite looking for firewood. There was a dried-up riverbed not far away, and along its banks were the skeletons of trees long dead. He snapped off armfuls of branches and brought them back in piles to Ratagan. He was soon helped by Madra and Isay, and the trio worked with a will in the growing twilight as the snow came down more thickly and visibility worsened. When they returned with one last load, Bicker stopped them from going out for more. He was sniffing the air worriedly, wondering where their scouts had gone. The fire was built up higher than usual to guide them back to the camp, but also, Riven thought, because they were imagining the packs of grypesh coming after them out of the heights of the hills.

Tagan and the other two Hearthwares reappeared some time later with snow covering them. They shook themselves before the fire and stood in the lee of the shelter.

'There were some tracks quartering the ground to the south,' Tagan said, rubbing his hands. 'But we could not follow them far in the snow. It was a small pack, maybe eight beasts. Not the one we fought. But there is at least one larger pack on our trail. This snowstorm might put them off, but we would do well to be extra watchful tonight.'

Bicker nodded. 'Two to each watch, then. But we'll eat before we fix them.' The lean-to trapped the heat of the fire, and the hobbled horses on the other side of the flames reflected the warmth also. It was crowded inside, but that made it warmer. They spread their bedrolls whilst Ratagan and Isay prepared food for the company. Madra lay next to Riven at the back, and he did not object when she piled the blankets over them both and pushed close to him.

The snow thickened as night fell, piling around their shelter and hissing at the fire. Ratagan and Luib took first watch, whilst the rest lay and listened to the wind, felt it tugging at the tarpaulin. It was hard to sleep with the image of the prowling packs on their trail. Ratagan stood with his hands spread to the fire and the flames winking on his axe blade. But he was looking outwards, to the wind-driven snow and the darkness.

'A wearisome night,' he said. 'And a long time till dawn. We need something to lighten the time. What about a story? Someone must have a tale to tell in our company.'

No one replied. He bent and threw a log on to the fire. 'Miserable wretches.'

'I have a story,' said Luib, surprising them all. His lined face was indecipherable in the firelight.

'It is a story of the Myrcans, and of the time when they first came to Minginish to take service with the people of the Vale and the Dales.' He paused for a second, staring into the fire. 'The Myrcans, when they were first created out of Dwarf-hewn and Giant-riven stone, took up residence in the broad Dale of Glen-arric, and in time that place became known as Merkadale, as it still is called today. They built homes throughout the Dale up to the borders of what is now Drinan, and their chief town was at Dun Merkadal. There they lived their lives, and prospered for a while; but there was a disquiet amongst them, for it was said that they had been created with a purpose in this life, and that the purpose had something to do with the manner of their creation. They were—and are—a hardy people, full of energy and unafraid. But they were never ones for the tilling of the soil; and they did not make great hunters. Only to one thing were their hands turned with skill, and that was killing. They thought then that they would set out as an army and conquer the rest of the land and rule over it; that was their mission. But some doubted and one, Rol, who was a great war leader, mistrusted the feelings which prompted the Myrcans to wage war and was sickened by the killing, so he set off into the mountains to seek the Dwarves and avail himself of their ancient wisdom.

'In the Greshorns, he wandered alone through the passes, climbed the peaks and was exhausted by the journey. Finally he lay down in the snow and determined to die, for his stamina had failed him and he had not found the Dwarves; and he did not want to go back to the life of killing he had led. It was then that the Dwarves came to him, fed him, warmed him in their mansions and asked his purpose, for no mortal man had ever travelled so far into the mountains. And he asked them what it was the Myrcans had been put on the earth to do, and they laughed.

'"If we knew that, we would know the purpose of our own lives, and mayhap the secret behind life itself," they said. "But no one can know that who breathes upon the earth."

'In despair, Rol asked them what he could do for his people except lead them in the killing of others in the land.

'They laughed again. "Not ours to answer that question," they said, "for you already have its answer within you. Look less far than the mountains the next time you wish your questions answered. Look at what has been given to you, and use it wisely." And then they were gone and he was lying in the snow of a mountainside, alone and cold.

'He journeyed back to his own people, with many adventures along the way; and when he was in Merkadale, he told the Myrcans that they had to stop the killing, that they were only trying to pick an apple that was already in their hands. He told them to go amongst the people of the land and offer them their service, to defend Minginish instead of conquering it; for the most earth a man ever needs is what is piled in his grave. So the Myrcans did so. In small groups they went out across the land and offered their services in its defence against the beasts, or against the wandering brigands which sometimes harried it.

'They were greeted with suspicion and hostility at first, and in more than one place they had to fight to prove they truly wanted to serve rather than to rule, to harbour rather than destroy. And some of the lords tried to misuse them, to pit them in small wars of conquest and pillage. But the Myrcans slew these lords, and sought better ones to replace them. Many faiths were broken before the people became convinced of the truth of the Myrcans' mission, but after a while, when no Myrcan had turned against the righteous lords, and they had not tried to usurp the rule of the Dales and the Vale, then they were at last accepted. This was long after Rol was dead. They became the guardians of the land, the scourge of any who tried to harm it, and every new generation issued out of Merkadale to take the place of those who had fallen for Minginish. The Myrcans found their purpose.'

The fire cracked, and Luib's story was ended. The wind rustled the loose flaps of the lean-to. Riven could feel Madra's soft breathing beside him.

Not a story. More like a sermon.

After a while he dozed, and then slid into a dreamless sleep. He disentangled himself from Madra before dawn to share his watch with Bicker, and the two of them saw the sun come up. The snow had stopped falling by then, and the sky was beginning to clear. The light grew over a white, silent world of vague hummocks and hollows, and the stars faded.

'A quiet night, after all,' Bicker said, his eyes on the flat land of the wide river valley ahead. 'And today we will leave the hills behind, and go to the places where men dwell.'

'The grypesh won't follow us, then?'

The dark man shook his head. 'I think they would have lost our trail in last night's snowstorm. If it had been Rime Giants following us, we would have had a more difficult time of it; they enjoy such conditions. But grypesh do much the same as we do: they hole up and wait for the weather to pass.' The first sunlight touched the snow and picked shadows out of their faces.

'It's so far away,' Riven murmured, but Bicker heard him.

'Are you that eager to get there?'

'I don't know. I was.'

'Maybe it is not only the Myrcans who are looking for a purpose.'

Riven barked a mirthless laugh, and remembered Guillamon shaking his hand.

I hope you find peace.

'I don't want anything,' he said roughly, though he was no longer sure if it were strictly true. He twisted away from the thought of the sleeping girl in the shelter.

THE SUN DAZZLED the company as they continued on their way. The horses seemed to have recovered, but they kept to an easy pace as the snow was deep. It was almost warm, and Riven hung his cloak by the saddle bow. The country rolled endlessly beyond his sight, and he abandoned himself to the routine of riding, resting, eating and sleeping.

Three days passed with no signs of pursuit. His limbs ceased to complain about the riding, and he slept more easily on the hard ground at night. Tagan roamed the country to the north of the company, but it was deserted, empty of both men and beasts. They saw a few hares, two of which the tracker managed to shoot for the pot, and there were buzzards overhead sometimes, but that was all.

Carnach Rorim was to their east as they continued, and Tagan saw one of its patrols once, far off, but the company went unnoticed. They had no more snow, and the streams they crossed were free of ice; the unnatural winter was less severe now that they were out of the hills.

Ten days after they had left Ralarth Rorim, they saw the silver sword-glitter of a river in the distance. Bicker shaded his eyes and peered north with satisfaction.

'The Great River. We have made good time. We shall reach it tonight, and tomorrow follow it northwards.' He grinned at Ratagan. 'And soon we will be within smelling distance of ale houses, my thirsty friend.'

'Praise be!' the big man responded. 'My stomach had all but resigned itself to a life of poverty.'

As the day wore on, they heard everywhere around them the rill of running water, and grass began to poke up through the snow in clumps. Riven even heard skylarks sporting over the open meadows. The company began to take off their winter clothes, and the saddle bows became piled with sheepskins.

'We leave winter behind us, it seems,' Tagan said, turning in the saddle to look back at the still-white hills. He shook his head. 'Strange times we live in.'

'When the real winter comes to the land, there will be lean times,' Corrary said, spitting over his mount's shoulder.

That evening they camped beside the broad river on ground that was free of snow. The sun spangled on the water as it went down into a red wrack of clouds. Luib studied it as the others set up camp.

'A fine day tomorrow, and no more snow in the air. We've been given back our summer.' He glanced at Riven, and then began unsaddling his horse.

'I am glad,' said Ratagan. 'Snow is a fine thing for children, but at my age it looks less pretty.'

'You are not so comely yourself,' Bicker laughed.

The river was almost half a mile wide, with several islets dotted throughout it that were alive with wildfowl. Riven glimpsed the blue flash of a kingfisher as he set out his bedroll, and paused, memories of wheelchairs and white-clad figures nagging at him.

It stayed light till late, the last scarlet wash of sunlight lingering in the clouds at the brim of the horizon. They sat around the fire, letting the horses graze freely with Rimir and Darmid to look after them, and listened to the birds that sang in the reeds thronging the riverbank. The sky remained clear, and a mist rose out of the river as it darkened. They brought in the horses, hobbled them and built up the fire. Then they lay like the spokes of a wheel around it and heard the sound of the river and the night fowl before drifting off to sleep.

In the morning, Riven lay half-awake, listening to the sound of the water close at hand, and for a few moments thought it was a quiet tide outside the bothy. He opened his eyes to be caught by the early morning sun, and to see that Bicker and the Myrcans were already awake and fixing breakfast. It was warm under the skin rugs, and now that Madra had taken off most of her winter clothing he could feel the shape of her, curved next to him. He moved his hand and touched her breast through the robe she wore, found the nipple and stroked it until it hardened and she stirred. Then he pulled himself out from under the rugs, feeling ashamed, and walked over to where the bank was free of weeds. He stared down at the slow-moving water, seeing a vague, bearded reflection. Then he knelt and thrust his head into the water, its coldness bringing a shout to his lips.

They moved on again with the river coursing slowly in the growing light beside them, and the birds darting out in front of their horses' knees. The Great River swept sluggishly through meads that were aflame with buttercups and dotted with the last patches of melting snow. Copses of beech and alder appeared, straggling along the banks with their roots lost in a tangle of briars and bracken. The sun set alight the water drops that speckled their leaves and shadowed the ground beneath them. Flies danced in the air.

It was Corrary who pointed, and drew their gaze to the dark shadow on the water. They squinted into the sun and made out the shape of a boat near the midstream. It was flat and broad, and a crowd of sweating men on the deck were poling it upstream amongst the bird-filled islets. Their voices were faint at this distance, but they could be seen gesturing towards the company. A tall, dark figure with no pole moved amongst them issuing commands, and slowly the flatboat drew over to the bank. Bicker reined in his horse, and the rest followed suit, the Myrcans sliding their staves out of their belts.

'River traders,' said Ratagan. 'Not pirates. They are probably heading up to Talisker.'

The poles slid glistening in and out of the water as the craft approached and then beached with a bump. Men jumped on to the bank to secure it, and the man who had given the orders leapt overboard with a silver plash, two others behind him. He held up an open hand in salute.

'Greetings, fellow travellers! We are well met on this fine day indeed. Finnan is my name, and you see my craft and my trade before you.' He bowed. He was very tall, taller even than Ratagan, though only half as broad. He had a bright head of closely cropped golden hair that the sun turned to silver, and a darker, neat moustache on his upper lip. He was dressed in weather-stained leather that was decorated with scarlet and yellow thread, and there was a slim sword hanging from his hip. The men behind him were brawny and short-haired, their bare arms reddened by sun and wind and their bare feet wet and muddy. They eyed the company, especially the striped faces of the Myrcans.

'For Talisker we are bound, with a pitifully small cargo of hides and grain that the weather has played havoc with.' Finnan had a cheeky grin that had nonetheless something guarded about it. He reminded Riven a little of the Bicker he had known at the bothy.

Bicker did not dismount, but leaned forward in the saddle and nodded to the river pilot.

'I was wondering,' Finnan went on, 'seeing your company so finely decked out for travelling, if you were by any chance headed the same way?'

'And if we were, would it concern you?' the dark man asked politely.

Finnan laughed. 'Why, of course. We can both aid the other here if we've a mind to. Passengers would make my trip profitable after all, and the river journey would be quicker and save the horses. It is a long way to Talisker, and there are fewer beasts to be met on the river than on the land these days. What do you say?'

'And how much do you charge for your ferrying?' Ratagan called out to him.

'A modest amount, no more. I am not a greedy man. Say a knuckle of silver from each of you; no more than you would balance on a fingertip. As I say, I am not a greedy man.'

'You are not,' Bicker admitted. 'That is a fair offer—but why be so generous?'

Finnan shrugged. 'I am tired of poling the river, telling the same stories and hearing the same ones in return. My crew would like to hear some new news from the Dales.'

'Indeed?' Bicker's gaze had suddenly sharpened. 'And is there no news forthcoming lately?'

'Much, but all of it hearsay. You have Hearthwares and Myrcans with you. Some of you have the look of lords, yet you bear the mark of hard travelling and your steeds are scarred. I have heard of a battle, of Myrcan fighting Myrcan, and many upheavals amongst the Rorim to the south. I am curious to know more. That to me is worth more than silver, for I think much about the state of the land in these strange times, with snow falling in midsummer and the Giants wandering the hills.'

'And you think we can sate the curiosity you harbour?'

Finnan smiled. 'I am sure of it. We carry beer on board. It is a fine thing to talk the evenings away, when the river work is done, with a mug in your hand. A weakness in me, some call it. I say, a foible that any man is entitled to.'

Ratagan let out a deep laugh. 'Well said, waterman. What do you think, Bicker? Do we take up Finnan's offer, or wear down our horses' hoofs further?'

Bicker stared at Finnan for a long moment, then turned to take in the rest of the company. 'Is anyone here against this?'

There were no answers, and he nodded.

'Very well, Finnan. Run out a ramp and we'll board our horses. You shall have your silver and your news, in return for a safe trip upstream to Talisker's Rivergate.' He spat on his hand, and Finnan stepped forward to slap it.

'A worthy bargain, and a wise course for us all. Welcome to the river, my friends.'

CHAPTER THIRTEEN

THE FLATBOAT WAS forty feet wide and at least twice as long. At the stern was a large, squat cabin which had the steering oar on its roof. There was an open hold half full of sacks and bundles of cured hides, and here the horses were put. Large tarpaulins were pulled over the hold whenever it rained, and most of the crew slept in their shelter. Finnan's passengers stowed most of their gear in the hold and the Hearthwares slept there, but there was room for the others in the three-sided cabin, though the roof was so low they bumped their heads. The boat had a crew of twenty, and they laboured from dawn to dusk in two shifts to keep the clumsy craft moving against the current, poling it away from sandbars and small, reed-covered islands.

But Finnan was true to his word, and there was beer that night to drink when they had beached and set the horses to graze ashore, and lit their fires on the bank. And they could see for the first time the lights of settlements off in the dark distance of the Vale. Finnan labelled them as they ate their evening meal.

'Corriad, Bemnor, Drum Larad; and that larger one there, that is Conwere. It used to be a good town for the hides trappers brought down out of the hills, but that trade is gone now, along with many another. Times are hard even here. They'll be harder before we see the spring, if the spring is to come when it should. The way the year is running, we could have a drought at midwinter and snowdrops at harvest time. Very unsettling.'

'Have you sailed the rivers long?' red-haired Darmid asked him.

'A fair number of years. A good way to see the land without getting bow-legged doing it, or flat-footed. The river is placid here, where it becomes patient in its long run to the sea and decides to slow and look at the land it passes through. A man can learn a lot from the river.'

Bicker leaned forward to toy with his mug. 'How have the lands in the Vale fared over the past year? It is months since I have been near them.'

Finnan was staring at Madra, and Riven could see her staring back with one eyebrow raised, eyes steady. The river pilot smiled crookedly and then turned to Bicker.

'The villages down near the river have been almost untouched, but many farms in the hills are now deserted, where their people have fled the grypesh and the Giants. Packs roam everywhere at will and the few towns have not 'Wares enough to police the whole countryside, so the farmers and herders are mostly left to fend for themselves and, as I said, the hunters are all but ruined. Many of them have been slain, and those who still pursue their craft do so in large bands, which means for bad hunting, even while it keeps them alive.'

'It is worse in the Dales,' Ratagan put in. 'There they raid right up to the walls of the fortresses, and within.'

Finnan looked down into his beer. 'I had heard that. I heard more, besides. How much of it is true?' He glanced at Isay and Luib, but the silent Myrcans did not appear to notice him.

'There was fighting,' Bicker admitted with a frown. 'There were misunderstandings, but all has settled down.'

'There was a battle?'

'Yes. Many died. The three western Dales are under one leader now.'

'Would it be a man named the Warbutt?' Finnan asked offhandedly.

Bicker shrugged. 'It might.'

Finnan was thoughtful. 'A great leader, if the rumours are true.'

Bicker scowled. 'I have heard that said about him.' He rose abruptly. 'I must go and see that the horses are secure,' and he left the fires for the darkness where Rimir and Corrary stood guard with two of Finnan's sailors. The river pilot watched him leave.

'A man with much on his shoulders, if I am not mistaken. How else can he ignore loveliness seated so close to him?' Here he raised his cup to Madra and then drained it with a flourish. 'Our journey will be the lighter for the sight of it.' Then he stood up and stretched. 'I have my own steed to see to, also.' He went off in the direction of the river and the dark bulk of the flatboat.

Riven threw back the last of his beer. None of my business. I don't own anyone.

He looked at Madra, but she was gazing into the fire and did not see him.

THE NEXT MORNING was fine and clear, after a mist was burnt off the water by the rising sun. Riven sat at the bow with his eyes in the dazzle of the water. To him the passing of the water was interminable, the shining poles like the dipping legs of a stranded insect. There were houses of turf and stone close by the river, and sometimes they passed rowboats, but the flatboat was sailing up against a rock wall it could not scale. This world was real. He had held it in his arms in the dark and kissed its eyes. Somehow he had been infused with some of its magic—that word again, he thought wryly. Well, it's as good as any other. So he was a wizard, in away. He made the seasons change and brought facsimiles of his own world's people into this one. But there was more to it than that. Minginish itself had its fair share of magic. Hence the dark-haired girl who did not know him and who wandered Skye and Minginish at will, searching for something she could not recognise. If Riven were responsible for Jinneth, then the land itself was responsible for Jenny's other incarnation. Two of them, here. But how much of his wife was in either?

And here the rub, the wall which always halted him. Was Jenny really dead? Was she at peace, or was there a part of her that was even now wandering Minginish? That idea he could not bear.

So he was travelling north, into the mountains. And if he could not find the Dwarves, then he was going to Sgurr Dearg and home. Try perhaps to write a happy ending for this world and the people in it. Perhaps that would be enough for them, if not for himself. Most of all, though, he had to make sure that his wife rested in peace.

So take it as it comes, for the moment. Enjoy the trip.

Unwillingly, he found his gaze dragged to Madra. She was on the cabin deck with Finnan, Bicker and Ratagan, a smile lighting her face. Did she smile more often these days?

He dragged his eyes away again and watched the labouring backs of the sailors. Darmid and Corrary sweated there too, whilst a grey-bearded, scrawny riverman criticised their poling. The Hearthware armour was a shining pile on the lower deck.

THREE QUIET DAYS went past in the slow slap and plop of the river. They had warm days and clear, cold nights, when they sat round the camp fires or stood guard over the horses. During that time, they stopped to talk to no one, though they passed other craft on the river whose occupants stared at the company. Apparently Myrcans and Hearthwares were a rarity in these parts.

There were straggling villages that trailed along the bank, with a boat to each house and nets hanging to dry or to be mended. The Great River was the highway for many towns and villages; the only highway that was still safe.

The horses of the company were making the most of their rest. Their wounds had healed and they were in full flesh again, frisking by the riverbank when they were disembarked to graze.

On the fourth evening of their waterborne journey, they tied up at a place which had thickets of hazel and birch growing near the water. The ground was boggy underfoot, though there was grass in abundance between the trees. They let the horses wander there with Rimir, Isay and two of Finnan's men watching over them, then found a relatively dry spot and set up camp in what had become their normal routine. The cooking fires were lit and pots were set over the flames to boil. Some of them gathered firewood, others drew water. Riven wandered away from the camp into the trees, and shook his head to Isay's questioning look.

'I won't go far. I want to be on my own.'

He rubbed the muzzle of a horse when it nosed up to him, and scratched its ears. Then he walked deeper into the trees as the twilight thickened around him and the stars began appearing among the branches over his head. He sat with his back to the pale bark of a birch and hugged his knees to his chest.

Been here long enough. Beginning to like it, that's my problem.

Leaves rustled behind, and he could not stop the smile when Madra sat down beside him.

'A pleasant night,' she said. 'There will be a moon later on, and we'll have mist by the morning.' She rested her head on his shoulder, and even at that slight touch he felt the familiar stirrings. He moved slightly away, and she had to lift her head.

'Why?' she asked thickly.

Why? Because there is a woman I love who may yet be out there with a heart that is beating.

But he said nothing.

'Finnan asked me if I was spoken for by you.' He looked at her for the first time and saw the tears on her cheeks, glistening in the starlight. He put his arm about her then, and drew her close.

Oh, you hero.

'I don't know what you want.'

He closed his eyes and leaned his head against the cool bark of the tree. 'I'm not sure I do any more. I'm sorry, Madra. Getting to know me was a bad idea.'

'But does it have to be that way?'

'It does if you want your world to survive.'

'But one moment you hold me, the next you push me away.'

He cursed softly. 'I'm just a weak fool who can't do what he should. I'm sorry.'

'What is it you are going to do in the mountains? Who is it you are going to meet?'

'I don't know. The Dwarves. My—my wife, maybe.'

She stiffened, and whispered, 'You said she was dead.'

Slowly, hopelessly, he said: 'She is, in my world. But somehow she is here, in Minginish. I have seen her... here.'

Madra pulled away from him. 'How can that be? How can she be here?'

Riven's hands fell to the earth and the leaf mould. 'I don't know. I don't know how any of this happened. I didn't ask for it.'

In a quiet voice, Madra said, 'Neither did I.'

They were silent for a long time. Her eyes were very dark in the dim light, her hair like a hood that shadowed her face.

'What was she like, your wife?'

It seemed he heard that question again, a thousand years ago and in another world.

'She was... a lot like you, in some ways,' he said at last, admitting it. 'More reckless, maybe, and afraid of nothing.' But that was what had killed her. That, and a rope he had forgotten to replace.

Madra touched his face, traced the old scars on his forehead.

'You saw her die.'

Michael!

'Yes.'

She pulled him to her and held him as though he were a child, kissing away his frown. They lay still. Off towards the river, one of the horses nickered loudly. Then the night was quiet again.

Except for the sound of feet on the leaves, thick as the patter of heavy rain on the floor of the wood. Riven sat up, then jumped to his feet as he saw the glitter of the eyes and the shadows moving amongst the trees. He bent and seized Madra's hand, pulling her to her feet.

'Come on!'

They pelted away, with the leaves flying at their heels and the sound of the pursuing feet closer, along with the squealing as they were sighted. They zigzagged around tree trunks and saw the dark shapes scurrying along out of the corner of their eyes. The breath sawed in their throats.

Madra tripped and fell headlong in the leaf mould,

and in an instant their pursuers were upon her. She disappeared with a scream as a grypesh leapt. Riven yelled incoherently and swept out his sword. He buried the blade in the beast's back and it jumped off her, snarling. Then a heavy body struck him from behind and knocked him down, the fetid breath on his cheek. He rolled, and felt claws rake his ribs, but gripped his sword and thrust upwards. Hot liquid and entrails spilled over him, and he scrambled out from under the thing. He threw himself forward, startling the beasts that were tearing at the prostrate girl on the ground, and arced his sword round with manic strength, tearing the blade through two of them with one swing. But there were others to take their place. He raged at the futility of it, and shouted for help as his blade hissed and crunched, but his arms were tiring and he could feel blood running down inside his tunic.

Then men burst into view under the trees, and there were half a dozen others there with him, their swords shining in the moon. Two Myrcan staves were splintering bones. Riven heard Bicker's voice.

'Get back to the boat before we're overrun!' Two figures bent and picked up Madra, and half-carried, half-dragged her away, whilst the rest fought a running battle with the maddened grypesh. They could not be forced away, but came on in ever greater numbers, shrilling with pain and anger.

They emerged from the trees, and Riven could see that the open space before the river was alive with the great grey-furred beasts and their cold eyes. They swarmed like lice over the camp, and there was a battle being waged at the boat. Some men were trying to push out of the shallows, whilst others held off the beasts. The moonlight splintered on the foaming water as they fought calf-deep in the river. Already bodies were floating sullenly at the bow, and others were drifting slowly downstream. But they were not all grypesh.

Riven's group cut and slashed their way to the river without respite. The animals which fought there gave little heed to defence; they massed around them and tried to engulf them. There was a sudden space when the man at Riven's shoulder went down with a cry. He did not come up again.

They splashed into the shallows and slipped on the smooth stones. The boat was drifting into the current, the long poles dipping in the dark water and pushing her away. They were floundering chest-deep, and Riven went to Madra's head, helping to hold it above the water. The grypesh swam out after them, and there were battles fought there in a welter of blood and foam. Riven could see nothing for the water in his eyes, but when the dark shape of the hull loomed up he pushed Madra towards it. Other hands took her from him, and he grasped the side of the craft, too tired to pull himself up.

Teeth sank into his leg, and he was jerked under the water. He choked for air, water gurgling into his ears and fighting to enter his mouth. The teeth shook him. His hands met a furry body and claws that flailed at him. He dug his thumbs into the eyes, a red bonfire blazing at his chest, and heard an underwater bubbling squeal. Then he was released, and whooping for air in the moonlight. Something hooked under his collar, hauling him upwards and choking him. He tried to fight it, but he had not the strength. He was lifted out of the water and dumped with a smack on hard wood. There he lay, gasping and looking into the unreadable eyes of Isay.

Finnan was shouting commands, and swords were still flashing at the beasts who fought to clamber on board. Riven had lost his in the river, but he snatched up one of the long river poles and stabbed it down on the crowds of hairy heads that thronged the water, clicking against skulls. But there were too many of them. They swarmed on board with the agility of rats and leapt for the defenders. The flatboat drifted helplessly downstream like a stricken beetle, as the crew fought for their lives against wet teeth and rabid eyes. Men went down with two or three of the beasts ripping at them; or fell overboard and were killed in a froth of churning water. Riven managed to prise a knife from a dead sailor's hand and stood between Isay and Darmid as they tried to keep their attackers away from Madra's still form on the deck. The Myrcan stave was almost invisible as it smashed bones and cracked skulls, hurling the animals into the river, and Darmid's sword wreaked havoc also. Riven darted in with a stab when he could, but there was little room between them. He stepped back and chanced a look at Madra. Blood marked her torn robe in many places and her eyes were closed, but she was breathing.

Darmid fell with his throat torn out and a grypesh worrying at it. Riven stabbed his knife in deep behind its ear and it went limp. Then he picked up Darmid's sword and met the next grypesh with a savage thrust that disembowelled it. There were fewer of them now. The flatboat was out in midstream and the current was carrying the swimming beasts away.

The defenders' plight was no longer so desperate. They advanced steadily along the boat, forcing the grypesh back until the grey beasts were scrabbling on the cabin deck. Bicker and Finnan killed the last one there. Its body fell with a loud splash, to be taken by the river. Then the fight was over.

Bodies lay in heaps on the deck, in the cabin, in the hold. The flatboat was dripping with blood. Wounded men were groaning quietly, and a crippled grypesh bubbled with pain until a sailor finished it off. Riven bent to Madra, but did not know what to do. He glanced at Isay helplessly. The Myrcan's face was a wilderness.

'Twice I have failed you, Michael Riven. Third time pays for all. It will never happen again.'

Ratagan stalked over the bodies towards them with his clothes in shreds. 'Is she alive?'

Riven nodded, but could not speak. He took off his bloody tunic and wrapped it around her, smoothed the hair away from her face.

There was a lurch and a bump. A grinding noise started from the hull, then was still. They looked up, and saw that the boat had drifted against an islet in the river. The current held it fast there, and it drifted no farther.

'OVER HALF MY crew are dead,' Finnan said. The firelight flickered over a face as grim as stone. He poked the embers with a stick. 'I am not even sure they will be enough to crew the boat upriver.'

'We will take the place of some of them,' Bicker said, 'though our people have suffered also. Three of our company were lost, Darmid, Rimir and Tagan, and the maid is grievously hurt. That leaves six to man the poles along with your eight. It should be enough.'

'Most of our gear has been lost, and all your horses,' Finnan went on as if he had not heard him. 'But why they attacked in such numbers and with such determination is beyond my ken. They even took to the river. Why would they behave in such a fashion?'

Bicker shrugged, but his eyes flicked over the fire for a second to Riven. And Riven sat beside Madra as she lay on most of the bedding they had left, with strips of cloak bound about the wounds which bit into her, and Ratagan on her other side with his face twisted in concern. She was conscious, but could not speak because of the gash at her throat. She smiled for Riven, though, and that smile was like a sword blade thrust in his chest. He gripped her hand with white knuckles, and could say nothing, to her or to anyone else. He felt he had finally been given the spade to bury himself with.

'How many days to Talisker?' Bicker was asking Finnan.

'Just over a week,' the pilot replied. 'Maybe somewhat longer for us, now, with everything.'

'Too long,' Bicker said with quiet savagery, burying his eyes in the fire.

They buried the bodies of those who had died on the boat, but had to leave the others where they were, for grypesh could be seen prowling on the bank. There were scores of the animals. They were all set to poling now, and it was hard work navigating the flatboat upstream. For Riven, it was agony. He seemed to have cracked bones complaining all over his body, and when they stopped at night, he ate, stayed by Madra for a while, and usually fell asleep beside her.

They moored in the evenings to various of the islets dotting the river. They did not dare camp on the western bank where the attack had been; the eastern bank showed no signs of life, but the tangled strips of trees continued along it and they mistrusted what they might hide. Even so, Bicker and Luib had to hunt on the eastern bank to supplement what food they had left. They found deserted houses, sometimes whole hamlets left lying empty with mutilated cattle in the fields around them. The land was dead and uninhabited, and the carrion birds were never out of the sky.

A week went past, and the picture did not change. Madra's wounds began to heal, but her voice did not come back. The rest of the crew and the company poled doggedly on, and most days the silence was broken only by the plop of the water and the odd cry of wild fowl. It grew warmer, and the mosquitoes that shimmered over the water began to plague them incessantly. They lit smoky fires at night to keep them at bay, but were soon itching with bites.

After nine days, they sighted Talisker through the haze. The river curved in wide sweeps through the flat of the Vale, with hedged fields surrounding it, and in the middle of one great meander there was a steep-sided hill on which the city was built. It was like a mountain of walls and houses and streets rising out of the Vale with the river curling round its feet, lapping at the high walls. The light glinted off a white tower at the very summit of the hill, and Riven caught the glitter of metal on the battlements as a helmet or spear blade caught the sun. In the river around the walls were crowds of boats filled with a multitude. Their noise could be heard even at this distance, and a hint of the smell drifted down the wind.

'And here we are,' said Finnan. All his gaiety was gone now. 'That is the river market you see before you in the water. On those boats you can buy anything from a loaf to a life. I have kept my half of the bargain, though I never guessed how costly it would be for me. Beyond the river market is the Rivergate. We shall pass through there to the city docks.' For a moment his eyes turned away from the city to the sleeping form of Madra. 'What will you be doing for her?'

'We must find a leech,' Bicker replied. 'In that great city it should not be hard.'

'I know one,' said Finnan. 'I will take you.'

After a while they were poling through crowds of anchored boats that teemed with people. The craft were tied together, and there were mazes of decks and gangways. It was almost like a second, floating city in the shadow of Talisker itself. Hundreds of voices were crying out their wares. There were drunken brawls that rolled from one vessel to another and ended with a splash in the cloudy river, and there were glimpses of painted female faces, bodies barely concealed by thin silk shafts. Invitations and threats, bargaining and cursing filled the air, coming from the mouths of men, women and ragged children and mingling with the sound of dogs barking, chickens fussing, mules braying. The surface of the water was littered with scraps of cloth, pieces of rotten fruit, mouldy vegetables and human detritus, and the air was as crowded, with the smell of excrement, rotting meat, unwashed bodies and a thin sting of strong spice. To try and take it in was like drinking too strong a wine. Riven turned his attention to Madra, and brushed the flies away from her face.

Somehow Finnan made sense of the tangled labyrinth, and brought them through the lanes and alleys of boats until they could see looming ahead of them the solid sunwashed stone of the city wall. It reared high above their heads and made the river market into a town of ants, the meaningless scurryings of insects. A great dark arch appeared, and then they passed into shadow, with the sounds of water glooping as echoes in the high tunnel and the light playing along the sides like silk in the wind. The splashes of their poles bounced round them, and when they spoke their voices bounced with them. Rats criss-crossed the water like caterpillars, their tiny *screes* a mocking reminder of grypesh.

Then the sun burned on the water ahead and they were dazzled by the sudden brightness. They came out into a wide waterway that ended in docks. The buildings of the city arced up steeply on all sides, covering the docks in shadow. There were large boats there that could have been called ships; they were webbed with a confusion of lines and ropes, and had the spider figures of men clinging to them. Cargoes were offloaded on to the stone docks, and again they caught the sharp pungency of unknown spices. Hoarse cries busied the air, and Riven heard the gulls screaming as they fought for odd fish on the quay and whirled round the masts of the ships, speckling the docks with guano.

Finnan knew the harbour master well, and found a berth for the flatboat. The company helped make her fast, and then gathered what was left of their things together. Luib carried Madra off the boat, and stood with her in his arms as they completed the formalities of berthing. Two of the crew stayed to oversee the unloading of the meagre cargo, and the rest were paid by Finnan with the same silver knuckles that Bicker had purchased the company's passage with. Then the sailors dispersed, shouting bawdy welcomes to others they knew who were busy at the bigger ships. Finnan led the company through the curious stares of many to the end of the docks, and the steep climb up the hill to the city proper. The streets were narrow, dirty and cobbled, and the gutters were clogged with all forms of evil-smelling filth. Pails were emptied from upper windows, making their way hazardous. More than once, they saw a passerby, soaking wet, shout threats and curses at an open window. The city was a vast maze of narrow alleys pocked with ale houses and middens, shops and smithies, brothels and moneylenders. Armed men stood in groups at many of the street corners. They would start to jeer at the company, but stopped when they saw the Hearthware sashes and the Myrcan staves and whispered amongst themselves.

'Sellswords,' Finnan said ominously. 'They have been hired in droves to police the lower city.'

They climbed ever more steeply, and the streets broadened, became cleaner. Stone began to replace the wood of the lower city, and there were fewer ambushes from above. They encountered taverns with painted signs hanging outside, and shops with their wares displayed in the windows. The people were better dressed, but just as curious. At last, Finnan stopped before a high stone house that had as its sign a serpent twisted round a staff.

He glanced at Madra, but she was asleep. Riven fidgeted and glowered beside Luib as the Myrcan cradled her. The river pilot turned to Bicker.

'We are here. Phrynius is a friend of mine.' He laid an odd emphasis on the word. 'Some folk in the city see him in a different light. It is said he is one of the Hidden Folk—a wizard of sorts—and as such he is not always popular. I stopped his neighbours burning his house once, and for that he owes me. I know not what you people think of his kind, but he has never harmed a soul that I know of. You have my word he will do his best to help the maid here.'

'Not all people shun the Hidden Folk,' Bicker told him quietly. 'I see no reason to doubt you, or your friend.'

Finnan nodded and smiled, then he hammered on the door with his fist. 'Open up, father greybeard. It is I, the river pirate, come to say hello!'

There was a long pause, then finally a rattle of bolts, and the door opened a fraction; in the crack appeared one bright black eye. The door was opened fully, and they saw a little dark man with a pointed grey beard and eyes like black pebbles. He beamed broadly at Finnan's grinning face, showing pink, empty gums.

'My dear boy, how good to see you! Come on in!' Then he seemed to squint and. see the others standing there. 'Company? Finnan, has there been trouble?'

'That could be said.' The pilot sighed. 'Your help is needed, your way with hurts. We have a patient.'

The little man stood back. 'My task in life. Come in, and bring your friends with you.'

They trooped inside and followed Phrynius down a shabby hall, then through another door to a larger room where the shutters were pulled down against the sun and which smelled slightly of ammonia and sulphur. There was a fire burning in a brazier, shelves of dusty books and a large table littered with papers, vials, bottles and jars. A threadbare rug covered the stone of the floor, and a human skull grinned to itself in the corner. Riven half-expected to see a crocodile hanging from the ceiling, but instead there were bulbs of garlic and bunches of other herbs which he could not identify. Their tang permeated the room along with the chemical smells, making him blink. He stared at the rows of glass jars below the books on the walls—and saw an eye staring back at him from one of them, and what could have been a human foetus in another.

Luib had laid Madra down on a faded red couch. She was awake now, and looking about her in bewilderment. Riven sat beside her and took her hand whilst Finnan introduced the company and told Phrynius something of what had befallen them.

The old man shook his head. 'What times! What times are upon us!' He shuffled across to where Madra lay and shooed Riven out of the way. Then he took his place and touched here and there with his thin, liver-spotted hands. She flinched, but made no sound. The old man spoke to them without looking round, and with surprising authority in his voice.

'Finnan, heat some water and rip some bindings in the kitchen. The rest of you must leave; no good in crowds. The poor girl doesn't want you staring at her. Get out. Have a drink, polish your swords. Go!'

They left, somewhat sheepishly, and followed Finnan into a tiny, grubby kitchen where he was setting a water-filled pot over the fire.

'He's a funny old goat,' the pilot said, 'but he has more goodness in him than the rest of the city put together. She's in excellent hands.'

'All right,' Bicker said. 'I believe you. So we wait.' He glanced about him. The company were crammed into the kitchen like a limpet in its shell. He laughed suddenly. 'But not here. There's not enough room to scratch our heads.'

'Beer,' said Ratagan suddenly. 'Beer! By all that's holy, I'd almost forgotten we were in a place where they sell beer. Our problem is solved. We'll go and wet our throats.'

'There is an inn, the Blackbird, just down the street,' Finnan put in. 'It has good ale, and the landlord has never cheated me yet.'

'Then we are off,' said Bicker.

'I will stay,' Luib said quietly.

The others trooped out of the healer's house on to the sunlit street, glad to breathe fresh air and to feel the breeze on their faces. They almost ran down the road, drawing looks from the passersby. But they did not care. They were glad to be free of the flatboat and the smell of death that had been with them ever since the battle. Even Riven laughed with the rest as they piled into the inn Finnan had told them of, and Ratagan wished the landlord good day in a roar that made the poor man cower. Soon they were kicking the bar with their toes, their noses buried in cold beer. Only Corrary was still subdued, remembering his brother lying in a makeshift grave far from his home Rorim. He had given Darmid's sword to Riven, to replace the one lost.

When the first beer had gone, they ordered another, and turned to survey the inn. It was quiet, but perhaps that was because their entrance had been so noisy. A scattered crowd of locals was eyeing them in silence. The landlord cleaned a tankard with nervous twists of his hand.

Ratagan belched, raised his mug to the other customers, then turned to lean on the bar again. Isay was the only one not drinking. He stood beside Riven, fingering his staff thoughtfully.

'So here we are,' Ratagan said, 'in Talisker, biggest city of the north, and the last before the mountains. What now, Bicker?'

The dark man sipped his beer, then rubbed his finger in the condensation dripping on the outside of the metal mug. 'The hardest part of the journey lies before us.'

'The mountains,' Riven murmured.

'And no horses,' said Corrary.

'That is no great thing. They would not get us far in the heights of the Greshorns anyway,' said Bicker.

'How far?' Riven asked.

'To the Staer, perhaps three weeks if the weather is kind. That is what it took me in the spring of last year, at any rate. It is a roundabout route we have to take to the mountain, avoiding the horseshoe of high peaks that arc out from it. If we leave the city by the north gate, we will travel through the fief of Armishir before coming to the foothills of the mountains themselves. Quirinus is lord there, and he knows me, for it is with he and his Myrcans that I took up service over a year ago. We can find help there...' He frowned. 'Though no doubt Quirinus would be more than slightly curious as to our errand in the Greshorns. He has a mind like a blade, does the Lord of Armishir.'

Familiar names were going through Riven's mind as he tried to tie in what was real in this Minginish and what was in his stories. Quirinus—the name rang in his head, and he remembered red wine and rich robes, a bald head and eyes like rain-scoured granite. A laugh with an edge in it. Quirinus.

'There are many Myrcans up here, around Talisker,' he said, making it half a statement and half a question.

Bicker looked at him in surprise, and then nodded. 'Talisker is not so far from Merkadale, and it is the largest population centre in Minginish. There are fifty of the Soldier-folk here in the city itself, under Odhar, and twice as many more in the surrounding fiefs. And Talisker boasts at least five hundred Hearthwares.'

'They have a job before them, in a place this size,' Corrary remarked, but he sounded impressed nonetheless. Riven saw him touch his sash unconsciously. The Hearthware was dressed in a plain hide jerkin; most of their armour had been lost in the flight north and was at the bottom of the river by now. There, or rusting around the bones of the dead. The company had the appearance of hunted refugees, travel-stained and weary. Only the faded sashes they wore, and the weapons they carried, marked them as anything but ordinary folk fleeing the marauders. Those, and Myrcans in their midst.

'Who rules here?' Corrary asked. 'I know nothing of this part of the world, except for the tales sometimes told in the hall about the mountains.'

Bicker gulped at his beer. 'Duke Godomar is head of the city council, and in theory has the last word when it comes to governing Talisker. But the council is made up of powerful men—Saffarac, Valentir and others. They head the guilds within the city itself, and control its trade. The Duke must compromise with them in order to keep his own authority. In the end, though, his Myrcans and Hearthwares are more than enough to overawe the retainers of the city lords, so there is a truce of sorts.'

'A fine-balanced arrangement, if I'm not mistaken,' Ratagan said absently, and downed more of his beer.

Conversation had started up among the customers in the tavern again, although two had left while the company had been talking amongst themselves. The landlord was still looking a little ill-at-ease, however, and he flinched when Ratagan banged his tankard down on the bar with a grin and demanded a refill.

'You're jumpy, my friend,' the big man told him. 'Why so nervous? We're not brigands—merely men who appreciate a fine ale when it hits our throats.'

The landlord filled up the tankard from a keg below the bar. As he straightened, something like resolution crept into his florid face.

'You're Sellswords, are you not, sir? You've come here to take up with Sergius?'

Ratagan's face clouded, but Bicker laid a hand on his arm.

'When did you last see a Myrcan Sellsword?' he asked lightly, nodding towards a frowning Isay.

The landlord swallowed. 'No offence was intended, sir, I assure you. It's just that in these times...'

'What times?' Riven asked him with a snap. He was suddenly tired and the beer was going to his head, making him think of Madra lying in the house they had left, and of the long journey ahead of them through the mountains. He wanted no more adventure at present.

The landlord's eyes flicked to the dirty remnants of the Teller's badge on Riven's breast. 'Forgive me. I see you have come far, gentlemen.' His voice steadied. 'It is just that we are wary of strangers in the city these days, with so many folk seeking safety behind the walls, and the... the Sellswords flocking to Sergius's banner, whether the Duke condones it or no. There are so many of them in the city at present, and you are armed...' He trailed off again.

Bicker sighed, and flipped a few coins on the bar. 'Intrigue. Politics. Have we not enough problems?'

'They say the Hidden Folk have come out of the mountains and attacked the Rorims to the south, in league with the beasts,' the landlord whispered confidentially. 'There are rumours that the Rorims have been overrun.'

Bicker and Ratagan leaned on the bar, eyes blazing.

'Who says this?' Bicker demanded.

The landlord quailed. 'It is a rumour—no more, sir. Some people fleeing from the south brought the news with them.'

'What people?' Ratagan asked, his red beard bristling.

'I don't know. Nobles. A lord, or a lady. Some say the Duke has a new bedfellow—a southern lady. I don't know.'

Bicker swore viciously. 'Jinneth.'

'A coincidence, maybe?' Ratagan suggested, but the dark man shook his head.

'It is her, I am sure of it. Talisker may not be a healthy place for us. I think it is best if we leave as soon as we can.'

Jinneth. Here. Riven felt somehow that it was fitting—Jenny's facsimile had come ahead of them. He remembered the black foam of hair, the grey eyes, the ivory shoulders with torchlight playing on them, and grimaced. No profit lay in that line of thinking.

A new bedfellow.

Oddly the thought still writhed within him—the thought of other men using the body he had loved himself, being given wholesale what he had been offered as an inestimable gift.

It's not the same.

But it writhed within him, nevertheless.

The door of the tavern banged open and a crowd of men entered with rain sheening their steel helms and the mail shirts under their cloaks. They looked rough and ready. They were unshaven or bearded, and dressed in leather and woollen breeches that were held together by scraps of hide with remnants of furs decorating their cloaks and the rims of their helms. Each had also a band of black linen with a white stripe running through it, tied round their upper arms, wound round their helmets or dangling from their sword hilts.

'The Free Company,' the landlord said in a whisper.

The newcomers spread out across the floor of the tavern, whilst customers dodged hurriedly out of their way. None of them spoke, but Riven could feel their eyes taking in the strength of the group—Ratagan's size, Bicker's wiry frame, Corrary's longsword and Isay's staff. They looked at each other, but still none said a word. Finally one of their number stepped forward. His black hair curled under the edge of his helmet and fell to his eyes, and there was a gap between his teeth.

'Who are you and whence come you?' he asked in a harsh rasp. Ratagan stiffened and Isay brought his staff up into the ready position with a small, bleak smile adorning his face. But it was Bicker who responded.

'Who wants to know?'

The gap-toothed mercenary frowned. 'I ask the questions here, and you answer them. I say again: who are you and where are you from?'

'Who gives you the authority to disturb honest men having a beer?' Ratagan asked reasonably, his metal tankard grasped in one vast fist. He grinned. 'Would it not be better if you were asking us such questions with a beer in front of yourself and the taste of it warming your throat? We could go about it in a friendly manner, then—like people who have just met. Would that not be better?' Abruptly, his fist tightened and the tankard crumpled in his grip like clay. Behind him, the landlord backed away as far along the bar as he could.

Riven became exasperated. It's like the fucking Wild West.

'We're from the south,' he said in the cracking silence. 'We're fleeing the beasts from the mountains. We came here seeking refuge.'

The mercenary leader's eyes did not leave Ratagan's. 'Where in the south?'

Riven blinked, and shared a glance with Bicker. The dark man shrugged slightly. 'Ralarth Rorim.'

The gap-toothed man nodded grimly. 'Then you will come with us.'

'Where?'

'To where we will take you.'

Ratagan threw the buckled tankard on to the stone of the floor with a clang, making the mercenaries jump. He was still grinning, but there was no humour in his eyes.

'Now this is hardly a courteous way to welcome visitors to your city. Why not explain to us why we must perforce accompany you, and where to and suchlike, and mayhap things will be a little clearer. That is the way for civilised men to behave, surely.'

'We are in the employ of the City Council,' the mercenary leader said in a strangled tone, 'tasked with the policing of this city and the investigation of all unusual strangers—especially those from the south and the southern Rorims in particular. Does that satisfy you?'

'Almost entirely,' Bicker said. 'You have investigated us, and now you can go. We are staying here to finish our drinks.'

'You will come with me.'

The dark man smiled. 'I think not.'

The mercenary looked them up and down once again, saw the almost joyful light in Isay's eyes, and then glanced at his own men behind him. There were five of them, and they appeared none too happy at the prospect of battling a Myrcan.

'I will return,' he snarled. 'And when I do, you will do my bidding.' Then he spun around and strode out of the door, his men following after without a word.

Bicker groaned. 'Isn't life difficult enough without Sellswords on our backs?' He spoke to the others. 'Time to leave. We'll go to... where the others are. It is not a great idea for us to be split up at this time.'

'It isn't. Talisker may not be too healthy for the likes of us at the moment, I'm thinking,' Ratagan said.

'And I'm thinking we need a talk with Finnan's healer friend,' Bicker told him. 'Come.' And they filed warily out of the tavern in his wake.

The street was busy as they made their way to Phrynius's house, and they had to push folk aside to make headway. The crowd was shouting and gesticulating, parents lifting children on shoulders to keep them out of the crush, fists punching the air, workmen's tools being waved like weapons.

The company had to halt as it became impossible to make any progress through the press of bodies. They stood in a tight bunch and craned their necks to see what was causing the commotion. It was Ratagan, with his great height, who saw first, and outrage and fury flooded his eyes.

'What is it?' Riven demanded of the big man.

Ratagan growled deep in his throat. 'Something I had thought the people of this land had done with. You'll see, soon enough.'

The roadway had cleared, the people packing themselves against the wall of the buildings that lined it. Armoured men were pushing the crowd back with the shafts of their spears. They were mercearies, wearing the black and white linen bands of the Free Company, but there were two or three others in full Hearthware armour who seemed to be in charge. Around their waists were black and white sashes, and swords were naked in their hands.

A ragged and halting procession made its way down the street, and the voices of the crowd rose into a single roar. Spittle flew into the air and hit the cobbles. A surge of people had to be thrust back by the Sellswords. Riven stood on tiptoe to try and see what was going on.

A group of people was being alternately shoved and pulled down the roadway, the shafts of Sellsword spears hastening them on their way. Their clothes were in tatters, and there was blood on their limbs. When they stumbled, a spear shaft was poked into their ribs.

There were both men and women there. The women were only half-dressed, and clutched rags in a pitiful attempt to cover themselves, but a grinning mercenary ripped away the scant tatters of one girl to send her sprawling nude on the cobbles. The crowd was delighted, and the Sellswords again had to push back those who tried to lean forward and seize her. She scrambled to her feet, sobbing, and continued on her way with her arms clamped around her breasts.

'What is this?' Riven asked in a daze.

Ratagan did not look at him. 'This is the clearance,' he said, his voice vicious with anger. 'The Hidden Folk are being sought out once again, and driven from the city.'

Riven shook his head. This was not the world of his books. This was not the land he had created. There was something terribly wrong here. Beside him, Ratagan was quivering like a nervous horse, his eyes on fire under the bristling brows, his hand clenched on the shaft of his axe.

'Ratagan!' Bicker said in a warning voice, and he reached across Riven to set a hand on the big man's arm.

A young blonde woman who had tripped against a Sellsword was shoved by him and sent flying across the roadway. There was an audible crack as her head connected with the cobbles, and the mercenary swore and drew his foot back to kick her. There had been something familiar about her, Riven realised.

'Ratagan!' Bicker shouted. But the red-beard had already let out a roar of fury, and launched himself forward.

Oh, shit. Now we're in trouble.

There was a desperate look on Bicker's face, though Isay's eyes were, oddly, as bright with anger as Ratagan's had been, and the Myrcan staff was out of his belt and cocked in his fists. Corrary's face was white, eyes blazing.

The big man powered forward like a train, flinging people out of his way as though they were dolls, that terrible roar coming from his throat. The mercenaries on the street looked up for one moment, eyes wide, and then he was upon them.

There was a confusion of bodies, a wave of pushing and shoving as the crowd recoiled. Riven was almost plucked from his feet, but Isay kept him upright. The air thickened with screaming. He pushed forward frantically, and together with Bicker, Isay and Corrary managed to force a path through the scrum to the roadway.

They almost tripped over the body of a Sellsword, his neck tilted at a weird angle; and then saw Ratagan. He towered over his foes, and was flailing at them two-handed. One fist gripped his axe, the other a mercenary sword, and together they wove a silver net of carnage around him. Already bodies littered the ground at his feet, but the mercenaries were pressing in and he was backing away, the mad fury still burning in his eye, but something else there now as well: a realisation of defeat.

Two Hearthwares, huge in their armour, lumbered over to join in the fray. Bicker cursed, then he swept out his sword.

'Ratagan!' he yelled, making it into a battle-cry, and he pelted forward.

Isay followed, his staff upraised. To his surprise, Riven found that he had joined them, and Darmid's sword was naked in his hand.

The two Hearthwares turned to meet the new foes, but Bicker's blade had already slid into the throat of one, and Isay's staff had split the skull of the other like a bruised apple. They crashed to the ground.

The four ran on, and the Sellswords became aware that they were being attacked in the rear. They split and retreated, Ratagan following them without respite. Riven held back as Bicker, Corrary and Isay piled into them. The crowds were peeling away from the fight in terror, and most of the ragged people of the procession had disappeared, been engulfed. The blonde girl lay as motionless as a corpse on the ground, a thread of blood ribboning her temple. Riven started towards her instinctively, but halted to check on the battle.

It was all but over. The last of the mercenaries were running, flinging away their weapons as they went. At least half a dozen of their comrades lay on the ground behind them.

Bicker spoke first, his eyes alight with anger.

'You damned fool!' he shouted at Ratagan. 'We've got to get away from here—now! There will be Sellswords crawling these streets in minutes.' He paused for breath. 'You fool!' he exclaimed again.

Ratagan said nothing, though fire still smouldered in his cavernous eyes. He dropped the mercenary sword, tucked his axe in his belt and then strode over the cobbles to the unconscious girl. He lifted her into his arms and straightened swiftly.

'Come on, then,' he said quietly, and began to jog down the bloody street. The crowd of people who remained there stared at him as though he were a ghost. No one hindered him.

The rest of the company followed, Bicker's face ugly with ire. Behind them they heard horns blowing the alarm in the upper city, but did not look back.

CHAPTER FOURTEEN

EVEN LUIB'S NORMALLY impassive face seemed dubious when they returned to Phrynius's house bearing another injured girl. They piled in through the narrow doorway, breathing hard, and Corrary sighed audibly with relief when the door was closed, cutting off the curious stares that had been following them through the streets from the scene of the fight. Bicker's eyes were hard with worry, however.

'They'll have no trouble trailing us here. We do not have much time. Take her to the old man. Isay, Corrary, guard the door.'

They clattered into the dim chemical-smell of Phrynius's main room to find Finnan feeding Madra a bowl of soup and the old healer muttering over a thick tome in the corner. Madra smiled at Riven as he entered, but he could not return it. He was angry with himself for the sudden stab of jealousy that had pricked him on seeing Finnan there.

The river pilot's face lost its usual mocking cast as Ratagan bent to lay the blonde-haired girl on the thick rug by the brazier. The big man gazed at her for a second, and pushed the blood-matted hair from her face. It was then that Riven saw the resemblance that had tugged at him earlier. The girl was so similar to Ratagan's wife that they might have been sisters.

Phrynius put down his book with a thud and made his slow way to the centre of the room.

'We have brought you more trouble, Phrynius,' Bicker said. 'There has been fighting. We have slain Sellswords, and doubtless they will be able to trace us here.'

Finnan swore. 'What in heaven did you want—'

But Phrynius cut him off. 'You know what to do, Finnan. I want the usual things.' He had knelt down on the floor, creaking and hissing with discomfort, and was now examining the wound on the girl's head. Madra made to get up and help Finnan in the kitchen, but the old man stopped her with a glare. 'You are a patient yet, not a nurse, so bide where you are.' And she sank back down on the couch.

They could hear Finnan swearing to himself as he clattered pots in the kitchen, but paid him no heed. Phrynius appeared unperturbed by the thought that a dozen mercenaries might break down his door at any moment, and Bicker seemed irritated by his composure.

'Did you hear what I said?' he asked. 'We will have the city around our ears at any moment.'

Phrynius looked up, the dark eyes like black stones set in his head. 'I heard you. I know also these things: first, the people of this part of the city will not aid the Sellswords in their enquiries if they can help it, for there is no love lost there. Second, this is not the first time I have had people in here who were fleeing Sergius's men. The Hidden Folk of this city know me, and know what I am.' His old, lined face hardened. 'They know also who I once was—personal physician to the Duke. Once upon a time, that is, but it still carries some weight here. And third, there are ways out of this house that cannot be seen by anyone but me, of which these mercenary scum know nothing. So seat yourself, and do not hinder me at my business for a while.'

The sharpness of his voice was at odds with his appearance. The withered, disreputable man had suddenly been invested with startling authority, and Bicker sat down wordlessly. Riven joined him. Ratagan kept his post at the senseless girl's head. His huge paws enveloped one of her hands, but Phrynius did not tell him to move away.

Finnan came in with a basin of steaming water, and the old healer began washing the blood away from his patient's face. There was silence in the room. Riven glanced at Bicker, and could see that the dark man expected the Sellswords to be hammering on the door in moments.

'How long has this been going on?' Ratagan broke the quiet unexpectedly. The old man did not pause in his work.

'I assume you mean the clearance. There have been rumours of it for weeks. Folk have been unsettled by the wreck of the seasons and the attacks of the beasts, as well they might be. It beggars my understanding. The Hidden Folk have been leaving the city quietly since it began, but now it seems'—he gestured to the prone girl—'they have little choice in the matter any more.' He paused, and then real venom seeped into his voice. 'It is the fault of that she-wolf from the south, the Lady Jinneth. She holds the Duke's heart in thrall. He was never a strong man, but he was at least swayed by the more sensible members of his council. Now—' He shrugged his thin shoulders. 'Now he has gone to ruin in the space of weeks, and these men of Sergius's are seen more on the streets than our own Hearthwares or Myrcans. Some say the Myrcans have withdrawn entirely to their barracks—certainly they have not been seen in the streets lately—and that they are considering what to do.' The healer's eyes darted suddenly to Luib, the grey-muzzled soldier who stood silent to one side.

'Your folk were ever ones for weighing up the moral niceties of things before acting. It remains to be seen what side you will choose.'

The Myrcan did not reply. On the floor, the girl stirred. Her fist tightened in Ratagan's, and then her eyes opened wide in fear. But Phrynius shushed her with a gentleness that was as much part of him, and as odd to see, as his sharp-tongued authority.

'You are with friends,' he soothed her. 'I am Phrynius. I am one of your own folk.'

'What happened?' she asked, tears crowding her eyes. 'Where are the others?'

'We rescued you,' Ratagan rumbled. He had released her hand, and seemed embarrassed. 'We took you from the mercenaries. I think the others who were with you escaped. They ran into the crowd.'

The girl looked at him, deep hazel eyes under coppery brows. 'You rescued me? Why?'

'You reminded me of someone,' the big man muttered, and then he glared around the room as though daring anyone to speak. 'And, besides, I do not like to see women thrown through the streets like sacks.'

The girl's hands fluttered to her head, but Phrynius grasped them firmly in his skeletal fingers.

'Leave it. I have things to do here. You have a hard skull, but a knock is a knock.'

'You are the healer who was once a member of the court,' the girl said suddenly. 'My father spoke of you.'

Phrynius grinned, showing empty gums. 'The very same. And who was—' He paused, and asked gently, 'Who is your father?'

'Mannir, the Apothecary.'

'I know him. He has mixed a few brews for me in his time.'

The girl began to weep. 'I don't know where they took him. Or my mother. They took them away, and they were going to throw them out of the city to the beasts.'

Madra left her seat and put her arm around the weeping girl. The head wound oozed blood on to her robe.

'You would be Mereth, then,' Phrynius said, and the girl nodded through her tears. Phrynius became grim. 'Your father was no magician. The Free Company is becoming less discriminatory, it seems. If they start throwing out every healer and 'cary in the city they'll have a good few less folk to worry about governing. Madness. It's madness. Worse than last time, if this is the way it is going.'

'A witch hunt,' Riven murmured. But the worst witch was the one who shared the Duke's bed. He felt a pang of fury at the thought. '*We'll meet again*,' she had said.

Not if I can help it.

But then he pondered on what Phrynius had said.

'Are you a magician as well as a healer?' he asked.

The old man paused in his binding up of Mereth's head. The bandage was stained yellow with some antiseptic-smelling substance he had gouged from a jar.

'What is a magician?' he asked, and stared at Riven with uncomfortably keen button eyes. 'Are you—who wears a Teller's badge, but who speaks so sparingly, and in a strange accent—are you a magician? Your voice comes from no land I have ever heard of.'

'Do you know about magic?' Riven persisted.

'What is magic?' the old man retorted. 'It may be that under my hands bones knit faster and skin closes quicker than with others. It may be that I can heal some of the body's inside hurts by merely laying my hands on it. Is that magic? If it is, then it harms no one. And Mereth's father: he heals with his potions, but there is no magic in them, just the lore he has taught himself; and the result is the same. The hurts are repaired. And here is the payment for it.' He looked for a moment as though he might spit, but then continued with his deft work. Riven subsided.

It was Finnan who spoke next. 'That's as may be, father greybeard,' he said lightly. 'But the rub of the matter is that the Sellswords will be here in the end, and maybe my tongue alone will not suffice this time to convince them that this house would not burn well.'

'Bah!' Phrynius exclaimed. 'They are afraid of me, as they are, at heart, of all the Hidden Folk.'

'They grow less afraid,' Bicker put in quietly. 'At least, the ones we encountered a while ago did not seem afraid of their charges.'

'Though they were not too enamoured of cold steel.' Ratagan laughed mirthlessly.

Phrynius finished his work and climbed shakily to his feet, accepting Madra's aid.

'Done.' He smiled down at Mereth's bandaged head. 'Now all you need is rest and peace for a while, which may be no small thing to hope for in times like these.'

'What I need is to find my family,' the blonde girl told him. Ratagan helped her on to the faded couch, and she drew her rags around her with an odd dignity. 'I cannot stay here.'

'You must,' the old man snapped, the gentleness flitting from his eyes. 'How far do you think you would get out in the streets? If a mercenary did not pick you up, you would faint within a quarter-hour. So let us hear no more of this foolishness.' He flicked an imperious finger at Ratagan. 'You, big man, take her upstairs and put her to bed, since you are so intent on rescuing her. And Finnan, take her would-be nurse up also.'

'At once, wise one,' Finnan said, and he offered Madra his arm. She looked at Riven, and he felt his face burn, but did nothing. The foursome left the room, Ratagan carrying Mereth in his arms and looking oddly content, Madra leaning on the river pilot's shoulder. Riven caught Bicker watching him quizzically, and grimaced.

Phrynius collapsed on to a high-backed armchair beside the glowing brazier and produced a deeply curved pipe, which he proceeded to light with a taper. Soon a blue haze writhed around his grey head, and he sighed deeply.

'You—dark man—you are a lord, or I know nothing. The giant man—he is also. Myrcans and a Hearthware travel with you, and there is old blood on your clothes, and the rents of teeth.' He puffed a moment, his face seamed with lines and his black eyes glittering. 'And with you is a Teller who says little, but whose face says much. I never yet met a storyteller who could shut his mouth for more than a minute at a time, but this man has no such trouble. I would go so far as to say you are bound on some errand, perhaps north of here.' He grinned toothlessly. 'Maybe it is none of my business, but you might have brought ruin to my door, so I am understandably curious. What say you?'

Bicker met his gaze. There were faint clumps from those upstairs and the fainter sounds of voices out on the street. Isay and Corrary were still keeping their vigil in the hall and Luib had not moved from his post at one wall, though his hard eyes missed nothing.

'You guess well,' Bicker said at last.

'Whither are you bound?' Phrynius asked him, the humour gone. He was like an enquiring stoat.

'Into the mountains. To seek the Dwarves, and maybe scale the Staer.'

'On what errand?'

'A high one. To save Minginish, maybe.'

Phrynius sat back in his chair. 'So,' he said thoughtfully. 'A high errand indeed.' His eyes shifted to Riven. 'And you with the scarred face and the old pain in your eyes. You are at the centre of it, are you not?'

'How do you know that?' Riven asked. He found he was relieved at Phrynius's shrewd guesses.

'Some say I have dwarven blood in me,' the old man said. 'At any rate I can smell strangeness when I meet it. There is something about you that is at odds with the very air in the room. And there is magic in you, as bright as day to those who can see it.'

Riven could not conceal his astonishment, and the old man nodded.

'But you have not seen it yourself. Interesting.' He puffed at the leaking pipe once again, seemingly untroubled.

'We must leave Talisker at once,' Bicker said, 'but we need supplies; pack animals, maybe.'

'These injured young women you keep chancing across will not be fit to travel for a week or more,' Phrynius said implacably.

'Then they must be left behind.'

Riven started. Leave Madra behind? The thought brought with it a strange pain, but he said nothing.

I don't own anyone.

Phrynius seemed to consider this. 'Finnan spoke truly, the whelp. The Sellswords will come in the end. I am too well known, and if you are found, then nothing will stop them putting this place to the torch—and me to the pyre, no doubt. I know places in Talisker—in the Upper City—that are yet untroubled by this madness. Places too near to the court to be touched by these animals. If we can move our two pretty patients there, they will be safe, for a while at least.'

'And you?' Bicker asked.

'I am good at weathering storms.' The old man's eyes twinkled, and for a second Riven was sure that his magic, if that was truly the word for it, extended farther than the healing of wounds.

'How has the Free Company gained so much power in the city?' Bicker asked. 'And how is it present in such numbers? Where are the 'Wares of the city? We've only seen a few since we arrived.'

And killed two of them, Riven thought.

'Godomar has hired over a thousand of the Company to aid the 'Wares in the policing of the city and the surrounding fiefs,' Phrynius explained. 'But men like Quirinus do not care to see Sellswords patrolling their lands, so the city's 'Wares have for the most part been given duties outside the walls, leaving Sergius and his minions in Talisker to do what they will.'

'He must answer to someone,' Riven put in. 'These men can't just do what they please with an entire city.'

'They do as they are told,' Phrynius said patiently. 'If they are told to expel those suspected of being of the Hidden Folk then that is what they do.'

'But no one tells them in what manner they should do it,' Bicker muttered, and the old healer nodded.

'There you have it. And this southern lady has the Duke trapped between her thighs. Some say she has an arrangement with Sergius, also.'

'She angles for bigger fish than once she did,' Bicker said.

'You know her?'

'We know her,' the dark man said heavily. 'Another reason for leaving Talisker as soon as may be.'

'You come from the south,' Phrynius said. 'How are the Rorims there? Is it true some are gone—overrun?'

'No. Those are the lies of the Lady Jinneth. The western Rorim are united now.' And Bicker told swiftly what had been happening in the south of Minginish over the past months, though he made no reference to Riven and his place in events. Phrynius appeared relieved, and then murderously angry.

'So this hysteria is whipped farther by lies. Sometimes I think these clearances are as much political as anything else.'

'Why did they happen the first time?' Riven asked.

The old man sucked at his pipe, but it had gone out. He cursed briefly. 'Twenty-eight years ago there appeared strange portents in the skies, and savage beasts in the mountains. Children were born to young girls who had never known a man. The magic of folk such as I went awry. There was something in the air that defeated it. People grew afraid. Those who had powers like mine were shunned, feared, and finally hated. They were driven from their homes into the wilderness. Some were burned. They disappeared into the mountains, and there they must have stayed. Some were fortunate, and laid low long enough to escape, to ride out the storm.' He smiled a thin smile. 'I was one such. The rest were never heard of again.'

Twenty-eight years ago. The year Riven had been born. 'Christ!' he breathed.

'And now it happens again. We have winter in summer, and Rime Giants roaming our fields in the night; so it is our fault. Our unholy practices have brought ruin to Minginish once again, and we must be punished.' Phrynius's voice was thick with bitterness. 'And some in high places seek to use this opportunity to garner more power for themselves, stepping over the bodies of the Hidden Folk to get to it.'

Minginish was real, as real as his own world, and his stories were mere reflections of it—not the other way around. But something had gone wrong. Behind the books, the stories Riven had told, something else had happened. A two-way channel had been opened up. He received inspiration from this world that he had never seen, but it was affected by him also, by the events in his own life—and that was where it had gone wrong. People like Bragad had no right to exist here. And Jinneth. Something had soured the characters he had drawn in his books. Riven's imagination was contaminating Minginish, giving it a history it should never have had. And people, too. The dark girl who wandered the mountains barefoot. Who was she? Something dredged up out of his own subconscious? He rubbed his eyes wearily. Even if the Dwarves had no answers for him, he knew now what had to be done. That channel had to be closed; he had to be sealed off in his own world again, and whatever umbilical it was that connected him to Minginish must be severed.

He felt real, surprising grief at the idea.

There was a clatter on the stairs as Finnan and Ratagan re-entered the room. The river pilot stretched until his knuckles scraped the ceiling.

'I need some space,' he said. 'Unlike you folk, who have been battling mercenaries and rescuing maidens all morning, I have been locked up here—in delightful company, it is true, but locked up nonetheless. I think I will go out and sniff the air, maybe see what sort of mayhem you have been stirring up in the city since I brought you here.'

'Is that wise?' Bicker asked.

'It is not I who have been knocking the heads of Sellswords together,' Finnan snorted.

'A good plan,' Phrynius said. 'Keep your eyes open and your nose out of too many taverns. It would be useful to know if our friends on the streets are searching the houses of the district and suchlike.'

Finnan bowed to them. 'Then farewell. Mayhap I'll bring something to eat. Not all of us are like Phrynius, and can subsist on brandy and pipe smoke.'

He left. They heard him exchange words with Isay and Corrary at the door before it closed behind him.

The afternoon wore on, and a tiredness crept over the company. At last, noting their nodding heads, Phrynius led them upstairs. His house was surprisingly spacious, and there was a room there that would serve to sleep them all. The company spread their bedrolls on the dusty floor and lay listening to the mice scuttling inside the walls as evening drew in and the sounds from the city outside lessened. They lit a brazier and sat dozing around it.

'An old house, this,' said Bicker quietly to the gathering dusk and the scratching mice. 'It is an old city. There was a tower on the height by the curve of the river before ever a Rorim was raised up in the Dales of the south, and the people lived by travelling on the Great River before the forests that once covered the whole land had been cleared.'

'There was magic in the forests, then,' Phrynius said, startling them, for they had not heard him enter the room. 'There were marvels in the deep woods, people who lived by leaf and tree and never saw a sky that was not covered by branches. But now only remnants of the Great Woods remain, and what was once hidden there has fled.'

'Scarall Wood is one remnant,' Bicker murmured, but Phrynius seemed not to hear.

'There are those who say that the magic began there, in the trees, running up from their roots, coursing out of the earth itself. And there are those who say the Dwarves discovered it in the ground, and mined it as one would a vein of silver. But whatever tale is true, it is from the land itself—from the earth and the stones and the trees of Minginish— that magic comes. Folk have chosen to forget that, and to persecute those who remember it. But I do not forget.' His pipe billowed blue smoke that spun around the ruddy light of the brazier, and his face was as lined as a walnut in the dimness. Riven wondered how old he was.

'I remember a time when the whole of the world was afloat with wizards and witches, as they are named now. They were, and are, ordinary folk with a gift, no more, and they were as much a part of the land as the Myrcans, and as necessary. The Dwarves lived lower down the mountains then, in their mansions, and they held fairs to which all and sundry came to trade and gawk. But with the clearances, that passed away. People ceased believing, or were afraid to, and the Dwarves withdrew to the high ranges and the deepest of their mines. And so the world became a poorer place.'

There was the sound of the laughter of revellers somewhere off in the streets. A dog barked, then became involved in a running battle with another. They snarled away into the night, leaving it peaceful.

'The city is very quiet tonight,' Phrynius said, and his head was cocked like a fox sniffing the air.

Riven threw aside his bedroll and stood up. He ignored the inquiring glances and shuffled out of the room, stirring dust in his wake. He felt it tickle his throat, but stifled the cough that threatened. Somehow he felt an unspoken need to make no noise, as if this were the last moment of peace he would know for a long time. He seemed heavy with mortality as he opened the other door on the landing and entered the room where Madra and Mereth were sleeping.

Two forms lying on the two narrow beds, a leaded window throwing faint starlight on to their faces. He sat on the creaking bed next to Madra and watched the slow rise and fall of her breasts under the blanket. An arm, white as ivory, lay folded across her stomach. Her hair was a dark hood that had fallen back from her face.

She breathed softly, the bandage collaring her, the tiny scar pale at one cheekbone where a Myrcan stave had knocked her down as she fought for Riven's life. He touched it, then brushed the velvet of her lips, her eyelids, one earlobe where the hair revealed it. And he knew that he had come to love that heart-shaped face, the stubborn brows, the level eyes, and the smile that was so grave and rare.

How many miles to Babylon?

Ah, Riven, be not bitter. You have loved and been loved. That's enough for anyone.

Enough for most lifetimes.

The tears broke his sight so that he was blind, the girl on the bed a blur in the darkened room.

Beggars would ride, if wishes were horses.

He stood up, leaving her behind, and made his way through the dust to the others.

THE NIGHT PASSED slowly and the company lay awake after a while, wondering what was delaying Finnan.

'He has probably found himself a girl and is even now trying to extricate himself from her clutches,' Phrynius said, but by the vast volumes of smoke he was pumping out, they could see even he was worried.

They took turns at the front door, and Corrary had just relieved Ratagan when the sounds on the street reached them, and they tensed in the dim red light of the coals, their low talk frozen in midair.

Scuffling in the street, and the murmur of voices, the chink of metal. They did not move. Hands halted halfway to weapons. A slow riband of smoke curled up unnoticed from Phrynius's pipe.

Then there was a crash from downstairs and a sudden bedlam of men shouting. Wood splintered under heavy blows, giving way to the clash of steel. Corrary's voice carried up the stairs, shouting Bicker's name.

The company leapt to their feet, weapons hissing free of scabbards. Phrynius hopped about like a goblin in the gloom. 'Follow me! Follow me! We must go downstairs. There is a way out there, from the cellar!' But they hardly heard him.

Ratagan and Riven dived out of the door on to the landing, meaning to fetch Madra and Mereth, but a tumult engulfed them as they piled through it. The landing was alive with men in armour, Hearthwares and Sellswords both, their feet skidding in the thick dust. Ratagan roared with rage and smashed into them like a battering ram, sending them thundering to the floorboards. One remained on his feet and his sword whistled down on the big man's back, but Riven twisted out his own blade in time to deflect it. The shock ran up his arm, and the enemy sword careered off in a flurry of sparks to bury itself in the plaster of the wall.

Bicker and Isay tumbled out of the room behind them. The landing was a mess of bodies, prone and upright, with weapons flashing and men shouting, trying to tell friend from foe.

'Alive!' someone shrieked. 'Take them alive!'

Ratagan was struggling to his feet, with armoured figures pounding him. Riven saw a sword pommel strike him in the temple and lay it open. More figures were running up the narrow stairs, with swords glinting in their hands. Some kicked down the other door on the landing and launched themselves inside. A girl screamed.

Something in Riven snapped. He bellowed and

launched himself over Ratagan's body, with Bicker and Isay in his wake. His sword swept in a short arc to cleave a man's skull, then snicked back to clang off a breastplate. A mailed fist struck him on the ear and a high hissing filled his head, deafening him. He caught a glimpse of burly figures retreating down the stairs with struggling bodies thrown over their shoulders, saw Madra's long hair cloaking a Sellsword's back, and charged forward again with the taste of blood in his mouth and a mad anger fuelling his muscles.

An armoured torso brought him up short, and another shattering blow to the jaw felled him. The Hearthware reared over him with elation in his face for a moment, and then Isay's staff had licked out like a snake, pounding him between the eyes, and he fell back into the arms of the others behind him. Isay propelled himself forward and landed bodily on the scrum of armoured men. They recoiled. One tumbled head over heels down the stairs, his armour digging chunks out of the frail walls. The Myrcan shortened his grip on the staff and punched it into faces. Bodies lay on the floor, but more of the enemy were powering on. They piled on to Isay and grasped his limbs, heedless of the savage blows he dealt out. He staggered as they weighed him down, a scream of pure frustration and rage coming from his throat, and then fell with half a dozen men clinging to him and sword hilts coming down in flurries upon his head. A last effort sent one Hearthware flying free of the tangle to smash into Riven. The man's metal-clad weight crushed him to the floor, constricting his ribs. His heartbeat was a red yammer in his head. He saw

Bicker lunging forward, his blade like a glittering needle, and old Luib battling away indomitably. But then there was a splintering of glass, and more Hearthwares were dropping on to the landing through the window behind. Riven tried to cry out; but he could not muster the breath in his chest to make a sound, and he watched helplessly as Luib was struck from behind and went down like a felled tree. Bicker spun and sent a fountain of blood flying from one of the new attackers, but he was alone and from two sides the enemy rushed him, standing on their comrades' bodies as they came. A foot stamped Riven's head, mashing his face into the wooden floor and for a while he could not see or hear, but could only feel the vibrations and blows of the fight in the wood underneath him. But eventually that, too, faded. The last thing he saw clearly was the face of the Sellsword who came last up the stairs. He was grinning widely, showing the gap between his front teeth, and his black hair fell in a curly mass over his forehead. He began kicking Ratagan's unconscious face with glee.

CHAPTER FIFTEEN

THE BLOOD WAS pounding in his head, hot as lava, heavy as lead. He could feel it trying to throb its way out of his temples. It washed across his shut eyes in waves of light and dark. A dry groan scraped out of his parched throat.

Slowly he became aware of other things. The painful stretching of his arms and constriction of his chest. The bright, bone-grating agony in his wrists. The nerveless weight of his legs pulling him floorwards.

Dull curiosity grew in him. He tried to open his eyes, but they seemed gummed shut. There was light beyond his eyelids, flickering torchlight—so they had not blinded him, at least. His fingers twitched, and there was the chink of metal. The manacles at his wrists shifted slightly, digging deep into lacerated flesh, and he almost cried out.

But the pain helped. It pushed the throbbing of his head away, poured light into his darkening mind.

He concentrated on moving his legs. The tingle of returning circulation pricked at him and he gritted his teeth, but that sent agony shooting through his jaw. For a moment, as his mind swam, he was at Beechfield again, and there were iron rods holding his face together. But he had beaten that pain, also. A hard school he had been to, but a good one.

He found his feet. Immediately his arms came down and the tearing pressure of the manacles eased. Air poured into his chest, and he leaned against the wall at his back, sucking it in, eating it up.

Not done yet, by God.

He had sufficient slack in his wrist chains to bring a hand to his face. He felt his eyes, the stickiness there, and then in one swift flick tore open the stuck eyelid.

When the pain had eased, he did the same for the other blood-glued eye.

He was in a dim stone room, ten feet square. Opposite him was an iron door, shiny with moisture. There was straw at his feet and water ran down the walls. The light came from a single clear-burning torch set in a wall hook to his right. The room was entirely silent.

A dungeon. A real-life dungeon. Terrific.

He was alone.

Not a sound. No jangling of keys, no piteous cries, no cackling jailers.

And a terrifying thought struck him.

They've left me to die here.

Ratagan, Bicker: where were they? He saw Isay go down again, saw Madra carried off on a Sellsword's shoulder. Where were they?

Panic fluttered at the edge of his mind, but he put it down ruthlessly.

Christ, I'm thirsty.

His dry tongue circled his split lips. He hadn't been in such bad shape since—

He cursed aloud, his voice startling in the silence.

A rat scrabbled through the straw of the floor, chittering to itself. It sat up on its hind legs, looked at him for a moment and chittered some more.

'Fuck off,' he said moodily.

The rat darted away, and then disappeared in the corner. He saw there was the grating of a drain there, eighteen inches square, and if he quelled the shifting of his feet in the straw he could hear the faint sound of running water echoing; the only sound in or out of his cell. He began to wish the rat had stayed to chitter at him.

Time passed. The torch burned lower. It would have to be replaced soon. His thirst increased and his legs grew weary from standing, but he dared not relax them. His wrists were no better than meat-wrapped bone. The panic welled in him again, and the fear for the others. Was Madra in another cell like this? Maybe she was enjoying the attentions of her jailers.

The thought made him twist in his chains, heedless of the pain. He shouted and screamed, the damp air scraping his arid throat, and finally he fell silent.

Hours passed. The torch guttered, sank, and finally went out, leaving him in impenetrable blackness. A whimper crept unbidden out of his throat, and he turned it into a snarl.

Eventually there was a rattle at the door, and a key turned in the lock. His heart jumped. He heard the door swish open through the straw, and then there was a glimmer of light, a low spill dancing in someone's hand. It shed a yellow glow of illumination that revealed fingers, a dark sleeve and a hood with the face shadowed.

The door swung shut again.

The spill was set in a niche to one side, and the monk-like figure approached him. Despite himself, he shrank against the wall.

The hood was thrown back and he was looking at Jinneth, her face a maze of shadow and light, black darkness and yellow flame; two diamond brilliances shone in her earlobes.

She came forward until her robe touched his chest, and her face tilted up to his.

'Greetings, Michael Riven,' she murmured, her voice a silken touch in the low light. 'I told you we would meet again. How do you find your new lodgings?'

Words crammed his mouth like a logjam. His breath clicked in his throat. He felt painful tears ooze out of his blood-covered eyes and streak his cheeks. This had been a face he loved, one he had never thought to see again. And here it was with the flame playing on it as though it were the glow of the peat in the bothy, looking at him with those eyes. And he had come to hate it.

'You're not my wife,' he croaked, and he saw surprise widen her eyes for a second.

'Indeed,' she said, her voice as low as the beat of a swan's wing. 'I am no one's wife now.' Her voice sharpened dangerously. 'You and your friends saw to that.'

'Where are they? What have you done with them?'

She smiled. 'They live yet, never fear.' The smile broadened. 'Is not irony a delicious thing? That I should flee you, only to have you delivered into the palm of my hand?'

'Hilarious,' he grated. Her nearness was dizzying him. He could sense the warmth of her under the thick robe, smell the perfume that rose from her throat.

'Who are you?' she asked him as she had once before. 'Where do you come from?'

He stared at her for a long moment, remembering other expressions on that face, other things in those eyes. He heard laughter that had died at the foot of a mountain long ago.

'I am Michael Riven, from Camasunary on the Isle of Skye, and I am a Teller of Tales,' he said clearly. And he felt that by saying it, he had somehow committed himself to something. A course of action, perhaps. A certain conclusion. But he did not care. He knew who he was and what he did, and that was enough.

'Strange names,' Jinneth said softly. There was an odd brightness in her eyes. Her hand came up and he flinched, but it caressed the old scars on his forehead. Her face creased with puzzlement. Dried blood flaked off under her touch.

He bent his head, with his heart thundering in his ears, and at the familiar angle his lips met hers. She did not draw back. Her tongue dipped delicately at his. His broken lips bled against hers, and he tasted the blood in both their mouths. His chains clinked. He had leeway enough to bury one hand in the rich darkness of her hair, to run his fingers on the nape of her neck—and then she pulled away.

He could have wept with loss. For a moment, an instant only, he had been kissing his dead wife.

There was a hardness about her face that he had not seen before; a hint of cruelty. She smiled again, and became a stranger, an enemy. His grief was shunted aside by rising anger.

'You bitch!' he spat.

His blood ringed her lips. She looked like a vampire.

'I wish to know more,' she said. 'I wish to know many things. I wish to know why you and your friends are here, where you are going. These things you will tell me.'

'Go to hell.'

'You will tell me, Teller of Tales. Or else the frowning girl who has accompanied you on your errand—and whom you care for, I think—will be lent to our Sellswords for a little while. We will see if the attentions of a dozen mercenaries cannot lift her frown.'

His fists clenched and unclenched helplessly in their chains. His eyes blazed, but he bit his mouth shut.

'You are stubborn and you are proud. Not altogether bad qualities in a man, but hardly suitable in your present situation. I will let you think on it for a while in the dark. Reason often comes more quickly when one is left alone without distractions. For now, farewell.' She curtsied to him as though he were a prince. Then the hood was thrown up again, the spill retrieved from its niche, and she left him with the darkness.

He heard no footsteps retreating after she had gone, and had noticed none approaching before she entered, so perhaps the heavy door blocked out sound. That was a small heartener. It meant he was not necessarily isolated from the others. They might be in the next cell, or down a corridor.

He slumped against the wall, his legs trembling with tiredness. What was she after? What could she hope to gain by this? Except revenge, of course. Maybe she believed him to be some sort of powerful wizard and hoped to harness him for her own ends.

But would a powerful wizard really have allowed himself to be captured so easily?

He moved his wrists in their chains, the iron slicing into his flesh. She would hurt Madra. No secret was worth that.

It was eerie. The woman who was his wife's image would hurt the girl he had come to love after her. Punishment for adultery. His laughter barked harshly in the cell, bouncing off the walls.

And halted abruptly. There was another sound in the cell—a scraping of iron on stone. He stiffened, his eyes stabbing the blackness uselessly.

Then he smelt it. A whiff of smoke in the stagnant air. The pungence of Phrynius's pipe.

Iron rattled in the corner, and there was a wheezing intake of breath. A voice cursed disgustedly. 'Blasted sewer muck!', and the straw rustled.

'Phrynius!' he exclaimed.

'Shut your noise! By all that's holy, I'm too damned old to be clambering about in storm drains, consorting with rats—even polite ones. A man of my station. What times these are!'

There was a breath of bad air on his face and a bony hand laid itself on his shoulder, making him jump.

'Light. Just a moment.'

A glow began in the cell, a blue-white radiance. It was a piece of straw. The healer was holding it aloft, and it shone like a lantern. He eyed it critically, and then nodded.

'Magic,' Riven breathed. Absurdly, he felt like laughing.

'Aye, magic.' The healer's eyes looked him up and down, and he sighed. 'A pretty mess you are in. I heard the she-wolf's visit.'

'She's been and gone.'

'Indeed. So we have some time.'

'Where are the others? Have you seen them? Are they all right?'

Phrynius raised a long finger to his lips, then he touched Riven's manacles with the tip of the glowing straw. They fell from his wrists at once, clattering to the wall, and the old man winced. Riven sagged forward and fell to his knees.

'No time for that!' Phrynius snapped. 'We have work to do, you and I. Places to go and people to see.' He cackled briefly, seeming diabolical in the werelight of the straw. 'Come.' And he hauled Riven to his feet with astonishing strength.

'Where are we?' Riven demanded.

'The Duke's dungeons. I know them well.' Phrynius cackled again. 'He used to put me down here when his gout lingered too long, but always he had need of me again.' His face grew petulant. 'I don't know why you needed me here. There is enough power in you to hoist yourself and your friends out of this scrape ten times over—if you could but use it.' He glanced around at the stone walls. 'This was my cell. There is water running in these hollow walls, over the ceiling and in the sewers beneath.' He grinned. 'It is a cell to contain magic, but no one needs magic to loosen a grating. The idiots. I never had the heart to tell them, but then they never put me here for long. A chastener, the Duke used to call it. And he would fill me with mulled wine and apologise afterwards. Nobility is a strange thing.'

'The door,' Riven said. 'Can you open it?'

'Oh no, my boy. Water in there too—and wards and spells. The Duke has magicians of his own, or had. No, not by the door are we going.' And he twitched the straw light back towards the hole in the floor with the displaced grating.

'The sewers,' Riven said slowly. Phrynius nodded, his black eyes gleaming. 'All the way back to my home. We could follow them, if they had not burnt it down.'

'How did you get away?'

'Their eyes did not see me. They are incurious things, soldiers. It took little effort on my part. You and your friends had given them such a battle that they were not inclined to stay longer. They torched my home, and left with your bodies trussed up in a wagon.'

'I'm sorry.'

'No matter,' Phrynius said crisply. 'I saved the most important of my books and a few other things are there yet, buried in iron. They'll keep. For now, liberty is on my mind, for you and your friends. And for the two maids especially.' His face darkened. 'This is not a good place for them. There are worse things than death for women. So come along.'

He tugged Riven over to the corner and peered down into the gurgling depths of the drain.

'I'll never make it down there,' Riven protested.

'I think you will,' the healer retorted, and promptly began lowering himself into the narrow hole, hissing and grimacing with effort. The last Riven saw of him was a clutch of bony fingers gripping the edge of the drain. Then they were gone, and there was a splash and a flurry of curses from below.

'Come on. We haven't all the time in the world to burn!' The old man's voice echoed out of the wet blackness.

Riven cursed as well. The hole was too narrow. But he lowered his legs through it nevertheless, his skinned wrists burning with effort. The edges of the hole caught at his pelvis, and then scraped at the flesh of his shoulders. He squirmed, terrified of getting stuck. His feet sank into chill water, and he wondered how deep it was. Then he could feel Phrynius's hands fastening on his legs. Like a cork from a bottle, he came through the hole all at once and pitched down into werelit water with a phosphorescent splash of spray, bowling the healer over. But Phrynius surfaced an instant later with the glowing straw gripped between his teeth, streaming evil-smelling liquid.

'Pah!' he spat, taking the straw out of his mouth. 'You are as clumsy as a pregnant cow, and as unaware of your potential. But there's no time for that. Put the grating back, and let's be on our way.'

Riven did as he was told, gagging at the smell of the dank air in the sewer. They were in an arched tunnel six feet high, the walls slimy with filth, and two feet of noisome water running through it. There was the odd plop of a wayfaring rat, but hardly any other sound. The current that tugged at his knees was sluggish and thick, and he shuddered at the thought of what it was doing to the open wounds that covered him.

He splashed down the sewer in Phrynius's wake, following the bobbing light of the glowing straw. The arch of the roof grew lower as they continued and he found he had to stoop, though the old healer in front of him was still able to walk erect.

'How far away are the others?' he asked in a whisper, but the curved walls echoed back the sound grotesquely over the plash and gloop of the water.

'Not far,' Phrynius hissed back. 'We go to meet friends first. Hold your noise. We are passing under the lower barracks.'

As if to prove his point, a torrent of liquid suddenly gushed down from an opening above them, and Riven had to leap aside to avoid it. He retched at the smell, and thought he saw Phrynius's teeth shine in a grin.

'That was a privy being emptied.' Then he had turned away, and was leading him onwards again.

Riven saw other tunnels to his left and right as they continued. Some were as wide as roads, others low as culverts and almost choked with water or mud. There were areas of moonlight as they negotiated past gratings open to the sky, and other areas black as pitch where the crude bricks that formed the sewers had slumped and spilled outwards, leaving spaces barely big enough to crawl through. On the whole, the tunnels they followed grew narrower, lower, more full of water, and more frequented by rats. Riven felt instinctively that they were travelling deeper all the time, making their way to the bowels of the city above. He began to wonder how deep the sewers went.

At last they halted. The narrow way they had been following dipped sharply, the filthy water rising up to meet its low ceiling. There seemed to be no way forward. Phrynius, however, seemed pleased.

'Nearly there,' he said, with obvious satisfaction.

Riven frowned at him. 'You mean—'

'Indeed. Here we take to the water. It is only a brief submersion, though a trifle unnerving, perhaps, for the faint-hearted.'

Riven swore.

'Hold your breath for twenty seconds and strike out upwards,' the old man said calmly. 'You will come to no harm.' And without further warning he dived into the black water like a wizened rat, still clutching his glowing straw. Riven saw its radiance flood the water for a moment or two; then it had moved off and disappeared, leaving him in utter night.

He stood there dripping in the cold, stinking water for perhaps half a minute, cursing the impulses that had ever brought him into his present predicament, and then dived.

It was very cold. The water swallowed him like a frigid womb, and he kicked out frantically, feeling his fingers scrape against the sewer walls at their farthest extension. He kept his eyes closed, not trusting to let the sewer water at them.

And there was air on his face after only a few seconds. He sucked it in, treading water and wiping muck out of his eyes. Light here—real light, firelight; figures moving around. Two of them bent and seized his arms, wrenching him out of the water and letting him flap on to hard stone like a landed fish. He flipped the unruly waterlogged hair out of his eyes and stared.

Phrynius was standing at the fire with a cloak thrown about his thin shoulders, his hands held out to the heat, and there were others with him. They were even shorter than he was, and they had the build of children. And their faces—

Their noses were black and button-like, set at the end of whisker-covered snouts. Their eyes were large and deep, their ears huge and cup-like. Rodent faces. Rodent faces set on the bodies of children. Riven shook his head as two of them helped him towards the fire. He glimpsed stone walls welling up like the sides of a beehive in the flicker of the yellow flames, the ceiling lost in shadow. His goosepimpled flesh hungered for the fire. He stood shivering before it and accepted a thick, dry cloak wordlessly.

Vyrmen. Rat-people. They lived in the sewers and ruins of Minginish's cities. They had been his own creation, but he had never written of them. He had intended them to appear in the third book as the quest to save the land was nearing its completion.

Maybe somebody is writing it for me. Maybe I'm just another character now.

The thought chilled him.

But they seemed to be friendly, at any rate. At least five or six of the diminutive figures were in the chamber. Phrynius was carrying on a conversation with one in a string of squeaks and chitters. The others were occupied with unwrapping bundled oilskins in the shadows, though Riven could see the green lamps of their eyes on him, reflecting back the firelight.

These things were just an idea in my head. I hadn't even got round to writing about them.

He soaked up the warmth of the fire. Minginish was playing games with him again.

Phrynius finished his conversation and regarded Riven once more.

'Well, Teller of Tales, this is Quoy, a raider of the Vyr-folk that some name the Vyrmen. He is a friend of mine, and this is one of the havens he and his people use in their travelling below Talisker. It is part of the street system of the old city which was buried and built over by the new one. Here the Vyrmen live, hidden from the eyes of the folk above, and here they have lived for centuries.'

Questions brimmed in Riven's mouth, but he knew better than to ask them. And anxiety for his friends was gnawing at him like a canker.

Unexpectedly Quoy spoke, his voice reedy and high-pitched, strangely at odds with the dark depths in his green-lit eyes.

'We have located your friends, and are even now arranging their freedom. They have been imprisoned in separate cells in the upper levels of the Duke's dungeons. As far as we can tell, none of them has suffered serious harm, though, like you, they have endured some discomfort.'

Discomfort. Well, that's one way of putting it.

'When do we leave?' Riven asked.

Quoy blinked slowly, and turned to look at Phrynius. 'He is to come with us?'

The healer scowled. 'Not by my reckoning. He's in no state to be running through the sewers, and perhaps battling with Sellswords. He was tripping over his own feet on the way here. Your folk alone would be better left to this.'

Riven swallowed anger. 'They're my friends. They're in this mess because of me. I'm going with you.'

Phrynius shook his head. 'There is no wisdom in that course, believe me. And, besides, there is a way you can help your friends by staying here. There is someone you must meet.'

He nodded at Quoy, and the Vyrman left them, joining his comrades at their work in the shadows. Metal glinted there, and Riven saw that they were unwrapping bundles of weapons and steel wires.

He looked at Phrynius bitterly. 'Who am I to meet then?'

'Quirinus,' the old man replied. 'Now hold your tongue and try to dry out a little.'

AFTER A WHILE, most of the Vyrmen left them to dive with thin splashes into the waterlogged exit of the chamber. They bore with them shining wires that Riven realised were garrottes, and slivers of steel that looked more like skewers than swords. Three of them remained sitting on their spindly haunches by the fire. They eyed him silently. Their hands were long and thin, the fingers covered with hair and terminating in black, sharp nails. He shifted uneasily under their gaze, and turned to Phrynius. The old man was puffing away on his convoluted pipe, steam rising faintly from his wet clothes.

'How are they going to rescue the others?' Riven asked irritably. He felt redundant and uncomfortable, but Phrynius appeared untroubled.

'There are hidden passageways and tunnels everywhere under the city,' he said between puffs on his pipe, 'and nowhere are they thicker than under the Duke's tower. His dungeons are only the highest level of the delvings that burrow deep into the hill of the city itself. Some say it was the Dwarves who began them, back in the time when woods covered the earth. No one has been down deep enough to find out, and the Dwarves say nothing.

'But these tunnels and sewers will allow the Vyr-folk to travel undetected into the heart of the dungeons. And locks are no barrier to their deft fingers. Nor are Sellswords any match for their noiseless feet and the garrottes they carry. Your friends will soon be freed, and it is best not to ask of the whys and wherefores of it. Just be grateful they are on our side.'

'Why are they on our side?'

'Because they believe in the purpose of your quest, and they can smell the magic in you as I can.'

'And this Quirinus—where does he come in?'

Phrynius smiled. 'Quirinus is a rare thing: a man of power who has an open mind. And he knows one of your company, apparently. He will help you to re-equip and leave the city as soon as may be, which is all to the good. There are things afoot in Talisker it would be best not to get mixed up in—games of power and prestige which have been brewing for some time, but which the arrival of the Southern Lady have quickened.' He sighed. 'Perhaps it is as well. There is a time of change upon us.'

The Southern Lady. Indeed.

After a time, when Riven had almost dried out, one of the Vyrmen began rummaging in a sack by his side. He produced thin strips of black, greasy stuff that stank of herbs and handed them round. Riven regarded one dubiously for a moment, and then began to follow his companions' example and ate. Though leathery, the strips were surprisingly palatable. It was some kind of cured meat, and he decided against asking what animal it had once been.

As they sat chewing in silence, the three Vyrmen seemed to suddenly stiffen. Their noses twitched and they pricked up their ears, for all the world like rats sniffing the air. A few words were exchanged in their high-pitched tongue, and then two of them left the fire to take up positions by the pool of water that was the chamber's only entrance.

Something broke surface with a whoop of air. A dark-haired head that whirled in the water, shaking off droplets in all directions. The two Vyrmen seized it and drew it on to dry stone; it was a man in leather armour with a long knife strapped to each thigh. He stood with the water pouring off him and, ignoring his hosts, bent over the pool once more. In a few moments another head broke the surface, spluttering. This one was bald as a mushroom, though it was barred by two thick, black eyebrows. The first man helped the second out of the water, and the cloaks which had warmed Phrynius and Riven were donated to the two soaked newcomers. The bald man ran one pale hand over his pate and laughed.

'You people get worse,' he said to the Vyrmen. 'Have you never heard of doors?' And then he spoke to them for a moment in their own language.

The two joined Riven and Phrynius at the fire, the bald man greeting the healer in a voice that bounced back off the stone walls. 'Phrynius, you old goat—still up to no good, I see. I hear you're looking for new lodgings at the moment.'

'It's an ill-mannered sot who will gloat at the misfortune of another,' the old man said with dignity. 'You are as lacking in courtesy now, my lord Quirinus, as you were when I used to sew up the many hurts you suffered in your youth in your chosen profession of rake. Age has not invested you with any more decorum.'

Quirinus boomed with laughter and sat down beside them, though his companion remained standing, his eyes watchful.

Following Phrynius's glance, Quirinus flicked a thumb at him. 'Don't mind Keigar: he worries about me in my old age.' His gaze shifted to Riven. 'So this is the Teller you told me of. He looks as though the Duke's men have already been having a word with him.'

'Indeed. He needs sanctuary, he and his friends, and gear for mountain travel. They must be on their way as soon as may be.' Phrynius paused. 'It is important, my lord.'

Quirinus looked at him. 'I don't doubt it, since the Vyr-folk have seen fit to aid him, you are homeless for his sake and the entire city garrison was put to the task of tracking him and his comrades down.' He chuckled. 'And a rare old time Sergius's men had of it, if I've heard right. Bicker has lost none of his skill with a blade since I last saw him. And now Godomar and his dark-haired witch have Talisker in a panic with tales of disaster in the southern Rorims, and malign magicians wandering the streets. Is it any wonder the population is in turmoil, or that we are seeing innocents tossed out of the city to the beasts?' For the first time humour fled his face, and the heavy brows made him appear momentarily savage. 'Even my own 'Wares are affected, whilst the Myrcans skulk in their barracks and keep themselves to themselves. They refuse to police the city any more, because the goings-on here leave a bad taste in their mouths. I do not blame them. There are rumours that some of them are leaving to take up with the lords of the border fiefs and do some real soldiering.'

'Which lords, I wonder,' Phrynius said archly, and Quirinus laughed, his good humour returning.

'Well, what can I do but accept their service? Besides, I need them. Whilst the nobles of the city squabble amongst themselves, we in the north are fighting for our very existence... Which brings me back to our friend here.' The heavy-brewed eyes were on Riven once more. 'You have the friendship of Bicker, I am told, which would make me trust you with no other token. I know that something happened to him whilst he was up in the mountains last year—something to do with you, perhaps. Something to do with what is presently besetting Minginish, for the Bad Time began the very day he said he had scaled the Staer. So what can you tell me?' Quirinus wiped at the water which still dripped down his face, and regarded Riven patiently.

Riven was taken aback by the bald man's forthright manner. He looked at Phrynius, but the old man's face was as seamed and shut as a walnut. He could feel the deep eyes of the Vyrmen on him, and the frowning gaze of Quirinus's bodyguard.

'All right, then,' he said, and began.

It was a long story, spanning two worlds and riddled with the inexplicable, but Riven's listeners remained silent throughout, and Phrynius did not seem to notice that he had puffed his pipe cold. Riven told them everything, fitting Bicker and Murtach's travels in with his own. When he had finished, one of the Vyrmen had to stoke up the fire, for it had sunk into glowing embers. The silence lingered long after he had finished speaking, until finally Phrynius sucked his pipe a last time, and then knocked it out against his boot heel. Quirinus's brows had contracted into a single black caterpillar across his forehead.

'A story, indeed!' he said quietly. 'You have been having a thin time of it lately, it would seem, and, hence, so have we.' He shook his head ruefully. 'This beggars the imagination. What say you, Phrynius?'

The old healer paused in the act of refilling his pipe. 'There have been rumours of other worlds for hundreds of years. Some of the Hidden Folk are even purported to have visited them, and it is said the Dwarves have discovered doors to other places in the deepest of their mines, but it is one thing to hear tales of such things and another to talk to a man who claims to actually come from such a place.' He lit his pipe from the fire and sighed heavily. 'I know this. I am disquietened, for two reasons. First there are the imponderables in the equation—this dark girl who is and is not our friend's wife, as is the Lady Jinneth.' He smiled. 'I will no longer refer to her as a she-wolf, for it would be hardly fitting. But there is something wrong here, something beyond what is in Riven at work, and I wish I knew what it was. And then there is the other thing. I do not know if even the Dwarves have any answers to this conundrum. If they had, would they not have done something themselves by now? They are reputed to be all-wise, if a little reclusive. Surely they know what is happening to the land. They are believed to be masters of the magic that is in the earth— but their hand is absent from this, nor do I think there is anything in them that could forestall what is happening. They may be as helpless as the rest of us, for they are inhabitants of the land even as we are. Another thing: we are told that the first clearance began in Minginish the year Riven was born in his own world. That suggests there is a deeper cause behind this link than simply his stories.'

'A two-way channel,' Riven broke in. 'That's what I thought it must be: a current of magic between me and Minginish. I receive pictures from this world, but in return it also receives something of me, and has done since the day I was born. I didn't create this place. I didn't.' He felt a moment of vast relief. It's not my fault, then, the killing and the destruction. There's something more at work.

'But what?' he asked aloud. 'What is doing it, and why?'

'The Dwarves may not know,' Quirinus said, 'but then again, they know much. They have been here since the first mountains were raised and the Great River first began its slow crawl to the southern sea. They may be able to tell you something of the past which will solve the riddle. I certainly cannot, and it seems Phrynius, who is almost as old as a Dwarf, cannot either, so I think your party's idea of going up into the mountains is a good one, though to be sure I am glad I will not be undertaking it myself.'

'The Greshorns,' Phrynius said reflectively. 'The Mountains of the World's End. It would have been hard to seek a more taxing journey.' He glanced at Quirinus. 'But you will help them? You will aid them on their way?'

'I will,' the bald man said. 'I would do it for Bicker's sake, if for no other reason. They shall find sanctuary in Armishir, and none of Sergius's minions shall touch them there. If any of your company wish to stay behind'—here he addressed Riven again—'then my fief shall be a home to them until they are prepared to go back south.'

Riven thanked him, thinking of the injuries the company had suffered. Madra, at least, could go no farther, and from what he could remember of the fight at Phrynius's house, Ratagan and Isay were likely to be hurt also.

The thought of Madra touched off a coldness in his belly, and he cursed himself for it. There was a time and a place for everything, but he had yet to find it.

'My friends are still locked up in a dungeon,' he said.

One of the Vyrmen leaned forward and said something in his own tongue, which made Quirinus nod.

'Not for much longer, it would seem. They are at this very moment in the tunnels, being led to the city walls. It will soon be time for us to leave as well.'

Riven looked from the Vyrman to Quirinus and back again, and the Lord of Armishir laughed. 'They speak to each other with their minds, my friend.

Sorcery of a sort. It is one of the reasons they needs must skulk down here.'

Quirinus's dour bodyguard spoke for the first time.

'If those we came for are at liberty then we must be on our way also, lord. We have a long way to go before daybreak, and the night is passing now above ground.'

'Indeed,' Quirinus mused. 'You are ever ready to remind me of my duties, Keigar, which is just as well. I'd have happily sat here and spun some talk a while longer.' He stood up, throwing aside his cloak. His clothes were still wet underneath. He beamed down on Phrynius, who squatted at his feet, reminding Riven irresistibly of a garden gnome.

'Time to go, my old friend. It seems that whenever I have a chance to talk with you these days, there is someone at my elbow making me hurry. I hope there will come a time when we can sit and yarn to our heart's content.'

Phrynius gazed at him gravely. 'I will look forward to it. Be careful of yourself.' He touched Riven on the shoulder. 'Quirinus will take you to your friends, and a place of safety. My job has been done.'

'You're not coming?' Riven asked stupidly. He knew suddenly that he would miss the odd little man.

'I stay here. The Vyrmen will find a place for me. But I wish you every blessing on your journey, for the sake of all the people of this land, but for your own sake as well.' He smiled. 'And now you must get wet again.'

The Vyrmen had already positioned themselves at the pool's edge and were talking to Quirinus. There was a splash, and Keigar had disappeared. The bald man beckoned to Riven once, and then followed.

Riven stood up reluctantly. The pool looked dark and cold and uninviting, and he shivered momentarily. One of the Vyrmen touched his forearm and said something.

'He wishes you a safe journey,' the healer said.

'Cheers,' Riven muttered, and he dived into the water.

CHAPTER SIXTEEN

THE JOURNEY WAS longer this time, and Riven was surprised to find they were travelling steeply downwards until he remembered that Talisker was built on a high-sided hill. If they were to leave the city by way of the tunnels, then they would have to descend to its foot.

He was exhausted, and stumbled as he trailed along in the wake of Quirinus and Keigar, his shoulders scraping the walls and his head banging against low spots in the passage. Thirst ravaged him also, though he was not yet desperate enough to consider the water running down the walls around him. It had an unwholesome look, though they had left the sewers behind.

The tunnels grew older in appearance, their walls sagging and crumbling, the floor becoming uneven and the black dagger-shapes of stalactites stabbing from the ceiling.

Quirinus led the way with a torch he had left on the far side of the entrance pool, the light throwing huge, vague shadows around the passageways and leaving floods of blackness in side tunnels and corners. There were no more rats, but several times Riven thought he saw quick, flurried movements out of the corner of his eye and he wondered if the Vyrmen were keeping a watch on them yet. Or perhaps there were other things creeping about in the darkness down here. The idea made the flesh between his shoulder blades crawl, and he wished he were not at the rear.

At last they halted, their breathing and the crackling of the torch the only sound in the subterranean quiet. Riven was grateful for the respite. He leant his back against the wet wall and sucked air in deeply. His legs were on fire, and there was a lightness in his head. His throat seemed to have contracted to a marble-sized hole.

Quirinus handed him a leather-covered flask. 'Drink this. We will be out of the tunnels soon, but there is a journey to make over the land, a ride of some miles, and you will need your strength.'

'How far?' Riven rasped, uncorking the flask. The contents smelled fruity and alcoholic.

'From the city walls to my home at Rim-Armishir is a dozen miles, and we will have to be swift. No doubt, at this moment, the city is humming with the news of you and your friends' disappearance. Sergius's mob will be out in force. Discretion is called for.' He smiled. 'Drink. It will put some strength in you.'

Riven drank. The liquid tasted of tangerines. It cooled his throat and warmed his stomach. His tongue began to feel its normal size again. He handed the flask back, but Quirinus refused it.

'Keep it. By the looks of you, you will have more need of it before the night is out.' Then he turned, nodded at Keigar, and led them onwards again.

This time it was not long before they halted once more. They had only gone a mile or so by Riven's blurred estimation when Quirinus held up his hand for silence and stood with his head cocked, listening. Off in front of them was the rush of running water, echoing up the passageway. Quirinus frowned.

'The water is high, higher than I had thought. Usually there is only a trickle in these levels.'

'It was raining when we took to the sewers,' Keigar offered. 'Perhaps it did not stop.'

'Perhaps,' Quirinus grunted. He shrugged. 'There is little choice for us in the matter, at any rate. Grab each others' belts. I am going to douse the torch.' He looked at Riven. 'This may be a struggle of sorts, getting through this next part, so hold tight.' He raised his arm, and then thrashed the torch out in an explosion of sparks and gledes, leaving them in darkness. The sound of the water seemed abruptly louder. Riven felt Keigar edging forward and tucked his fist into the rear of his belt. They inched along like a trio of blind men.

There was water underfoot, rising rapidly; It climbed over Riven's toes, lipped his ankles and kept rising. When it was up to mid-thigh, he uncorked Quirinus's flask with his free hand and took a few generous swallows. If he was going to be immersed in freezing water yet again, he felt he deserved it.

When it was chest-deep, he could feel the current trying to sweep him off his feet, and his grip on

Keigar's belt tightened. He had visions of being swept away to be lost down unknown tunnels in the bowels of the city, lost for ever inside his own story. He smiled wryly into the darkness.

The water had become a roaring torrent that buffeted and thrust at them, but there was a faint light ahead, grey as cobweb. Riven saw that the tunnel was arching up overhead, widening, and there were squares of grey light set in its ceiling high above. But the water was still rising.

'Keep to the wall!' Quirinus yelled. 'There is a ladder on the right-hand wall. Feel with your hands!'

They struggled along blindly, spray smashing into their faces and filling their gasping mouths. Riven had to struggle to breathe. The air seemed full of furious liquid that beat and thrust at him like storm-tossed branches. For a moment, he lost his feet entirely and was trailing in the rapids, hanging on to Keigar's belt grimly. But he regained his feet and battled along again, keeping the wall close to his right hand, his fingers searching it for a purchase that would help him along.

Keigar stopped, and there were shouted words which Riven could not hear. Then he began to ascend. Riven felt along the wall frantically until he came across a metal rung set in the stone. He pulled himself upwards in Keigar's wake, leaving the water behind. Above, he could see the round shape of Quirinus's head outlined against a square of night sky. He and Keigar pulled him up through the hole, and then he was lying on the shining cobbles of a dark alleyway, with the roar of the water far below him and a soft rain pouring down on his face.

He began to chuckle. A soft night, indeed.

But there was to be no rest. His companions hauled him to his feet and half-carried him along the alley. He blinked water out of his eyes. There were horses here, and men in the shadows wearing rain-silvered armour. He stiffened. A trap, then, after all? But someone wrapped a cloak around his shoulders and shoved him towards a riderless horse.

'Mount!' Keigar's voice hissed in his ear. 'We must be gone!'

He pulled himself wearily into the saddle, feeling the cold water in his clothes gather round his buttocks. Someone else took his reins, and then hoofs were clattering in the street. He pulled the cloak's hood over his head against the insistent rain, and as they rode off, he became dimly aware that Talisker's great walls were looming up around them in the night. The hoofbeats echoed in a tunnel and they passed through a great gateway, then the land was open and dark before them, rolling out into expanses of shadowed hills and the dark pinnacles of the mountains beyond. His mount lurched into a canter along with the others, and he cursed feebly, clinging to the saddle. They were leaving Talisker behind at last, but he felt too tired and beaten to care.

THEY PUSHED THE horses without mercy, seldom slowing from a canter. The ground rose and fell under them, and several times their mounts crashed through the sparkle of shallow streams. The air bit at Riven's wet face, whipping the hood of the cloak back on to his shoulders. He shivered uncontrollably as it froze his sopping clothes to his skin and iced his beard. It was truly winter now, and they were climbing into the foothills of the Greshorn Mountains, the highest of this world. From his glimpses of them, they were many times higher than anything he had climbed on Skye. He put the thought of scaling them out of his head. Warmth was what he wanted now, warmth and sleep. He felt for Quirinus's flask again, but it was gone, lost in the maelstrom of the sewers. He cursed silently and endured the long pain of the ride, losing all sense of time and distance and feeling his toes grow numb in his water-filled boots.

He must have slept or dozed, or at least lost consciousness for a while, for a jolt roused him and he had to struggle to stay in the saddle. They had stopped, and around them was the golden, wind-whipped bloom of torchlight and people on foot taking the horses' heads. A wall reared up, grey and massive, packed with arrowslits and dominated by the yawning chasm of a gate. For a second, Riven thought they were back in Talisker, but people were helping him off his horse, and Quirinus was standing with his face grey in the torchlight and his eyebrows encrusted with rime, telling them to be careful with him. His helpers caught him as his legs crumpled, and someone gathered his frozen form up in their arms. It was Isay, Riven noted without surprise. The Myrcan's face was savage with bruises and gashes, but the flat eyes were as unreadable as ever.

'Well met, Michael Riven,' Isay said, and Riven shut his aching eyes.

'Yeah, right,' he replied, and felt himself carried out of the reach of the wind and the searching rain.

* * *

FACES CAME AND went. He was aware of a fire, of heat baking him. Someone undressed him and wiped the ice from his face, and then he was laid down in a bed; a real bed. And he was able to leave this dream for a while and go back to the real world.

But he woke again with the light of an afternoon steaming in through narrow windows to bar the coverlet. The room was warm, the fire glowing in the hearth. He was stiff and sore, but he found that his scratches had been bandaged and he could feel his toes, which was an improvement.

He sat up. He was alone in the room, though there was a chair by his bed. Outside, he could hear the wind in the eaves, and voices from elsewhere in the house. He lay back again comfortably, memories of dungeons and sewers and rat-people coming and going in his head like the shards of a nightmare. What a place. What a bloody place!

And then he remembered Isay from the night before. So they were safe. They were here. Thank Christ.

There were clothes on a low table to the right of the bed, and he flung aside his coverings to examine them. More Minginish clothes. He was building up quite a wardrobe—or would be, if he were not destroying them all the time.

The door opened, and Madra stood there, joy lighting her face as she saw him sitting up. He grinned at her, and she ran across the room to fling herself into his arms, tumbling him to his back on the bed. He laughed out loud and kissed her soundly. She had a dressing still bound around her throat. He held her face in his hands and gazed into the grave eyes that were dancing with gladness. The sight of them took ten years off him.

'Can you talk yet?'

Her face clouded slightly, and she shook her head. He kissed her on the forehead.

'Are you all right? Did they treat you badly?'

She nodded and shook her head, unable to look away from him. There was incredulity in the eyes now, and her fingers ran through his hair, over his chest, as though to verify that it was really he who was asking her this, who had kissed her so unrestrainedly.

'What about the others? Ratagan—is he all right? I saw him—'

She nodded again, then kissed him into silence.

'Ratagan is alive and well, and I see that you are not in such ill health either, my friend,' the familiar deep voice said from the doorway.

Madra rolled off him and he saw that Ratagan, Bicker, Finnan and the rest of the company were clustered there. Even Luib's face seemed to hold a flicker of amusement.

'There's a time and a place for everything,' Bicker laughed, and they came in like a gale with Quirinus at their rear, his thick brows halfway up his forehead.

Riven threw his legs off the bed and found himself in a bearlike embrace as the big man crushed him to his chest. His face was a purple swollen mess with a livid scab running from temple to nose, but the blue eyes were as unsullied as ever in the middle of it.

The rest of the company were in a similar condition. Even Finnan had his fair share of bruises, whilst Bicker had a linen bandanna stained vermilion around his skull. The dark man grasped Riven's shoulder and shook him.

'Quirinus tells us you have been consorting with wizards and Vyrmen, exploring the hidden passages of Talisker and swimming in the sewers. None of us believes him, of course. For a time, there, you almost had us concerned, Michael Riven.'

Riven grinned. For some reason it seemed remarkably easy to do so.

'I'm as fit as a fiddle. When do we leave?'

'Soon, but not too soon,' Quirinus put in dryly. 'You and your friends had best rest for a day or two before setting out for the mountains. Bicker will explain.'

'Indeed,' the dark man said, his face sobering. 'We are all suffering the after-effects of the Lady Jinneth's hospitality, and her Sellswords are combing the foothills for us.'

'We are, you might say, a trifle sought after,' Ratagan interjected.

'We are outlawed,' Finnan said. He looked glum, probably thinking of his flatboat, still moored inside Talisker's Rivergate. 'They took me soon after I left Phrynius's house. They had been watching it.'

'What happened?' Riven asked. 'How did the Vyrmen free you?'

'With stealth and skill, and some luck.' Bicker nodded towards the bald man in the corner who was watching them intently. 'Quirinus's men helped once we were out of the cells, but even so we had to dispose of a few mercenaries before we quit the city.'

'Not such a distasteful task,' Ratagan said. There

was a perilous light in his eye that made him look oddly like Isay.

'And now my Hearthwares have joined in the hunt for you,' Quirinus added with heavy irony. 'It need not be said that Keigar and I have them well-briefed. You should have a clear route up into the higher foothills at least.'

'Supplies have been readied,' Bicker said. 'We can leave within two days, perhaps even in one, depending on how able we feel.'

Riven asked the question that had been occurring to him even in Phrynius's house.

'Who goes?'

'Yourself, Ratagan and I.' The dark man glanced round the company a trifle uncomfortably. 'Isay insists on joining us. That is all. Madra, you are not fit for it—'

Riven felt her stiffen.

'—and Corrary and Luib will stay to try and see you safely home.'

Corrary made a swift movement of protest, instantly stifled by a look from Bicker.

'I got your brother killed,' the dark man said softly. 'One is enough.' Luib remained impassive.

'At least that is sorted,' Quirinus said, the dry tone back in his voice, and he moved out of his place in the corner. 'And it is almost time to eat. I like my food, and will be happy for whoever of you it pleases to join me.' He left unobtrusively, followed closely by a thoughtful-looking Finnan.

'Our waterborne friend is after a new job,' Ratagan remarked when they had gone.

'And who can blame him?' Bicker asked. The

gladness had leeched out of him, and he was worn and drawn again. 'Come. We will eat. Join us if you feel up to it, Michael Riven. Quirinus lays a good board.' He smiled. 'Though his steward is not yet up to our Colban. I will see you later.'

And he left also, ushering out Corrary and the two Myrcans. Ratagan lingered a moment longer. He strode over to one of the windows and stared out at the snow-flecked mountains beyond.

'Almost there,' he said. He turned around. 'Mereth is doing well. She is a fine girl. A fine woman, indeed. Quirinus is trying to locate her father—discreetly, of course...' He trailed off, and bent his great grizzled head to look at his hands. There was grey in his hair, Riven noted with something like a shock. He seemed battered and mortal, and suddenly unsure; a Thor facing Ragnarok. But when he looked up, there was the usual grin on his face. 'I had best go. I will miss the best of the beer. And I think you two may have a few things to talk around. Be good.' He exited quietly.

Riven sat back on the bed and Madra's arm encircled his waist. She laid her cheek on his shoulder. Almost there. And for the first time the thought held no terror for him. He felt that the many strands in this story were finally coming together.

Everything is meant to be.

He hugged Madra closer to him, feeling strangely whole.

AND LATER, WHEN night had come and he was watching the snow pile up in crescents at the windows, and the fire was a red eye in the darkness of the room, she came to him again. She was barefoot, and wore a long cloak that hung to her ankles. As she stood by his bed, with her dark hair like a hood about her face, he was reminded of Jinneth in the dungeon. But she cast the cloak aside with a twitch of her shoulders and stood nude before him, the low glow of the coals bathing her skin in scarlet and shadow. She slipped into the bed with the cold air about her, seeking his warmth. He gave it to her without stint, taking and receiving all she offered. And none of the old ghosts came to crowd at his shoulder. He was a boy again, a youth with questions in his eyes and wonder at the sheer delight of touching her and joining himself to her. Again, he felt that fleeting sense of wholeness, of rightness. He was one with the slowly falling snow outside, the savage splendour of the mountains, the frozen earth and the people who walked it. He was splicing himself into the fabric of a world that had claimed him before his birth, and was happy to do so, for it was fitting. And he felt himself healed.

It was time, at last, to seek the mountains.

CHAPTER SEVENTEEN

TALISKER WAS A hazy hill with the grey blade of the Great River winding around its feet. They stopped in their upward trek to look back at it, at the vast open plain of the Vale shining white in the weak sunlight, the black smudges of villages with their wisps of smoke, the beetle-like clutter of buildings that were Rim-Armishir already distant.

Riven, Bicker, Ratagan, Isay. And then there were four. They were on the last leg of the Quest, climbing slowly but steadily into the foothills of the mountains. The Greshorns. And in their midst the Red Mountain; the Staer. Arat Gor to the Dwarves, and, in another world, Sgurr Dearg.

Three weeks, perhaps, if the weather holds. Not long left. Riven's legs were stiff and sore, his collar bone aching with the weight of the pack perched high on his shoulders. There was a wind picking up to stir the dry snow and whirl it in clouds about them. It was cold. The snow had stopped falling, and was even now beginning to melt, but there was more of it on the bitter wind and he could see where the distant heights were dusted with it. He peered ahead though the pain in his skull and his sucking lungs to see great ragged masses of stone rearing up to the sky in twisting ridges and peaks, veined with snow, bare as gravestones. The very sight ate away his strength, made him want to turn and stumble back down the steep way they had come, perhaps even to take his place at the side of a frowning woman who could not speak.

But no. He had things to do. Places to see and people to meet. He smiled into the wind.

They stopped their staring and continued on their way wordlessly, with Talisker and its fiefs at their backs and the stony hills in front.

The day went past in a tired upward haul and the quiver of thigh muscles forcing themselves to flex and straighten time after time. They shed clothing as they walked, and sweated and laboured over boulder fields wet with slush, through ankle-deep mountain streams as clear as wet glass.

There were curlews here, and once they startled a brace of grouse that launched themselves from under their feet as they trudged along. Where the snow melted, there was copper-coloured bracken on the sides of the hills and rabbit droppings on grassy slopes. And once they saw an eagle circling with his fingered feathers spread against the grey sky.

Speed, bonny boat...

At the fall of the first night, they camped below a profusion of rock buttresses that leered down at them, naked of vegetation. The ground was hard and chill, and Riven was grimly satisfied. Somehow it seemed more concrete with every step. There were no warriors here, no fortresses or monsters. Only the gaunt emptiness of the hills taking him back to what he had once been. He felt he could trust the cruelty of the granite cliffs and the icefields, the sullen massiveness of the mountains. He was at home here, as he had always been in the high, desolate places of Skye.

More days went by, and the silence of the mountains became infectious. Even Ratagan was quiet and subdued, whereas Bicker wore a constant frown under his bandaged skull. All of them found the going hard, their recent sufferings having taken a toll of stamina and fitness. But they had not objected when Riven announced on their second morning in Quirinus's home that they must leave at once. They seemed to recognise that there was something in him that was calling for urgency. It was almost as though they had an appointment to keep.

Their way began to take them through the peaks proper and they found themselves treading the narrow ways at the foot of massive acned scree slopes with snow peppering the stones. The wind was cut off, and there was only the rattle of the rock and the far shriek of the eagles as they circled tirelessly in another world far above.

Could be they can see Glenbrittle from where they fly, maybe even out to sea, and the dark cliffs of Rhum with Muck and Eigg somewhere behind it. Maybe they can even glimpse the fishing boats around Mallaig, and hear the gulls.

Higher up, the snow was not melting, and they began to sink ankle-deep as they walked farther in to the mountains. The sky remained overcast and dull, and the aching, bone-numbing cold seemed to defeat the efforts of every fire they lit and soak its way through their bedding every night.

The lower paths disappeared, and they began to ascend, seeking the knife ridges for the easiest way to maintain altitude. Here the wind could launch itself at them, and it tore at their clothing, numbing their faces and making their way among the ice-covered rocks treacherous.

Apart from eagles, they saw no other living thing this high, but they all sensed that there were others in the mountains, other things watching them; following them, perhaps. The feeling grew so strong that they would stop often as if by common consent and scan the surrounding slopes for movement. There was the rattle of stone that could have been furtive steps, or may have been the wind in the rocks.

'Sellswords would never follow us this high,' Bicker said, voicing their fears. 'There is no profit in it.' And they nodded, but remained watchful just the same.

They found themselves travelling through a desert of stone and ice, and lacking stuff to burn, huddled like children at night for the warmth, chewed their food cold and swallowed the snow they walked across until it made their throats ache. Soon it seemed that they had left any memory of warmth and comfort behind and were being transformed into creatures of the mountains themselves, chill and hard as the granite of the winding ridges and peaks, dumb as pebbles, scoured by the whining wind into new shapes, new hardnesses.

Two weeks went by in a grinding march after Bicker's lead. They were following a horseshoe course through the Greshorns, to come upon the long ridge from which jutted the steep peak of the Staer, the backbone of the entire range. If there were Dwarves in the mountains, it was said that it was here they dwelt, in the shadow of the Red Mountain, looking out over a vast gulf on to the land of men below. Myrcans had used the place as a lookout post for centuries, and had had many dealings with the Dwarves, but that had ended with the clearances. It was said that the Hidden Folk who had fled into the Greshorns had been taken in by the Stone-folk, as they were called. None had ever returned to the lands below to confirm the rumour.

They halted on the twist of a sharp ridge, the steam of their breath whipping away in the wind. Bicker scanned the ground ahead.

'We follow this one down, and should come to that bit of valley with the wide stream in the bottom. We'll camp there. The way becomes easier for a while before we come to the last few ascents.'

They jammed their feet into crevices to fight the tearing air and looked down from the ridge to a flat, gravel-floored valley with a shallow stream steel-grey on its floor and some dark shrubs clinging to life along its banks.

'By all that's holy,' Ratagan said, 'we may have something to burn tonight besides snow, and warm food in our bellies.'

'Best make the most of it,' the dark man retorted. 'After tonight I doubt if we will have a fire again in these mountains. We will be going too high.'

In the evening, it grew dark earlier than usual, with the clouds thick and dark enfolding the peaks around their heads. They sat around their small fire and listened to the wind and the promise of bitter weather in its noise. Close by, the stream burbled quietly to itself.

Ratagan held his big hands out to the fire like fans, his eyes reflecting the flame above his beard. They blinked slowly.

'How much farther do you think it is?' he asked the company in general. 'Where do you find Dwarves in these mountains?'

No one spoke. Bicker looked tired, and Isay's face was empty. Even his Myrcan sternness seemed weary. Riven poked an ember back into the fire with his boot. He could have told them he was sure something had to happen before the Dwarves would reveal themselves, but that would have sounded ridiculous, so he held his tongue.

And something did happen.

Rocks cracked and tumbled beyond the light of the fire. Dark shapes moved and boots crunched on the wiry heather. Others splashed through the stream to their side.

'We are attacked!' Ratagan roared. 'Beware!'

Instantly the four of them were on their feet, travel-weariness forgotten, weapons in hand. Riven was hefting a longsword which Quirinus had given him, Ratagan a borrowed battleaxe, Bicker a short sword and Isay an ironbound staff that had been dug out of the armoury at Rim-Armishir. They stood in a circle with their backs to the fire and met their attackers squarely.

They came in a rush, skidding on scree or charging up out of the stream. Bicker killed one as he slipped on the bank and kicked another back into the water in an explosion of spray. Ratagan clanged another's sword aside and shoved him to the ground, stamping his heel in the man's face and then catching the weapon arm of his comrade and slinging him out of the firelight to collide with a boulder. He split the skull of the first man as he struggled on the ground, with a bark that was half laughter, half the cry of a triumphant animal.

More of the enemy poured in around them. Isay knocked the feet out from under two in a swift blur of movement, and poked his staff butt viciously into their breastbones. There were two loud cracks, sharp and high through the tumult, as the men's rib cages collapsed. There was a wild light in Isay's eyes, and Riven thought he heard him humming above the noise of the fighting.

A snarling face ran up against Riven out of the darkness, and their sword hilts crashed together. He threw his attacker back and the man stumbled, slipping on loose stone. Riven plunged his blade in at the neck and saw blood spurt black in the firelight, then he had to wrench free as another came at him, and twist his sword round frantically to ward off a blow. A voice shouted, clear and high in the night: 'The Teller must live! Harm him not!' A woman's voice. Riven felt an absurd need to laugh, but the effort of parrying another blow took away his breath. The appointment had been kept, but would they live to see what happened after?

He killed the man without thought, his body using reflexes he had learned in the past months. But another took his place.

A body crashed down on the fire, filling the air with sparks. For a moment they were fighting in the middle of a firework display, before the wind caught the flying embers and took them and snuffed them out, and then they were fighting in near-darkness with the glint of swords reflecting the faint luminescence of the clouds above the mountains, and the snarling faces of their enemies pale blurs in the night.

But the fight slackened. It trickled away. Their foes backed off, cursing, bumping into each other. A woman's voice screeched at them to stand fast, to do their job, to earn their money, but they would have none of it. Ratagan's savage laughter followed their running backs out into the night. Isay darted after them with murder in his eye, ignoring Bicker's order to stay put. Riven felt the foul sweat on him turning cold and smarting his cuts. The smell of the burning man on the ruin of the fire filled the air with a stench that even the mountain breeze could not dispel. And then Isay came struggling back, pulling with him a frantic figure that fought him like a cat. He threw her down by the side of the fire, and she looked up at them with her eyes flaming. Isay's stave had bruised her right temple and there was a thin thread of blood there, trickling slowly down to her neck.

'My Lady Jinneth,' Bicker panted, his face wolfish. 'We are well met this winter's evening.'

The wind whistled round their heads in the darkness, and there was a cold touch on Riven's face. He raised his head and it kissed his eyelids, melted on his lips. Ratagan lifted his eyes to the high peaks and stared.

'Snow,' he said.

THE BLIZZARD WAS swift in rising. In minutes, a curtain of snow had enveloped them on all sides and was coating their clothes and hair, thickening on their eyelashes, covering the corpses that littered the campsite.

'We'll not last the night in this if we can't find shelter,' Bicker shouted over the strengthening wind. 'Pack up!'

'What about her?' Riven asked, gesturing towards the woman who crouched on the ground beside them as though ready to spring.

'She comes with us. Isay, guard her!'

They retrieved their gear from where the fighting had scattered it, and bundled it into their holdalls. They could hardly see in the spinning murk. Isay lashed a leather strap about Jinneth's wrists and tethered it to his belt. When she tugged on it, Riven saw him turn and put the tip of his staff against her throat, a thin smile bleakening his face. Then he tugged her onwards.

They ploughed through the blizzard, the snow piling on their faces. Riven could feel the ground rising under their feet and wondered how Bicker knew where he was taking them, but the dark man did not falter. As they continued to slog uphill, Riven realised they were scaling the ridge at the end of the valley that he had seen before nightfall, the one that coiled westwards like a dragon's backbone and led into the high peaks. But what shelter would there be for them up there?

They pushed on silently, struggling against the wind and the driving snow. Ice formed in Riven's beard and eyebrows. His hands stiffened even in the fur mittens that Quirinus had supplied for them all. The snow became deeper, lapping at his calves, and it was agony to force his legs to bend and stretch through it. At the same time, he was keeping his eyes fixed grimly on Bicker's back, terrified of losing sight of the dark man in the whirling gloom.

Suddenly Bicker let out a cry and sank out of sight in the snow. Riven rushed forward, and found himself sinking in a deep drift that had accumulated in a dip of rock. He floundered in the snow uselessly, chest-deep—then Ratagan had extended a brawny fist to him and was pulling him up and out. Behind him, Bicker's head could be seen sticking out of the whiteness, almost invisible through the snow curtain.

Riven lay gasping in the shallower snow, but in a second he had joined Ratagan in trying to throw a rope to the dark man. They saw his hand reach up out of the drift to grab it, but the wind was blowing it back towards them.

'You'll have to weight it with something!' Riven yelled over the roar of the storm. Ratagan nodded. It was impossible to see any expression on his face under its covering of ice. He fumbled with his mittens, stuffed them down the front of his sheepskins and then began laboriously tying the rope around the haft of his axe with slow, cold-numbed fingers.

Isay joined them, dragging Jinneth with him. She sank to her knees in the snow as he halted, and Riven saw that her hair had frozen to her shoulders.

'Damn these hands!' Ratagan raged, struggling to make his fingers tie the knot. He stopped to beat his arms against his side.

'Let me!' Riven shouted. He discarded his own mittens and began fumbling with the rope, marvelling at how so simple an action could be rendered so difficult.

A sound bit through the tumult of the storm: a high-pitched howl that carried above the wind's fury for a moment and then was dampened by the snow. Riven paused.

'What was that?'

'Tie the damn knot!' Ratagan screamed, his head up and his eyes scanning the blankness of the storm. 'We don't have much time!'

It was done. Riven threw the axe to where Bicker's head was still faintly visible against the snow, praying belatedly that it wouldn't split his skull. As he did, they heard the howling on the wind again. It seemed to be coming from farther down the ridge, but it was louder now, gaining ground.

Bicker tugged on the rope, and immediately the three of them began hauling him in like an overweight fish. Finally he was with them, bulky with clinging snow, his face grey.

'Rime Giant,' he gasped with stiff lips. 'Did you hear it?'

Ratagan and Riven helped him up, and he shook snow off himself like a dog. The cry on the wind came again—very close, now. It was somewhere to their left, hidden by the blizzard.

'It knows we're here,' Ratagan told them. 'It stalks us.'

'Christ!' Riven said, remembering the dream at Beechfield where he had encountered a giant in the snow.

'Come on!' Bicker shouted, breaking the spell of immobility. 'We must keep moving!'

He forged off to the right, flanking the drift before them. Riven saw him tug his short sword out of its scabbard. His own fingers felt too numb to do anything, much less fight a Rime Giant. Once again he wondered if Bicker knew where he was going.

The right-hand way seemed to be the northern slope of a sharp ridge. Riven found he was trudging with his left leg higher than his right. He slipped and skidded on ice beneath the snow, falling to his knees. A blast of wind struck him like a great hand and knocked him sideways. He fought himself upright, almost blind. Ratagan bumped into him from behind and helped him fight his way forward. They both yelled at Bicker to slow down, to wait, and he looked back at them impatiently.

Something happened to the storm. It was as if it had suddenly climbed a dozen octaves. The wind shrieked across the mountainside like a gleeful and demented being, tearing the breath out of their throats and clubbing them to the rock. It gouged chunks of snow out of overhangs and hollows and sent them flailing along the ground like tumbleweed. They were beaten flat by its blast, and sank their numb fingers into ice and snow, seeking a purchase there to prevent them being plucked off the mountain. Riven felt Ratagan gripping one of his pack straps, anchoring him. Ahead Bicker clung to an ice-covered boulder like a desperate spider.

And then the howling came over the wind, loud and gloating—and very close. Riven's head snapped up instinctively into the blast of the wind, but the raging snow forced his eyes shut.

Behind them Jinneth screamed into the storm.

Riven twisted in Ratagan's grip and looked back, shielding his eyes in one hand. It was hard to see, but he thought he could make out movement there—figures tumbling in the blizzard. Shards of other cries were swept away by the wind.

Ratagan hauled himself upright. 'It attacks!' he cried, fumbling for his axe, but he slipped and the wind pushed him off his feet. Riven reached out for him frantically as he slithered through the snow.

Jinneth ran into view, her hands still bound in front of her. She fell to the ground and crawled through the snow, which whipped up in a cloud around her. She was shouting something that Riven could not hear. Snow had invaded every crevice of his features, had filled his ears and fought to seal shut his eyes. He grabbed her as she came to him.

'Where is Isay? What happened?' But the storm snatched the words out of his mouth.

He saw it then, looming out of the blizzard like winter incarnate, the icy points of its eyes glowing like stars. Its fur was matted with snow and ice hung in great spears from its blunt jaw.

Incredibly Isay was upright, fighting it. His staff was battering the Giant as it advanced, and it tried

to ward off his blows with great sweeps of its arms.
But he was faltering. His feet could find no sure grip
in the snow and ice and loose rock, and time and
time again he half fell only to redeem himself with
the skill of an acrobat.

Even as Riven watched, the Myrcan's staff snapped
in his grip, shivering into two pieces, and Isay was
smashed aside by one slap of a shaggy arm. The
Rime Giant howled again, and met Riven's eyes.

It knows who I am.

He was frozen to the ground, Jinneth's weight half
on him, anchoring him there. He could not move.

I'm going to die.

He heard Ratagan yelling into the wind and Bicker
answering, but they were too far away. Nothing
could stop those eyes. The Giant rushed on him
like a mountain, its mouth agape—and flinched as
a football-sized chunk of rock struck it in the head.

Ratagan was up the slope with Bicker, and they
were raining lumps of frozen stone down on the
creature, their faces contorted with shouting that
Riven could not hear.

Another rock struck the Giant in the jaw and
splintered blood into the wind. It roared with fury
and started upslope.

Isay appeared from nowhere with the broken end
of his staff in his hand. He stumbled behind the
giant, and in a thrust that took his feet out from
under him, stabbed the splintered end into its groin.

The Giant screamed shrilly and spun round, falling
to one knee with its blood pouring out in a black,
steaming rush on to the snow. Isay rolled away
like a man possessed as it tumbled forward after

him. It fell on its face, still screaming, and began dragging itself in pursuit, its legs kicking feebly, but Ratagan and Bicker climbed on its back like intrepid mountaineers. Riven saw Bicker's sword sink to the hilt and Ratagan's axe split the great skull. The Rime Giant stopped moving. Its blood began to freeze on the snow.

Riven became aware that Jinneth was clinging to him, her face buried in his chest. He pushed her away and stood up, swaying against the battery of the wind. His three friends were staggering towards him, sculpted in white, their faces frozen masks.

'I know where there is shelter!' Bicker shouted in his ear. 'We must be quick, or the woman will die.' He pointed at Jinneth, and Riven saw she was only half-conscious. The shock of the Giant had almost finished her. He bent and slapped her face roughly until the eyes had regained a measure of awareness. Then he grasped her wrist strap and pulled her to her feet. They forged on into the storm, leaving the Rime Giant corpse a hill of snow behind them.

THE BLIZZARD CONTINUED unabated, and they battled their way forward, bent almost double under its fury. They could hardly see and were reduced to their hands and knees, scrabbling through the ice-cocooned rocks of the mountainside. Riven was nearing his end. Only the fact that he could pull Jinneth on behind him kept him going—that, and the terror at the thought of losing sight of Bicker. So he ploughed forward relentlessly in the dark man's wake, his feet and hands becoming suspiciously comfortable with their lack of feeling, and a drowsiness that he knew was the onset of hypothermia creeping up on him.

Hands shook him, punching him, and he opened his eyes irritably. He had stopped to lie down in the snow. Jinneth was pummelling him, her hair a helmet of ice about her head and her eyes dull. He laboured to his feet, and set off again. Bicker had been fibbing. There was no shelter here. There was nothing but the snow and the stone and the Giants. He would lie down again in a moment, and get some sleep. He was not cold at all.

His boots scraped on stone, and the wind disappeared. It was cut off at once. He opened his eyes again, but there was no light. He could see nothing. His shoulders hurt, and encrusted ice was cracking away there. He realised that two people were hauling him along, his legs trailing on the ground. The absence of the storm's roar was like a great hissing sound in his head, filling his brain.

'Where are we?' he asked in a mumble, but no one answered.

He heard Bicker exclaim in surprise, and was placed on the floor next to Jinneth. Someone threw blankets over them both and began chafing his hands and slapping his cheeks. He snarled at them. Couldn't they leave him alone? But then warmth lapped his face, light flickered beyond his iced-up eyelids, and he forced himself to look.

A fire. There was a fire burning in the blackness, revealing rough rock walls all around. He thought he was back in the sewers for a moment, but no: it was Bicker and Isay who were building up the flames, taking thick faggots from a high pile by the wall and creating a bright, burning blaze. The smoke caught at Riven's throat and he coughed, whilst at the same time he felt the first agony of returning feeling in his hands and groaned aloud. Ratagan ceased his chafing and buffeted him good-naturedly on the side of the head, dislodging half-melted ice.

'Good of you to join us, my friend. Now keep your eyes open and count your toes. Take your clothes off and get warm. Bicker has worked a miracle.'

Riven groaned again. There was a flaming pain in his extremities. His ears and nose were on fire. But he forced himself to wriggle out of his pack and limp over to the fire.

Bicker and Isay seemed almost maniacal in the light of the flames, feeding the fire with feverish urgency. They had stripped down to their breeches and meltwater was glittering in their hair. Riven began peeling off his own sopping garments.

'How the hell did you find this place?' he asked Bicker.

The dark man shrugged. 'Luck, mainly. The Myrcans use it sometimes when they come this high. We have been fortunate. They—or someone—have left a goodly store of wood, which is a precious thing at this height. It has saved our lives, in all likelihood. How are your fingers and toes? Have you feeling back in them?'

'And some. It's been a long night,' he said tiredly. The warmth was lulling him into drowsiness even as he spoke.

Ratagan came to the fire, half-carrying Jinneth. He had thrown a blanket around her and she was naked underneath. Her thawed hair hung about her face in dark tails.

'The lady here is not feeling herself, I think,' he said.

There was an edge to his voice. He laid her down close to the blaze and arranged the blanket about her limbs with a gruff gentleness that made Riven smile. Beer was not Ratagan's only weakness. He was a sucker for ladies in distress, even those who had tried to have him killed.

Jinneth stirred feebly and moaned, and moments later, she opened her eyes. Her gaze sprang to the fire and to the four men around it. She sat up and the blanket fell away, revealing breasts with cold-hard nipples. Her eyes blazed, and she covered herself. 'Animals!' she spat.

Bicker regarded her wearily. 'We animals saved your life after you had tried to take ours, so save your outrage and give us some answers instead.'

She glared at him but said nothing. He sighed and poked at the fire.

'Why did you come after us?' Riven asked her. 'What was the point?' His voice shook a little. He wished he had not seen her nakedness. It brought back too many secret memories.

'You have power in you. I wanted it,' she said simply, but her words did not ring true. There was bafflement on her face for a second, and she shook her head as if exasperated. 'I don't know. I had to follow you. I don't know why.' She sounded bewildered, and Riven had to stop himself from reaching out to her. Here, with the trappings of wealth and intrigue missing, she was more than ever like Jenny. She was young, adrift. He swallowed and looked away.

Skeins of smoke hung in the air like streamers. There was no sound in the cave except for the crackling of the fire. Jinneth glanced round at their closed faces.

'Where are you going?' She sounded almost plaintive.

'We seek the Dwarves,' Ratagan rumbled. 'We seek answers, a way to end the torment of Minginish.'

'And you are the key,' she said to Riven.

He nodded dumbly.

'You are fools,' she told them.

'And what are you?' Bicker asked her quietly, but his eyes were hard. 'What manner of woman are you—or are you a woman at all?'

'Put her out into the blizzard,' Isay said levelly, startling them. 'I see nothing but ill in her.'

'No!' Riven exclaimed at once. They stared at him and he stammered under their scrutiny. 'She has to come along with us. I don't know why, but she's supposed to be here, with us.'

'Is it because of who she resembles?' Bicker asked.

Riven bent his head. 'I don't know. Maybe. I think it's no accident she is here. I think she was drawn here as surely as I was.'

Jinneth regarded Riven with wonder. 'Who do I resemble? Why would I be drawn into this?'

He looked at her. 'You are the twin of my wife, who is dead.'

She blinked. 'You are a wizard,' she whispered. 'You and your companions. How else could you have escaped from the cells?'

Ratagan barked with laughter. 'We had help, lady, from a source you have never dreamed of. We used no magic. But what if we had? Would that then entitle you to hound us out of the lands of men and into these mountains, to mistreat our children, to confiscate our property? I think not.' And he spat into the fire.

Jinneth did not answer, but gazed at them across the fire. Isay's implacable eyes, Bicker's wariness, Ratagan's anger; Riven's twisted mouth.

'You are men,' she said bitterly. 'What do you know of being a woman in this world, where you must warm a bed to get what you want? You who blunder through this life with your swords and your armour—what do you know?'

'You have not done so badly for yourself,' Bicker said.

'Not so badly? Do you know how many times I have had to endure the slaverings of a man I loathe to reach my aim, how many times I have had to lie under a man at night and make noises like an imbecile to make him think I take pleasure in it? Do you? And you think it is a courageous thing to swing a sword...' She trailed off.

'Not every woman is so obsessed by the trappings of power that she must needs open her legs to every lord who comes along,' Ratagan snapped.

Jinneth stood up suddenly and discarded her blanket. She stood naked before them, with her hands on her hips, the firelight painting her skin in dancing colours. Riven stared at her for a moment and then closed his eyes with a low groan. Ratagan looked away with a flush creeping up his neck.

Bicker buried his gaze in the flames, scowling. Only Isay continued to stare at her, a frown biting a deep line between his brows.

'There is not one of you here who, given some wine and privacy, would not be happy to take this body of mine and use it for your own pleasure. Why then should I not get something in exchange?'

She sat down again and tugged the blanket about her, a silver brightness welling up in her eyes.

'It doesn't have to be like that,' Riven whispered, but she did not hear him. There was an uncomfortable silence.

Abruptly Bicker began rummaging through the packs. 'Time we ate. Some hot food would do us good,' he said.

Isay helped him break out some of the soup blocks he had been hoarding since they left Rim-Armishir. Soon two blocks were bubbling and swelling in the party's single copper pot. They were getting low on food. There was dried beef and fruit, more soup blocks and a small bag of flour, but it was over two weeks since they had set out and the packs that had once seemed so crushingly heavy now seemed feather-light, weighed down only by their personal gear.

While the food was being prepared, Riven took the opportunity to take a brand from the fire and walk down the cave away. He was curious to know how deep it went, and he wanted Jinneth out of his sight for a while. Ratagan followed him, and together the pair explored in silence. The cavern continued off into the darkness for as far as their makeshift torch would let them see. It was narrow but high-roofed, and the floor was smooth. Their footsteps echoed off the walls.

'More like a passage than a cave,' Riven murmured, his voice loud in the quiet. They could no longer hear the others or see the glow of the fire. The smoke from his burning stick made him cough.

'Perhaps we are in the hallway of a Dwarf's mansion,' Ratagan said, only half in jest. He perched himself on a blunt stalagmite comfortably and folded his arms. 'Does it still hurt, to see her so near?' he asked gently.

Riven looked at him. He seemed part of the stone in the dim light. 'Yes. More so, up here. They have become even more similar.'

'And she is meant to be here, you say,' Ratagan mused. 'By who? I wonder. And is it a good thing, or a bad thing?'

Riven shook his head. 'I don't think there's any good or bad in this. It's just the way it's turned out, like an equation. Something that must happen. Meeting the Dwarves may be the catalyst to some sort of reaction.'

'Ah.' Ratagan tried not to look mystified, making Riven smile.

'Do you believe she is evil?' he asked the big man.

Ratagan's brow furrowed. 'Evil! What a word. A mighty term to be throwing about. No, I do not believe she is evil, though she does miserable things for pitiful ends. I think she does not truly know what she wants.' He wrung his hands together as though washing them. 'Killing is evil—taking a joy in it. Making laughter out of it. That is evil.' His voice was heavy with grief.

Riven remembered him slaughtering the Sellswords at the campsite, his savage laughter following their retreating backs. 'We all get carried away,' he said lamely.

Ratagan looked up at him and smiled wryly. 'Aye.'

A cold air blew up the passage and they both shivered, for they were half-naked, their clothes drying at the fire. The brand in Riven's hand fluttered like a trapped bird and almost went out.

'We'd better get back,' he said, but for some reason neither of them moved. It was as though they were waiting for something to happen.

They listened, and heard nothing but the slow drip of water somewhere and their own quickening breathing. Then the brand went out, and they were smothered in darkness. Riven moved instinctively to Ratagan's side, dropping the brand to the floor. His heartbeat rose like a dull thunder in his throat.

And then there was a light, a blue-white aura that slowly grew in the passage, lighting the walls and the high ceiling, spreading up and down in all directions; allowing them to see the four figures that surrounded them.

Four figures no more than five feet high, but massively broad, their shoulders wide as doors. They had long, thick beards and their huge fists gripped heavy hammers. Their foreheads were bald and gnarled, and in the pits below them, their eyes glittered with a red light.

'Dwarves,' Ratagan said hoarsely.

CHAPTER EIGHTEEN

'WE ARE THE Graijhnehr, the Folk of Stone,' one Dwarf said. His voice was as deep as the rumbling of a subterranean avalanche, and the red light flashed from his eyes like the glow of coals in a fire.

'We are the oldest of all the peoples of the world, and we live the longest. We have seen the life of Minginish running from the time when the great woods covered the Vale and the hill of Talisker was uncrowned by any tower, to the present, when winter has replaced summer, beasts roam the land and men turn on each other to no good end.'

The cavern was low-ceilinged, Ratagan's head scraping stone, but it stretched out to an immense distance on every side, the roof supported by thick pillars hewn out of the living rock. On the pillars were carved the shapes of men, women, animals—even Rime Giants and grypesh. Riven saw a gogwolf snarling on one, a Vyrman crouched on another, and a Myrcan standing stolidly on a third.

Set in the floor of the cavern at irregular intervals were circular pits filled with fire. The flames licked up to bathe the pillars and the entire cavern, making it a vision of hell. A dozen Dwarves were sitting in high-backed chairs before the company, their eyes glowing with a light to match the fiery pits in the floor. At their rear were a line of pillars different from the others. Each was sculpted in the shape of a gigantic Dwarf struggling to hold up the rock of the granite ceiling, his face contorted with effort. There were twelve of them, all different, all straining with agony written in every eye. They looked unnervingly real.

The cavern was uncomfortably warm, and sweat beaded Riven's forehead. He stood before the Dwarves with the rest of the company in silence. They had been disarmed and brought here by the four Dwarves he and Ratagan had encountered in the passageway. Now they stood as if they were on trial.

And the Dwarf who was addressing them had the face of Calum MacKinnon, Jenny's father.

'We have seen many men enter these mountains. Many of them have left their bones here. Some we have assisted, some we have ignored, some we have slain. You have a Myrcan with you. That is good, for the Soldier-folk were hewn out of Dwarf-crafted stone. You have a tall man and a dark man. You have a lady. And you have one who has power locked up inside him like the water in a dam. One who is not made out of the stuff of this world, who is so alien that we could smell him as his feet touched the very stones of the mountains. An interesting company, indeed. And it is pursued across the peaks by Giants and men. The Vyr-folk have aided it, and the Hidden Folk are friends with it. An interesting company.'

The Dwarf fell silent as if pondering them. None of his comrades moved or spoke. They might have been made out of stone themselves. But there was a low humming in Riven's mind, like a far-off mutter of talk. He stared at the Dwarf who was Calum again. The beard changed the face and the eyes were strange, but it was him, down to the humorous quirk at the side of the mouth; a quirk Jenny had inherited and Jinneth shared. But the Dwarf's face was impassive, with none of the dancing life in it that had made Calum's so mobile. The red eyes made it look inhuman.

Standing behind the company were other Dwarves, a great crowd of them. Riven and his companions had run the gauntlet of their stares as they had entered, the Stone-folk clearing a path for them to the twelve high seats. They varied in size and appearance. Some were almost as tall as a man, though twice as broad. Others were so short as to be grotesque, their heads not reaching Riven's waist and their knuckles dangling on the floor. They were all huge-limbed, with hands like spades, their thighs as thick as tree trunks, their chests like barrels. Most were bearded, the hair on their chins either cropped bristling and short or grown long as a woman's hair and tucked into broad belts. Some wore it braided. Others had moustaches whose ends drooped past their chins, or were stiffened with what looked like lime so they had the appearance of pale tusks. Some were bald, their wrinkled scalps shining in the red heat of the hall; others had thick, long hair combed into ponytails or trailing down their backs; They all appeared old, their faces lined and their noses long, their eyes sunk in cavern-like sockets over which sprouted thick, angry eyebrows. Their eyes glowed in the dimness, shining like the eyes of an animal caught in a searchlight, but with a red radiance as if inside each of their skulls was a tiny inferno.

They had made a low murmur as the company entered the hall, but now they were silent, though Riven could feel the pressure of their stares on his back.

'What is your errand in these mountains?' the Dwarf asked. It was Bicker who answered.

'We came seeking you, Lord of Stone. We sought to avail ourselves of your wisdom.'

The Dwarf raised one eyebrow. 'Indeed? And you have found us. What questions would you put to the Folk of Stone?'

Bicker hesitated and glanced at Riven, who nodded to the dark man and stepped forward.

'I must tell you a story first,' he said.

He stood there for a long time in the red light, with the sweat gathering and the eyes of the Dwarves set on him unwaveringly, and he told them the story he and Minginish had become. He told them of his own adventures in the land above, and of what had befallen him in his own world. He told them of Jenny and Hugh, Calum and the dark girl. He spoke of the wanderings of Murtach and Bicker, the battles that had taken place in Talisker and the Dales, the plight of the Hidden Folk and the timing of the clearances. And he told them of his own books. He drew their plots out in the firelight and pointed out the similarities and the differences between what he had written and what was real. He told them he had seen this hall of theirs long before he had ever entered it. It was a scene out of his third book that he had not yet written but had visualised. He knew that the name of the Dwarf who looked like Calum was Thormod, and he thought that the name of this place might be Kasnrim Jhaar, the Place of the Iron Fort in their own tongue.

There was a stir amongst the Dwarves at this, and some of them muttered angrily. But most regarded Riven with open wonder, and Thormod had a half-smile on his face that made him look more than ever like Calum.

'We have a sorcerer of the human kind among us,' one of the other Dwarves said. 'He is not the first and he has a facility with tales, it is true, but can we believe what he says?'

'He spoke the name of this place in our own tongue. No man has ever done that before,' another said.

'There is power in him such as I have never seen before in a man,' a third rumbled thoughtfully.

'His description of events in the land above is accurate,' said a fourth. 'There, at least, he told the truth.'

'He travels with a Myrcan. They do not offer their services lightly,' one put in, and there was a bass murmur of agreement from all of the seated Dwarves.

Thormod spoke, cutting short the discussion.

'What do you seek from us?' he asked, almost gently.

Riven returned his gaze wearily. His clothes were soaked with sweat and his head was beginning to spin. His throat was as dry as sand from speaking. He swayed where he stood, and felt Isay's hand steady him.

'Answers,' he said. 'I want you to tell me about magic, and how it came into Minginish.'

One of the Dwarves snorted with derision, but Thormod frowned.

'What is it you wish to do?'

Riven sighed. 'I thought I had made it clear. To close the doors between Minginish and my world. To stop what is happening to this place.'

And I want my wife to rest in peace. But somehow he could not say that with Jinneth standing behind him.

Thormod regarded him in silence for a moment.

'We knew you were coming,' he admitted at last. 'And I at least knew your errand. We retain contacts with the Vyr-folk of the cities and the Hidden Folk of the mountains. We know Phrynius, though he was a young man when last I saw him. You tell the truth, and you frighten me. There is enough power in you to tear this world apart and rebuild it again. Maybe that is what you and your stories are doing.

'We know also of the existence of the door on Arat Gor, the Red Mountain, though none of my people have ventured through it. We have placed a guard on it and none has passed that way in the last months. But we have seen this dark girl who is the sister to the lady in your company. She has been wandering the mountains, and none of the beasts will touch her. Nor can our powers affect her, or the hunters of the Hidden Folk catch her. But we can sense her, even in the depths of Kasnrim Jhaar. She is not human. She is made of the stuff of pure magic, the stuff from which Minginish was created.'

'Tell me about magic,' Riven repeated in a cracked voice.

Thormod shook his head. 'You and your company need rest and food before we start trying to bang our heads against the walls of this puzzle. You will think better after a sleep and some nourishment. Your company has been through hardship. Let me offer you the hospitality of the Jhaar, and apologise for our mistrust.'

'I'd settle for some beer,' Ratagan muttered, none too softly. Several of the Dwarves chuckled.

'A man who appreciates the good things of life. We shall dig up some beer for you, big man, never fear. And after tasting dwarvish ale you will never be content with any other.'

Ratagan bowed deeply.

'Hyval and Thiof will show you to some quarters in the lower levels where you can wash and rest. I will join you there later.'

Thormod nodded at the Dwarves behind the company and, turning, they found that a way had been cleared in the crowd once more and two very short Dwarves were gesturing towards the back of the hall.

'Later, then,' Riven echoed. He stumbled along in the wake of their two squat guides with Ratagan, Isay, Jinneth and Bicker following after. Thormod was right, he realised. He felt as though he could sleep for a week. At the same time there was high excitement running through him like a fever.

*   *   *

THE QUARTERS THEY had been given turned out to be a pair of spacious rooms hewn out of solid rock, complete with stone fireplaces. Wood was burning in both of them, making Bicker ponder aloud on the difficulty of transporting it this high. Or this low, Ratagan reminded him, grinning. They had no way of knowing how deep inside the mountains they were, but the journey from the cave of their fire had not been short and the four Dwarves who had discovered them had hastened them the whole way.

The rooms were furnished with low tables and benches that seemed to be carved out of marble, though there were couches by the walls piled high with furs. Earthenware vessels clustered thickly on the tables, some giving off tendrils of steam and smells that brought the water into their mouths. They had forgotten the last time they had had a proper hot meal.

Their two guides, Hyval and Thiof, set the tables for the company, dragging the heavy benches around as though they were made of plywood. They poured beer into deep cups and carved haunches of what looked like deer expertly. Then they bowed to the company and left without another word, closing the stone door behind them.

The first thing Bicker did was to try and open it. He strained at the stone until the sweat rolled off his face, but even after Isay and Ratagan went to his aid, the door remained stubbornly shut.

'So we are prisoners,' Ratagan said, wiping his brow and eyeing the dark beer with interest. He did not seem unduly worried by the thought.

'In a sense,' the dark man said. 'Dwarves are secretive folk. Perhaps they did not like the thought of us running about their mansions and peering into corners.'

Ratagan was swallowing his drink with a look of ecstasy on his face. 'By all that's holy!' he exclaimed. 'Any folk who make ale as good as this cannot be all bad. They can keep me here as long as they will, if they continue to top up my cup with this stuff. It makes Colban's ale taste like riverwater, and he is no mean brewer.'

Bicker laughed. 'Little pleases the innocent,' he said, but his face changed as he, too, tasted the dwarven ale.

For a while there was little talk as the company helped themselves to food and drink, occasionally commenting aloud on the amazing selection. There were apples and pears, fresh cheese, bread warm from the oven, pickles, onions, tomatoes, honey on the comb, hot broth and prime cuts of pork and venison with the skin on them crackling and the meat pink inside. And, of course, there was the beer: a huge jug of it, dark and cold with a head on it like cream. Jinneth had two cupfuls of the stuff, throwing it back as though she were dying of thirst: Then she tore herself a chunk of bread and cheese and nursed it by the fire, turning her back on them.

Riven looked at Bicker, and the dark man shrugged. Ratagan, Isay, Bicker and Riven retired to the next room to leave her in peace, dragging stone settles over to the hearth and lounging on them shoulder to shoulder. Tiredness was bearing down on them like a dark cloud. Even Isay looked half-asleep.

Ratagan chuckled suddenly and Riven looked at him. 'What?'

'Our hosts' faces when you told them the name of this place. I'll wager there are not many in this world who have seen a council of Dwarves at a loss.'

'It was a well-told story,' Bicker said, 'even for a Teller.'

Isay shook himself out of his doze. 'In the stories, all Dwarves love to argue and discuss, and they love problems to unravel. They hate to fight. It is said that is one of the reasons they helped create the Myrcans, to defend Minginish for them. Some have called my people the Hammer of the Stone-folk, and some have said there is dwarven blood in us, hence our hardiness and our long lives. I know I feel at home here as if I were in Dun Merkadal itself. I believe they will aid us.' He took another swallow of the potent beer.

Ratagan nudged him. 'Dwarven ale is strong stuff, indeed. Isay, I think that is the longest speech I have ever heard you make.'

Sleep claimed them soon after. They laid themselves down on the fur-piled couches around the walls and were unconscious almost at once. Only Riven remained awake, debating within himself. At last, cursing silently, he made his way to the firelit gloom of the other room and saw Jinneth slumped by the dying flames with her empty cup lying by her side.

He knelt on the hearthstone and stared. Her mouth was open slightly in sleep, dark lashes shut, her cheeks flushed with warmth. The flames danced a troop of shadows over her face and in the recesses of her raven hair.

'Jenny,' he said in a whisper, tucking the hair back from her face. He would have sold his soul to see her wake up and be the woman he had once known. But as Guillamon had once said, death was final—even in the land of dreams and stories.

And he had come to accept that at last. Madra's doing. Admitting to himself that he loved his frowning young nurse had been like casting aside a final, irrational hope. His wife was dead and this sleeping woman was not her, had never been her. But he was human, nonetheless, and he could not stop himself gazing at this face he had once loved, as if he were trying to get its contours right in his mind, make it imperishable.

He kissed Jinneth on the forehead with infinite gentleness, and then gathered her up in his arms and laid her on one of the fur-laden couches. He covered her, and then returned to his own sleeping space without a backward glance.

IT WAS TALK that woke him, the murmur of voices in the room, along with the clink of cups. He dragged himself out of a deep, dark womb of oblivion and knuckled his eyes until they could open without squinting. The fire had been built up, and there were thick candles burning on the table. Riven sat up. The dwarf, Thormod, was seated by the hearth smoking a long-stemmed clay pipe and engaged in conversation with Ratagan and Bicker. Isay stood to one side, listening. It seemed Jinneth was still asleep. A beer jug was propped against the leg of the settle and they all held cups in their hands.

The Dwarf noticed him. 'Good morning, my friend, for it is such outside. I hope your first night in the Jhaar was a pleasant one.'

Riven mumbled something incomprehensible. The beer of the night before had left him feeling thick-headed and dull. He did not feel ready for conversation.

The Dwarf smiled and continued smoking his pipe in silence whilst Ratagan and Bicker threw back their beer.

There was a jug of water and a towel by Riven's couch. He splashed himself vigorously, the coldness smarting his skin. But he felt more awake afterwards, and joined the others at the fire. The room was brighter now in the candlelight. He wondered how Thormod knew whether it was morning or night down here.

'What's happening?' he asked as he creaked over to the table and selected an apple from the bowl there. Ratagan gave him a cup of beer.

Thormod took the pipe out of his mouth and inspected it for a moment, a gesture so like Calum that Riven stared.

'This morning, the council meets to wrangle out a few details of the story we are going to tell you later on in the day,' Thormod said. 'Our Teller is burnishing his skills and mining old lore from the eldest among us, so that he may present you with a polished tale the like of which you have never heard before.'

'A tale!' Riven exclaimed. 'You mean he's going to tell us stories?'

'A story,' Thormod corrected him.

'A story.' Exasperation crept into Riven's voice and Bicker shot him a warning glance, which he ignored. 'We haven't time to sit here telling stories. I need answers, so we can decide where to go next, what to do.'

Thormod puffed out blue smoke that writhed snakelike in the candlelight. His voice was mild, but the red light of his eyes had brightened.

'This story will give you your answers,' he said, his voice a bass register that Riven half-fancied he could feel vibrating in his bones. He subsided. Stories and magic. He knew the Dwarf was right. Stories and magic were at the heart of Minginish, and at the core of its connection with his own life. And the mountain, also. Sgurr Dearg had a role yet to play, of that he was sure.

Jinneth came into the room and helped herself to a cup of the ale. Thormod regarded her from under his eyebrows. Calum watching his daughter. Riven shook his head and bit into cold bread.

'Why do you stare?' Jinneth asked the Dwarf defiantly. 'Have I a flaw which interests you?'

Thormod took the pipe out of his mouth and tamped down the bowl with one thick thumb. 'Exactly,' he said, taking her aback. 'A flaw. I couldn't have put it better myself.' His eyes were like candlelit rubies shining above his beard.

'Explain!' Jinneth demanded, and her voice shook. Riven took a seat beside Ratagan.

'You are flawed. There is something wrong with you,' Thormod said. 'The Teller here'—he gestured towards Riven—'has something wrong with him also, but with him it is in the nature of a surfeit.

He has too much in him, whereas you—you lack something. There is a hollowness in you I cannot plumb. Were it not for the suspicion within me that you are needed in this thing, I would have considered having you and your band of bravos slain as soon as you entered these mountains, but Orquil, one of the oldest of the council, said we should let you be, confirming my own instincts. You are a murderess, but not, I think, entirely evil.'

Ratagan and Riven exchanged glances.

'And the Teller here would not allow us to harm you, I believe, even if it meant harm to himself.'

Isay opened his mouth as if to speak and then shut it again, frowning.

'There you have it. You are here, and living, because others would have it so, not through any merit of your own. So hold your tongue, if you cannot keep it civil.'

Thormod had spoken in the same mild tone throughout, but Jinneth looked as though he had struck her. Her fingers fumbled at her cup and sent it tumbling to be broken on the floor, making them all start. Riven could not look at her, and lost his gaze in the creamy head of his beer.

'What do you want of me?' Jinneth whispered.

'We do not yet know,' Thormod told her, 'but we will find out.' His face was as stark as stone, his eyes lava-filled holes in his head. And yet it was still Calum's face. Calum angry was something Riven had rarely seen, but never forgotten. And he had never seen him lose his temper with his daughter. He was strangely ashamed at being a spectator to this.

'Was it you and your kind who made me come

here?' Jinneth asked. Her face was flushed, her hair awry from sleep. She was like a child who had just been chastised.

Thormod cocked an eyebrow. 'Made you come here? No one forced you to take this road you have set yourself upon. You chose it yourself.'

She shook her head, and there were tears trickling down her cheeks, brilliant in the candlelight. Her bare feet were in a puddle of spilled beer, but she did not seem to notice or care.

'No,' she said brokenly. 'Something made me come here. Something has drawn me to him since the first time I saw him.' She stared at Riven, but he could not meet her gaze.

Bicker's eyes were filled with anger. 'You have a queer way of showing your attraction, if that is the case.'

'Attraction!' And now the hardness was in her voice and she drew herself up as though she were a queen addressing a peasant. 'Attraction! Is that the only word you can dredge up for yourself? You have no idea about what you speak, so close your mouth.'

Surprisingly, Bicker did so. Ratagan rubbed a hand over his beard in an effort to hide his smile.

Riven's heart was thudding in his chest. So she had been drawn to him. Was there then something of Jenny in her, after all?

He downed his beer, cursing silently. 'When are we going to hear this story of yours?' he asked Thormod.

The Dwarf shrugged with a twitch of his massive shoulders. 'We had thought to let you rest for a while. Your company looked as though it needed it.' Unexpectedly, he grinned, white teeth flashing in his beard. 'I have a feeling that if we leave you to rest much longer you will be fighting amongst yourselves.'

'The woman is not of our company,' Isay snapped.

'I think you err, brother Myrcan. Whether it seems good to you or not, she is needed.' Thormod paused. 'I will ask my kindred to assemble for you once again, as soon as may be, though as I have said our Teller will need time to put together his story from the scraps he will garner from our eldest counsellors.'

'Must be quite a tale,' Ratagan said.

'Perhaps. I know this. It begins where all good tales should: at the beginning.'

'I have a question,' Bicker said abruptly. 'Our tales say that the Hidden Folk who fled the clearances made their way into the heights of the mountains and were taken in by the Dwarves. Is this truly the way of it, or is it a mere legend?'

Thormod took a few puffs to revive his flagging pipe before replying. 'Some came,' he conceded at last. 'Most went into the Eastern Mountains, and some crossed them and made the trek across the desert to Nalbeni—so it is said. Few came to the Greshorns. They are too high, too bleak. Nothing can live in these mountains except the beasts and the Dwarves, yet some came seeking us. For a while they stayed and we made them welcome, but my own people were under pressure at that time also. They abandoned their mansions and mines in the lower foothills and the marts and fairs they had once held in concert with the folk of Drinan and Talisker, Idrigill and Ullinish; they ceased, and the

Folk of Stone slowly withdrew. They were no longer welcome in the affairs of men.

'So these poor folk from the cities and the Vale came seeking us in the heights of the mountains, in the grip of a witch winter such as is upon us now. Oh, they were folk of magic, yes, but most of them worked with charms and spells that were beneficial, primitive. Very few had any of the raw stuff of the high magic about them. Only one or two were sorcerers of might, and they kept themselves to themselves.' Thormod smiled coldly. 'Wizards are not as common as some of the folk of this land would like to make out.

'But they stayed with us for a while, until they began to hanker after the light of the sun and moon and the feel of the wind on their faces again. A man called Birkinlig—an old man who came, he said, from beyond the Greshorns—appeared and led them away. They followed him into the heart of the Greshorn range, meaning to find an end to it, an unknown land which existed beyond, and they disappeared. None returned, and no word was sent back to the Dwarves. It was as if they had vanished. There were Hearthwares with them, and even some Myrcans who were following banished lords. But none returned. We searched for them, but found no trace. Their company kept north; that much we could find out. But the mountains there are savage and there is nothing that will hold tracks, and our own powers do not extend there. Something baffles them that far into the Greshorn massif. We lost them.'

'What lies beyond the Greshorns?' Riven asked.

'We do not know. The world's end, perhaps, or perhaps there is another land there—another world, indeed, where the exiles are living in peace. Who knows?'

'Birkinlig is a figure of myth, the man who was given magic by the Stone-folk to take to the people of Minginish,' Bicker stated. 'How can it be the same man?'

'It was the name he gave,' Thormod said.

'All those people,' Bicker said. 'Did they die, then, and leave their bones in the peaks?'

No one answered him. Thormod tapped out his pipe into the fire and stretched.

'Time for me to depart and see how this tale of ours is coming along. I will have Hyval and Thiof send you more food and drink, if you wish.'

'Where is our gear?' Riven asked.

'In a safe place. It has suffered rough treatment, and we are refurbishing it for you. We can fit you out in winter clothing more effective than anything you will chance across in the lands below.' He looked at Ratagan's massive frame with amusement, Calum's quirk at the corner of his mouth. 'Though most of it will need to be altered somewhat. You will be summoned later.'

Without another word, he strode over to the door and pushed it open with one hand. It swung back after him and boomed shut. The fire crackled to itself in the sudden silence.

'So the Dwarves are not all-knowing,' Bicker said ruminatively. 'Even they are ignorant about some things.'

Riven realised he had been hoping the Dwarves

could tell him what exactly to do, but he understood now that he knew as much as they—or would, once he heard this story of theirs.

So it's all left to me in the end. Some hero.

He felt weary, though he had only just woken up. He noticed the beer puddle on the floor and saw wet footprints leading out of it into the adjoining room. Jinneth had left them again, it seemed. He was both glad and sad. Her words had opened up too many possibilities, and up here she was becoming too similar to the Jenny he had known. But perhaps that was meant to happen.

He followed her footprints unwillingly into the other chamber. It was darker in there, the only light that of the fire in the hearth. She sat staring into the flames, but looked up when he joined her. Irritation flitted across her face, and her eyes were full of the writhing firelight, but she said nothing. They sat together in a bright semi-circle that spilled outwards from the hearth, and for minutes Riven was both content and tortured to remain silent and gaze at her.

'Why do you stare at me so?' she asked him, and then sneered. 'No. I know, of course. Your dead wife—I am her image. No wonder your eyes follow me.'

'That's right,' Riven said harshly. 'You're her image, but you're not her. You're nothing like her. Nothing.'

She studied him then. 'You said I was needed here, on this quest you and your confederates have taken up. How? What do you think my role is in your mission?' The sneer was still in her voice.

'I don't know.' He kicked a recalcitrant faggot into the fire. He could smell her; the beer she had spilled clung to her and there was another odour underlying it. Sweat. Blood, perhaps. He remembered her standing nude in the cave and shook his head angrily. She smiled.

'You loved this wife of yours, it is plain. You loathe me, yet you cannot leave me be. I am a thorn in your flesh.'

I am a dark room you never entered. He heard the voice of his dream once again, mocking him.

'It doesn't matter,' he rasped, and started to get up. There was no profit in torturing himself here.

But she grasped his arm and drew him down, pulled him towards her.

'No. Don't leave me.'

She took his hand and held it in her lap, an odd smile twisting her mouth. Gradually his fingers uncurled from the fist they had become and she interlaced her own with them.

'Who was the girl in Talisker who could not speak?' she asked him. 'The one you cared for.'

'The one you threatened to have raped,' Riven said, and her fingers tensed in his.

'Yes.'

'She was my... nurse.'

'Did you love her?'

He thought of Madra's grave smile and mobile brows, her agelessness. The calm she seemed to carry with her.

'Yes, I did.' I do.

Jinneth bent her head so that her hair threw her face into shadow. 'What would you say to your wife if I were she?'

Riven grimaced. 'You're not.'

'But if I were?'

He tried to pull his hand away, but she would not let go.

'Please.'

He shook his head in bafflement and pain. Was this another game she was playing with him?

'She's dead, for God's sake.'

'Maybe she is not. Maybe she is in me. Perhaps that is why I find myself here, why I did not have you slain in Talisker, why I followed you into these mountains.'

There was something like bewilderment in her voice, and he felt a thrill of fear chill his belly.

'Death is final,' he said.

'Are you and your friends taking me to mine?'

'No, of course not. We're not assassins.'

'You play for high stakes. That would make certain things expendable. Like myself. Your Myrcan friend would slay me without a thought.'

'It was the lies you and Bragad spread that set him against his own people. Are you surprised Isay wishes you dead?'

'Do you?'

'No.'

She began to laugh. 'I don't think you know. You want me, it's plain, but you hate me too.'

Riven could not answer. He wondered why he was sitting here listening to this.

Suddenly Jinneth sprang. He tumbled backwards with her weight on top of him, her hands fastened on his wrists like fetters, and fell to the warm stone. Raven hair cascaded over his face. She was surprisingly strong, and for an instant he wondered if he were about to receive a knife in his ribs. But he felt her body shaking. She was laughing silently, her mouth muffled in his neck. Her fingers left his wrists and entwined with his.

She nuzzled his cheek, let her lips trail over his eyes. He freed one hand and ran it up her buttocks and back, the muscles quivering beneath his fingers. Then he grasped her nape and forced her mouth over his. Their teeth jarred and then their lips had joined. He could feel the smile and kissed it off savagely. They half rolled away from the fire, locked together as though in mortal contest. He swung her beneath him, her legs locked round his hips. There was a laugh still on her face and in the firelight her eyes seemed to glow like a wolf's.

'Did your wife do this?' she asked him with a grin that was more a baring of teeth.

He slapped her, hard enough to spin her face to the side, but the grip on his hips remained. He hit her again, and saw blood fall from her lip. Her grip on him loosened. She lay still beneath him, her face strangely empty, the eyes alight with sudden tears.

'It would seem she did not,' she murmured thickly, the tears tracing lines of firelight down the side of her face, disappearing into her hair.

'I'm sorry,' Riven said, his voice strangled and hoarse.

She pulled him to her. 'No matter.' And they lay in each other's arms before the fire, faces close, her blood on his hand as he wiped it from her mouth.

'Why?' he asked her softly.

'I love and loathe you,' she said, holding him tighter. 'And you are to be the death of me.' Then she pushed him away. 'Go now. Leave me alone. Go back to your friends and leave the she-wolf in peace.'

He stood and stared down at her for a long moment, at the blood on her face and the swelling there. The eyes mocking him through their tears. Then he left her and rejoined the others.

HOURS WENT ROUND and Riven waited. There was little talk amongst them. They felt that they were close to the end of their quest, but as of yet none of them knew what that end might be. Riven suspected, with some of the same foresight that had convinced him they were to meet with someone in the mountains; but as always, he could not be sure. It was like having the idea for a story in his head that was vague and unformed, knowing how things should turn out but unsure as to how it could be done. Knowing and not knowing; the same feeling that had gripped him ever since he had wandered into this world of his in the company of one of his own characters. Somehow he had been marked down for this since his birth.

But he would have given a lot to find out how exactly it could happen, how it was possible. He believed in magic, for it was all around him, but in his own world there was nothing like it, nothing whatsoever.

The dead cannot rise again.

At last the door to their chamber grated open, and the two squat Dwarves, Hyval and Thiof, stood on the threshold. They bowed to the company, their beards sweeping the floor.

'It is time,' one of them said. 'Our people await you.'

Ratagan stood up first, stretching. 'Never keep a Dwarf or a woman waiting,' he said with a smile.

They tugged themselves to their feet. Jinneth joined them from the other room, a cloak pulled about her lower face. To hide her bruises, Riven realised, and his face burned with self-disgust and shame. He had never struck a woman in his life before.

They followed their two guides out of the chamber.

IT WAS A different place they were taken to this time, farther away—deeper in the mountain, Riven thought. He could almost feel the awful pressure of the titanic gutrock above his head. The passageways they trod were mere wrinkles in its flesh. A twitch of the mountain's shoulders and they would disappear, and Riven would be fossilised in the bowels of his own story.

Their guides led them unerringly along narrow corridors and broad thoroughfares, through intersections and crossroads, past yawning chasms and castle-sized emptinesses. And they were not alone. Everywhere in the darkness there were lights, the embers of dwarven eyes moving with them, the low stump of feet, the murmur of conversation, harsh laughs, sepulchral voices humming unknown tunes. There were crowds on the move in the darkness, both behind and before the company. The inhabitants of the Jhaar seemed to be congregating to hear the story that was to be told that evening.

They entered a vast darkness, so large that there were air currents moving in it like wind. They could see nothing but the firefly-flicker of eyes scattered throughout it, strewn like forgotten gems in a mine. There were hundreds of them, some near, some so far away that they were visible only as a faint glimmer on the edge of sight. The space spun with whispered voices and scraping feet. Riven stumbled in the blackness and felt Isay and Ratagan steady him. He put his hand out to grasp at Bicker and was tugged forward again. The company stumbled along blindly, Ratagan cursing in a low tone as he tripped over something.

Then they halted, and suddenly there was a blue-white radiance about their two guides such as they had seen once before. Hyval and Thiof gestured to the floor and they saw that there were stone benches there, seemingly hewn out of the solid rock. They sprouted out of the floor like a weird fungus. The company sat down and the light went out. They were left to listen to the massive black space around them, the sound of the Dwarves moving about within it, the cold feel of the stone beneath them.

After a while the shuffling stopped, the movement ceased. A stillness fell in the place.

And a light grew around them. It was a warm, saffron light that seemed to have no source. It welled out of nowhere, revealing rock walls that arched around them steeply and rose for ever above their heads to an unguessable height, leaning closer as they rose, perfect as the beams of a cathedral— except the space they enclosed could have held ten cathedrals.

The cavern was round, and in the middle was a black pit, surrounded by benches such as the one the company occupied. Five thousand people could have found a place there with ease. The benches rose in row after row from the centre towards the titanic walls. And from the pit, now, the light of flames licked out, throwing shadows over the faces of the crowd that sat there unmoving. Riven heard Bicker's breath rasp sharply in his throat.

'I didn't think there were so many Dwarves in all the world,' he breathed, staring at the bearded figures, their eyes shining in the dimness, smoke rising in reams from some as they smoked long pipes.

Then one Dwarf left his seat and strode to the lip of the flame-filled pit in the centre of the cavern. He was taller than most of his comrades, and his beard was short and grey. Sewn into the breast of his leather jerkin was a flame emblem such as Riven had once worn: the mark of a Teller. The Dwarf paused and let his eyes sweep the occupants of the hall, lingering for a moment on the benches where the company perched, Ratagan's shoulders hulking and huge in the firelight.

'Kirgaern,' Riven heard one of their dwarvish guides whisper. 'The Teller of Kasnrim Jhaar.'

Kirgaern finished his scrutiny and stared into the fire pit with his hands tucked into his belt, as though lost in meditation. Riven saw Thormod's face behind him in the dimmer light—Calum's face, flame-lit and thoughtful.

Then Kirgaern spoke.

'In the beginning, there was the Face of the Water, looking up into darkness above. And below the water there was mud and stone, and more darkness yet. Nothing moved on the face of the water or in its depths, and the darkness above it held no light.'

His voice was low, deep like the voices of all the Dwarves, but it had a lilt to it that was something like music, and he made the words of his story into a song.

'Then it was that something stirred in the deeps of the waters, something moved and shifted and opened its eyes and looked out on to the blackness. It was a Dwarf, and his name was Modi.

'Modi pushed a stone with his hand, and who knows if it was by chance or design? But the stone moved under his fingers. The stone shifted and touched another, which toppled and brushed a third, and so it went until the depths of the waters were alive with the rumblings and the crashings of stone, the grinding of boulders and the grate of rock.

'And so it was that the Beginning truly began. Immense piles of rock and stone and mud built up and rose and collapsed again, but in the main went ever upwards until there was a break in the surface of the waters as the topmost point of the highest pebble was pushed out of the seas. More followed— jagged heaps and points of stone, the round heads of boulders and the grey sweeps of scree and shingle—until at long last there was a mountain standing there in the midst of the waters, with its head and shoulders blunt and wet in the dark. And that mountain the Dwarves call Arat Gor, the First Berg. It was so high that its peak scraped the dark mass of the sky above, and holed it there so that light from the worlds beyond spilled in and set the oceans ablaze with the first dawn.

'Then the Dwarf Modi dug his way out of the depths of the rock with his bare fingers, and clawed his way upwards until the light lit his eyes and the wind was on his face; and he stared in wonder at what he had wrought.

'But the oceans were wrathful at him for making land that was dry underfoot and usurping their hegemony, and they sent their legions, the waves of the sea, to assault the mountain and the Dwarf, so that the water smashed on to Arat Gor like a furious storm and sought to tear Modi from his place there. And little by little, the stone began to break and crack and split under the battery of the sea. The mountain began to slump and tilt in the waters, and Modi with it. And the oceans laughed in glee, thinking that soon they would be lords over all again.

'And then Modi shouted into the tumult of waters and spray, begging the oceans to cease their assault and leave him be and let the mountain live, and they laughed again and asked him why should they? So Modi tried to bargain. He offered to tell them a riddle, and they scorned him. And then he offered to sing them a song, but they would have none of it. And finally he said he would tell them a story, the finest story ever heard, and the waves ceased their blows, the waters calmed, and the seas agreed to listen and spare him until his story was done.

'So the Dwarf Modi began his story, and it was a tale never to be heard again. Years he sat there on the cold stone of the first mountain with the seas crowding round to listen to his words, and he told the first story ever to be told.

'He spoke of water, its fury and its majesty, the might of waves in storm. And then he spoke of the calm blue of windless seas, the stillness of a pond without ripples, and he spoke of the music of running water, of streams and rills, rivers and lakes, waterfalls and cataracts. And as he spoke, springs started bubbling out of the rock of the mountain around him, and one grew in size, hurrying down through the stone and the bare mud to join its brethren in the sea; and that was the Great River.

'He spoke then of the stubbornness of stone, the obdurate endurance of granite. He spoke of mountains and peaks, valleys and cliffs, rock falls and boulder fields, and as he talked there reared up around the First Berg a host, a horde, a crowd of its brothers and sisters—fellow mountains grinding into the light of that first day. The Greshorns.

'His tale continued. He spoke of the warmth and richness of soil, the goodness in loam, the sustenance in the very dirt of the earth. And around him things stirred where the mud had gathered. Heather sprouted, and grass, and snowdrops, the first of the flowers after winter. And the great trees put out their roots and stretched themselves and thrust leafy heads into the sun, becoming ever larger as the light touched them.

'And such was the power of Modi's tale that the worlds beyond the sky paused to listen, and they came crowding around the holes the first mountain had created in the sky, the pinpricks its fellow mountains had caused, and the light from them blazed through as stars. But as the other worlds leaned close to listen their inhabitants tumbled out of them, through the holes in the sky into our world, and they fell on to the land that was birthing below. And thus came the giants, and Vyrmen, the wolves, and grypesh, the horses and men. They fell upon the ground and lay amid the roots of the trees, and looked up at the worlds they had fallen from, and had no choice but to make a home for themselves where they were. In this land of ours, named Minginish, they prospered and throve and grew in numbers. And still Modi's tale was not done.

'Now the seas knew they had been tricked by Modi. The land of his story had grown great and strong, and the mountains high and indomitable. In fury they threw themselves at it and battered the coasts of the world, seeking to destroy it, but they could not. And they are there still, fighting the stone of the world and breaking it into sand, seeking to swallow it. One day they will, but the world has a while to run before they do.

'Modi's tale was finished and he lay with the life leaking out of him, for he had given it to make his tale come to life. And as he died, the mountains reverenced him. They took his bones and buried him. From his skull they fashioned Talisker Hill, and in his beard the forests thickened and covered the land. And the life that was in him seeped down into the very rock and earth of the world, and became the magic that sustains it.

'But from his bones, the mountains crafted others in his likeness, and the Dwarves opened their eyes and wrenched themselves free of the grave of their father. They dwelt in the mountains as men dwelt in the forests, and they plumbed the dark recesses in the bowels of the mountains, seeking the magic that was their father's legacy.

'Aeons passed. Tens of centuries came and went like the leaves of an autumn tree. The Dwarves delved deep, men tamed the forests and built cities, the first of which was on the high hill of Talisker beside the Great River. And the Giants dwindled, became degenerate. They grew stunted and evil, and their intelligence waned. They became creatures of the snows and the high peaks, marauders of winter, and were called the Rime-folk and were much feared.

'Only some retained their former stature and of these one was Myrca, from whose statue the Dwarves created the Myrcans. The Folk of Stone had spent untold years subduing the beasts of the mountains and the deep woods, to safeguard the world from their ravaging. They had fought battles in the depths of their mines and on the peaks of the mountains, and they were tired of it. So the Myrcans took this task upon themselves, as the Dwarves had known they would.

'There was magic in the world, then. Tunnelling deep, the Dwarves found the essence of their father and refined it, working wonders with its powers. They built Jhaars all through the mountains, so that the Greshorns became a vast city, riddled with their mines and their fortresses. But the magic was too powerful for one race. Dwarf fought Dwarf for it, and there were civil wars in the mountains that crippled the Folk of Stone. Many of their great works were abandoned and their dwellings were left empty, and the Greshorns were given a name by men for evil sorcery and wicked weather.

'So the Dwarves met in council, and decided that the magic was not theirs to wield alone. They gave some of it to a cripple named Birkinlig, who had come seeking them in the mountains, and told him to distribute it through the folk of Minginish; and this he did. And the most powerful magic they took and sealed in the peak of Arat Gor, that men now called the Staer, and there it lay locked in the stone of the Inaccesible Pinnacle, harming no one. And Minginish prospered. Men began calling the passage of years their history, and they wrote books on it, and chained down the seasons with a count of the years. They felled the forests and mastered the land, and fought wars among themselves, while the Dwarves watched them from the mountains and said nothing.

'Some say that Modi's tale never finished, that he is somewhere yet, speaking still, and that the day the tale ends will be the day the seas rush in to claim the land at last. And some say the tale can never end, for there will always be another to take it up and tell another chapter. That is beyond our knowledge, for we are within the story and cannot see out of it. All we can do—man and Dwarf and Vyrman and Giant—is live a life that makes the story worth the telling.'

The Dwarf's powerful voice fell into silence in the cavern and for a moment there was no sound. Even the rock of the walls seemed to be listening, waiting for more. Then he smiled, bowed to his audience and stepped back to his place on the bench.

A thumping noise began in the cavern, like the sound of far-off drums, and Riven saw that the Dwarves were beating their breasts with their fists in applause. He sat as the noise grew to a crescendo and, beside him, Isay, Bicker and Ratagan joined in.

He stared at the floor. He had been given his answers at last, and knew what it was that Minginish wanted of him.

He looked at Jinneth. She had let the cloak fall from her face, and the bruise at her mouth was visible even in the firelight. Her eyes were empty, face expressionless.

Sgurr Dearg, or Arat Gor as the Dwarves had named it. He had known all along that it was the key, that something had happened that summer morning of Jenny's death. He knew the quest would end on a certain ledge below the Inaccessible Pinnacle, as it had begun there.

Magic and storytelling. Always it had come down to those. And now he knew why.

Somehow what had happened on Sgurr Dearg had released the magic the Dwarves had buried there. And he had taken it to himself, ripping a door from his world to this one. Thormod had said the dark girl was composed of pure magic, and so she was— the same magic he now held within him. He and Jenny had together been invested with the power to make or break this world, a world that even in its own myths was but a continuing story. Riven had become the storyteller. He was not only inspired by Minginish; he controlled it. Jenny was dead, but the magic had taken something of her and sent it walking Minginish, looking for him.

He had another appointment to keep.

But it went further. There had been a link between himself and this world long before Jenny's death—

hence his novels. And Jinneth, who was becoming more like Jenny with every step she took closer to the Red Mountain: her role had yet to be seen.

The Dwarves were standing up, leaving the hall in thick streams. Riven realised he had been blind to his surroundings for minutes. Thormod was standing before him.

'Have you found your answers?' the Dwarf asked gently.

Riven hauled himself to his feet. The company were staring at him as though they expected some great revelation. He smiled despite himself.

'I think so. I know where I have to go. And I have an idea about what there is to do.'

Thormod nodded, satisfied. 'You must leave soon. The bad weather is breaking outside, I am told, and the Greshorns are pitiless to travellers at the best of times. Your gear is ready as we speak.'

'You've been busy,' Riven noted.

'You have not far to go,' Thormod said, 'if your destination is what I believe it to be, but the way is hard. We will set you on the straight path to the mountain.'

'Thank you.' Riven scanned the faces of the company. Isay with his eyes narrowed and eager, Ratagan humorous as always but with lines etched deeply around his brows. Bicker ruminative, but with a smile for him, half-mocking. And Jinneth with her accusing bruises and a hopeless look that made his heart twist within him.

'I guess we're ready now,' he said.

CHAPTER NINETEEN

THE SNOW WAS blinding in its whiteness, the bright sunlight setting it alight so they had to narrow their eyes against its glare. Above them, the sky was a flawless blue, a vast arch that rested on the peaks of the mountains that covered every horizon. Riven estimated their height at some twelve thousand feet. He sucked the thin air into his lungs and breathed out again in a nimbus of steam. He knew these mountains. They were too high, too big, but he recognised them. He could see the long curved sweep of the Cuillin Range from where he stood. He could make out Sgurr nan Gillean, Sgurr a Ghreadaidh, Sgurr na Banachdich... all those mountains he had once clambered upon, there in front of him, the heights of Alps now. The traverse of their peaks would not be easy. If the weather turned bad again, it could prove well-nigh impossible.

He glanced at Jinneth. The raw air had put colour

into her cheeks and made her eyes sparkle. Her hair was flying free in the stiff breeze that blew snow off the high peaks in banners. There seemed nothing alien about her now; her face was as familiar to him as his own. He looked away.

The Dwarves had led them up winding stairs of countless steps that coiled inside the mountains, and had brought them out here, on the snow-hooded slopes of a high peak that overlooked the rest of the Greshorn Range to the north. The Staer, Thormod had told them, was just over a day's journey away, and the guard the Dwarves had set upon the mountain had been recalled. Riven did not ask how. He had a feeling that the Vyrmen were not the only race of this world that could speak to each others' minds.

And then the Dwarves had closed the stone of their door after them and retreated into their underworld mansion, leaving the mountainside as bare and unmarked as before, except where the snow had been disturbed.

And that was that. There were no longer any people whose advice could be sought, no sages whose wisdom would show him what to do. He was alone in this thing.

Almost done.

'I hope you know the way, Bicker,' he said to the dark man.

'I could never forget it,' Bicker said. 'I did not come out here, though. I travelled lower down, along a shallow valley that lies on the other side of the ridge ahead. It will be a simple matter to pick up the trail.'

Riven tugged at a pack strap that was eating into his collar bone. 'Let's be off, then.'

The Dwarves had outfitted them well, equipping the five of them with thick clothing fashioned out of reindeer hide and trimmed with what looked suspiciously like Rime Giant fur. On their feet were spiked iron frames not unlike crampons, and they carried ropes and ice axes. The Dwarves had seen enough winters in the mountains to encourage them to develop such equipment, though Ratagan and Isay eyed it a trifle dubiously.

They trudged forward in Bicker's wake, Riven behind the dark man, Isay next, then Jinneth, and Ratagan bringing up the rear. Their feet sank ankle-deep in the snow before the spikes on their boots gripped the ice beneath. They leaned on their axes and ploughed on doggedly, with the wind bringing tears to their eyes and whipping the hair back from their foreheads. It was a bitter blast, lashing the mountains and raising plumes of powdery snow from their summits so they seemed to be trailing white smoke into the clear sky. Their breath puffed out in clouds before it was snatched away, misting the fur of their clothes with rime. It searched for every seam, every gap, and wormed its way under their garments to steal the warmth from them. Despite their exertions, they were shuddering with cold as they walked. Riven wondered if snow was lying in the Dales, if Talisker was dusted with it, if Madra was even now watching it pile up at a window in Quirinus's house and thinking about him. And was it falling at the bothy, on his home? It was rare to get snow there, since they were on the shore, but it had happened one year, one fine, cold winter's day, and he and his wife had marvelled at it like children, and made an expedition of climbing the ridge and forging through the snow to the post office at Elgol, six miles away. They had arrived thick with snow, chilled to the bone, happy as summer swallows. A day to tell tall tales about, to mull over afterward when the fire was bright in the hearth and the driftwood was burning blue in the midst of the peat. That was luxury. Those were riches. He had been a wealthy man, and had not even known it.

And here he was again, in the midst of those mountains, only now they stood tall as dreams before him, savage and unforgiving, beautiful as a sword blade. He was glad that he knew enough now to be grateful for such things. They were worth hoarding, the bitter along with the sweet.

All day they plodded on, slowly losing height and making their way down to the path that Bicker knew. They dug their axes into the ice and stabbed their feet into the snow, cutting steps for themselves in places, roping themselves together in others; stumbling, tripping, slipping and sliding, helping each other and being helped without a word. Riven even saw Isay supporting Jinneth over a sheer ice sheet. They had come too far, he realised, to worry about treachery now, or to debate anything. There was only the one road left to travel.

They reached Bicker's path after four hours of descent, the muscles in their legs quivering with strain, and set off without pause up the ridge beyond. Once they gained its height, they would be on the traverse itself, and would maintain altitude. Riven could not help wondering about where they would sleep that night if a storm crept up on them.

The sky was still almost clear, but there were clouds skirmishing at the horizon's rim, veiling the summits there with grey fog, and the wind was picking up farther. Even the Dwarf-made clothing could not keep out its bite.

They paused to look around, the air fighting to press them down on to the snow and ice of the ridge. They were almost a third of the way up. Another five or six thousand feet and they would be on the level of the peaks.

'Work ahead,' Ratagan said, peering at the summit above. 'A long, weary way.'

'We must do it before nightfall,' Bicker said crisply. 'The other side of the ridge is in the lee of the wind, and we will be able to make camp there.'

'And burn snow for our fire, maybe,' the big man retorted.

Bicker laughed. 'The Stone-folk put enough faggots in our packs to give us a few hours' warmth, so do not despair entirely.'

Ratagan brightened. 'There is that. There is also the thought that I have a jar of their ale stowed away somewhere, which is bound to improve our outlook.'

'What it is to think ahead,' said Bicker. And he gestured them onwards again.

They laboured up the southern face of the ridge, as the day waned and a gale-bitten night loomed at them. The snow they trod became a bright luminescence as the sky darkened, clouds piling around the heads of the mountains. By the time they reached the top, it was almost wholly dark, and the wind was screaming around their heads, slamming into the southern side of the ridge like a wall. They scrambled over the knife-edge that was the summit and half-tumbled down the other side, their linking ropes pulling them down together. Isay and Ratagan anchored them like two rocks, their ironshod feet sinking deep into snow and ice, and the wind lessened as the bulk of the summit cut it off. They could see nothing in the gloom except the dark shapes of each other, sprawled, panting, in the snow. There was snow in the air, too. It whirled in eddies of wind and began to speckle them in the dusk. Bicker shrugged off his rope first and lurched to his feet. 'We need better shelter than this. Come on!'

They followed him, cursing, the snow building on their eyelashes and cutting down visibility to yards. The thickening snowstorm forced them to halt again after a few minutes. Massive, monolithic rocks rose to their left, and the company wormed their way through them, finding at last a space big enough to accommodate them all. Riven sank to his haunches, for there was not room enough for them to stretch their legs. The wind shrilled about the tops of the sheltering stones. Ratagan was already struggling to dig the tinderbox out of his pack, whilst Bicker and Isay were tossing chunks of wood out of theirs. Riven and Jinneth joined them, but it was a shivering half-hour before Ratagan could get the tinder to catch and had warded the feeble flame well enough to kindle their meagre supply of wood. The rising flames conjured their faces out of the snow-woven darkness, easing the cramp that was settling into Riven's confined limbs.

'How long can we keep it going?' he asked Ratagan, shouting to be heard above the wind.

The big man grimaced. 'Not long enough. We can have a decent blaze for a couple of hours, not more, or a small one for twice that. But we need warmth. I'll keep it high and see if the snow abates.'

They huddled together in the coruscating firelight, with the snow powdering their shoulders and the storm shrieking above. It would be a long night, even longer once the fire died.

One by one they fumbled their hide sleeping bags out of their packs and shared them. There was not room enough to clamber inside, so they draped them about their knees and shoulders and crept so close to the fire that they could smell the fur on the bags singeing.

Riven dozed, becoming used to the lost circulation in his cramped limbs. He dreamed, vaguely, his mind's eye whirling with images of Giants and Dwarves, underground halls and high-walled cities. So much, so many pictures, and all of it he knew and recognised. But there was more, he realised: another chapter, perhaps, or a face which had yet to be seen. His dreams made him uneasy, and he swam out of sleep into the red gloom of the dying fire and the coldness of unmelting snow on his face. It was still dark, and the wind sounded as relentless as ever. He felt a moment of hate for the weather, the mountains, for everything that had conspired to bring him here.

Life's a bitch.

He looked at his companions. They were asleep, even Isay. Bicker had volunteered to take first watch, but was crunched up with his eyes closed next to Ratagan, a frown marking his thin face as if, even in sleep, he was aware that he was failing in his duty. He was clearly exhausted. They had depended on him from the moment they had entered the mountains. It was for Bicker to lead, Isay to fight and Ratagan to make them laugh. Riven and Jinneth had been set aside for other purposes.

What a story it would make, if I could ever tell it.

It would not be easy to take these people, who had been his characters and who had become his friends, and make them into characters again.

But perhaps he would not be called upon to make up any more stories.

The fire died at last, guttering down into chill darkness, and the snow settled on the rest of the company as they dozed underneath the thick hide bags the Dwarves had given them. Slowly but surely the cold seeped into them, and Riven watched their shapes twitch and shiver in sleep, felt Jinneth push closer to him for warmth. He could not sleep himself. There was a jangling feeling that something had yet to happen. He had felt it before, prior to encountering Jinneth and her mercenaries, but now it was sharper, more precise. The closer he drew to the Red Mountain, the more keenly aware he was of... things. As though he were already stepping out of this world and becoming its author once more. The thought grieved him. He had roots here now, some running as deep as, or deeper than, any he had in the world where he belonged. He was not sure if he was prepared to sever them so easily, to wake from the dream. For if a man loves to dream more than remain awake, why should he open his eyes?

And he smiled at his own absurdity.

Bicker woke at some time during the night. Riven heard him swearing and cursing himself. Then he shook each of the company awake and and asked them their names to check that they had not slipped into hypothermia in the dark, fireless hours. Ratagan swore at him and told him to go jump off the mountain and leave him to sleep. Only Jinneth seemed slow to answer, as if confused, and the dark man spent some time checking that she was fully conscious. It was only when she roused herself and told him to leave her alone in much the same tones as Ratagan that he left her, his teeth shining in a grin.

The snow had stopped falling. Riven could feel its weight on his shoulders and knees, pressing the bag down on him. The space where the fire had been was a blank whiteness, but he was not cold. It seemed as if the snow were insulating him. Only his face was chill, and he rubbed feeling back into his nose and cheeks for some minutes. His eyes were like orbs of frozen glass set in his skull, and he blinked his stiff eyelids furiously. There was a blueness about the air above that heralded the approach of dawn. Bicker was already out of the shelter of the stones and scanning the way ahead for the day. The last day. Sgurr Dearg was very close.

They hauled themselves out from under the combined weight of snow and their sodden sleeping bags, having to dig for their packs. Riven was shivering uncontrollably as he crammed the wet bag into his pack. Around them, the dark shapes of the high mountains began to become clearer as the light strengthened, moving from blue to grey. They packed in silence, except for mutterings against the cold and hisses of breath that plumed in the frigid air. Riven felt as though the ice had insinuated its way into his brain; he was torpid and dull. Ratagan's sudden cry of triumph roused him from his stupor. The big man was holding up an earthenware jar and levering the seal from its neck with feverish care. Then he offered it round.

'I had an idea this might do us good at some point.'

Dwarven ale. Riven took two generous swallows and the stuff warmed his throat and ignited a glow in his stomach a second later. His shivering ceased. He stood and watched the slow seep of pale light in the east that was the dawning sun, the ice in his mind melting away. He returned Ratagan's grin and Bicker's wry look, nodded at Isay, who looked incredibly young with his lengthening crew cut and cold-pinched face. And he studied Jinneth until she cocked an eyebrow at him and drank from the jar. He knew it was the last morning he would ever see with these people, and while the thought grieved him, he knew also that it had to be, that the best things are better not savoured too long. Jenny had shown him that, but Madra had made him believe it. That was something this world had given him. It was enough, perhaps. Perhaps. He felt like a child hauled away from a toyshop window. There had been no time, no chance to stop and stare. Now all there was to see were the mountains, where it had begun. This story's Teller had a sense of fitness, at least.

When they had squared away their belongings and wolfed down some cold food, they relashed their crampons and started out again into the grey morning, following Bicker's lead. Even though Riven now knew the way ahead better than he.

THEY WERE ON a level with the high peaks and they could now look the Greshorns in the eye. Range after range twisted and arched away, and blue gaps appeared in the clouds as they crunched forward. There was actually sunshine to light their way, making the snow blaze. The mountains were vast, barren, sharp as spears. Riven felt he had entered a different kingdom, a place where the affairs of men were irrelevant and ignored. He was as insignificant as a beetle. But that was not true. There was something in him that had the potential to dwarf even these mountains.

Their path forward became uncomfortably exposed: a jagged ridge of adjoining peaks that rose and fell like a breaker hitting a beach. The pace slowed, and once more they roped themselves together, using their axes as walking sticks. There were places where great buttresses of stone thrust up out of the ridge to form minor peaks, and these they had to climb, one by one, someone—usually Bicker—belaying from the top. Riven could not bring himself to contemplate that task.

The sky cleared farther and the wind dropped somewhat. They began to sweat in their heavy clothes, their palms becoming slick inside the thick mittens. There was no sound except the scrape of the snow, their own breathing and a far soughing of air through the teeth of the mountains.

In the middle of the day, they halted to rest and eat, breaking out bread and fruit and dried meat, slugging at their canteens and then stuffing them full of snow. Riven's eyes were full of the dazzle of the snow, and he kept them slitted against its glare. His lips were cracked and split and he had to lick them into mobility.

They set off again. The Dwarves had reckoned on the journey to the Staer taking them a day and a half, but they were making slower progress than they had planned. They were tired, even Isay, and it was as much as they could do to keep lurching forward, with Bicker leading them like a recalcitrant shadow. The Red Mountain was not only higher here than on Skye, it was also higher in relation to its fellows, its pinnacle towering above the rest of the range, whereas in Riven's world it was not the highest of the Cuillins. Its outline remained the same, however, as familiar to him as Jinneth's profile.

The afternoon wore round quickly. It was almost with a start that Riven realised the sky was darkening. The air was calm, with hardly a breath moving, but snow had started to drift down in a silent curtain.

They stopped and stared at what was before them. They had come to a vast curve in the mountain, the peak arching up savagely to their left and a huge expanse of smooth ice cupped within its maw, stretching out as wide and unbroken as a white lake, tilted down towards the northern flanks of the traverse at a sharp angle.

'We have a choice,' Bicker said into the quiet that had enfolded them. 'We can scale the peak or cross the ice field. But either way the mountain must be reached tonight. We cannot stop any more. There is nothing to burn, this high, and we would be hard put to it to last out another night up here.' He did not mention what they would do after the mountain had been reached, how they would find a way back to the Jhaar.

'The ice field,' Riven said abruptly. 'It's getting too dark to climb.'

'My thought also,' Bicker said.

They were still roped together, and shuffled off the rock of the mountain and on to the face of the ice like a procession of blind men. The field's tilt was some thirty degrees, and they leaned into it with their axes, digging into the ice with their fanged feet, kicking every step home. The field loomed off below into an unknown distance down the flank of the mountain.

Riven's ears were full of the rasp of his own breath, the crunch and scrape of his feet, the cracking of his joints as they ached to do his will. The falling snow clamped all other noise down, muffled what he could hear of the others. The quiet was almost surreal, even the ever-present sound of the air currents in the peaks inaudible.

There was the crack of ice breaking upslope, loud as a gunshot in the gathering twilight. Shards and pieces of the stuff tumbled down towards the company in a small avalanche, and they paused, breath misting the air in front of their eyes. Riven looked at Bicker questioningly and saw that the dark man's face had gone as pale as paper.

'What is it?'

'I don't know. Keep moving! Don't stop!' And the rope at Riven's waist tugged him on again. He glared upslope but could see nothing there except the blankness of smooth ice. Cursing, he did as he was told.

Then the ice beneath his feet exploded.

He glimpsed something grey and snake-like launching itself out of the ice like a blunt-headed missile, and then it hit him in the chest and he was catapulted away, blasted from the slope. He somersaulted and came down hard on the ice once more, hearing it creak under him. The rope at his waist was biting into his flesh like a wire, and he screamed. There were shouts in the air around him. He swung like a trapped fly, and felt his rope sing with strain. Desperately, he scraped at the ice with his axe, trying to halt his mad jerking. He looked up to see a huge stone-grey column looming over him, and a screech rent the air, hurting his ears.

'Ice worm!' Ratagan's voice yelled.

He heard Bicker shriek, saw the creature hurtle at him and knock him sprawling, and then the dark man was loose and was sliding down the ice field. Riven's rope tore at his waist and the shock clashed his teeth together. He tasted blood in his mouth, and then was torn free of his hold once more, and the ice was sliding away under him. He was caught again with a jerk that sent lights and darkness spangling before his eyes, and then was swinging there by the rope with Bicker's weight suspended below him. Isay. Isay and Ratagan must be supporting them.

There was another screech, like that of a large bird of prey, and he heard the hiss and crack of weapons, the splinter of ice. They were fighting above.

He struggled round to face the slope and swung the axe into it as hard as he could. It had been thonged to his wrist, or he would have lost it. He kicked his feet in and grunted with the effort to anchor himself. But then the awful limp weight that was pulling on him lessened, and he looked down between his legs to see Bicker climbing upslope with his eyes glittering.

'Cut the rope!' the dark man hissed, and Riven severed it unquestioningly with the axe. They were free of each other.

Something massive crashed into the ice, making the entire area shake and groan. 'It dives!' Isay shouted up above. They climbed to meet him and found the ice churned into a maze of broken blocks and splinters. Ratagan, Isay and Jinneth were crouched in its midst with wild eyes, their ice axes at the ready.

'It'll be back. It'll come again,' Bicker croaked. 'We must get off the ice, get on to stone. We have no chance here.'

But there was a sudden fountain of rime and ice among them, and the thing was towering before them again, mouth agape. It was as thick as an old beech tree, with a crested dragon's head and eyes like green fires. It reared up to twice Ratagan's height, and then turned to regard Riven.

Isay leapt forward and sank his ice axe into it with a cry. The thing screamed, and whipped back and forth like a pinned worm. The Myrcan was smashed aside, his rope pulling Jinneth with him and yanking Ratagan to his knees. Then the worm plummeted down on Isay, and the great jaws closed about his leg.

'No!' Riven shouted, lurching forward with his axe upraised. The worm lifted Isay into the air and shook him like a dog shaking a rat, the connecting rope lifting up a screaming Jinneth also. Riven swung his axe, and the rope severed, letting her tumble to the ice. The worm discarded Isay, flinging him off into the falling snow. They heard the ice twenty yards away shatter as he struck it.

Ratagan surged forward, bellowing with fury. His axe scored a long crimson line about the worm's trunk, and it reared backwards, hissing with anger and pain. It stabbed down at him, but he flung himself aside, scrabbling through the broken ice, and the beast's head missed him by a foot. The body followed it, and Riven realised it was tunnelling down into the ice at unbelievable speed. Even as he watched, the tapering tail disappeared down the hole it had created. It was gone.

They stood immobile, gasping for breath for perhaps a second, and then Bicker grabbed Riven's arm. 'Take the woman—make for the safety of stone. We will hold it here.'

'Isay—' Riven said brokenly.

'Go! We will see to him. You must go now!'

Riven wanted to weep. He seized Jinneth's arm and dragged her away, but he had not gone ten feet when there was the sound of splintering ice and the worm erupted into the air beside him, knocking him aside. The green eyes bore down on him and he raised his axe feebly, but then Ratagan's great bulk had collided bodily with the creature and his axe had been buried up to the shaft in its body. Riven thought the scream it uttered would burst his ears. It writhed backwards, slithering away across the ice whilst Ratagan stood like a blood-smeared giant over Riven and Jinneth. They heard him laugh, a laugh as free and unforced as any Riven had ever heard him utter.

'Come on then, you damned worm! Try Dwarf-forged steel once more. Try the thews of Ratagan and see how you like it!'

Bicker and Isay stumbled out of the snow to join him. The Myrcan had splinters of bone sticking out from one dangling forearm and his face was shining and dark with blood, but he wielded an axe in his good hand and his eyes were bright as stars. Bicker steadied him with one hand whilst in the other his short sword glittered. The snow was piling on their heads and shoulders.

The worm hissed hatred at them, dark fluid pulsing from the deep wound Ratagan had inflicted. Its eyes lit the spinning snowflakes with green. The head swayed a moment, and then it dived into the ground with a spray of shattered ice and disappeared with a grinding noise. The ice field quivered under their feet for a moment, then was still.

Isay half-sat, half-fell down to the ground, and Riven noticed for the first time that his leg was a ragged blood-soaked mess from the thigh down. The ice around was already blushing scarlet, a dark stain in the dimming light. Bicker joined him and began cutting away his clothing on arm and leg to get at the wounds.

'Will it come back?' Jinneth asked them hoarsely.

'Maybe,' the dark man replied. He was wincing unconsciously as he tightened a thong about the top of Isay's thigh to halt the streaming blood.

'There may be others, I'm thinking,' Ratagan said. 'I have heard of these creatures. They are seldom encountered alone.'

'Leave me,' Isay managed to whisper, but Bicker glared at him.

'We'll patch Isay up as best we can and then get off this ice field. They are creatures of the snow and ice, the worms, and they don't like being met on stone.'

Riven bent down beside Bicker and the fallen Myrcan. The blood was already beginning to freeze in the snow.

'How is he?'

'Not so good. He will be dancing no jigs for a while, and his blood will draw the worms to us.'

'Arm,' Isay mumbled. He was slipping in and out of consciousness. It was a shock to see him so helpless, so crippled.

I looked like this once, after I had fallen off the mountain. All blood and splintered bones.

'He'll be all right,' Riven said firmly, dragging his eyes away from the slivers of bone that poked out of the flesh of Isay's forearm.

A sudden, far-off screech battered the air, muffled by the snow. Another sounded below them, down in the darkness.

'They smell us,' Ratagan said, beating his weapon hand on his breeches. His mittens were clogged with snow. 'It is not going to be too healthy around here in a few moments. Are you finished, Bicker?'

The dark man nodded. Isay was unconscious, his leg bound with an assortment of furs and linen and leather. Bicker had wrapped his arm in a thick cloak and immobilised it with the shaft of an axe. 'Rough and ready, but it'll have to do for now,' he said. 'Let's go.'

Ratagan bent and lifted Isay as tenderly as a baby, placing him over one shoulder so that his smashed arm hung stiff and straight over the big man's pack. Then they set off again, unroped this time. They moved more slowly than before. Riven's legs were trembling with the aftermath of the fight and he had to help Jinneth along as though she were lame, his arm muscles on fire as he stabbed his axe into the ice and supported both of them.

It was getting harder to see. The night was deepening and the snow fell as steadily and noiselessly as ever. Riven was sure that the Red Mountain could not be too far ahead, but it was impossible to tell. The great size of these mountains and the confusing darkness had disorientated him. And they were barely halfway across the ice field.

There was a roar and a crash upslope, and a hail of broken ice showered down on them. They paused, searching the gloom frantically for movement.

'They're closing in,' Bicker said calmly. 'They smell the blood.'

'How much farther to stone?' Ratagan asked. He sounded weary now, though it was impossible to read his face in the darkness.

'Too far. We won't make it.'

Again, there was that roar, like the scream of a caged raptor. It was answered by two others. The worms were above, below and behind them. They heard none in front.

'We can still go on,' Riven said.

Ratagan laid Isay gently down on the surface of the ice and anchored him by planting an ice axe beside him. Riven thought he was smiling. He addressed Bicker. 'Shall you tell him, or shall I?'

The dark man leaned on the haft of his axe for support, head bent. They could hear movement from upslope in the darkness, the sound of a heavy body swishing across the ice. Jinneth started as she heard it and clutched at Riven's arm. Behind was a distant crash and crunch that made the ice underfoot shake minutely. They were closing fast.

'They are making for the blood,' Bicker said matter-of-factly. 'They smell it. You and Jinneth go on and we will stay here and hold them off for a while. We will buy you time to get onto stone.'

Riven stared at him. 'No.'

'You must do this, my friend,' Ratagan said. 'You must get away at all costs, or everything that has happened will have been for nothing. You have this thing to do—and the lady must go with you.'

'No,' Riven whispered.

'You must, Michael,' Bicker said, and he laid a hand on Riven's arm. 'This is why we came: to see you do this thing, to make sure you get there. Do not fail us now—and do not fail Minginish.'

'I can't,' Riven croaked. 'I can't go on without you. I can't do it alone.'

'You must,' Ratagan insisted. 'Besides, you have a beautiful lady with you. You are not alone.'

'You will never be alone,' Bicker told him. 'Not so long as this story continues.'

It seemed he heard another voice say, from a long time ago: 'There is always a story. Maybe the people within it are different, maybe it is even someone else's to tell. But it continues.'

It continues.

Magnificent, make-believe characters. He had made them, had met them, had loved them. He counted them his friends, perhaps the best he had ever known. And now he was to leave them, to let them die.

I won't do it.

Ice creaked off in the darkness. Something hissed close by, and then they saw the green glitter of eyes through the snow. Ratagan hefted his axe thoughtfully.

'You must go, Michael Riven.'

I know.

His throat had narrowed. He could not speak. Bicker and Ratagan were no longer looking at him, but were staring at the eyes that blazed on the edge of vision. Three pairs of them.

'Don't get caught,' Ratagan warned him. 'Go now, while you can.'

The cold burned the tears on Riven's cheeks. He backed away.

'I'll tell a story of you two some day,' he managed to say. Then he lurched off across the ice with his ironbound feet anchoring him, Jinneth trailing after. He heard the worms shriek as they closed in, and Ratagan's laugh rose in the night, clear as a bell.

'Make our story a good one!' he shouted. Then the sounds of the fighting began and Riven turned away from it. He left them behind, his face set towards the mountain ahead, which reared up out of the night like a cathedral.

CHAPTER TWENTY

SGURR DEARG. THEY were on its lower slopes, labouring up a scarp that was treacherous with scree and ice-welded stone. The snow had stopped falling, and Riven thought there was a light behind the clouds that was the rising of the moon. He heard his crampons screech on bare rock and slipped to his knees. Only then did he realise that he was weeping as he walked. He bent his head, his face gnarled with grief. They were gone, now. He was almost alone.

Jinneth knelt beside him, and her arm encircled his shoulders. The night was almost entirely silent. If the fighting continued, then the bulk of the spur was blotting out the sound of it.

He twisted the sob that ached out of his throat into a snarl, and rose to his feet.

Make an end, Riven.

He started forward again without a word to his companion. He was afraid, this close, that if he spoke to her, he might find his wife speaking back, and that would have been too much. His mind was about to give up its ghost. Or meet it, perhaps.

There were too many faces in his head, too many pictures. He was claimed by two worlds, torn apart by opposing loyalties. At this moment, most of him wanted to be back on the ice, fighting with his friends. They had saved his life times beyond count, and he had left them to die in exchange. And Ratagan had laughed.

He saw the river at Beechfield glittering under the moon, waves rushing up the shore at Camasunary, the Red Mountain on a summer's afternoon with the sun warming the stone. He felt Nurse Cohen's arms around him, her lips on his forehead, but she changed into Madra, sitting with a wolf's head laid in her lap.

Too many things. Too many impossible images.

The clouds drifted apart and they found their way lit by moonlight, a grey, eldritch radiance that made the shadows seem like dark pools, the mountains as grey as ash. He grinned at the emptiness and the surrounding silence, but at the memory of Ratagan's laugh, the grin faded. No matter. No matter. His dream was behind him. There was nothing in front of him but the mountain.

And Jenny.

Sgurr Dearg filled half the sky, looming black in the moonlight, the summit wisped with silver cloud.

It was a clear winter's night on Skye, and he was walking the mountains with the bright memory of a dream veiling the edges of his mind; walking back into his own world, with a ghost at his side.

They stopped to remove their crampons, and then the way became harder, steeper, the scree sliding under their feet to rattle off down the slopes. The wind had allowed no purchase to the snow here. It gathered in drifts where there was some shelter, but for the most part, the mountain was as bare as a gravestone, rocks shining with ice under the moon.

His limbs were complaining. All over him there seemed to be once-broken bones clamouring for attention. Beside him, he could hear the breath sawing in and out of Jinneth's throat. She was keeping pace with him. He could see her face, stark in the livid light. It looked cold as a statue, and the eyes were silver glints, under brows that met in the middle.

He had to stop and rest after a while, gasping, and she sank down beside him. Pictures of himself, clean-shaven and healthy, ploughing up mountainsides in Brecon with scarcely a pause. Lieutenant Riven.

Off again, breath whooping; like the sound of George's chest wound in Derry.

Soldier no more.

The first of the steep cliffs leading to the summit reared in front of them, black and glistening with snow in odd corners that sparkled in the moonlight.

Climbing, now.

They no longer had any rope. The rags of it were tied about their waists, but the rest was down with Bicker and Ratagan and Isay, and the worms. He threw off his mittens, knowing he would need his fingers for this, and he made Jinneth do the same. She seemed to be in a trance or daze, as helpless as a transfixed rabbit, but she followed him without question.

He began to pull himself upwards, the handholds easy to find in the bright moonlight, but his feet slipping on unseen pockets of ice.

False summits came and went. Sharp rock numbed and bled his hands, making him fumble clumsily for a grip. Twice he had to lever his axe into a cleft and reach back to draw Jinneth after him. She was shuddering, and her teeth were clenched with cold or fear. There was blood on her hands.

The vertical rock came to an end, and they found themselves on a flat, exposed space that was near the Pinnacle. They crunched and clinked across it, exhausted. Halfway to the Pinnacle, he shrugged off his pack and let it fall to the ground. Then he levered Jinneth's from her back, and caught her in his arms as she swayed. They stood there for a moment on the last approach to the peak, and she leaned her forehead against his shoulder.

'My death is here,' she whispered, and sobbed silently. He stroked her ice-clogged hair, but had nothing to say. He had come too far. When they started forward again, they walked hand in hand, like children drawing comfort from one another.

And at last they were there.

He had half-expected to see the rope dangling, the frayed end hanging loose, but there was nothing except the bare granite, the scattered snow, the darkness beyond and the gulf of the valley he knew was waiting below. There was a fall as long as a river there, out in the moonlit night, and at the end of it Minginish slept. If it were daylight, he would be able to see the fiefs and villages around Talisker, perhaps even the high-sided shape of the city itself, with the river coiling round its feet and the expanse of the Vale looming off into infinite space. Or perhaps he would only see Glenbrittle, the houses trailing along the narrow road in the bottom of the glen. The house where Jenny had been born that was empty now.

He and Jinneth crouched on the ledge where he had belayed from, a year and a century ago, and knew they were not alone.

She was with them, on the ledge. Jinneth shrank from her, but Riven stared, frozen. He could not move.

The dark girl.

She wore her thin shift still, and her hands and feet were bloody. She was starvation-thin, the face below the cheekbones sucked in and emaciated. It seemed as though her bones were ready to break through her skin. She was smiling.

Jinneth screamed and leapt up, but one look from the grey eyes paralysed her. The two women stared at each other, the face of one suffused with terror, the other inhumanly peaceful, calm as a corpse. Riven was rooted to the rock between them.

A creaking gasp of breath came from Jinneth's mouth. She shook her head wildly, her eyes never leaving those of her twin. Then, slowly, she stepped outwards—

'No!' Riven shouted, and he lunged forward. Too late.

She toppled over the lip of the ledge without a sound, spun once, her face a flash in the moonlight, and then was gone.

Jesus Christ!

Riven pressed his mouth against the stone of the ledge and put his hands over his ears. He did not want to see, did not want to hear—he did not want to hear the thud, could not bear to hear her scream. He thought he heard his own voice shouting frantically, far away, had a momentary impression of sunshine on his back. Then it was gone. The stone was as cold as death on his cheek. There was ice between his fingers.

And a tentative hand on his arm. He jumped back from the edge like a hare, eyes wide.

'Michael,' she said.

Jennifer MacKinnon sat on the stone before him, concern on her face, a smile wavering on her lips; that smile, with the quirk at the corner she had got from her father.

His wife. Not some facsimile, not a vision or a dream. His wife, here before him on the mountain that had killed her.

He reached out one chapped, rock-scored hand towards her, and her cool fingers entwined with his and gripped them. Human. Real.

'Jenny?' he whispered, his voice cracked and raw.

She looked puzzled a moment, and thoughtful. Then her brow cleared. 'Jenny. Yes. I suppose that is who I am.'

'You—you're alive.'

She smiled again. 'I am more than alive. I am in the story, as are you now. There will be tales told of you from these mountains to the sea. You have become a hero, Michael.'

His eyes filled with tears. 'I don't want to be. I want you back. I want you home.'

She shook her head. 'That part of the tale is finished. It cannot be told again. I cannot go back.'

He knew then that this was not the woman who had climbed Sgurr Dearg with him that day. Not her, not entirely. And the mourning rose in him as he realised anew that his Jenny was lost for ever.

'Minginish is the name of the land where you made your home,' she said. 'It is here, also, because you never left it. It surrounds and is part of the world you know as your own, even as the people you knew in one world became people in another.'

'Who was Jinneth?' Riven asked.

'She was part of you, and part of me. She was the fears you had for me, and more. Magic, Michael. Do you believe in it now?'

There was a dull ache in him, a pain he had known before.

'Yes, I do. Now.'

'Minginish is made of magic. It is not immutable, as the world of Skye is. It changes constantly, and you are what changes it. You were born with a story in your head, a story that was so close to the truth of this world that it was drawn to you and entered you. Who knows why or how? Maybe you will find out some day. But you were given some of this world's magic. You became its arbiter. You changed it and it changed you. But too much of the essence of this world was taken by you. The connection became too strong, and when—when I died, it was like an explosion. For a time all the magic came back in one direction—to Minginish, creating... Jennifer. The dark girl who has shadowed you since you came here. Because she loved you.'

He looked up at that, and saw that her eyes were fixed out in the yawning gulf below, and her face was twisted with baffled grief.

'The magic was in me,' she went on, 'trapped in me. And the land began to die. Only when I was made whole was it released.'

'Jinneth, and I, coming here?' Riven asked her, and she nodded.

'Now the land can heal itself, and I am whole.'

He tried to pull her close to him, but she would not move.

'Why?' he asked.

'Death is final,' she said in a soft voice. 'Yet the story continues.'

'Oh, yes, I forgot. Life goes on,' he said harshly, blinking the treacherous tears from his eyes. 'And what am I left with?'

Her hand stroked his cheek. 'A tale worth telling, perhaps. A reason to go on.'

'It's gone, isn't it? I'm back again.'

She nodded once more, silent.

'Will I ever enter Minginish again?'

'You are going home now, and you are going to forget. You would never be content, otherwise.'

'Forget everything?' he asked, and he remembered Giants and Dwarves, mountains and cities, friends and foes, and a lover who had been almost a child.

Everything.

A BREEZE HAD picked up, and was curling round the mountain as though on an errand. He was cold. His clothes were worn and thin and the stones were eating into his back. Dawn was bleeding into the eastern sky, blooming over the jagged darkness of the Cuillin Mountains. He shivered, wrapping his arms around his chest.

What in hell?

The glen loomed below him in the gathering brightness. Already there were a few lights on in the windows of the houses. He stood unsteadily, wondering why his clothes felt so odd on him. He was hungry, and his hands were racked with pain.

He sat down once more. There was something at the fringe of his mind, like a picture barely viewed. He felt terrible. But alive—strangely alive. He felt he could laugh at the high peaks and hear his voice bounce back at him exuberantly.

Can't sit up here all day.

He stood up again. He was quite a way from the bothy, but the sky was clearing and it looked like being a fine day, clear as water. He smiled to the emptiness, the surrounding mountains, the blue sky and the far-off wash of the sea on the shore of Skye.

Then he started off for home hurriedly, because he had a story to write.

Paul Kearney

'One of the very best writers of fantasy around'
Steven Erikson

A DIFFERENT KINGDOM

Michael Fay is a normal boy, living with his grandparents on their family farm in rural Ireland. In the woods—once thought safe and well-explored—there are wolves; and other, stranger things. He keeps them from his family, even his Aunt Rose, his closest friend, until the day he finds himself in the Other Place. There are wild people, and terrible monsters, and a girl called Cat.

When the wolves follow him from the Other Place to his family's doorstep, Michael must choose between locking the doors and looking away—or following Cat on an adventure that may take an entire lifetime in the Other Place. He will become a man, and a warrior, and confront the Devil himself: the terrible Dark Horseman...

 WWW.SOLARISBOOKS.COM

Follow us on Twitter! www.twitter.com/solarisbooks